C000213171

ABOUT THE AUTHOR

Peter Gray has been writing in various guises since he was twelve years old and he has never been able to stop. From plays to magazine articles Peter has produced a plethora of work.

His first 'Sam Series' book "A Certain Summer" has had excellent reviews, one from TV presenter and ex England soccer coach Bob Wilson who grew up in the same area and could easily identify with the character in the book.

With many short stories, articles and celebrated Mummers Plays plus many touring productions under his belt. Peter is always busy writing something or other. He has also acted in and directed some of those productions and one such production played at Warwick Castle for six full seasons. He has also written several scripts for advertisements, mostly with a humorous theme as well as several live shows for the stage. He has now embarked on a new series of Adventure Novels of which more details can be found on this website at www.petergrayauthor.co.uk.

He currently lives in the Highlands of Scotland.

ALSO BY PETER GRAY

A Certain Summer
Sam's Kingdom
With Feeling

FROM THE AVALON SERIES

The Drums of Drumnadrochit
Auld Clootie
The Brollachan
The Black Clan
Caledonian Flame - out 2019

The Brollachan

by
Peter Gray

Tricky Imp Publishing

The Brollachan

First edition first published November 2017
Reprinted April 2018

Tricky Imp Publishers
Highlands, Scotland.
Email: books@trickyimppublishing.co.uk

A CIP catalogue record for this title is available from
The British Library.

ISBN 978-0-9572668-5-8

Cover artwork by the author.

More Information at:
www.petergrayauthor.co.uk
www.trickyimppublishing.co.uk

Printed and bound in the UK by 4 Edge.

With thanks to Jonathon McColl
for his invaluable work on the manuscript.

Brollachan:-
"Shapeless, deformed creature; senseless creature.
A shapeless, malevolent supernatural being in Scottish
Gaelic folklore, a child of the 'fuath'."

Chapter One

The blue flashing lights reflecting off the rocks at the side of the glen could be seen by other motorists long before the sirens were audible. Soon after, a plain black BMW came hurtling round the corner as if the hounds of hell were in chase. All along the A82 main road that ran down the side of Loch Ness, cars were trying to get out of its way, as it was clear the car was stopping for nothing. Once the manic police car passed, the drivers of the vehicles that had pulled out of its way gradually came to their senses and continued on their way wondering what could possibly cause such a hurry.

"Jesus Christ Ross, you're gonna get us killed," demanded Detective Inspector Lasiter, gripping the underneath of the passenger seat as the car squealed around another corner.

"You're in safe hands, just relax," replied DS Ross as he swung the car in the opposite lock.

"Relax?" squeaked Lasiter, "I'd be more relaxed as a passenger with Stevie Wonder."

"This over-steers a bit more than mine," explained Ross as he flew past another line of cars.

"Et's not the steerin' I'm worried about," frowned Lasiter pressing his fingers into the seat, "et's the friggin' driver."

"Whoops," said Ross as the car seemed to slide loose for a second but he instantly corrected it and the car straightened out. Lasiter just couldn't believe that the only comment Ross made was a complete understatement. The DI had almost lost control of his bowels as the car slid and all Ross could say was 'whoops', as if he had spilled his tea or something. From that point on Lasiter was silent. He wondered what he would regret not doing most in his life if he was to die at that moment. Ross was just grateful that the DI had shut up and let him get on with his driving. The police had spent their time and money training him to drive fast, why not let him just get on with it? After all, if there *had* been a terrorist attack at Fort Augustus then they needed to get there as soon as they could, he knew damn well that the Armed Response Vehicle would be following soon and so it was a matter of pride to Ross that *he* was first at the scene. Though both Ross and Lasiter had admitted that they didn't think that Fort Augustus was on the terrorist top one hundred places to attack list, they had to respond, particularly in the light of the Westminster Bridge attack the week previous. With the Prime Minister visiting Scotland for talks about security, the last thing that Police Scotland needed was an under-reaction to a terror attack. So, Ross was in a hurry. All they really knew was that a car had driven into a shop at speed injuring several people. As they neared Fort Augustus the traffic was slowing due to the incident ahead, making it difficult to pass on the winding road and soon the traffic heading towards Fort Augustus was at a complete standstill. Ross managed to squeeze past most of it but it was difficult to drive into the village, so he 'parked' the car at the north end of the bridge slewed

8

across the road. He could see a marked police car a little further down, so obviously the local officers had arrived. They both got out and moved towards the bridge, there were many cars and people around the area but in the distance could be heard sirens approaching. It was likely that all manner of emergency services were on their way and a couple of local uniformed officers were trying to make a path through. Lasiter and Ross made their way to the officers and asked what was happening.

"The officer in charge is down there inspector," pointed the PC over the bridge, "I think it's all under control though." Lasiter nodded and continued over the bridge to where a car could be seen on its roof resting against the front of a shop. Two more uniformed officers were attending the car with what seemed to be a man in motorcycle clothing.

"That looks like DI Avalon," announced Lasiter as they approached.

"I thought it was your day off?" asked Lasiter as they got closer. Avalon turned with a deep frown.

"It was until this arsehole decided otherwise," he nodded towards a prostrate figure on the ground besides the overturned car. The officer kneeling by the figure stood.

"I think he'll survive," he announced to Avalon who nodded. He then turned back to Ross and Lasiter.

"I've told them to stand down the emergency, it's not a terror attack just some 'dick-head' driving faster than his capabilities," spat Avalon looking down to the bleeding figure on the pavement.

"We didn't hear anything on the radio," said Lasiter.

"I've only just sent someone to radio HQ. We were trying to get him out of the vehicle as there's fuel leaking out." He nodded down to the figure on the floor once more.

"Reports said there were people injured," insisted Ross.

"Yeah, just from flying glass fortunately," replied Avalon, "I don't know how the car missed some of the people on the pavement."

"Anyone still in the shop?" asked Lasiter trying to peer over the crippled car.

"No, one of the PCs said he checked through before I got here," replied Avalon. As he looked down the street the ambulance could be seen threading its way through the mass of cars at a standstill prior to the bridge, uniformed officers trying their best to clear the area. The fire tender was close behind and as soon as it was possible the driver of the crashed car was taken to the ambulance. The firemen then made the vehicle safe as Avalon walked away and found a place to sit. It wasn't long before he was joined by Ross and Lasiter.

"So what're you doing here, I can't imagine you came to spend a day at Fort Augustus?" grinned Ross.

"I went down to have a look at Ben Nevis, I'd never seen it before and I was on my way back," he shrugged, "the plan was to have a look at the locks on the canal," he shrugged again.

"Et's probably a good thing you were here then, they were sending everything down here thinking et was a terror attack," explained Lasiter.

"Yeah, one of the PCs explained that, that's why I got them to radio in as soon as we got the driver out of the car and knew the situation."

"Well y' can go and have a look at the canal locks now, we better wait for the RTA investigator tae arrive and then we'll get off," smiled Lasiter.

"I'll probably just get off home now, the wind seems to be getting up again," said Avalon looking up at the trees swaying in the breeze. He looked up to Lasiter and asked,

"So why are you two teamed up, this seems an odd coupling?"

"Well, someone had to get the old man down here in double quick time," explained Ross with a grin, "he'd still be in the car park trying to get the handbrake off," he continued nodding towards Lasiter.

"Old man? you cheeky..." Lasiter was about to swear but he suddenly checked himself seeing the public close by.

"Come on DI, you have to be knocking on in years, at least pre-decimalisation," said Ross with a wink to Avalon. Lasiter looked around at the people passing by, he clearly wanted to swear at Ross but looked down to Avalon and asked,

"Can you find something particularly crappy for him tae do en the mornin'?"

"I'll find something," nodded Avalon and then he stood, "right, I'll get off then and hope that nothing else comes along to ruin my day off," and he walked over to a police car close by and opened the rear door. He took out his helmet and gloves and returned across the road, a little to the side where a path ran by the bridge, there was his bike on its side stand. Avalon zipped up his jacket, put on the helmet and gloves and pushed the bike towards the road and then sat on it.

"I thought you were going to push it all the way back," smiled Ross, "is it steam powered?" he added. Avalon looked up to Lasiter as he prepared to start the bike.

"Definitely something crappy," he nodded and

11

then stood on the kick-starter and gave a deep lunge.

"That was uneventful," smiled Ross folding his arms.

"That es a classic machine you Philistine," frowned Lasiter pointing to the bike. The second kick brought the Thunderbird to life and everyone within twenty yards stopped and looked at it. Avalon nodded and then carefully threaded his way through the people and the cars, as more uniformed police arrived to clear up the mess. Ross and Lasiter watched him carefully make his way over the bridge and once he was clear, the unmistakable sound of an old British twin could be heard threading its way up the A82 and into the trees by the side of Loch Ness.

On the way back, Lasiter turned to Ross and asked,

"Is he still driving that shabby old Ford?"

"Yeah," nodded Ross not taking his eyes off the road, "one side mirror is red, there is a scratch down the side where an eager shopper scraped past and the front valance is held on with duck tape and a tie wrap."

"Someone ought tae have a word with em I suppose," frowned Lasiter.

"Not me, he's not been in the best sort of mood lately."

"Oh, why's that?"

"Dunno," shrugged Ross, "but it's probably woman trouble."

"I didnae know he was seeing anyone," answered Lasiter in a questioning tone.

"He isn't," replied Ross turning to him for a second, "that's the trouble."

"My, my," grinned Lasiter looking ahead, "Auld Clootie es pining for the feminine touch."

"Who told you about the nick-name?" asked Ross

looking quickly over to the DI.

"I don't know," shrugged Lasiter, "probably somebody downstairs but I thought everyone knew et." Ross sighed, he thought only 'C' section knew Avalon's nick-name but then again, it was difficult to keep secrets at a police station. "I thenk et suits em," added Lasiter with a slight grin.

"Probably," sighed Ross once more, "he's certainly the devil to work for at the moment."

"Well et's hardly surprising, et's been busy of late and this must be his first day off en a month," offered Lasiter knowing he too was due a few days off.

"He usually copes well though, I think there is more to it this time."

"Like what?" asked Lasiter. Ross just shrugged and shook his head. He didn't want to go too deep into Avalon's personal life and neither did he think it was right discussing the matter in detail, Avalon was a friend as well as a colleague. Lasiter saw Ross's reaction and changed the subject to some inane police matter, Ross listened and added his piece now and then as they drove back to Inverness.

Avalon left his bike just outside the shed to cool down before it was put away, the familiar 'ticking' sound coming from the machine as the exhaust pipes embraced the cool air from an easterly breeze that was rushing through the estate and over the garden. He was still sharing a house with Angolina Carbonna, a friend of PC Kirk, an arrangement that would soon come to a halt as Avalon had sold his terrace house in Wolverhampton. He had been at Inverness just over a year now and he felt he had integrated fully into Scottish life, he really couldn't see himself ever leaving. He could hardly believe he had lived a different life in Wolverhampton, it seemed a world away and even the connection he had with his ex-wife Carol was being eroded. They still spoke now and then on the phone but the gaps between calls were widening and Avalon was beginning to feel that her life in the south wasn't exactly as rosy as the picture she painted during their phone calls. On several occasions he had considered asking her if she ever wanted a few days away, she was welcome to come and see him but he had resisted. How could he anyway? There wasn't room for her to stay at the shared house and he didn't have the time, he always seemed too busy. He would have to find some more time off though as he was thinking of looking for his own house, somewhere not too far out of the centre of Inverness but far enough to be reasonably quiet. He pulled off his bike clothing and decided to make something to eat, Angie was out doing some shopping, so he had the rest of Sunday to himself and he considered devoting a little time practising his guitar. He was getting better, not good but better, at least the sounds were similar to the songs he was trying to play. He had even tried his hand at writing a song. It hadn't ended up quite as he imagined and it still needed work but he found he could play it much easier than some of the other songs he had tried. He considered lessons but he knew it was difficult to commit to regular times so he abandoned that idea and continued playing when he managed to grab a little time, mainly before he went to bed. He still had very little social life, except for the odd pint of beer with Ross or someone's birthday party from 'the nick', other than that he saw no one and had few friends. Then again, it had always been the same, it was the job, if he wasn't at work he was in bed. Days off were rare and it seemed to him that even when he got a

14

full Sunday away from the office, some retard in a hatchback tried to wipe up a pavement full of tourists and the whole of the Highland police force assume there had been a terror attack. He slumped into the kitchen chair to face the sausage sandwich he had just cooked. As usual, brown sauce was in abundance but as he bit into it he thought about Sarah Underwood from police forensics. It wasn't the brown sauce or even the sandwich, which reminded him of her, it was the fact that the sausage in the sandwich was not meat. Sarah Underwood was a vegan and not that long ago, Avalon had harboured some interest in her, he still did but the only time they met was in a professional circumstance, well almost the only time. He did see her in Drumnadrochit once and though he had been to the village on many other occasions he had not seen her there again. He had cut down on his intake of meat and had considered becoming vegetarian if not vegan and indeed he had become so used to the non-meat sausages, he had bought nothing else since. He no longer bought cows milk and had changed to Soya, his burgers were always vegetarian but he could not make the leap to the other side of the bridge. He told himself it was the lack of time, another attempt to blame the job but in his heart he knew it was all a shallow gesture, because he had done it to impress Sarah. Ironic that he had never told her. Since then, he had accepted that *he*, like so many others, would not find himself in the affections of Miss Underwood and resigned himself to that fact. He had however continued to eat more healthily, at home at least though he had been seduced by a full fry-up breakfast at the odd roadside cafe when he was out with Ross.

After washing the plate and 'downing' a mug of tea, he went to the laptop and looked at the work schedule for

15

Monday morning. There were a few loose ends to chase up but there was nothing major on at the moment, just a few petty incidents and a few old cases to rework. DS Wilson and DC MacDonald were winding up a couple of break-ins and Ross and DC Boyd had been looking at two 'cold cases' from the previous year. DC Mackinnon had come on leaps and bounds and was seen as an important member of the team but DC Pottinger was another matter. Though most of the team were ambivalent to Pottinger, Avalon disliked him. He disliked his approach to both the work and the team and saw him as a weak link in the section. If he could have, he would have moved him on but they needed the staff and so Avalon usually kept him in reserve.

The rest of his evening was the usual mix of a little reading, a glass of something strong, some little time struggling with his guitar and the inevitable check to see what was on the television until Angie returned home from her shopping in the city. Sunday was just about the only time he and Angie got to chat but on occasions it had been a pleasant distraction. That night, he took the opportunity to tell Angie he was considering buying a house but he didn't think it would be anytime soon, the information at least let her consider finding another house-mate. By the time he was ready for bed he had more or less felt reasonably relaxed but even so, he didn't sleep very well. He needed some time off, not just a Sunday but a longer break and if things stayed as quiet as they were at the moment it may be a possibility.

When Monday morning arrived, Avalon pulled into the car park behind the police station into the usual spot and walked towards the building. He nodded to a couple of 'uniforms' exiting the building, he knew people talked about the car, he knew by their expressions it was a joke to them but he didn't care. If he had to go out he used a pool car or asked one of the uniformed officers to drive him. He had no interest in cars, it was a method to get him to and from work and what was the use in having anything that looked nice? In the minuscule parking spaces provided in most car parks it was inevitable that someone would open their door into the side of the vehicle or rest a shopping trolley against it as they loaded their cheap booze and ready meals into the back of their four-by-four. Even when Avalon had bought a reasonable car, someone tried to park a large delivery van inside it. Yes, he had a tatty old Ford but the bonus was, if someone drove into it then they would come off worse, after all, what could they do to it that would make it look any more tatty than it did? As he reached the door of the station he looked quickly back to see how bad it actually looked.

"It looks fine from this distance," he said to himself and he turned and walked into the building. Most of the team were already in the Cave, the name they had given to the office from which they worked, Ross and MacDonald arrived soon after. As the office came to life and the team began their daily rituals, Avalon looked out from his glass booth checking their body language and their attitude to each other. Pottinger as usual had little to do with any of the them, he was almost as antisocial as Frazer. With this thought, Avalon looked at the empty desk where Frazer had once worked. It stood out like a beacon, tidy and unused, like a no-go area and Avalon had still not told anyone in the team anything about the reason for DC Megan Frazer's disappearance. He couldn't tell them the truth and he didn't want to lie to them so he had said very little, he just insisted they keep it clear. Even that puzzled them, as usual they had given the desk its own name, 'Area Fifty-One', the name given to the secret airbase in the USA. He shook from his thoughts, looked down to his computer and began sifting through his work for the day. It wasn't long before Wilson came to the booth and gave a slight knock on the glass as he arrived. Avalon looked up and said,

"Gordon, I expect you'll be off to the quarry?" Wilson nodded,

"Aye, there's a load of people tae interview so we better get an early start." An excavator had been stolen from a quarry to the south of Inverness and to everyone's surprise nothing had been seen of it since. The quarry manager was sure it had to be an, 'insider' but the official police opinion was that there was no evidence to suggest that.

"Well it can't be that far away, it's not exactly a getaway vehicle is it?" smiled Avalon.

"Not really but Mack thenks et could have been put on the back of a truck." Avalon shrugged at this and just added,

"Could be, should be easier to track then I would think." DS Wilson nodded, then he and MacDonald left to pursue their lines of inquiry. The next at the booth was Ross, he sat in the chair opposite and sighed.

"What is it?" asked Avalon looking up from his screen.

"It seems quiet."

"Bored are you, I can find you some more work if you like?"

"No, I have plenty to do, it just seems..." Ross didn't complete the reply, he looked back into the office and then up to the ceiling.

"Are you hinting at some time off?" asked Avalon, this time looking straight at Ross.

"I was thinking more about you, this is the quietest it's been for almost twelve months."

"True, but there's still a mountain of paperwork to get through, there are still three main cases pending, five court cases, this quarry theft and a host of minor cases so I doubt that it's the time to take a break," replied Avalon before he turned back to his screen. Ross sniffed and then sighed again.

"You forgot two missing persons."

"I forgot them on purpose, I'm tired of missing persons, they either turn up several days later as if nothing has happened or they end up dead tied to a gravestone in a crumbling priory." Ross nodded to the reference to the Beauly Priory incident the year previous and then stood.

"Well, I'm just saying that if you were to feel the need for a few days off..." and Ross slowly returned to his desk. Avalon felt slightly agitated, was Ross suggesting that he was burning out or was he trying to get him out of the way? No of course not, he knew Ross had his best interest at heart but *he* would decide when he would have time off not one of his Detective Sergeants. Maybe the job *was* getting to him, maybe he simply wasn't cut out to be a DI, either way, he decided to change his tack and think about something else. He looked at the report sheets that had been filed and then through case notes, it *was* certainly quiet. Maybe it was the calm before the storm. He then noticed in the corner of his eye Mackinnon approaching the booth.

"You got a minute boss?" asked the young DC.

"Yeah, what is it Rory?" Mackinnon looked down at a file he was carrying.

19

"I've just been going through the statements on the burglaries over at Muir, I've found several inconsistencies in two of the statements."

"Good work, you better see that they are re-interviewed then," nodded Avalon.

"Do you want me to pass the file to DS Ross?" asked Mackinnon.

"No, you sort it," frowned Avalon, "take Pottinger with you when you go." Mackinnon was a little surprised and it showed. "What's wrong detective, don't you think you need to do anything for the vast amount of money the Scottish tax payer gives you?"

"No sir, er no it's not that I just thought..." he paused and then continued, "yes boss, I'll get straight on it," he turned and went off to speak to Pottinger. Avalon was pleased with the way young Mackinnon had developed, he was quick thinking and thorough but he just lacked a little confidence. This was an opportunity for him to use his skill and find that confidence.

It was a long, slow day and Avalon found himself walking to the large windows of the office on several occasions and just staring out. He would pour a coffee from their private machine near the door and return to his seat and continue either writing or reading reports. Ross was right, it was quiet, relatively quiet anyway, and he was now beginning to wish something interesting would walk through the door. It didn't, the only thing to come through the door was PC Dowd bringing in the mail. Even the enigmatic Dowd had little to say for himself and uncharacteristically mentioned the weather and how nice it was that it wasn't raining. Avalon went back to his work in the knowledge that some major catastrophe was about to befall them. Fortunately he was wrong, though there was a slight scare in the late afternoon when the coffee machine blew a fuse. Once a new fuse was fitted to the plug, all was well with the world once more. Inverness could be flooded, blown apart by a hurricane or attacked by aliens but Avalon wouldn't be able to cope if the coffee machine wasn't working. Just previous to Avalon thinking about calling it a day, Ross came over to the booth.

"Fancy a beer tonight?" Avalon looked up and tried not to look excited by the prospect.

"Yeah, why not?" he shrugged and then stood, "what time and where?" Ross thought for a moment and then had an idea.

"Let's go somewhere different, how about the Castle, about eight thirty?"

"Okay, I've not been in there yet but I think I know where it is," replied Avalon and then added, "right I'm away, see you later."

Avalon regretted the decision to walk into town, the Castle Tavern was only about a mile from his house and about half an hour walk, but he considered that it could rain at any moment. The pub was easy to find and Ross was already there, seated in a slightly raised part of the pub and he stood as Avalon entered.

"Name your poison," he announced as he reached into his pocket.

"Just a pint of that," said Avalon pointing to the nearest hand pump. He still wasn't a fan of beer but he was taking a break from whisky.

"A pint of that one and another lager for me," announced Ross to the bartender. They took their drinks and sat. They sat in silence, the sort of silence that picks up a pencil and pokes it in your ear, the sort of silence

21

that screams at you. They both suspected the other one wanted to say something or had something on their mind but neither wanted to be the first one to break the quiet. Avalon took another sip of his beer and eventually said,

"This seems a nice place," it was an innocuous statement, neither admitting to an uncomfortable feeling, or surrendering to the lack of conversation.

"Yeah," nodded Ross equally noncommittal, "I thought we ought to try somewhere different," and he too took a sip of his drink. Both of them looked around the pub, to Ross it was ideal, he didn't know a soul in there and more importantly they didn't know him. Avalon was more detailed in his appraisal. He thought the place was more like the town pubs he had been used to in England. He had found some great places to drink in the Black Country during his days in Wolverhampton and this pub was similar to those. There was conversation all around the pub, all except the table they were seated at. The silence between them was palpable, Ross folding his arms looking somewhat uncomfortable.

"So what is it?" asked Avalon.

"What is what?"

"This thing you want to ask me," frowned Avalon. Ross shrugged and replied with,

"I didn't say I wanted to ask you anything," and he unfolded his arms.

"You didn't but I know you do."

"Well you're wrong," insisted Ross taking another drink in a slightly agitated way.

"I know you well enough now to see in your body language and the fact that you haven't cracked an inane joke for several minutes that you've something on your mind." Ross raised his eyebrows at this.

"What body language?" he insisted. Avalon gave

a big sigh and looked up at the ceiling and then back at Ross.

"Just spit it out man," he glared. Ross seemed to fidget a little at this but then began to speak.

"It's not what *I* have on my mind," he simply stated emphasising the 'I'.

"What's that supposed to mean?" asked Avalon a little taken aback.

"Well you have had something on *your* mind for some time now and you just won't talk about it even though I have offered to listen," he stopped for breath, "and it's starting to impact on the team."

"In what way?" asked Avalon with some surprise.

"So there is something?" said Ross raising the tone of his voice slightly. Avalon frowned once more but seemed to be searching his mind for something or other.

"No," he said emphatically, then he revised the reply and added, "well nothing important anyway." Ross kept his gaze on Avalon as if he was expecting more but Avalon simply looked away, casually taking in the interior of the pub.

"If you don't want to talk about it..." shrugged Ross picking up his glass.

"There's nothing to talk about," insisted Avalon looking back to Ross, "nothing like that anyway," he eventually added.

"Go on," smiled Ross replacing his glass on the table after a gulp of lager.

"Pottinger!" announced Avalon. Ross shrugged slightly.

"I know you don't like him but he's just another career copper who can't make his mind up, no mystery just a very ordinary, humourless dick-head."

"So you don't like him either?" questioned

Avalon.

"I don't like him no, but neither do I find him an irritant as you seem to."

"I've come across people like him before, officers that squeeze their way through your armour and then drop you in the shit," scowled Avalon.

"You think he's like that?" asked Ross raising his eyebrows.

"Probably," replied Avalon without emotion, "I'm just not prepared to give him the benefit of the doubt and if I had options I would try and move him on but as it stands..." he trailed off.

"Yeah, we need the staff," replied Ross and then his brow creased slightly as he continued, "and on that theme, are you ready to explain what happened with Frazer?" Avalon was obviously uncomfortable with this.

"What do you mean, I thought I had explained all that?" he replied. Ross looked down to his drink, he was thinking through the next part of the conversation, trying to figure out the best way to get the most out of his friend rather than his DI.

"Well yes, you told us the official line that she was being moved and all the shite about it being a 'good career move' for her but you never explained the *real* reason." Avalon looked into Ross's piercing gaze and remembered that he had told him about her loss of control during an interview, the fact that DC Frazer had struck a suspect in an interview room with a pair of handcuffs.

"It's tricky," he admitted, "I told you months ago I couldn't tell you everything about Frazer."

"You did," nodded Ross, "but that was before all that crap that came during the 'people trafficking' case."

"What do you mean?" asked Avalon with a deep

24

frown.

"Oh come on," insisted Ross, "it's one thing to say you couldn't reveal all the details about Frazer, but after the McCabe case she returned to work for just over a month."

"So what's your point?" shrugged Avalon, still frowning.

"Do I really have to point it out?" asked Ross but seeing Avalon wasn't about to offer information he continued with a deep sigh. "Okay, why would she be relieved of duty seven weeks after you found out about her attack in the interview room and not with immediate effect, and why would she be singled out after the cover up by DI Lasiter, after all, Lasiter still has a job last time I looked?" Avalon shrugged and took a drink of his beer. Ross shook his head with disappointment. "So you're not going to tell me, I see, so why does Frazer's desk remain in aspic as though you're waiting for her to suddenly come walking through the door?" There was still no answer from Avalon. Ross shook his head once more and lifted his drink to his lips, paused and then downed its contents and stood. "Okay, I'm off, see you in the morning."

"Where're you going?" asked Avalon looking up at him.

"Somewhere more sociable," replied Ross and he left. Avalon sat looking at Ross's empty glass and all he could think about was why Ross had left the glass there when he had to walk past the bar?

"Stupid," he said to himself but he didn't know if the comment was directed to the fact, or to himself for not being able to tell Ross the truth about Frazer. As 'mates', he should be able to let Ross in, but his past experience made him very cautious and in his heart he knew he didn't trust anyone when it came to his job. The job, the damn job! It was all-pervasive and it was getting to him, it had caused him a divorce and it still played games with his private life. He shrugged and sipped his beer but he was now wishing is was a single malt, so he left it half finished and took the glass to the bar along with Ross's.

"Anything wrong with it mate?" asked the bartender.

"Sorry?" asked Avalon.

"The beer," pointed the young man, "was it not right?"

"Oh, no," smiled Avalon realising what he meant, "it was fine, perfect in fact, I'm just not in the mood."

"Aye," smiled back the man, "Mondays can be like that," he shrugged and he walked off with the glasses to attend to another customer. Avalon exited the pub and walked down by the castle. Not just Mondays, thought Avalon, every damn day could be 'like that'. He always had doubts, about his life, the job, his capabilities but now those doubts were evolving into something different, mutating into a totally different emotion. They were becoming 'hates' and 'regrets', a much more destructive species. As he walked down Church Street he considered his options, he knew Ross would be fine about it, they had argued about many things in the last year but they had always forgotten about it the day after. He was more worried about everyone else, he had already obtained a disparaging nick-name due to his lack of patience when things didn't go to plan, or was it his mood swings? A nick-name was one thing, a lack of respect was something else, something he just couldn't afford. Maybe, as he previously expected, he just may not be right for the job, balancing protocol against his connection to his colleagues may just be something that couldn't be done, by him at any rate. By the time he was close to home he had convinced himself that he was right not to tell Ross the details about DC Frazer and what mattered was getting the job done and *that* was more important than what Ross or anyone else thought of him, and if that meant having no friends, so be it.

He didn't sleep well, but then again he hardly ever did. As usual in the mornings, he showered, he drank his coffee and ate a small slice of toast watching out for a neighbour across the road he called Mrs Pink. As she came through her front door and walked to her car Avalon was astonished to see she wasn't wearing any pink whatsoever. This was new, Mrs Pink always wore *some* pink, always, and as Avalon was thinking if it was simply the case that her pink apparel *was* being worn but unseen, maybe in the form of matronly underwear or similar, he almost missed her waving to him. They had spoken on occasions, and of late she had taken to waving as she walked to her car. The shock of neutral colours and the mental image of an ancient set of pink bloomers set his mind ablaze to the degree he almost didn't wave back. Well the mystery would have to wait, if Mrs Pink was leaving he would have to follow soon and what of the name? Would he have to think of her as Mrs Plain?

In the Cave, all seemed well and the activity of the morning soon settled down as mail arrived and those going out left and those staying worked tirelessly at their computers. Ross as expected, reacted as he usually did and seemed to have forgotten about the conversation the previous evening. Avalon hadn't. It had reminded him exactly why Frazer was no longer at her desk and he had to admit that ensuring that the desk remained clear did seem odd, he couldn't do anything about that though. Mackinnon brought him out of his thoughts.

"I have to go out again Boss, should I take DC Pottinger or not?"

"Oh, yes, of course..." he hesitated, "how did you go on Rory?"

"Okay, I think there is something they aren't telling us but we have the other suspect to interview again today," replied the young DC.

"Keep at it," smiled Avalon and Mackinnon left with Pottinger in tow. Avalon liked the lad, he was good at his job, he just hoped Pottinger wasn't taking advantage of him in any way. Rory was easy going and with Pottinger being slightly senior he was probably giving the lad a hard time. There was just Ross and Boyd left in the office so Avalon went to get a second cup of coffee from the machine.

"We'll seriously have to look at getting a bigger coffee machine," he said to no one in particular.

"The Toad will love that, he glares at the thing every time he comes in here," frowned Ross. 'The Toad' was a name given to their immediate boss, DCI Croker and normally Avalon would reprimand those who openly used it but with just the three of them in the room he let it go.

"Fortunately, he rarely comes in here," he replied with a slight frown.

"He's been a bit more easy going of late," replied Ross.

"I think he had his arse chewed over the demarcation system he set up," shrugged Avalon with reference to the DCI setting areas for each section.

"So how come it's still in place?" asked Ross

with a questioning look.

"He still wants us to keep to it but now he accepts that if B section have a big job or it gets busy in the city, we can help out or take on some of their cases."

"Does that work both ways Boss?" asked DC Boyd, her face giving away a hint of doubt.

"Yes, if we have to, we can ask B section to help out in the rural areas," nodded Avalon.

"Hell, he must have had a serious arse kicking then," grinned Ross.

"It's just what I heard, that's all," answered Avalon as he made his way back to the glass booth. He sat and looked at the glass partition between him and the main office that, for a short time, had seen blinds fitted to it, but he couldn't work out how to use them and in one transitory, impatient moment, he pulled much too hard on one of the cords bringing the lot down. The blinds were now leaning in the corner in a very dishevelled manner, a reminder that sometimes, he *did* lose his temper. He glanced down at the blinds as he sipped his coffee.

"That's what happens when you mess with Avalon," he said quietly to himself. The phone rang. "Avalon," he barked.

"Ah, Detective Avalon, I have some results for you, it's the DNA report from the burglaries at Muir," it was the dulcet tones of Sarah Underwood.

"Ah, oh, er right," he was slightly taken aback as he wasn't expecting her to call with the results, "right... DC Mackinnon is dealing with that case at the moment, I can give him the results," he half stuttered.

"Oh that's okay, I'll send them over, I just thought I'd ring them in to save time."

"Well thanks anyway," he replied, "I doubt he
29

will get time to read through them until the morning."

"*Fine, I'll send them over, bye*," and she was gone. What a fool he was, Ross had worked on that case and he was here in the Cave.

"Damn it!" he called out and looked up to see both Ross and Boyd look towards him.

"Bad news?" called Ross, Avalon shook his head and replaced the receiver before turning to his computer. Was he losing his marbles? Just because Sarah Underwood had phoned he had gone to pieces. Yes, it was obvious he needed some time off or he would become a liability to the team. He reviewed the current cases, there was plenty of work to do but with no major cases waiting, there was nothing urgent, nothing really pressing, nothing that needed his personal touch. As Ross had stated, it was the quietest it had been since his arrival and even the laconic Lasiter had intimated that B section were not particularly busy either. He picked up his diary and checked through it, there was nothing there to prevent him having a few days off. He began to wonder what he would do with the time, maybe take the bike out, or even a few days away? That was unlikely. Two nights at a secluded bed and breakfast sounded like an idea, somewhere near a nice little pub with a selection of single malts behind the bar. He had no idea how long he had been dreaming but long enough for him to be slightly 'snappy' when he answered the phone, which annoyingly decided to ring again.

"What is it?" he barked.

"*Er, Inspector Avalon, it's Dowd.*"

"Oh sorry Neil, what can I do for you?"

"*A chap has just delivered a package from forensics, do y' want me to bring it up?*"

"There's no rush, it's for DC Mackinnon and he's

out at the mo," explained Avalon.

"Oh it's okay, it'll get me off the desk for ten minutes," replied the PC. It wasn't long before a slight knock was heard and in walked Dowd with the package, he was reading a folded newspaper. Avalon stood and walked in to the main room.

"Do you want a coffee Neil?" Dowd handed over the package and shook his head.

"No ta Inspector, I can't be away long, I just wanted to have a wee peep at the line-up for tonight," he smiled as he raised the paper. Avalon poured a cup then said,

"I've heard that before, here you go," and he handed the PC a mug. Dowd smiled and sat briefly still reading the paper.

"Who are they playing tonight Neil?" asked Ross.

"Aberdeen, they drew one all Saturday, gave away a stupid penalty, luckily Billy McKay did the stuff so I'm expecting big things tonight," announced Dowd looking up to Ross.

"Don't get your hopes up," he laughed.

"Men and football," announced Boyd shaking her head. Avalon wondered if Dowd was about to impart one of his 'snippets of wisdom' as he looked up to Boyd from the paper. He wasn't disappointed.

"But you have to understand Constable Boyd, it isn't football at all," and he held his gaze upon her. She didn't look away, in truth Avalon saw a glint of devilment in her eyes, but she didn't know Dowd like he and Ross did.

"Okay PC Dowd, pray, tell me, if it's not football, what exactly is it?" Dowd lowered the newspaper a little and replied.

"It's tribal, it's the warriors of the village putting

31

paint on their faces and wearing their best mojo beads, making their hair stand up with sticky resin and picking up their finest spear and shield. It's ten thousand years of evolution in a format that modern society can understand and deal with, that's what it is constable." Though both were using the formal titles both had a slight grin in the corners of their respective mouths.

"So tell me exactly where throwing a wheelie bin through the Co-op window comes in to your assessment of ten thousands years of evolution," asked Boyd. Dowd raised his eyebrows and gave a slight nod.

"That is the granting of the spoils of war, it's the taking of the enemies land, the rape of his women, the slaughter of his children," replied Dowd and even Avalon was taken aback by the reply. Boyd wasn't and simply said,

"Well I can see how throwing Highland Council refuse bins through shop windows may be preferable to rape or murder, but to my civilised eye, it's still unacceptable behaviour and has no place on our streets," and she glared before returning to her work. Dowd looked to Ross and gave a tight-lipped smile before going back to the pages of his paper. Ross smiled over to Avalon shaking his head slightly then back to Dowd.

"I think I need you to be my official press release writer," but Dowd seemed to have found something of interest in the pages of the local tome.

"That is really odd," he said, still reading the story.

"You mean like someone dying a natural death in Glasgow?" asked Ross but Dowd was still reading. He seemed to finish the article and then looked up.

"Er what? No, this article is about a missing person but it seems quite odd, are you working on any

32

missing person cases?"

"Yeah, there are a few, there always are. Nothing new there," replied Ross continuing with his work.

"Oh well, I suppose you have it under control, right must get off," he stood and looked over to Avalon, "thanks for the coffee Inspector," he called as he placed the cup on the table near the machine and left.

"He's an odd sort, I think he's wasted in the force," smiled Ross.

"He's a bright chap, exactly what we could do with in the CID instead of the mediocre riff-raff I have to put up with in C section," smiled Avalon as he walked into his booth.

"Thanks for the vote of confidence," called Ross. Avalon went back to trying to plan a couple of days off, he reopened his diary as if he hadn't believed it the first time and confirmed he had nothing pressing. He stood, took his empty cup into the office and turned to speak to Ross.

"I was thinking," he began.

"That's new," replied Ross, "go on."

"With things as they are-" there was a quick knock at the door and in walked DI Lasiter. He glanced over at the coffee pot, it was usually a measure of how busy C section were, the pot was just about empty so they weren't all that busy. He noticed a folded newspaper.

"Bloody hell, d' ye have the papers delivered now as well?" his thick accent accompanying a frown as he picked up the paper and sat at the nearest table.

"PC Dowd brought it earlier, he must have forgotten it," explained Avalon as he leaned on one of the desks.

"I think he was seeing if the team were match

fit," offered Ross.

"They're playing Aberdeen the-night, they've no chance," frowned Lasiter reading parts of the paper.

"Aberdeen or Inverness?" asked Avalon.

"Look," interrupted Boyd, "we've established that Inverness had a draw Saturday, we now know that they need to win but will likely lose," the constable looked up to Lasiter, "and please, Detective Inspector, don't tell me it's tribal, or do we have to go through this same conversation every time a man walks in?"

"Who's upset the cleaning staff?" asked Lasiter to Avalon.

"You have my permission to staple his nuts to the chair DC Boyd," said Avalon to Boyd, she just made a tutting sound. "So what can we do for B section?" he asked, "or have you just come to sample the recreational delights of the Cave?" Lasiter looked up from the paper and said,

"Oh aye," he paused recalling why he had come, "have y' heard o' somethen called Operation Brew?" Avalon thought for a moment, the name rang a bell but he couldn't think where and then he recalled it.

"Sort of, not sure where though," he replied.

"It's an internal isn't it?" asked Ross.

"If it's internal how come you know about it?" asked Boyd. Ross shrugged but Lasiter added a little.

"I thenk some info got out, but yeah et's internal. I heard on the grape vine that *we* may be under investigation."

"Inverness, why?" asked Avalon.

"Well we have a past, the last few years have seen some people cross the line and go down," explained Lasiter.

"Yeah but nothing recent, nothing I have heard of

anyway," said Avalon folding his arms.

"It could be just rumour, some people get jumpy when something like this is knocking about," added Ross.

"Probably," nodded Lasiter, "I just thought I'd let y' know." Avalon nodded and then turned to look out of the window, the sky was overcast and it looked like rain would visit.

"That's an odd one," began Lasiter suddenly.

"Here we go again," cut in Boyd.

"Thes isnae tae do wi' footba' hen,"

"I know it's a missing person but it still sounds like the record's stuck," insisted Boyd. Lasiter dropped the paper on the table and raised his hands as he stood.

"Okay, a detective inspector can take a hint, I'll come back when the fire goes out," and he left. Ross and Avalon gave each other a knowing look, DC Boyd didn't stand on ceremony just because the target was a DI.

"You know, that's got my interest now," grinned Ross and he moved to the table where the paper was, "why would an article about a missing person be so 'odd', particularly as we haven't issued any press releases on missing persons." Avalon continued gazing through the window wondering if a few days off in the sort of weather that was brewing outside was worth it. He was about to put the idea to Ross when the DS spoke.

"They were right, this *is* odd," he said and he sat at his desk. Avalon wasn't really interested in what the local press might invent, Ross on the other hand was reading through the whole article. Eventually he stood by Boyd's desk and asked,

"We have a missing person logged as Muiranne Stodart, just have a look at it will you?" Boyd tutted and looked for the file. Avalon was ahead of them.

"Yes, we do, Mack went up north just over a week ago. Neither he nor SOCO found any evidence of foul play so we shelved it."

"Here it is," interrupted Dowd, "Muiranne Stodart, reported missing on the twenty second of March this year by a Mr David Sutherland."

"That's the chap in this interview," explained Ross, "are there any other details on Mack's report?"

"Not much," shrugged Boyd, "just what you'd expect, she went missing while out in her vehicle and nothing has been seen of her since. The case was logged by PC Gunn at Golspie and investigated by DC MacDonald."

"Then there's nothing to indicate that she disappeared into thin air?" asked Ross. Boyd read through it again but slowly shook her head.

"No, just that her vehicle had been found at the entrance to a field and it was reported by David Sutherland," she explained looking up from the screen. Avalon then interrupted again.

"I told you, nothing was found, Mack said the chap was insistent that she had just disappeared but we can't write that in as evidence can we?" he insisted, Ross puckered his lips and then raised his eyebrows. Boyd was still looking at the notes added to the case.

"There are other documents such as the interview with her husband and her friends if you want me to read through them," she added.

"No," shrugged Ross, "as the DI says, it seems far fetched anyway."

"What's the newspaper article say?" asked Avalon.

"Well, this chap," Ross looked down at the newspaper again, "David Sutherland, says that the police have refused to take him seriously, he says that under the circumstances he would have expected Police Scotland to have taken more interest in the disappearance of a high profile citizen."

"Is she a high profile citizen?" asked Avalon directing his question to Boyd but this time *she* was ahead of *him* and tapping at the keys of her computer.

"She doesn't appear on the internet with any regularity, she opened a local gala last year and judged at the East Sutherland vegetable show."

"Not my idea of high profile," smiled Ross just as Mackinnon returned to the room.

"Have you done already Rory?" asked Avalon turning to see who it was.

"Not quite boss, Ewan is tidying loose ends and I've come back to start writing this up," smiled the DC. Avalon wondered if that meant Pottinger was impressing his will on Mackinnon.

"Let Rory have a scan through that case until Mack comes back," he said to Boyd and then looked back to Mackinnon. "Let DC Pottinger sort out the paperwork, I want you to have a look at a missing person case, here have a read," he took the newspaper from Ross and handed it to Mackinnon. The lad took the paper and sat to read it as Avalon turned to head back to the booth.

"Is there something I need to know sir?" asked Mackinnon knowing that there usually had to be new evidence before a missing person case made headway.

"Not really," began Avalon as he stopped and turned, "it's just that we have more or less been accused of ignoring the case so just give it a once over." Rory shrugged and nodded at the same time and continued reading. It wasn't long before he said,

"Well that's odd..."

"If I hear that phrase again I'm going to throw something heavy," interrupted Boyd. Rory was taken aback and looked to Ross for an explanation.

"It's okay mate," Ross began, "every time she hears that phrase she assumes people are referring to her." Boyd turned quickly on Ross.

"And you can button it or I will tell everyone about your new little habit in the car." Avalon smiled and returned to his paperwork as the playful argument continued in the main part of the Cave. He was happy when the banter was being bounced around the room, he saw it as a way for the team to connect. That's why he thought Pottinger would never make it in the section, he never connected, similar to Frazer but *she* did at least have a sense of humour. That got him thinking about Frazer again, he shifted his thoughts quickly to return to his planning of a few days away. He then realised that he had tried to talk to Ross about it but got distracted by the newspaper article. He would probably wait until DS Wilson returned to the office and discuss it with him, after all, Wilson was technically second in command.

It wasn't all that long before Mackinnon could be heard tapping at the frame of the booth and entering.

"What have you found?" asked Avalon ceasing his typing to look up at the lad.

"Well nothing really boss 'cause I don't know how much of this is newspaper stuffing."

"Sit down Rory," Avalon nodded to the chair and Mackinnon sat, "so why does everyone who reads the article say," he looked through the glass at DC Boyd and lowered his voice to say, "That's Odd," and he looked to see if Boyd had heard him. She hadn't so he continued, "if there is nothing in the article?"

38

"Well, that's what I mean," continued the young DC, "the article says that the woman disappeared into thin air from what the witness says and that beggars belief, so we have to assume that this is no more than a cheap attempt to sell papers," he insisted raising the paper for a second.

"You said 'witness', I wasn't apprised of the fact there was a 'witness'."

"If the statement he made is correct he was there when she vanished and yet there is nothing to that degree in the report from the local plod, or from DC MacDonald's report." he raised his eyebrows before adding, "well..." Rory paused, "he does mention that the witness said the woman had mysteriously vanished."

"Have you got the case number?" asked Avalon and Mackinnon read the case number as Avalon typed it into his computer. The screen brought up all the relevant files on the case including all the statements and what seemed to be a report from the forensics team on the vehicle. "It says that the fingerprints were mainly that of Mrs Stodart with a few that matched her husband and Mr Sutherland's thumb print on one of the doors."

"Yes," nodded Mackinnon, what you'd expect I suppose."

"It says the locality is a place called Golspie, that's north isn't it?" asked Avalon.

"Dunno boss, I'm a stranger in these parts too." Avalon smiled and then opened Google Maps and typed in the place name.

"It's certainly north, it's some miles up the A9 on the coast."

"Do you want me to follow it up?" asked Mackinnon a little unsure if he should ask.

"No, I can't see the point until something crops

up but just in case, see if she or her husband are on the database, I just need some facts in case someone asks for a comment, I'll have a word with Mack about it later," answered Avalon. He then pushed a package towards Mackinnon.

"This is the forensics report from Sarah Underwood on your Muir case," he added. Mackinnon nodded and left with the package to return to his desk. Once again Avalon drifted back to the idea of a short break and then the phone rang. He tutted involuntarily.

"Avalon,"

"Hello it's Sergeant Brooks from the Brunet Road nick, I'm trying to contact Detective Sergeant Ross,"

"Just a mo," replied Avalon and he knocked on the glass panel of the booth and held up the phone. Ross understood and he stood but he had a puzzled expression on his face. As he reached the booth, he mouthed,

"Who is it?" to Avalon.

"Don't know," shrugged Avalon, "Burnet Road for you." Ross took the phone and said,

"DS Ross, how can I help?" There was an amount of silence as Ross's face took on a serious look and eventually asked, "When did it happen?" There was more silence until he continued with, "Aye okay, thanks for the info, I'll get straight off," and he handed the phone back to Avalon. "I've got to go out, one of my old sources has been found dead."

"Foul play?" asked Avalon.

"No, it doesn't sound like it. He was homeless most of the time and took a wee bit too much of the sauce," explained Ross, "I have to go and ID him as I doubt there's anyone else who can do it." Avalon nodded and said,

"If you need anything give me a call," and he

looked at the clock on the wall, "better call it a day when you've done there." Ross also glanced at the clock and then his wristwatch to confirm it.

"Okay, see you in the morning." As he left, Avalon knew that on occasions, the people who provided information could become important to a detective and sometimes it was easy to strike up a relationship with certain ones. By the look on Ross's face, this man was one of those cases. Avalon sighed and for the last time he considered some time off, if he was interrupted again he would forget the whole thing. It wasn't so much as an interruption as a barrage of interruptions. First Pottinger returned to the office and straight after, DS Wilson and DC Macdonald returned, and Wilson came to the booth to let his boss know how he was doing with his cases, not before having a joke with Mackinnon. Wilson sat and as usual didn't bother with the minutiae of the case, just the relevant facts and a rough idea how they were going on. When he had done Avalon thought the timing was a good as ever to tell him his plans.

"Before you go," he began, "I was thinking about-" but then he saw Mackinnon making his way back to the booth.

"What is it Rory?" asked Avalon trying to hold back any signs of being impatient.

"Sorry to bother you Boss," he gave Wilson a quick glance, "but the husband does have a bit of a police record, nothing heavy but I just thought I would let you know." Avalon thought for a moment, it may need a bit more digging into Mr and Mrs Stodart.

"Okay," nodded Avalon, "thanks for that and let me know if you find anything else," and Mackinnon turned, "oh and tell Mack to come and see me," he added as Rory returned to his desk.

41

"You were saying?" smiled Wilson.

"Yeah, I was saying that seeing as it's not all that busy I was thinking of having some time off, just a couple of-" but there was another interruption as the door to the Cave opened and in walked someone else. Avalon sighed but as everyone looked up to see who entered, the room went into a stunned silence.

Chapter Two

Detective Sergeant Ian Ross could easily seem like the sort of person that didn't give a damn about anything or anybody, but his few close friends knew he could also be very empathic and emotional. Avalon knew this, he had seen Ross come apart when he found his wife was having an affair and he had seen him react when they were out on cases in such a way it was clear he was a deeply caring individual. Ross was about 'front', it was all bluster and what was seen on the surface wasn't even slightly similar to who he really was. Ross hadn't known the man on the mortuary slab particularly well, as a source of information, he had only provided occasional and low key intelligence but he had done it because it was right, not because the police had something on him. Arty Struther had been a drunk for sure, he could often be seen down by the riverside with a bottle in a brown bag, drinking 'loch water' from a paper cup and talking to himself. The 'loch water' was inevitably gin or vodka and the talk was gibberish but behind Arty's red-rimmed eyes and weather beaten face, had been a sharp intellect and a sense of humour. He had been homeless most of his life, generally by choice, not finding the 'ordinary' life to his choosing. He had grown up in Govan, moved out when he was fifteen years old and joined the crew of a fishing boat soon after. He had made enough money to marry, buy a house and have a reasonable car but one day, soon after his thirtieth birthday, he 'dropped out' and left the car and the house with his wife, never to be seen by her or his family again. He had travelled the width of the country on foot and eventually settled in the Inverness area just over eight years ago and was known to many of the locals around the riverside area. He was totally harmless and would help anyone if he had the means to do it. Here he was, stiff and cold and never more to tell Ross one of his old jokes that he and everyone else had heard a hundred times. On occasions, Ross had given him money, he knew Arty would buy booze but it also helped him make ends meet in the colder weather. Ross nodded to the mortician.

"Yes, that's Arthur William Struther alright," and he added in a quieter tone, "see you old timer, I'll have a dram for you tonight," and then walked out of the building. He then went over to Burnet Road police station to find out the details.

"He was found by a passer-by," explained the sergeant, "it looks like he tripped up and banged his head, not seriously but he was so drunk he just lay where he fell. It seems he drowned in two inches of water from a puddle." This confirmed what the mortuary had said, there were no signs of foul play whatsoever.

"How did you know to ring me?" asked Ross.

"His personal effects, these were found in his pockets," and he placed a plastic bag on the counter. There was a combined bottle and tin opener, a Yale type key and a business card that said Detective Constable Ross and his phone number. Ross recalled giving him

44

the item some years previous but why he kept it was anyone's guess, he had known the number by memory. "We tried the number on the card but there was no answer," explained the sergeant. Ross looked to him with a sheepish glance.

"I dropped the phone in a burn last week," he shrugged, the sergeant nodded and asked.

"Do you know if there are any family?"

"No family," replied Ross as he picked up the bag. He took the items out and placed them on the desk. "You can throw these in the bin, I'll take the key, it may belong to a shelter charity or something." The sergeant nodded and did as he was asked and Ross left to walk to his car. The key was an odd one, Ross didn't recall him having a key, or at least he had never seen it before. Certainly, it *could* belong to a charity organisation, god knows Ross had sent him to enough of them but how the hell would he know which one? He looked at it several times but eventually threw it in the glove box of the car and drove home. When he finally arrived, he felt suddenly tired and decided to skip food and went straight into the shower. He stood, letting the hot water run over him, hoping it would wash away the depression he was feeling that had haunted him since leaving the mortuary. He wasn't even sure why it was so. True, Arty was dead but he knew in his heart that the old chap was going down a slippery slope and when he considered it, so did Arty. He felt it was something deeper. Just over a year ago the same black cloud had been overhead but when Avalon arrived at Inverness, that seemed to change. He had enjoyed the first six months working with Avalon, it had been refreshing to work with someone that he felt he could trust and get on with. They made a good team but now Avalon was a DI, they rarely worked together, although he did think that he would eventually get a similar relationship with DC Boyd. She wasn't Avalon though, they were similar, but Boyd although headstrong and quick witted, didn't connect as Avalon did. He turned the heat down on the shower and finished with cold water as usual and then stepped out of the tiny cubicle and into his robe. He combed his close-cropped hair with nothing more than his hand and towelled his face dry, noticing the beginning of lines around the eyes.

"It's not the best job in the world for your complexion," he thought to himself. He sat in the only easy chair in his flat. Since leaving his wife and taking on his own place he had decided on a minimalist approach, there was little furniture and next to no ornaments. A Mitre rugby ball that was signed by all the members of his old rugby club on the occasion of his birthday sat on a wooden plinth above the TV. That was seven years ago but it seemed like yesterday. He smiled when he thought back to that evening. His old mate Kenny Robertson had calculated that they had drunk so much that night that their alcohol levels were ridiculously high and technically they should have been dead. He had joked himself that the body parts at the university's biology lab had never experienced so much alcohol. That reminded him, he walked into the tiny kitchen area and poured himself a shot of Jack Daniels. Avalon found the drink disgusting and if the truth was known, Ross didn't like it all that much either, but he found its rasping haze comforting at that moment, and there wasn't anything else. He began to get hungry and made himself a peanut butter sandwich, which he also wasn't fond of but it seemed to be an evening of doing things that were not particularly to his taste.

"Poor old Arty," he said to himself, "drowned in two inches of puddle water." He took a bite of the sandwich and thought about the old tramp, he probably knew nothing about it and that was the best way to go. Drowning in alcohol and then in puddle water, "If the booze don't get you the water will," he thought to himself. "Here's to you Arty, cheers," he said and raised his glass to the heavens before gulping the contents in one.

When he awoke, he was still sitting in the easy chair and he felt as if someone had emptied the contents of a litter bin in his mouth. He soon spotted the reason, the bottle of Jack Daniels was now just 'bottle' and close by was the empty glass where it had obviously fallen from his grip as he nodded off to sleep. He pushed his hand down to raise himself up.

"Oh shit!" he exclaimed as his hand squashed something soft. For a moment he considered he may have soiled himself but thankfully it was a part eaten peanut butter sandwich and now it was compressed into the easy chair. He looked at the clock, it was six thirty but by the time he had cleaned up the mess and had another shower, he decided it wasn't worth going back to bed. Five cups of coffee later he was beginning to feel mildly better but nothing approaching human. The bottle of booze hadn't been full but there had been enough to make him feel that his brain had turned to gravel and his stomach to pure sulphuric acid. As he dropped the empty bottle into the bin, he once more thought of Arty Struther, it was sad but that kind of thing happened every day of the week in one town or another and he just had to make sure it never happened to him. He looked back to check the room, noticed the wet patch on the chair where he had scrubbed it clean and then left for the office.

He had stopped off at the shop to get a drink as he was suddenly feeling thirsty, so he was a little late, but Ross knew it was almost expected of him. As he walked into the Cave the first thing that struck him was how quiet it was, the second thing was someone sitting at Frazer's desk. For a moment he almost rubbed his eyes, it looked a little like Frazer but, he had to admit, better looking. The woman looked up at him and said,

"Jesus Christ, *you* don't get any easier on the eye, you look like shite."

"Megan?" he said then he did indeed wipe his eyes, "what?" and then he looked over to the booth. Avalon had his head down and was pretending to write something but even at this angle he could see Avalon was grinning. He tried again. "What are you doing here?" The woman frowned and said,

"Well et's my fu-" she stopped and gave a glance to the booth noticing Avalon looking over, then started again, "et's my desk esn't et?" She knew Avalon frowned on his team swearing and as she was on a sort of probation she thought she had better 'toe the line'.

"I thought you had taken another post," said Ross with a questioning look.

"What! Me leave you, who would carry you around and wipe your arse for you?" she frowned. Ross could see now how different she looked, if he had passed her in the street he wouldn't have recognised her. She had her hair down and it was cut in a short but modern style, she was wearing some make up and had put on a little weight. She was still slim but she didn't have the pinched look of the previous incarnation. Avalon was

48

making his way towards them, he still had a smile on his face.

"Meet our newest recruit, DC Megan Frazer," he grinned.

"Well thanks for letting me know," frowned Ross.

"I didn't know she was back until she walked in late yesterday," explained Avalon.

"So where have you been?" asked Ross. Frazer looked up to Avalon.

"Can I tell 'em?" she asked. Avalon nodded.

"As far as I can see you've been debriefed so why not?" and he sat on the edge of the desk.

"I was seconded tae Internal Investigations, they wanted tae put a large surveillance team together and I was asked to join et," she replied, "but I can't tell y' where et was yet."

"Was this something to do with this Operation Brew?" he asked.

"Aye," she nodded, "et seems pointless having a secret operation ef everyone knows what et's called but I wes part o' that."

"We heard Inverness was under investigation," frowned Ross.

"No chance, they only took officers from areas that *weren't* under surveillance," insisted Frazer.

"Well," smiled Ross, "I never thought I would hear myself say this but I'm glad to see you."

"Well I can't say the same, I thought I'd seen the last o' your sorry arse," she frowned in reply. Ross knew that meant exactly the opposite from Frazer, for her to even speak to you, you had to be in her good books.

"You look so different," said Ross shaking his head with a smile.

"Aye, I'm a real fat cow now, et's all the sittin'

49

around en cafés and the like, eating donuts an' pretending to be one o' the general public," she frowned, I had tae change the way I looked tae blend in." She rolled her eyes, "me blend en, that's a joke." Ross continued to smile at her. "What's up wi' you? Have y' got nothin' better to do?" she frowned even deeper.

"Well, I was thinking of asking you out," he smiled.

"Right that's et, he's gone too far," she looked up to Avalon, "I want him reported for sexual harassment." The room burst into laughter, Ross shook his head and Frazer continued with, "I look like going on a crash diet, I must look real freaky ef this numpty finds me attractive."

"You look smashing as you are and it's nice to have you back," smiled Avalon and he turned to Ross, "you got a mo?" and they walked back to the booth. There was still some laughter in the room as they sat.

"I really never thought I would miss her you know," said Ross in a more serious tone. Avalon nodded and then asked,

"How did it go last night?" Ross dropped the smile and shrugged.

"Well, it's a sad end for anyone, he fell down drunk and downed in a puddle." Avalon frowned and slowly shook his head, Ross continued, "he'd been homeless for some years and all he had in possession was a carrier bag of food scraps, a combined tin and bottle opener, an almost empty bottle of gin and a key."

"A key, I thought you said he was homeless?"

"He was, he wasn't much into a regular roof over his head so he walked the streets, he also had an old card of mine, I gave it him years ago but he knew the number off by heart. I can't imagine why he kept it," added Ross.

50

"What sort of key was it?" asked Avalon.

"A sort of latch key, a Yale type, why?"

"And you've no idea what it's for?" asked Avalon with a slight frown.

"Well, I know it's not for the Caledonian Gentleman's Club if that's what you mean?" sighed Ross, "but no, I've no idea." Avalon looked to be thinking for a moment and then he asked,

"Did you get on with the man, I mean on a personal basis?"

"You mean did I introduce him to my family and take him to the cinema? Course not," spat Ross, "I wouldn't even let him in my car, his clothes had more bugs than Windows 10."

"I don't mean like that, did you chat, pass the time of day?" insisted Avalon.

"Yeah," admitted Ross, "he had some interesting stories to tell, I suppose in another life we could have got on. I gave him some of my old clothes now and then and sometimes a few quid to be going on with but I suppose a lot of that was because he sometimes gave me some reasonable info." Avalon could see he was being defensive, he wanted to admit to liking the chap but didn't like letting his guard down.

"You're not making the same connection here as me are you?"

"What connection?" asked Ross doubtfully. Avalon thought for a moment again and then explained.

"Look at it this way, the old chap had no possessions, he probably never wanted possessions from what you have said, so..." Avalon paused for a moment to let it sink in, "his one and only important item he kept in his pocket. A tool that can open tins and open bottles. It's his lifeline, his way to always be able to eat or drink." Ross nodded at this.

"Yeah, I would say that sums him up."

"So," continued Avalon staring directly at Ross and leaning forward slightly, "the only other items he kept close at hand with that important tool was a key, and a phone number, *your* phone number."

"I admit, the key could have meant something to him but that old dog-eared card of mine? It wasn't even current, it was the number of the phone I dropped in the burn last week, the card still had me as a DC!" he exclaimed but then thought for a moment, "we got on alright but apart from the odd chat on a bench by the river..." Ross trailed off, he didn't even know why he was being so defensive.

"You're still missing the point," insisted Avalon slightly frustrated, "he kept your number with the key, he was ensuring that if anything happened to him, the first thing people would do was ring you. You admitted he knew your number by memory so why would he keep it?" Ross suddenly began to see what Avalon was getting at, it seemed odd, but it did make sense.

"Oh shit," Ross eventually said. Avalon nodded, smiled and leaned back to let the implication sink in. "The old dog wanted me to get the key and then find out what it was for." Avalon nodded again. "But it could even have been a key he just found and was looking for a lock for it to fit."

"That could be," admitted Avalon, "but equally it could be something he intended you to sort out for him after his death."

"Shit," Ross said again, "it could take a lifetime to find what it fits."

"What you need is a good detective," smiled Avalon.

"Do you know where I might find one?" asked Ross as he stood.

"Ask Sarah Underwood if they have any experts with key identification, there must be a forensic locksmith somewhere."

"Yeah, that's not a bad idea," agreed Ross as he slowly made his way back to his desk. Avalon watched Ross as he blew Frazer a kiss, she immediately held up her middle finger, it was nice to see the team complete again and the break seemed to have done Frazer the world of good.

"It's great when a plan comes together," said Avalon to himself.

~~~~~~

The file that dropped on Ross's desk just after lunchtime wasn't a hefty chunk of literature but the look on Avalon's face and the "Take a look at this for me," said more than he was going to find inside it.

"It's one of the missing person cases, the woman near Golspie I'm guessing," shrugged Ross without having to open it.

"Good work, you'll make Superintendent yet," frowned Avalon, "have a closer look." Ross did as he was asked while Avalon looked out of the window with his hands linked in the small of his back, watching the rain cascade slowly down the glass. It didn't take Ross long to finish it.

"Well as Rory pointed out, the report is somewhat at odds with the newspaper but I'm thinking I would rather take the facts as written down by," he looked down to find the name of the reporting officer, "PC Gunn and Mack, over the excited statement made by David Sutherland. I mean, the paper actually mentions some kind of 'moor spirit' that comes down from the hills for Christ's sake."

"That's just newspaper hype but this Mr Sutherland says he was there, actually there when she went missing."

"Exaggeration?" suggested Ross.

"Maybe, but I spoke to Mack last night and he says Sutherland was adamant that the woman vanished from her car as it was travelling down the road. As Mack said, if he had put that in the report he would have been a laughing stock," mused Avalon.

"And there was me thinking you would have told him that it's not his job to speculate just report the facts?"

"Well I did," grinned Avalon, "but I can also understand that he wrote down facts and didn't go into any great detail about the ramblings of Mr Sutherland. It's quite clear that she didn't disappear into thin air which means either the woman chose to go missing or Mr Sutherland is lying and is responsible for her disappearance."

"I would agree with that but what now?"

"Her husband has a bit of lightweight form, nothing big time but *form* nonetheless."

"It doesn't mean he's done away with his wife though does it?" replied Ross raising his brows.

"No," admitted Avalon, "but what makes my inquisitive gland itch is the fact that a friend of the missing woman is making a song and dance about it and yet her loving spouse has been as quiet as a deaf-mute church mouse."

"I take your point but it's not conclusive."

"Not at all," agreed Avalon, "but I think we ought

to take another look at this one. I trust Mack but we can't take chances that we've missed something."

"Send Rory up there, he knows the story now," suggested Ross.

"I was going to but he and Pottinger have some work to do yet and I would prefer more experienced eyes on the job."

"What about Miss Sexy over there?" Ross nodded towards Frazer as she heard the comment and stopped typing and turned to face him.

"Listen arse wipe," she began, "I don't need the likes o' you tae volunteer me for extra duties, get off yer fat arse and do et yerself."

"Isn't she gorgeous when she's angry," purred Ross.

"Spin on et," replied Frazer with the usual middle finger.

"Now, now children, I'll take your toys away," cut in Avalon, "Megan has enough paperwork to sort out for the next three years," he explained.

"Well," began Ross without any enthusiasm and a sigh, "I suppose me and Ali could go and have a quick sniff around, it's just over an hour journey I would think." Avalon nodded and then he thought more about it. He had an embryo of an idea, it would mean he was working but it was only asking a few questions here and there.

"I was going to have a couple of days leave but I suppose I could find a bed and breakfast up there and have a day looking around," he suggested.

"It's not the metropolis up there you know, it's just a coastal village," replied Ross with a cautionary tone to his voice.

"But that's it, it's coastal and I love those kind of

places."

"Inverness is coastal," added Ross. It was true and though water could be seen all over the place and seagulls could be heard all around the city, he never really thought of it as coastal.

"Yeah," nodded Avalon, "it is but it's not the same, I like these old fishing villages, there's just something about them."

"So when were you thinking of going?" asked Ross.

"I'll maybe wait until the weekend now, we'll see," he smiled and Ross nodded, then Avalon remembered something, "did you contact Sarah Underwood about the key?"

"Yes," nodded Ross, "she told me to send it over to her, she thinks she knows someone who may be able to tell me something about it."

"Well, it's a start," agreed Avalon and he went back to the booth trying to think through what he would have to do in Golspie and how long he could afford to stay there. He considered that if he travelled up sometime on Friday he could stay until Sunday night and make the drive back around early evening. He began to look for bed and breakfast on the internet but the village seemed to have more than its fair share of places to stay. He decided not to book, it wasn't exactly holiday season after all.

Most of the afternoon he spent catching up on reports and paperwork and every now and then he looked up to watch Ross and Frazer throw some insult or other banter across the room. He kept looking at Frazer too, she looked so different and she seemed as if the cloud that had been hovering above her had lifted. If a change of scenery could do that for her he was sure it would be of great benefit to him. He then looked at Ross, he seemed in his element. Both Boyd and Frazer were giving him a hard time and he revelled in it. It probably took his mind off the dark side of the job, every police officer had their own ways to deal with the poison. Wilson had his home life, he put his heart and soul into that. MacDonald had his hobbies, Mackinnon had his hobbies too and Ross played the fool, others Avalon knew had fast bikes, cars and sometimes boats. DS Murrey in B section sometimes jumped out of airplanes with a parachute on his back for some charity or other, DI Lasiter spent any free time fishing. Avalon? Well, he had his bike but in the past no amount of distractions had stopped the poison almost reaching his heart. His ex-wife Carol had been the only antidote to it. Now she wasn't there he knew he would need something else, but what? Maybe he would get time to consider it sat in a bar somewhere up the east coast of Sutherland?

~~~~~~

Avalon stood with DS Wilson on a cloudy but dry Wednesday morning on a mound of earth, watching an excavator working away at a growing hole. Other police officers stood around with several quarry workers looking on. To the rear of the scene stood three forensics technicians headed by the chap Avalon knew as Hendry, already suited up and ready for action.

"Have you found out who the tip-off was from yet?" asked Avalon not taking his eyes off the action.

"Nope," replied Wilson shaking his head, "and I would think we're not gonna find out either."

"It's to be hoped that the damn thing is here

then."

"It seems a good chance unless somebody es just arsing us about," replied Wilson, "but et's looking pretty obvious that the security man wasn't on site." DC MacDonald was climbing up the mound to join them. "What did y' find out Mack?"

"Nothen' much, the manager says this area es used for parking so et's unlikely they would have noticed ef et had been disturbed anyway," announced MacDonald in a shout. The wind and the sound of the excavator's engine was making it difficult to communicate.

"Et's probably the place then," nodded Wilson as another massive bucketful of earth and gravel was pulled out of the hole.

"He has a bit of a theory," added Mack.

"Who does about what?" asked Wilson looking over to the young DC.

"The manager, he reckons that one of the drivers probably sent in the tip-off," he said missing his footing slightly in the loose earth.

"How's that?" asked Wilson being buffeted about in the strong breeze.

"He reckons they would have had to use one of the other machines to bury it which would mean it would be running for a few hours," explained Mack.

"Aye, but et's unlikely it would still be warm in the mornin' in this god-forsaken place," insisted Wilson with a frown.

"He says it's tae do weth the hours that the machine records in the cab, the drivers log them each night. Ef a driver noticed extra hours on his machine et would make him suspicious. The manager es checking records at the moment," replied MacDonald.

"Is he going to let you know who it is?" interrupted Avalon.

"Yes boss, he's checking through the-" Mack's phone rang, "that might be hem," said MacDonald as he answered. "DC MacDonald," he seemed to be listening, "an' es he here today?" questioned Mack to the phone, "Aye, okay, thanks for that," and he put the phone in his pocket. "The manager says it must be a chap called Rob Watson, he's actually the chap who is on the big digger," said Mack pointing to the large excavator. The three of them continued to watch as yet another bucketful came out and then a man at the side of the hole who was acting as a banksman took off his hard hat and held up his hand. He then dismissed the big excavator, which slowly drove away to be replaced by a smaller version.

"That's your cue," said Wilson to MacDonald as he nodded to the big excavator. Mack went dutifully off to interview the driver.

"Looks like they may have found something, I pity the security man if this is it," said Avalon. Wilson stood quietly with his hands thrust deep in his trouser pockets, the wind playing havoc with his rather large and unfashionable tie. After a few small scrapes with the bucket, the banksman told him to stop and jumped in the hole with a shovel, two other quarrymen joined him and moved more earth. There in the bottom of the hole showed some yellow painted metal.

"Bingo," announced Wilson as the banksman looked up and held up his thumb in the time honoured way. "I'm wonderin' ef the security man was in on it," Wilson's phone then rang. "Go on Mack," he said, the young DC had rung to tell him the news from where the big excavator was now parked the other side of the hole. "Okay, get his details and a statement," added Wilson and then he turned to Avalon. "Mack has confirmed the driver of the big excavator gave us the tip off, he noticed that the machine was low on diesel, he also noticed cigarette butts en the cab and white gravel on the bucket. He put two and two together and phoned et en."

"Why stay anonymous?" asked Avalon knowing that it was the nature of some people. Wilson shrugged.

"Don't know, he too probably suspected the security man," he said, "but et's clear they thought that they could bury et until the whole thing blew over and then come back to claim et."

"It seems a lot of work and trouble for a digger," added Avalon.

"They're worth a shitload of dosh those things."

"I suppose so," nodded Avalon, "right I'm off, good luck with the paperwork," he grinned and left Wilson to it.

As he left the quarry and headed back to Inverness he contemplated the rest of the day. He had to go over to the Procurator Fiscal's office in the afternoon and he had the inevitable pile of paperwork but he considered stopping off to get a few things for his trip at the weekend. He then noticed the steering seemed unusually heavy and it wasn't long before he realised he had a puncture. He couldn't remember ever going in the boot and that had been a mistake as there was no spare wheel. He banged his fist on the roof of the car in frustration and kicked the front, which loosened the front valance even more.

"Damn pile of crap!" he shouted at the car. Where was he? He looked around. There was nothing he recognised, he just knew he was south of Inverness on the A9. He got back into the car and pulled it off the road onto the grass verge and then noticed a large sign down the road in the direction he had just come. He walked down to it and phoned the office.

"*DS Ross*," said the voice on the other end.

"It's Avalon, I've got a puncture and there is no spare wheel in this damn car." To Avalon's surprise Ross said nothing, he was probably laughing or telling everyone else what had happened. "Are you there?" he asked.

"*Er yeah*," came the reply, "*what do you want me to do?*"

"Send someone to pick me up, I'll phone someone to tow the car back, I think it's time to get rid."

"*Well it's probably cheaper to scrap it than buy a new wheel for it,*" Ross replied and Avalon was sure he could tell Ross was grinning. "*Where are you?*" he asked.

"I'm on the A9, near a big brown sign that says 'Loch Ness and Attractions', you know, one of those tourist signs."

"*Anything else?*"

"What do you mean anything else, I'm a detective not a sodding tour operator?" replied Avalon scornfully.

"*I'm just trying to ascertain how far away you are that's all,*" insisted Ross's calm voice.

"Oh, right," replied Avalon apologetically, "it says," he paused, "Jacobite Cruises five miles, er, Loch Ness Centre and exhibition seventeen miles and Urquhart Castle nineteen."

"*Anything else?*"

"Are you trying to wind me up?"

"*Not at all we're trying to find the sign on Google Maps, it looks like you're near Bogbain,*" replied Ross.

"Just get a bloody car down here pronto," demanded Avalon and ended the call. He then kicked his car one more time.

By the time Avalon got back to the office it had been too late to consider going into the city and so he had gone straight back to work. Wilson, Mack and Frazer were the only ones there when he walked in.

"Where is everyone?" he asked.

"Ross and Alison have gone out tae get a sandwich," explained Wilson, "and Potty Pottinger has gone down tae the archive. Poor young Flicks es with the DCI."

"Bloody hell, why?" asked Avalon with surprise.

"DCI Croker wanted tae know what was happening about one o' the missing person cases and Rory said he knew a bit about et, so he volunteered," smiled Wilson.

"I bet the poor lad is crapping himself," said Avalon raising his brows.

"He'll be doing fine," replied the DS, "Rory has a good head on hes shoulders, not like this muppet," he nodded and pointed his thumb towards MacDonald who just gave a big toothy grin and said,

"Someone your age needs young blood tae get y' across the road safely."

"No respect for their elders," concluded Wilson shaking his head. Avalon was about to return to his booth when in walked Mackinnon. He looked calm and was carrying a folder of case notes. He became slightly embarrassed as he noticed everyone looking at him expectantly.

"What?" he asked scanning the blank faces.

"How was the DCI?" asked Avalon.

"Fine, I just briefed him on the missing woman case," replied Mackinnon innocently.

"Why was he interested in that?" asked Avalon.

"His wife had read the article we saw in the paper, it just set alarm bells ringing with the DCI." Avalon nodded and then gave Rory a brief smile. He was really pleased by the way Mackinnon was shaping up. He hadn't even been fazed by the DCI and there were a few older officers that couldn't say that. Avalon turned to move to the booth but hesitantly Mackinnon asked,

"Have you got a minute boss?" Avalon turned back for a moment and replied.

"Of course, walk this way," and they both went to the DI's partition. Avalon told Mackinnon to sit and then asked,

"What's on your mind?"

"It may not have any relevance to this case but when I knew I had to go and see DCI Croker I did a bit of research."

"It's my understanding you didn't actually have to go and see the DCI, I hear you offered to go," said Avalon raising his eyebrows a little in a questioning manner.

"Well, sir, it made perfect sense," he seemed embarrassed again, "DS Wilson would have had to read through the whole case notes but I already knew most of the details."

"Go on, what have you found?" smiled Avalon.

"It seems after searching our database, Mrs Stodart isn't the first person to go missing in that area," offered Mackinnon.

"Are we talking recently or not?" asked Avalon cautiously as Rory could easily become fixated on a case.

"One of them is reasonably recent, but there are others..." he shrugged.

"Is this to do with the newspaper mentioning

something coming down from the hills?" asked Avalon tilting his head slightly.

"Er," hesitated Mackinnon, "no, well er, sort of." He looked slightly embarrassed. "There is a sort of curse or legend in Sutherland but I..." and he trailed off.

"Keep to the facts," glared Avalon, "and tell me about the other recent one."

"Another woman actually, eighteen months ago, she went missing in similar circumstances. She told her husband she was going to see her sister and she pulled the car out of the garage, her husband became suspicious when he noticed the car was still parked in front of the open garage with the engine running."

"And the outcome?"

"There wasn't an outcome, she has never been seen since, her handbag was still in the car and nothing was taken from the garage," insisted Rory.

"The husband did it," smiled Avalon but Mackinnon stayed serious.

"Maybe, but if he did, he got away with it, I have even checked through the notes, there were no clues then and still aren't now."

"Have you found anything to link it to the more recent case?" asked the DI.

"No, nothing," replied Mackinnon with a frown and a slight shake of the head. Avalon looked beyond him for a moment as he saw Ross and Boyd return to the Cave, they seemed to be having an in-depth discussion.

"Well the recent case is all that we are interested in, we'll leave the other one to whoever was assigned to it," insisted Avalon. He hadn't asked for the information but Mackinnon volunteered it anyway.

"DS Murrey and DS McGill." Avalon raised his eyebrows.

"DS McGill has retired but DS Murrey is still in B section," he said but Rory made no reaction. "Still," he continued, "it's not our baby," he looked at the folder that Rory still had in his hand, "are those the case notes?"

"Yes," he nodded, "do you want me to take them back to the archive?"

"No leave them with me," said Avalon reaching for them, "I'm off to Golspie at the weekend to re-interview Mr Stodart, I need to read up before I go." Mackinnon had been on the internet to see exactly where the village was, it was north but Avalon was making it sound like an expedition. He just nodded and stood. "Oh, and well done with the DCI, quick thinking that man," said Avalon raising his eyebrows once more. Rory smiled and nodded then returned to his desk. Avalon placed the folder in the draw and went to pour a coffee.

As usual, the machine was almost empty but he squeezed out enough for one cup as he listened to Ross and Boyd arguing about Scottish politics. Rory noticed the coffee machine and began to refill it.

"That's utter bullshit and you know it," insisted Boyd raising the volume of her voice.

"It's true," retorted Ross, "since she came to power the Scots have a much greater say in Westminster than any time I can think of previously."

"All that she is achieving is making Scotland and the Scottish people less popular in England than any time since Culloden, that dry-faced crone is nothing but a racist xenophobe and the sooner there is an election to get rid of her the better." Avalon sipped his coffee watching the heated argument over the rim of his cup.

"That's not true, there needs to be a stronger, national identity and this is the way to go about it," replied Ross with an almost laughing countenance.

"So why is it when anyone out of Scotland is asked what they think of us, the universal answer is, '*if it's so good up there why don't they sod off back*?' As I see it, the 'stronger identity' doesn't exist and she just making us seem more isolationist," snapped Boyd.

"That's bullshit, not *everyone* hates us and that kind of answer only comes from people who have never been here, answered Ross letting some of the smile leave his face. He paused for a moment seeing Avalon looking on, "Okay then," he announced, "let's ask our resident Englishman what *he* thinks." And all faces turned to Avalon.

"Me?" he asked almost hiding behind his cup, "it's no good asking me, I don't even begin to understand the fish thing," he shrugged.

"What fish thing?" asked Boyd the fire still in her eyes.

"Well, you had a Salmon, now a Sturgeon, what next, Billy Bloater or Willie Whitebait?"

"And that's it?" asked Ross, "the Englishman's take on the Scottish political situation is a joke about fish?" Avalon shrugged again.

"It worked for Douglas Adams," he smiled, "anyway," he continued more seriously, "take my advice, as a copper you should never have an opinion on politics, religion or..." he paused and then raised his eyebrows to Boyd, "football," and he turned to walk to the booth before calling back, "and as for the Scots in Westminster, with the likes of Callaghan, Brown, Blair, Campbell, Kennedy and a raft of others over the years, I would think that the Scots had already invaded that insidious house before the SNP got there, now get back to work and leave politics to the Scottish people," there was a pause as he turned back to them, "I'm trying to sleep in here."

As he sat, he could see the frustration in Boyd's face, he hadn't got her down as a political sort and Ross certainly wasn't. He was winding her up as he had admitted on several occasions that all politicians and political parties were the same, career politicians worked to *'feather their nest, not further their country'*, he thought it was a great quote and since then he had used it himself. Boyd however seemed as if she could have opinions and liked to let people know, he would keep his eye on her, Frazer however had been unusually tight lipped. She had listened and sighed but offered no comment into the argument. Everyone else had just enjoyed the spectacle of Ross being Ross and creating friction for the sake of it. The debate had however slacked off and left Ross grinning and making the odd comment very quietly and Boyd shaking her head or rolling her eyes. She and Ross got on pretty well and as he had noted previously, these short 'spats' usually bonded people together. It was then he noticed that Pottinger was not in the Cave.

"Where's DC Pottinger?" asked Avalon returning to the room. Rory hadn't seen or heard Avalon approach, he had noticed that about his DI, he could be like a damn ghost.

"Er," Mackinnon looked over to where Pottinger usually sat, "I'm not sure boss, he went to the archive but I don't know where he is now," he looked apologetically at Avalon, "shall I look for him?" he asked.

"No, I'll take a look," said Avalon and he made the journey downstairs and into the archive. A civilian archivist sat at the computer in there and she was busily typing away while a PC, who Avalon recognised as John Makin, was scanning through some old files.

"Is DC Pottinger in the archive?" he said to the

girl. She momentarily looked up and then glanced through the entries of her book to check.

"No he isn't, he was here about an hour ago, he returned some files according to the ledger." Avalon thanked her and nodded to the PC who had turned to look over, then left. Where the hell was Pottinger? For certain, if Avalon really wanted rid of the man here was his chance. He went to the front desk and asked if they had seen him but they hadn't, even in the control room no one had laid eyes on Pottinger. Avalon trudged back upstairs and back to the Cave and with very little surprise he found Pottinger at his desk looking very apprehensive.

DC Pottinger, my office now," he growled. It was a grand title for the booth but everyone in the room caught the seriousness of the command.

"Sit down Detective Constable," he said as calmly as he could muster. "Where have you been?"

"To the archive, I went to-"

"I checked the record, that was some considerable time ago," interrupted Avalon.

"I made a phone call afterwards and then I er," it was clear that the man hadn't quite formulated his excuses, "I... went outside for a smoke."

"So you will still have the packet with you?"

"I have to protest sir, as a Detective I have to have freedom to manoeuvre surely-"

"I'll tell it as it is detective," interrupted Avalon again, "I know you don't smoke and I consider lies from any detective very shoddy never mind someone from my section, I will not accept it on any account and more importantly, you were told to work closely with DC Mackinnon and you have left him to try and make excuses for you, which is an obvious flaw in your character. It is also tantamount to serious misconduct." Pottinger just glared at Avalon, he looked as if he was going to say something and then thought better of it. "You can consider yourself on report pending an investigation of your whereabouts."

"This is a nonsense," insisted Pottinger, "everyone has freedom to work as they see fit but me?"

"I expect my officers to work with their team mates not leave them to take the flak, and you have offered no explanation of why you were missing or where you have been. Lies are all I have heard." Avalon leaned back to let it sink in. There was no reply, Pottinger just sighed, folded his arms and looked to one side. Avalon leaned forward and quietly said,

"Have you got nothing to say?" Pottinger looked at Avalon and he too leaned forward and spoke quietly.

"It's clear you don't like me Avalon, from the very start you had it in for me, I never stood a chance so as far as I'm concerned, put me on report, it won't be the first time."

"I don't doubt that," replied Avalon, he sat upright and said in a louder voice, "you're dismissed, go home until I decide how to proceed." Pottinger shook his head and stood, he looked like he was about to speak to everyone in the Cave but he left without another word.

~~~~~~

Thursday morning was cloudy but dry, as Avalon sat in Frazer's car ready to leave the car park.

"Anywhere in particular?" she asked.

"Not really, I just need to buy a car, I'm not fussed what it is or where it's from, it just needs to be reasonably cheap but reliable," he announced.

"Well et's not my thing but we'll give et a go," and she drove off.

"There are a few car lots on Harbour Road, I would try there first," suggested Avalon and Frazer nodded and drove on. Avalon looked over to her and asked,

"So how did you go on with your 'Special Ops'?" She looked at him for a second.

"Special Ops? that makes et sound much better organised than et was, et was okay, a bit boring at times but that's the nature o' the beast."

"I'm guessing it was a good change from the run of the mill here though," he smiled.

"For a while et was," she agreed, "but et's the same thing every day and that soon becomes an arse ache if y' catch my meaning?"

"How did you get on with the rest of the team?" asked Avalon trying not to make it obvious why he was asking.

"Et was quite a big team but some o' the ones I was with were okay," she grinned a little and then added, "they were nearly all Scottish but two of them couldn't tell what I was saying."

"I always wondered about that," smiled Avalon, "you have a much broader accent than most people from round here and yet you were brought up in Beauly," there was a moments silence and he added, "oh, it doesn't matter if you don't want to tell me, it's not an order or anything," he laughed.

"No, et's okay," she sighed a little and then began to explain. "My mother was from Glasgow and my dad was from Edinburgh," she glanced over to him, "that's probably why I'm such a misfit," and then she paused. "Oh, y' probably don't mind about the Glasgow-

Edinburgh thing?"

"I sort of understand it, I know there is a sort of rivalry," he admitted, "it was once put into perspective by a comedian I saw on television once," he glanced towards her, "Kevin Bridges his name."

"Aye, 'ave heard of him," she replied.

"Well he stood on stage and he said to the audience, 'what's the difference between Glasgow and Edinburgh?'" Avalon used his generic Scottish voice to tell the story, it wasn't the rich Glasgow sound of the comedian but it did sound Scottish, "In Glasgow, no one wakes up when a gun is discharged at one o' clock in the morning." Frazer glanced over for a second with a straight face and then continued to drive. "It probably works better with the correct accent," said Avalon slightly embarrassed, "but I found it funny."

"There es a rivalry, but that's the nature of we Scots. The people en the west don't get on with the people o' the east and conversely the easterners don't get on with the westerners. The Catholics hate the protestants and vice-versa the Islanders don't trust the Highlanders, the Highlanders dislike the Islanders and the lowlanders and the lowlanders hate everyone including the English," she shrugged, "none intended." she added as an afterthought.

"None taken," replied Avalon.

"Et's just the way we are, no matter where we live, we'll find someone we don't like."

"And yet," he began but noticed something. He pointed to a car lot and they pulled in, then he continued, "you can be so tolerant of other cultures. I read a great deal about Scottish history when I first came north, I was amazed by the Scottish acceptance of new ideas but lack of trust of their leaders."

"How do y' mean?" said Frazer as they got out of the car.

"Well, they would raise an army under one leader or another and march off to raid into England, when it came time to bring in the crops they would return north and sell out their leaders for a few pieces of gold. If there was no gold they would hang their leader under a bridge," he explained.

"Well we've had some unscrupulous villains en our history but the bridge thing I havnae heard before," confessed Frazer with a shrug as they walked round a few cars.

"Let's put it this way, I don't think there are many old bridges in Scotland that haven't had one leader or another hanging from it at some time." He bent down to look inside a BMW.

"Maybe et's a tradition we should resurrect," she made a slight grin, which was unusual for her, "present company excepted of course."

"None taken," he repeated then he said, "so, back to your parents," Frazer looked over to him.

"Oh, aye, well as you'd expect given their heritage they argued a great deal, my mother had the loudest voice and so et was her I ended up copying I suppose."

"So how did you end up in Beauly?" asked Avalon looking round the rear of some sort of Asian estate car.

"There were relations living there," she explained, "when my parents first married that's where they lived due tae an uncle giving my dad some work, et didnae last though. Soon after my eighth birthday they split up and my dad left tae go back tae Edinburgh."

"That's sad," frowned Avalon.

"Not really, they argued so much I was glad things settled down, and I grew up en Beauly with a cross between a Glasgow and a Beauly accent." Avalon looked over to her and nodded, she seemed to be looking at a black car with interest. "This looks okay," she said.

"I'm not lucky with black cars," he said raising his brows.

"You're not lucky with cars!" she glowered.

"None taken," said Avalon for the third time.

"It's not too expensive and et looks quite tidy," she said taking a closer look. Avalon saw it was an Audi and he agreed it did seem to tick all the boxes. He walked to the small showroom to find out more about the vehicle.

They were back in the office around lunchtime and Avalon told Ross he had purchased an Audi A6 and Ross seemed reasonably comfortable with the idea.

"They're getting it ready for this evening so I need to tax and insure it."

"Colour?" asked Ross.

"Black again, I just hope that van drivers can see this one when it's parked up."

"I'm guessing it's an old bus knowing you,"

"Old-ish, but it was less than four grand," he nodded.

"Bloody hell, four grand, were Audi making cars back then, does it come with a guy to walk ahead of it with a red flag?"

"I needed a car to go north at the weekend and quite frankly, I like it," he smiled.

"At least old Audis *can* be reliable, does it have a spare wheel?" grinned Ross. Avalon gave him a slight glare and walked to his booth. "Oh and PC Kirk was here to see you earlier," he called, "said she'd come back."

Avalon phoned PC Kirk but she insisted she needed to talk to him in private so he arranged to see her in the rest room.

"What's the problem?" he asked in a low voice. Kirk looked very apprehensive, Avalon had not seen her quite like this before.

"There es a friend, well a colleague," she began, "and she's in a wee bit of trouble, well not trouble but..."

"Well that's as clear as mud," stared Avalon, "you have to give me more to work with." Kirk shuffled her feet around and then looked round the room before continuing.

"This friend has been seeing another police officer," she admitted.

"There's nothing wrong with that, well nothing morally wrong anyway."

"No, true but..." she hesitated, "she has just found out she es pregnant..." there was a long pause until Avalon's face took on a realisation.

"You mean you..." he paused but Kirk saw his expression and her Glasgow temper kicked in.

"No for Christ sakes et's no' me..." and then she composed herself, "et's not me, I'm not quite that stupid, et's one of the staff of the control room," she insisted in a quieter voice. "The problem es, the other half of this coupling is from *your* section," and she waited for Avalon to explode, but he didn't. He sat with a blank expression and then shook his head slightly.

"Well unless he was committing the act on our time or on these premises I can't really make a comment, I'm not happy about it but..." and he trailed off. Kirk was feeling more confident with the reaction and continued.

"The thing is, I told her tae come and see y' but she won't, I think she's embarrassed so I have come tae tell you, she doesn't know I'm here."

"Oh?" was his only comment.

"She only had et confirmed yesterday morning and the trouble was she got her partner en crime into some bother when he came tae find out how she was."

"Pottinger!" exclaimed Avalon putting the facts together, "the dirty little toe-rag," he then growled. Kirk nodded. Avalon looked into the middle distance for a moment. "I take it he intends to do the honourable thing?"

"Aye, I think they intended living together anyway, I'm guessing they would get married but from what I can gather, well..." she hesitated, "he's in some bother with his boss."

"Don't give me those sad kitten eyes Kirk, it doesn't quite work when *you* do it," he frowned, "leave it with me, I'll give it some thought." He sighed then said, "Why couldn't the stupid arsehole just come and tell me?"

"I don't know, maybe just pride, maybe he's just a private person."

"Yes, well, there are some things he needs to put more thought into," he said as he stood to leave, "I hope your friend finds out one day just how good you are to her," and he exited the room.

Chapter Three

Avalon was a little late to the office, it had taken longer than he had expected to pack for his trip to Golspie. He had watched the indomitable Mrs Pink leave in her car and then loaded his vehicle with his items. Only then did he realise he hadn't left Angie a note to say he was away for a few days. By the time he arrived, everyone was in the office including Pottinger. Avalon had sent him a text the previous night and told him to be in the office first thing under pain of death. He called DS Wilson into the office and left him all the details he needed for current cases and a rough outline of what he wanted doing.

"Jim, for Christ's sakes yer only goin' for a couple o' nights, we can cope well enough," smiled Wilson folding his arms.

"I know, but it's the first time I've been away and left all the children with a neighbour," smiled back Avalon. He then had words with Mack to find out exactly what had happened on the day he went up to Golspie and he made some notes. The whole story of a crime was never to be found in case notes, if it were, they would be solved on the same day as they happened. In this instance, Avalon was beginning to think there wasn't a crime at all. That was good too, it meant he could relax for at least some of the time up there. He then picked up his briefcase and walked into the main office.

"Right, I'm off," he announced to the room, "I'm leaving C section in the capable hands of DS Wilson and I'll be back Monday morning," he looked over to Pottinger. "DC Pottinger, I have something for you in my car," and he left the room with everyone calling 'bye' or 'have a nice investigation'. Pottinger followed the DI to the car park where Avalon placed his briefcase on the passenger seat and then he turned to Pottinger leaning on the car.

"I know why you were missing," his voice was calm but had an element of menace about it, "I don't like lies however honourable they seem at the time."

"You know about Ka..?" he paused wondering if Avalon had set a trap for him.

"Yes, I know you have had a liaison but I don't know who she is and don't wish to, but here is a warning," and Avalon pointed at him, "if you ever call me by name without using my title, I'll cut your nuts off with a blunt knife and feed them to DS Wilson's Labrador, is that clear?" Pottinger nodded.

"Yes boss."

"Good, get back to work and do your best not to put DS Wilson under this sort of pressure," and he walked round to the drivers side.

"I'm guessing it was a ruse about there being something in the car?" asked Pottinger not knowing if he had been excused.

"Oh, no, it wasn't as it happens," and he reached across to the glove compartment and then handed Pottinger a large pink envelope. Pottinger just stood staring down at the thing wondering if Avalon had lost his marbles and given him something that he had intended for someone else. Avalon's new car pulled out of the car park and vanished around the corner with him in it. Pottinger looked at the envelope and decided to open it. It contained a large card that had yellow stars and cartoon lambs holding multicoloured balloons, above the ridiculous image were the words 'Congratulations on your good news' and inside more stupid imagery. This time the words were in biro, scrawled in Avalon's distinctive writing, 'You better marry the girl pronto or I'll arrest you for wasting police time!' Pottinger blinked several times, looked back to the gates where Avalon had just vanished and then down to the card again. He read through it all again and then closed it. He shrugged, looked around the car park to find himself alone and he shrugged again. Then a slight smile came to his lips, it wasn't something he experienced a great deal and so his face resisted it for a moment, but inside he knew it was a real, honest to goodness smile.

~~~~~~~

The black Audi A6 headed north over the Kessock Bridge and on into uncharted country under an overcast and angry looking sky. Avalon had never been any further north than Dingwall, a place he attended on a minor case just after Christmas and so as he crossed the bridge over the Cromarty Firth he knew as soon as he turned right at the other end he would be seeing places new to him. The A9 was a more sedate road north of Inverness, free of its dual carriageways and speed cameras, it seemed more like an 'A' road of years ago.

He could feel the pace of his life slowing down and he was already becoming more relaxed. As he passed the turnoff for Bonar Bridge, the firth opened up to his right and to him it was quite spectacular, dotted here and there with what looked like oilrigs. On he drove through acres of meadowland and newly planted fields, past lush woodland and moors of bracken and gorse. This part of the road was nothing like the A9 he had grown to loathe, this was a road that he could see himself riding his motorbike on and he was regretting not being on it at that moment. At the Nigg Roundabout the road bore left and the scenery changed again to flatter, farming country but the ever-present coastline could be seen now and then to the right. At Tain he was amazed to see the Glenmorangie distillery sail by and he considered what golden treasures were stored away in the maturation sheds there, then on to discover Dornoch Firth and another crossing of the water. To both left and right the views were stunning and more than once he pulled over to let traffic pass as he was driving so slow. What surprised him more than anything was the fact that as he crossed the firth and entered the county of Sutherland, the landscape became almost mountainous. He had expected a flatter, more restful and typically coastal look to the place and when Mack had told him, 'Look for a massive monument on a hill,' the hill he had in mind wasn't at all what he was seeing. He noticed it too, way off in the distance he saw a monument that seemed to be almost in the clouds, the monument that he was told overlooked Golspie. Even the A9 changed again and became full of sweeping bends through thick woodland and forest with clearings of farmland here and there. The road then became as straight as an arrow and dropped down and then climbed once more obscuring any chance of an horizon, and at the end of it a sweeping left hand turn that made the top of the rise. There, ahead of him was a black wall. In the shadow of the scudding clouds the massive hills ahead looked dark and foreboding as if guarding the coastline, which stretched out before them, on one hand holding up the sky, on the other holding back the water. He was impressed with that view and more than once had to check his steering and concentrate on driving. Surprises still awaited, the A9 snaked down a large bay and crossed the River Fleet and then climbed the other side past an unfeasibly shaped promontory. His trip to Glen Affric had taught him that Scotland had much to offer but he now realised that there was so much more still left to see. As he closed in on the monument it began to disappear as the cloud dropped and covered it and drizzle began to fall. The wipers of the Audi cleared the rain well enough but they couldn't clear the mist that now shrouded the view and the visibility obscured the scenery. The wind had risen too and Avalon wondered if this was the downside of being so far north. As he saw the road sign that announced Golspie and its award-winning beach, Avalon considered he may just give the beach a miss but as he entered the main street of the centre, the rain ceased and the visibility began to return. The street was made up of rows of stone built houses, mostly small in stature with the odd Victorian taller building here and there. There seemed to be a broad selection of shops and to his right he noticed a car park. He pulled in and looked out over the sea and parked the car. As he exited he glanced up at the sky and wondered about pulling his overcoat out of the boot, it wasn't particularly cold but the stiff breeze felt like it would eventually cut into him. The sky was threatening too even though the visibility was improving. He looked back up at the monument on a large wooded hillside and then decided his first port of call would be the police station. He had been told that the station shared its location with another organisation so as he set off walking north he kept his eyes open. He noticed that there was a newspaper office in the village, that could be a resource for local information, then he saw the sign for the police station and as he approached he noticed it did indeed share its locus with another organisation, namely the Highland Council. He entered and found two ladies within. Avalon produced his warrant card and asked if PC Gunn was available.

"He's out in his car I believe, I can check if you like?" and she stood to go and find out.

"No, it's okay, I'm sure he's busy but if you'll pass this on to him and ask him to give me a call when he has the time," and he handed her his card. She read it and said,

"Oh." Avalon had no idea what that meant but he thanked her for her help and left. Certainly his first interaction with Golspie had been pleasant enough and he wondered in what order he should structure his day. He needed to speak to Muiranne Stodart's husband but he was also considering speaking to David Sutherland. He had saved all the phone numbers he may need onto his mobile and so he decided to give Mr Sutherland a call to see if he was available.

"Hello, Mr Sutherland?"

"*Yes it is.*" He had a slight Scottish accent but nothing Avalon could pinpoint with his limited experience.

"It's Detective Inspector Avalon from Inverness,"

"*Oh cripes, is this about the newspaper article?*"

"No not really, I need to ask you some further

81

questions about the disappearance of Mrs Stodart."

"*So it is about the article, I'm afraid they exaggerated a little,*" he replied apologetically.

"That's as may be but I need to speak, it won't take long."

"*When were you thinking of coming up*?" he asked. Avalon felt the rain begin again and so he retreated into a bus shelter.

"I'm already here, I'm in Golspie at this moment."

"*Oh, er... right... well,*" stuttered Sutherland, "*well I suppose now is as good a time as any. My address is-*"

"I have your address Mr Sutherland, I'll be about twenty minutes," said Avalon and felt glad he had decided on the overcoat.

By the time he reached the location the satnav had brought him to, the rain had stopped and the sky was breaking up. Here and there blue could be seen forcing its way through the ash coloured clouds that sped off over the hills into the west. The road was single track and Sutherland's house was a small bungalow slotted into the hillside with an extension to one side. Avalon noticed the curtains move as he entered the small driveway. As he approached the house the door opened and a person he assumed to be Mr Sutherland stood at the door with an approximation of a smile. The man was probably in his sixties but looked fit and tall for his age.

"Detective Avalon did you say?" he asked.

"Yes, Mr Sutherland?" and he held his hand out and Sutherland shook it with a strong grip.

"Come in, would you like a cup of tea?" asked the man.

"Thank you but I'll pass on that, I have a great deal to do." This was Avalon's stock answer, he rarely took a drink at anyone's house just in case the coffee was instant or the tea was 'Poundshop' fifty pence a hundredweight stuff. "I just want to go over your statement about the incident on the twenty second of last month."

"Oh, is there a problem with it?" he asked.

"Not as such but I gather from the investigating officer that you insisted Mrs Stodart vanished from the vehicle as it was driving along?" frowned Avalon.

"As I said, the newspaper exaggerated what I told them, but she did seem to just vanish," insisted Sutherland. Avalon had been studying the man he didn't seem the sort of chap who would be prone to fantasy or lying just for effect. It was clear he needed to look more closely.

"What do you know about Mrs Stodart, Mr Sutherland?" he asked.

"I'm certainly not going to gossip about their private life detective if that's what you're getting at."

"That's not what I asked, do you mind if I sit?" and he pointed to the chair.

"No not at all," said Sutherland opening his arm in a sweeping movement and as Avalon sat he too took to the easy chair opposite.

"It's just that all I have heard *is* gossip," Avalon was trying to feed the man an opening, "and to be honest I would just like to hear about her character."

"I don't really know her that well, they live further up the road in a large house, I understand her family is an old Scottish land owning set."

"Really?" said Avalon raising his eyebrows.

"Related to the Dalrymple family I believe but I don't know how closely." Avalon nodded, the name didn't ring any bells.

"Do they still own land here?" asked Avalon trying to ease the man into his confidence.

"I don't think so, most of these families have sold out to land collectors like Anders Povlsen," he frowned as he spoke.

"I don't know the name," offered Avalon.

"Why would you?" shrugged Sutherland, "the man is left to do as he pleases, did you know detective just 432 individuals like Povlsen own more than half of Scotland's non-public land. In European countries like Norway a country seven times the size of Scotland there are only twenty-three estates bigger than 10,000 hectares. In Scotland there are 144. Does that seem wrong to you?" Avalon shrugged, he didn't care all that much but he had obviously hit on an obsession of David Sutherland's.

"No, I didn't," was all he said.

"If some of the larger British companies established such dominance in their field, they would find themselves falling foul of EU competition rules detective and furthermore-"

"I can see this is important to you Mr Sutherland," interrupted Avalon, "but if we could get back to the Stodarts?"

"Oh, yes of course, but as I said I know very little about them. The money was hers of course, Peter Stodart is a... well let's just say he's not been one to work for his money," replied Sutherland looking downcast. Avalon had hit a nerve and he now knew where he had to pressurise that nerve.

"I assume they don't get on," he began.

"No they don't," replied Sutherland surprised at how easily Avalon had got to him. He paused but then considered he was about to impart nothing that wasn't already talked about, "I don't think he has actually struck her but I believe she has a hard time with him."

"They argued?"

"That I can't say but I doubt it, Muir is a gentle creature, I would say she would just walk away rather than argue," replied Sutherland looking into the middle distance.

"Are you married Mr Sutherland?"

"Yes I am, my wife works part time in Golspie."

"Does your wife get on with Mrs Stodart?" asked Avalon.

"I think they have only met on a couple of occasions, she certainly hasn't expressed any feeling one way or the other."

"But *you* get on very well with her I assume?" Avalon was going for the throat.

"If you mean what I think you mean I would have to say you are pushing the limits of my hospitality," replied Sutherland angrily.

"Don't look at it as hospitality Mr Sutherland, more like answering questions for an investigation into a missing person that could turn into something far more serious," replied Avalon with equal anger, "now, were you having an affair with Mrs Stodart?"

"Certainly not," replied Sutherland and then he began to calm and Avalon saw him thinking through something. "She is a wonderful person, so petite and demure, any man would give a lifetime to spend a day with her but there was never anything like that between us, and I doubt if she would ever stray from her marriage."

"Why do you say that?" Avalon asked in a quieter voice.

"She has a loyalty that is old fashioned and honourable, even through her miserable existence she has never said a bad word about her husband." Avalon nodded, he could see the man was infatuated by her. Maybe it was his fantasy, the connection to the 'lady of the manor', or maybe she was just the sort of person who attracted fantasists? Avalon needed to move forward and after a moment he said,

"I wonder Mr Sutherland," and after a pause, "would you be prepared to indulge me and walk me through the events leading up to her disappearance?" The man thought for a moment.

"Yes, I don't see why not, it happened just outside."

"Outside your property?" asked Avalon.

"Yes, well more or less. I'll just put my wellies on," and he walked to the door and pulled on a pair of Wellington boots. Avalon looked at his own shoes, was this going to ruin them he thought?

"Is it muddy out there?" he asked.

"Not particularly, I always wear wellies when I go out. I used to leave them in the porch but a pair went missing so I bring them in now,"

"I wouldn't have thought this was a high crime area Mr Sutherland?"

"No it's not, he said as he stood, "I assume a playful fox ran off with them as I found the right one in a field close by," he gave a slight smile and walked to the door.

They walked past Avalon's car and onto the single-track road.

"It was just down there, near the gate to the field," said Sutherland pointing down the hill. There was a bank to the right with a copse of trees growing on it

86

and to the left just open fields bordered by hedging and a few trees.

"So can you take me through the events prior to her going missing?" asked Avalon.

"Well, I was in the drive clearing leaves up and I heard a vehicle stop on the road, it was Muir," he began but Avalon interrupted.

"That's what you called her?"

"Yes, I think all her friends called her that."

"You say you didn't know her all that well but now you intimate that you are a friend, but carry on Mr Sutherland," insisted Avalon. This put Sutherland on the back foot for a moment, he blinked and considered explaining why called her Muir, but then relented and continued.

"She leaned from the drivers seat so I went to speak to her and opened the passenger door, she asked if I had another water butt as the one I sold her had a leak," he explained and quickly turned to Avalon, "I did offer to replace it free of charge if she brought it back but she said she had another use for it."

"Water butt?" asked Avalon.

"Yes," nodded Sutherland, "I bought five of them, it was so much cheaper and sold the others for a wee profit." He looked around, "the same as that one by the greenhouse," he said pointing to the glasshouse through some shrubs. It was a plain, plastic, forty-five gallon type with a small tap at the bottom, a black plastic lid sat on the top with a short drainpipe entering through a hole.

"Go on," insisted Avalon.

"I told her I had one left and to back her truck in the drive. The road can be busy even though it's single track," explained the man.

"By truck I assume to refer to the Land Rover she

was driving?"

"Yes," nodded Sutherland, "she had a car but she wouldn't have got the barrel in that." Avalon didn't react so the man continued his story. "When she had backed it in we placed the barrel in the rear and she had brought one of those small ratchet ties to hold it in, she told me the last one had been bouncing about in the back, it was probably how it got damaged. We tied it down and I put the lid in but she said she didn't need it as she still had the old one."

"How was the butt placed?" asked Avalon.

"What do you mean?

"Was it length ways? Was it standing upright?" explained Avalon.

"Oh, I see, it was lying down and the open end facing the rear door."

"I see," nodded Avalon and he pulled out his notebook to make a rough sketch, "go on please," he added.

"Er, well, she gave me the money which I refused to take and then she said goodbye and got in the truck."

"Then what happened?" asked Avalon placing the notepad back in his pocket.

"She started the truck and pulled out of the drive and went down the hill, she hooted the horn, I waved and headed back to the house and then I heard the engine rev," he explained.

"So you did take your eyes off the vehicle?" asked Avalon.

"Well, yes but only for a second," he insisted.

"Then let us try an experiment Mr Sutherland," said Avalon and he walked slightly down the hill and looked back. "I want you to wave to me, and then to the best of your knowledge do exactly what you did on that

88

day considering the noise of the engine from the Land Rover," explained Avalon. Sutherland looked a little embarrassed at having to wave but he did as he was asked and was shocked to see Avalon standing not a foot away when he returned to the roadside.

"I take your point detective," he nodded.

"I'm guessing the vehicle was out of sight for several seconds, enough time for me to walk about ten yards at a steady pace," explained Avalon.

"But that still doesn't explain where she went to," insisted Sutherland.

"Then let us continue with the story," he nodded and Sutherland did as he was bid.

"Well, I looked down the hill and saw the truck had driven into the gate of that field down there," he pointed to a position about a hundred yards down the hill. Avalon walked to the position accompanied by Sutherland noticing a broken gate and then asked him to explain what happened next.

"I came straight down and ran to the driver's door but when I looked through the window there was no sign of her, I opened the door and looked inside, the water butt was in the back but no sign of Muir. I even opened the back door and had a look but she was nowhere to be seen."

"What did you do then Mr Sutherland?"

"I... I think I must have scratched my head as I couldn't believe what I was seeing. I looked over the fields and even climbed the bank," he pointed to the other side of the road, "just in case she had wondered off but except for a few trees and hedges you can see some considerable way. I returned to the truck, had another look inside and switched off the engine."

"It was still running at that point?" asked Avalon.

"Yes, she had just vanished out of the driver's seat."

"What happened next?"

"I walked back up the hill and back to the house and phoned the police. They sent an officer from Golspie and he was very kind but I don't think he believed me. He made some calls and a team came and checked the vehicle and the surrounding area. They took my fingerprints and my footwear and cordoned the area off. Apart from a young detective coming to see me from your neck of the woods I can't say much more."

"Am I correct in saying that Mrs Stodart lives further up the hill?" asked Avalon, Sutherland was still clearly shaken by the event as it took time to answer.

"Yes, she lives about a half a mile from here."

"Did she say where she was going then, as she turned left it would seem she wasn't going straight home?"

"No she didn't," said the man looking slightly upset, "I never really considered that, though she may have had something to do in Golspie."

"And one last thing Mr Sutherland," continued Avalon, "and I want you to think deeply about this, when you first looked down the lane from your house and saw the vehicle in the field, were the brake lights on or not?" Sutherland raised his eyebrows and held his chin, he was deep in thought as if he was running it through his brain like a movie.

"I... er, I think... no that's right, they were on and then they went off."

"Are you sure?"

"Yes positive," he said.

"And I'm guessing from that point on the vehicle would be in sight right up to the time you reached it."

90

Sutherland nodded.

Avalon had returned to the village, he needed to find somewhere to stay so he parked up once more and walked onto the main street, just then his phone rang.

"Avalon."

"*Hello, et's PC Gunn, you wanted me tae give you a ring.*" The voice was clear and deliberate with an accent similar to if not stronger than the Inverness brogue.

"Oh, thanks for calling, I wanted to have a word with you about Mrs Stodart going missing, I believe you recorded the case?"

"*Aye, I'm off soon but ef you're close by I'm en the office.*"

Avalon made his way back to the building that housed the police office and he was shown into a room at the rear.

"How can I help you?" asked the PC as they sat.

"I wondered what you made of Mr Sutherland's story."

"I think he believes what he said," shrugged Gunn.

"And you?" asked Avalon.

"Et's not my place tae speculate, the SOCO team found no footprints en the mud other than his and the only fingerprints on the vehicle were from Mr Sutherland or Mrs Stodart and her husband. They are the facts. I have tae assume that she wasn't en the vehicle when Mr Sutherland says et went off the road."

"Meaning she jumped from the vehicle and made off?" asked Avalon.

"Aye, possibly, I can't imagine why but what else es there?" Avalon also established that the PC didn't know either of the Stodarts well enough to give him more and he only knew Sutherland by sight. Outside the office as he and the PC left he added little more.

"The problem you might have DI Avalon es that there are a few people round here that have good imaginations, there are all manner of legends and the like, et's an ancient coastal settlement so et's to be expected."

"You mean there are already rumours?" smiled Avalon.

"Aye, one or two, there's even one about the moor spirit," grinned the PC.

"I noticed the newspapers have picked up on that one," frowned Avalon.

"Aye, some people love a good mystery or conspiracy theory, the Brollachan had to come into a disappearance I suppose," shrugged the officer.

"That's strange," frowned Avalon, "I think I have heard that name before?" he searched the rear shelves of his over-packed memory but couldn't remember where he had heard it.

"There are legends all over this area, ef et's legends y' want tae know about ask Frankie Osborne, he swears the Brollachan es responsible for everything that goes wrong around here," shrugged Gunn.

"Where would I find him?" The PC pointed to a building down the street, it was a pub.

"He can be found en there now and then," smiled PC Gunn, "but I would take what he tells y' with a pinch o' salt," smiled Gunn.

"Thanks for your time," said Avalon holding out his hand.

"Anytime, ef you need anything just leave a message at the office," and the PC went on his way.

Avalon noticed the fish and chip shop, he was hungry for sure so he treated himself to a fish supper, his new found vegetarianism notwithstanding, and sat on the front looking out to sea. He considered the new information he had. He knew if Sutherland was correct about the brake lights being on, Mrs Stodart was still in the vehicle prior to his arrival at the driver's door, but where had she gone? He knew forensics had checked the vehicle so the idea of hidden compartments was out of the question, he was missing something, however the seagulls weren't. Avalon's fish supper had caught the attention of the local gastronomic critics so he ate with care. Avalon liked the gulls, he knew people who lived at the coast hated them but what would be the point of the coast if it didn't have seagulls? Their cries and calls were all part of the experience for him, the smells and the sounds had to go together and compliment each other. He was also struck by the beauty of the birds, close up they looked so white and bold. He finished what he needed and contrary to what the locals would have probably wished he unloaded the remains of the meal onto the rocks on the beach. They were soon gone. He considered that here, without the commercialism of the southern resorts the seagulls must have a much harder life having to cope with the harsher weather. He stood and decided he needed a dram.

Avalon sat at the bar with his glass of single malt, not before he visited his car to make a quick change of clothes to blend in. He had removed his suit jacket and the tie and worn a casual 'bomber' style jacket and was ensconced on a high stool scanning the room every now and then. He asked the barman if he knew Frankie Osborne.

"Aye, he comes en here now and again, he'll probably be en later." Avalon nodded and sipped at the whisky as if it didn't matter. It didn't, Avalon wasn't interested in local legend but it was a way to get a local to open up, it was a method he used on a regular basis. A little bit of chat could sometimes lead a new line of questioning in a case. He shot a quick glance down to his watch, the time was passing and he still had to find a room for the evening. There had been more rain and the sky was overcast, the wind was still brisk too and he was thinking that his day off would probably be spent indoors if the weather didn't change.

"Can you suggest anywhere for a room for the night?" he asked behind the bar.

"You shouldn't have any trouble this time o' year, there are plenty of hotels and bed and breakfasts, et depends ef y' want sea views or no'," smiled the man. Avalon just wanted a comfortable bed and hopefully he could relax into a good nights sleep. A small built man entered the pub and walked up to the bar and ordered a drink.

"By the way Frankie," said the barkeeper nodding towards Avalon, "this guy says he's looking for you." The man was thin and slightly built, he eyes were small and close together which Avalon thought gave him the look of a small marsupial. He looked Avalon up and down and then said,

"Now why whood a copper be loo'kin' for Frankie?" His accent was different to the locals, the vowels were rounded and the intonation slightly flatter.

"Very observant Mr Osborne," smiled Avalon taking another sip of his drink.

"We might be fifty miles from Inverness," his speech was slow and deliberate as if he couldn't rush it if he tried, "but whee're not wet behind the ears," and he took several gulps of his drink. Avalon ordered another drink for Osborne.

"Bribery is it?" he asked winking to the bartender.

"The information I'm after isn't about anything to do with police work," smiled Avalon.

"Oh, I can't imagine you want to know about creel fishing Mr..." said Osborne waiting for the policeman to give his name.

"Avalon, Jim," he added the 'Jim' as an afterthought. The man nodded at the name and took another drink.

"That sounds like an ancient name," he nodded again and then turned to Avalon with an unblinking stare, "so how can I help you 'Jim'?" He emphasised the name.

"From what I hear you are prone to put the blame of certain incidents on something called..." he hesitated, for the life of him he couldn't remember the word properly, "well, I can't remember what it's called, a legendary creature that begins with 'B'."

"The Brollachan?" asked Osborne.

"That's the one," nodded Avalon.

"So why whood you be wanting t' know about such things?" asked Osborne.

"I keep hearing about it," Avalon remembered suddenly where he had first heard the name. A chap called Arnold Burnside had warned him against it. That was over a year ago when he was investigating the mysterious drumming sounds at Drumnadrochit. "I thought that if I keep hearing about it so much I ought to know what it is." Osborne looked towards the rear of the bar for a few seconds and then back to Avalon.

"Whell Jim, not many folks around here take such things seriously so I'm doubting you will either," and he finished his drink and ordered the one Avalon had paid for. The man lifted the full glass and said,

"Slarncha," which Avalon assumed was the correct way to pronounce 'Slàinte', the word that he now habitually pronounced as 'Sludge'.

"Good health," was his reply as he gave a slight smile to Osborne.

"I'm not an expert in the field, you whood need to speak to others about it," he added rather languidly.

"Anyone in mind?" asked Avalon finishing his drink.

"Probably Tom Bell, he used to teach the subject, but..." Osborne stopped and took a drink.

"Go on," insisted Avalon.

"Well, hees not so well in the heid sometimes," and Osborne pointed to his own skull.

"Where would I find him?"

"Oh, he comes in here when he's not so mixed up," nodded Osborne. Avalon was bored, it was seven o' clock and so he decided it was time to leave the pub.

"Well thanks for the information Mr Osborne," smiled Avalon and he stood.

"Thank you for the drink Jim, and if I was you..." he paused again and looked seriously at Avalon, "I whouldn't dismiss the old creatures of the Highlands, not at all, this is their last natural environment you see," and he gave a slight 'knowing' nod and turned back to the bar.

Avalon walked to the car and drove slightly south to where he remembered seeing a 'B and B' sign and so he followed it and chose a place at random. The landlady was friendly and the rooms were pleasant and it did indeed have a sea view, just, squashed in between two other houses. He unloaded the car and had a shower and with a lack of anything else to pass the time, he changed and made his way back to the pub he had been in earlier. The barman recognised him and said,

"Back so soon?" Osborne wasn't to be seen and so Avalon asked about Tom Bell.

"He doesnea come en much these days,"

"I saw him earlier on," said another customer on a barstool. "I saw him twenty minutes ago by the pier, do you know him?" asked the man.

"No, I was told he may be able to point me to some information," explained Avalon. The man shrugged.

"Good luck, he's not been the same since his wife croaked," and he gulped at his drink.

"When did she die?" asked Avalon.

"About seven or eight years ago I think," was the answer. Avalon thanked him, paid for another drink for *him* and left to find Mr Bell. Leaning on the railings near the pier was a man short in stature holding tight on the metal as if he was out at sea and the surf was up. Avalon wondered if he had been drinking.

"Mr Bell?" he asked but there was no reaction. "Mr Tom Bell?" he asked again. Without turning to Avalon the man began to speak.

"*Oh, - we do like - to be beside - the sea side...*" the words to the old song were not sung but spoken out, clearly and slowly, with gaps between the phrases, "*oh we do - like to be besides - the sea...*" Avalon leaned a little and thought he could see tears in the man's eyes. He didn't think he was much over sixty-five, maybe in his early sixties. His face however looked wracked with pain, something behind his features seemed tortured, or

97

at least in turmoil. "*oh, we do love to walk - along the prom, - prom, - prom...*"

"Mr Bell, are you alright?" asked Avalon, this seemed to work and the man looked directly at him, tears streaming down his face.

"Hello, do I know you?" asked the man wiping the tears away with the back of his hand.

"Someone said you may be able to tell me something about the local legends?" he explained.

"Local? I'm not really local, I don't know why they told you that, I'm from Invergarry..." he paused and Avalon was about to give up on the man. Bell let go of the railings and took a handkerchief from his pocket, dried his eyes and blew his nose. He took a deep breath of the clear air and then said, "I'm sorry for that, I don't know what came over me. Who did you say you were?" There wasn't much of an accent, he was probably educated in England.

"Avalon, Jim Avalon, someone said you may know something about local legends."

"Well I used to teach ancient Scottish culture in Glasgow, mainly about the Picts but I did cover some of the legends of our country," he sniffled a little and then asked, "anything in particular?" He was now like a different man, he looked younger and though his eyes were now ringed with red, a bright mind likely lurked behind them.

"Are you sure you are alright, do you want me to get you home?" asked Avalon with concern.

"I lost my wife you see, I still haven't quite got over it," he explained. Avalon assumed the man in the pub had exaggerated so he asked,

"I'm sorry to hear that, when was it?"

"Oh," the man looked out to sea and he eyes

skipped along the horizon as if he was thinking through the horror of it all over again, "er, it will be five years ago this month." Avalon considered it was a long time to mourn, but who was he to decide how long a person was sad for a lost partner? "Yes, I know it's a long time, I just never got over it like some people do," he explained as if he knew what Avalon was thinking. "I used to lecture in Glasgow, mainly Scottish history but also folk law, we lived in the Cumbernauld area and so when I retired, Harriet said she would love to live on the coast. It was her dearest wish. She was brought up in Invergarry but had been to this coast for days out and holidays, it made perfect sense to buy a retirement property in Golspie." Tears were once more running down his face. "She loved it here and was so happy that we'd come, two weeks later she collapsed and died," his head lowered and the tears ran off his face and crashed to the ground, "they said it was her heart..." he stopped talking.

"I'll leave you alone Mr Bell, I'm sorry for your loss," said Avalon but the man turned.

"No, it's alright Mr, er..." he looked apologetic and wiped the tears with his sleeve, "I'll be fine, now what was it you wished to know?" Avalon wasn't sure, he was beginning to wish he had stayed in his room.

"I was trying to find out about the Brollachan," explained Avalon, pleased that he remembered the name at last.

"Ah, the Brollachan, a nasty creature for sure, what do you wish to know about it."

"Shall we take a seat?" said Avalon pointing to a bench behind them. He had a quick glance at the sky, it was still overcast but the rain seemed to have left them alone. When they were seated Avalon asked him to tell him about the creature. The reason for engaging him in

99

conversation seemed pointless now but he considered that if the man was left alone he would drift back into the place he had just come from.

"In most Scottish legends the Brollachan is the child of the Fuath, but in some parts it is a mist elemental. It generally has no shape due to being young and not yet able to find a suitable host. Children are its most common prey as the young are not strong enough to resist, and of course it prefers the mist moors rather than the forests."

"Sounds dreadful," nodded Avalon with a smile.

"It is dreadful, mainly because it possesses other people, it is even said that while a person is possessed it can still turn back into mist whilst keeping the host." Bell seemed to come alive explaining the legend and though Avalon was ready to go, he let the man continue a little. "You can tell if someone is possessed however because the Brollachan has limited powers of speech, in some legends it is just a disembodied mouth with eyes." He paused for breath, "Ask it a question and it will struggle to answer and its eyes will glow red."

"Well that was very informative Mr Bell, I think you have given me what I wanted to know," and he stood.

"I'm glad I could be of some assistance," and he stood too, "of course it's just a story that was invented to keep children from straying too far from home but there are still people who live near the lochs that say when the mists roll over the moors, something comes down with it, and doesn't always go back," he frowned slightly, his swollen red eyes showing an inquisitive glare, "why the interest in the creature?"

"It seems to crop up now and then in my line of work and I can't find out much on the subject. I thought

100

it would be best to ask people who are closer to the legends," explained Avalon. Bell was nodding slowly but a dark pallor once again flushed through his features.

"I think there is always something more tangible at the back of legends," he said. Avalon remembered a similar idiom voiced by PC Dowd some time ago.

"Well thanks again, nice to have spoken," and he turned and walked away. When he was thirty or forty yards away he looked back and saw Tom Bell return to the railing and start to chant again.

"*Where the brass band plays, - tiddly om, - pom pom...*"

~~~~~~

Avalon slept reasonably well and awoke to another breezy and overcast morning but as he returned from breakfast he thought about his day. He still had to interview Peter Stodart but after that, the day was his own, he just hoped the weather picked up a little.

"Mr Stodart?" he said into the phone.

"*Yes, what can I do for you?*" The accent was mainly English, there was a hint of Scottish to it but probably just what he had picked up living there.

"It's Detective Inspector Avalon, I wonder if I can come round and ask you a few questions about your wife's disappearance?"

"*Well, it's not really convenient,*" he replied.

"I'm just round the corner, it won't take long," explained Avalon.

"*As I said it's not really convenient and I have given several statements already.*"

"I realise that Mr Stodart, then maybe you would rather come down to Inverness and have the interview

101

there?" There was a long pause, the tactic usually worked.

"*Okay*," sighed the man, "*I am busy so I hope it won't take long.*"

The house was rather grand, not country mansion grand but late Victorian, servant's quarters and small stable block grand. Even this far north it would be well beyond Avalon's salary. There was a once pretty summerhouse to the left, now looking somewhat forlorn but still showing its former grandeur. Inside the main house, the theme didn't continue. There was little furniture and what was there was cheap and ordinary. The house felt as if the owners didn't quite have the money to keep the place as it ought to be. Even the curtains looked like they had been there since the blackouts during the war. He was taken to the kitchen where they sat at a farmhouse style pine table. There were dirty pots in the sink so there was obviously no 'hired help' and all that was in the room other than the table and chairs was a Welsh dresser and laptop on the table beside an empty cup.

"So what do you need to know?" asked Stodart. He was of normal build and height and had a thick head of dark hair. He was dressed expensively if not well, Avalon noticed a label sticking out of the top of his shirt and his trousers were creased. He had a fidgety way about him, some would describe it as shifty but Avalon recognised it for what it was, the man was a drug user.

"I'm just chasing some loose ends and wanted to ask you a few questions." The man sat impassive. "I assume you have heard nothing from your wife," he asked. Stodart shook his head and said simply,

"Nothing."

"Have you any idea where she might be?"

"No not at all but she's probably abroad

102

somewhere."

"What makes you say that?" asked Avalon.

"She cleared out her account before she left, I didn't know until a few days ago, she's taken almost two hundred grand with her."

"I see," said Avalon raising his brows.

"No you don't, you're here to look for an excuse to point the finger at me and all the time she is laughing behind our backs," the man said with a bitter tone.

"You said 'her account', does that mean you had separate finances?"

"To a degree, yes..." he paused as he answered, Avalon saw him glance down at the laptop, "she kept an account for her own money, we both did, it meant that my business accounts stayed separate."

"Then if it was her personal money I would say she was free to do with it as she pleased," shrugged Avalon, he wasn't trying to annoy the man, just get him off his guard.

"Not when our life is crashing down around our ears," he spat, "that money could have given us the time to get ourselves sorted out," he was quite emotional now but he managed to calm before he continued, "you can see the house Inspector, we are in some financial trouble and she has done nothing to alleviate our little problems."

"What is your business Mr Stodart?" The man sat motionless for a moment and then turned to answer.

"I run an online gambling website."

"I would have thought that would be lucrative," replied Avalon raising a slightly questioning look into his features.

"It used to be, too much competition now," he replied and looked at the laptop again.

"Was your wife insured Mr Stodart?" asked Avalon calmly.

"Oh I see," answered the man becoming agitated once more, "I've done away with her to claim on the insurance, is that it?"

"I have to pursue all lines of inquiry," insisted Avalon.

"But if you check Inspector, you'll find I haven't claimed."

"You wouldn't be able to either unless we find that something unfortunate has happened to her," said Avalon with a slight smile. The man calmed a little and shrugged. Avalon didn't like the man, he didn't like him at all and he could see why a woman may want to be rid of him, but he didn't see anything in Stodart that pointed to him being directly involved in her disappearance. "I gather you have the Land Rover returned to you, may I have a look at it?" he added.

"It's in the garage, it's still covered in the mess your people left on it, be quick, I'm thinking of selling it." Avalon nodded, then stood and went to check the double garage at the back, Stodart didn't follow. There was just the Land Rover in the garage, it was still covered in black powder from the fingerprints team, it looked like Peter Stodart wasn't the tidiest man but there was no sign of any other vehicle, which meant if the man sold the vehicle he would be without transport. There was no sign of the water butt either so Avalon returned to the house. He considered looking at the summerhouse as the door looked slightly ajar but he decided not to waste any more time. As he passed the kitchen he looked through the window and saw Stodart furiously typing on the laptop, Avalon couldn't see any details but by the time he returned to the kitchen the laptop was closed once more.

"I was under the impression your wife owned a car," commented Avalon as he entered.

"She does, I have no idea where it is but I expect if you find that you'll find her," he replied. Avalon placed his notebook on the table with a pencil and asked Stodart to write down the make, model and colour of the car with the registration number and then asked,

"I'm just wondering why the car is missing, I gather she was in the Land Rover when she disappeared?"

"I really have no idea, I hadn't seen it for several days, and then she decides to run off with the truck and leave me without transport," he replied unconcerned and then he suddenly asked, "Are you married?"

"No," replied Avalon, "but I was."

"Then you can probably understand my anger at being treated this way by her."

"Not really," replied Avalon as he read the notebook and then placed it in his jacket pocket, "certainly in my case it was *my* fault," he then glared at Stodart, "and I bitterly regret that," and he turned to leave. "I'll see myself out, you must be busy."

~~~~~~

Sunday was already wearing thin and he hadn't even had a good look around the village. He parked in the car park he had previously visited and walked all the way down the sea front. The bite of the sea air and the calling of the gulls brought clear thoughts to his head. It seemed that there was nothing more to do on the case, it was clear to him that Mrs Stodart had formulated an elaborate plan to make herself vanish and walked away with what

105

remained of her money. Why she had done it in the way she had was a mystery and one that Avalon couldn't fathom, it would have been much easier to just walk out. Maybe she didn't want any paper trail for her husband to follow, maybe she had something to hide. There was nagging doubt however about the car. If she had taken the Land Rover to pick up the water butt, where was the car? Had an accomplice given her a lift back so that she would still have the car for her own use after? Either way he could see no reason to put further time or resources into the case. As he reached the end of the promenade he cut through to the main road and doubled back the way he had come but down the high street. He walked past the bank and on toward the Co-op trying to figure out how she got out of the vehicle without being seen. To his right he saw movement but it was too late, there was a crash of sorts and shopping seemed to be falling from the sky. He had walked into someone coming out of the shop, or rather they had walked into him. He began to apologise immediately and helped to pick up the shopping. As he stood he noticed the woman looked a little stressed.

"Here, let me sort this out for you," he said as he began to repack the bags.

"It's not your fault, I just wasn't looking where I was going," she admitted. They soon had things under control with the help from another shopper who gave them an extra bag to replace the torn one. "Thank you," she smiled. He hadn't noticed at first but she was quite attractive, she had a wide, pleasant smile and her reddish hair was pulled up into a bun. She was fairly tall too but her clothing style wasn't particularly to Avalon's taste, which was probably why he had only just noticed her attractiveness. She had a baggy brown pullover over

106

what seemed to be muddy jeans and very worn sandals that did little to make her stand out. She didn't have movie star looks but Avalon was taken in by her and inevitably, his shallow side began to assess her against his watershed that was Sarah Underwood. He almost had an 'Underwood scale', but he was so embarrassed about it and would never admit it to a soul.

"Let me help you," insisted Avalon keeping hold of two of the shopping bags.

"There's no need," she smiled, "my car is parked just round the back of the shop."

"Then it's no trouble at all, lead the way," he said. She thanked him as he tried to work out her accent, it wasn't all that broad and he thought it was maybe Inverness or that area. They reached the car quickly, it was almost as shabby as Avalon's previous wreck and was also an estate car but the rear of it was full of various items. "You're a painter?" he asked.

"No, well I used to be but no one wanted to buy them so I became a potter," she shrugged.

"And did you have more success?" he asked.

"No not really," she said closing the back of the car, "do you paint?" she hesitated, "I mean you seem to know what all this junk is for," she nodded to the rear of her car.

"Not me," laughed Avalon, "I can only just draw breath never mind paint a landscape," he looked down at the artists paraphernalia and it brought back memories, "my ex-wife took to it for a while but all the gear eventually ended up in the loft." She smiled and nodded.

"I confess, if I had a loft it would be overflowing," she smiled again. "Do you live in the village?" she asked as she fumbled in her pockets for her keys.

"No, I'm..." he wondered what to tell her, "here on business you might say." She raised her eyebrows.

"Business?" she walked to the driver's door, "sounds interesting." Avalon noticed there was a café at the back of the car park, he was thinking quick, maybe it was the northern air.

"Look, can I buy you a coffee?" he then became slightly nervous, "and you can tell me about your pottery." She looked at the cafe and then began to shake her head, but then looked to him slowly.

"Okay, why not? but I'm buying," she smiled.

~~~~~~~

Peter Stodart closed the lid of his laptop and paced the room, he looked at the kettle and wondered if he needed another coffee, maybe not, maybe something stronger, but he filled it and flicked the switch. He then sat once more and opened his laptop again and checked his emails for the twentieth time. Still nothing, he composed another message and sent it quickly.

"Why don't you damn well answer?" he growled and banged his hand on the table. He stood again and habitually closed the lid of the laptop, the kettle clicked proving the water had boiled but he ignored it and quickly went to his bedroom. He pulled open the top drawer by his bed and took out a little black box and took it with him downstairs gripping it tightly to his chest. He heard a noise in the kitchen. "I bet it's that damn copper snooping around," he thought to himself and he burst into the room. He instinctively looked at the laptop, it was still there and untouched. He picked up his cup and walked to the sink placing the black box on the drainer. Again he heard a noise so he quickly turned.

"You!" he exclaimed, "what are *you* doing here?" He sighed and turned to reach for another cup from a rack but his world went black, the last thing he knew was a falling sensation and in the distance something smashing.

Chapter Four

True, the sky was the usual canvas of cloud and there was a promise of more rain in the wind's breath but Avalon awoke from one of the best nights sleep he had enjoyed for some time. He slept so well he almost missed breakfast, but the poached eggs and toast washed down with two strong cups of excellent coffee, hit the spot and set him up for the day. The trip hadn't been a waste of time for sure, even if it was just the rejuvenated feel from a little relaxation, he felt that it had been truly worth staying over. The previous afternoon and evening had been pleasant if brief, he had spent a short time in the afternoon in the company of Julia Beattie, the woman he had bumped into outside the shop. It had been a short meeting, he had just about found out her name, the fact that she was originally from the Dundee area and her age of forty-four due to her stating she was born the same month as Pink Floyd's 'Dark Side of the Moon' album was released. He wasn't sure if it was the type of information tucked away in his head a dedicated detective should admit to, but it was there anyway. He wasn't able to find out if she was married, had children, what her favourite movie was and more importantly, if he could see her again. A sudden phone call from her neighbour saying she had a visitor meant she had made her apologies and left before they had time to get to know each other. The great irony was that she had explained that she had a little 'bothy' at the side of her house, a word Avalon now knew was what the Scots called the tiniest house that human habitation was possible in. She told him that he could have stayed in it for a few days though it wasn't plush, but cosy and inexpensive. It seemed she had been considering renting it out to try and make a little money to supplement her meagre income. Yes, okay, she had taken his phone number as she rushed off and even said she would call but he knew she was just being polite. He would be on his way back to Inverness in a few hours so all the possible scenarios from that chance meeting were now just a list of 'what could have been' and he sighed. He had also spent a pleasant hour in the pub the previous evening, chatting and finding out what he could about the area. He had casually inquired about the Stodarts and tried to glean any information he could without raising too much suspicion about the case. He had been told little at first but as a couple of customers enjoyed Avalon's hospitality they began to talk. Most of it gossip of how the husband was a drunk, how he treated her badly, how he tried to live a playboy life without playboy money and generally how he was disliked locally. *She*, on the other hand had the sympathy of most of the locals. When he tried loaded questions on how she had vanished, there were shrugs and blank faces but the subject of the moor spirits and the Brollachan raised its murky head on at least one occasion.

He liked the village though, it was friendly and had much of what Avalon loved about small communities. He sighed and pushed the remaining clothes into his kit bag and checked around the room of the B&B. There was one last call to make and that was to the police station to update them on his findings and thank them for their help. He then decided to take a last walk onto the sea front. That tangy, sea smell bit into his nasal passages and brought a slight smile as he watched the light waves struggle up the beach. Above him seagulls twisted in the growing breeze, trying to keep aloft without ever having to flap their wings as Oystercatchers swept by blowing their boson's whistles as they passed. It wasn't cold but the south-westerly was gaining in force and darker patches of cloud were climbing over the tops of the hills in the distance and so Avalon took a last look out to sea and returned to his car. The journey back was pleasant, the views were spectacular until the clouds dropped and the inevitable rain came. As soon as he was home Avalon sent a text to Ross to ask if everything had been okay. The answer was quick arriving and said simply, 'YES!'. Soon after as Avalon slumped in the chair watching the rain falling outside, another text came in from Ross. It said, 'Fancy a pint tonight?' and so Avalon agreed and asked where.

It was still raining as Avalon reached the Castle Tavern and once again saw Ross was already there. He was seated in the raised section again and stood with his already empty glass to join Avalon at the bar.

"What can I get you?" asked the bartender. Avalon looked at the ample selection of single malts and creased his eyes trying to see what was there.

"I'll have a lager John while he decides, it could take some time," winked Ross to the landlord. Avalon looked across to Ross with some surprise.

"So you're on first name terms, I've only been away for a couple of nights and you've moved your

112

furniture in here?" he frowned.

"Oh aye," cut in the man behind the bar, we've even swapped holiday snaps and the lot."

"I haven't been in that much have I?" asked Ross to the landlord but he simply shrugged and smiled.

"That would be a breach of landlord-customer confidentiality," the smile broke into a slight grin as he placed Ross's drink on the bar and then he handed Avalon a whisky menu.

"A la carte whisky, I like it," smiled Avalon as he peered down the list.

"That's gonna confuse him," sighed Ross taking a sip of his drink, "too much choice for you, have you decided yet or shall I order myself a second drink?"

"Yeah," nodded Avalon, "I'll have the Dalmore, it's the most expensive," and he gave a slight grin to the landlord.

"Thanks for that," frowned Ross as he turned and headed back to his seat. Avalon joined him with his drink and sat with a sigh.

"So how was your trip?" asked Ross taking another sip from his glass.

"Good," nodded Avalon, "the weather could have been better but I managed to get some time to relax," and he too took a sip of his single malt.

"What about the case?"

"Nothing much to report, the wife seems to have planned an escape route, it's a bit elaborate but, she probably wanted out very badly."

"What do you mean?" asked Ross with a slight frown.

"Well, the husband," began Avalon, "is probably a dreamer and I suspect a user. The money is from *her* family and he seems to have a talent for throwing it away on bad business ideas. The wife seems to have come up with a plan to go missing in a manner that would be difficult to trace for someone as incompetent as the husband."

"Does that mean you know where she is?" asked Ross taking another gulp of lager.

"Not at all," replied Avalon shaking his head, "I don't even know how she did it, but I think she must have had some help."

"Why?" asked Ross, not quite sure what Avalon was getting at. Avalon shrugged.

"I've been to the place where she is supposed to have vanished and on the face of it I can't fathom how she managed to just disappear into thin air. Another thing is that she had a car, and *it's* missing too."

"So if she had help," offered Ross, "maybe this Sutherland chap is the accomplice?" he suggested.

"That's what I thought, he certainly fits the bill because he admires the woman and is probably besotted by her but certain things don't add up."

"Such as?" shrugged Ross. Avalon folded his arms and thought about his answer.

"He had just loaded her vehicle with a water butt, if he had designed this escape why would he have included this little detail in the story? It doesn't make sense if he was involved. I rather think that Mrs Stodart went to get the water butt because Sutherland was an unwitting part of the plan. She had to let him see she was in the vehicle when she set off but missing, just a few hundred yards further down the road." Ross nodded, he saw what Avalon was getting at.

"So she had planned a perfect witness into her scheme," he said.

"Exactly, and after talking to Sutherland he seems

114

truly baffled by it," Avalon picked up his glass, "and I don't think he's a very good liar, he seems the sort who would get all the details too precise."

"So there is another accomplice."

"That I can't say," shrugged Avalon.

"Well there must be if the car is missing, it seems obvious if she was driving the Land Rover and the car isn't there, someone had to drive her back to the house," insisted Ross lifting his glass for a drink.

"I realise that, but there isn't an obvious candidate," replied Avalon staring across the room.

"Well," began Ross, "I'm betting she's found in the boot of her own car." Avalon turned to him.

"Well I'm hoping for a happier ending than that," he said with a frown.

"So that's the end of it then?" nodded Ross.

"Yep, unless we get any information to the contrary, Mrs Stodart has done a runner, plain and simple," he raised his glass slightly, "and from what I've seen of the husband, good luck to her," and he took a drink. Ross noticed there was something else on his mind, just for a second he saw trouble in his expression.

"So what was that little nagging doubt I just saw in your eyes?" smiled Ross. Avalon stared ahead again for a moment and then blinked and looked over to Ross.

"Not a doubt as such," said Avalon raising an eyebrow, "I just can't come up with a reason why the woman made such a theatrical exit." Ross looked around the room.

"I suppose you would have to know her to work that one out," Ross shrugged.

"Maybe, but my instinct says there is more to that side of the story."

"Probably," nodded Ross, "didn't you get

anything from the locals?"

"Not much," sighed Avalon, "most have no idea why or how it happened and a minority even blame it all on local folk law, I can't understand that in these days of enlightenment."

"I suppose because of the landscape and in some places the isolation," answered Ross.

"PC Neil Dowd would say there is no smoke without fire," smiled Avalon.

"Yes but Dowd is slightly crazy, you have to realise that, anyway," continued Ross, "why the interest if you are dropping the investigation?" Avalon looked at Ross and sighed.

"I heard the name Brollachan again, it keeps cropping up, Arnold Burnside warned me about the Brollachan over a year ago."

"And he was another 'crazy' from what I remember," nodded Ross after taking a drink.

"He was certainly a character but there are still a few people in the Golspie area that talk about something that comes down from the moors with the mists and fog and sits at the edge of settlements waiting for a victim," explained Avalon, Ross made a slight 'humph' noise

"It's probably the nature of coastal village life," he smiled finally draining his glass.

"No, not at all," replied Avalon realising it was his turn to buy the drinks, "most people laugh when it's mentioned and many haven't even heard of the Brollachan."

"Well," shrugged Ross, "it's probably a great tourism ploy, making the place seem spooky and edgy brings tourists in to see the secret side of Scotland." Avalon picked up Ross's glass and drained his own,

"Another?" he asked and as Ross nodded he

stood. "Could be, though some people talk about the legends with a sort of affection," and he walked to the bar trying to recall the landlord's name.

"A pint of cat wee for my friend please John and I'll have an Aberlour," smiled Avalon.

"I heard that," cut in Ross as he approached the bar.

"Well, I don't know how you can drink that stuff," replied Avalon.

"I don't mean that, I meant the bit about 'friend'," frowned Ross, "I'm not even sure I want people thinking I know you." Avalon shook his head at this and then said,

"We make a wonderful national drink that is the envy of the world and you drink this homogenised garbage," said Avalon pointing to the lager font.

"We?" questioned Ross with a frown, "I assume you mean 'we Scottish'?"

"Don't get the hump about national identity," said Avalon handing over the money for the drinks.

"Well it's too late, the floodgates are open," frowned Ross, "it didn't take you long to become Scottish," Avalon shook his head, he didn't want to get into an argument about national identity, particularly in a pub.

"Not Scottish but certainly proud that I live and work here, is there another word for that? I have the strong belief that if you join any community be it a village, a town, a county or even a country, you should throw all in and be connected to that place to the degree you regard yourself as a native."

"Highly commendable," replied Ross with a slight amount of sarcasm in his voice, "there's more to it than that though."

117

"So," said Avalon, "you are one of those people who would move to France and seek out the British quarter and look for the nearest fish and chip shop are you?"

"Not quite, but then again I wouldn't go to France," frowned Ross.

"I was just trying to make a point," said Avalon returning the frown.

"I grant you," began Ross, "if you had moved to another country in Europe, indeed even France, you would have to live and work there for some years and then you'd have to prove you could support yourself and only then would they consider you for citizenship, and you would probably be tested as well."

"So what's your point?" asked Avalon taking a trial sip of the whisky.

"The point is, you have had it handed to you on a plate by the Scottish nation."

"Had what handed on a plate?" asked Avalon with an even deeper frown.

"National identity," insisted Ross looking directly into Avalon's eyes.

"I think I just admitted that I wasn't Scottish," replied Avalon shaking his head slightly and giving Ross a bemused expression. Ross's face broke into a slight smile and he said,

"But here comes a slight twist in the unusual circumstances of this group of islands we call Britain." Avalon looked to the landlord and asked,

"Do you know what he's on about?" but he shrugged and said,

"I wasn't listening," then he gave a wink.

"For a detective," continued Ross raising his eyebrows, "you're particularly slow." He then held up his

118

index finger in front of his nose and continued. "I'll explain but please keep up." He took a deep breath and continued. "As a British citizen, you came to live in Scotland, which means you are now on the electoral roll, that means my unenlightened friend, that you can vote on the future of this fine country." For a moment Avalon was stuck for words, he could see Ross's argument but it didn't feel right and he wanted to contradict him, he couldn't, the argument was sound but he didn't like where it was going. "So," continued Ross, "what we have here is an English detective and a Scottish detective but both are Scotsmen by right of vote."

"I see what you're getting at," interrupted Avalon, "and I can see why it would be an issue if I was here just because of the job, but that isn't the case."

"But you are here because of the job," insisted Ross,

"True, I took the job," explained Avalon, "but if Croker sacks me tomorrow, I'm not going back south, I'm here to stay, like it or not."

"Maybe, but you see my point," said Ross.

"Yes, o' course I do," agreed Avalon, "the way you see it, you have a birthright to vote, *I* on the other hand, bought that right," and he looked to see Ross's reaction, there wasn't much of any reaction. He continued. "Your name is Ross and *Ross* is such an old Scottish family that it is etched into the fabric of the landscape, you even have county named after you, and have a clan too, Clan Ross is a proud and integral part of this country, I understand that, and I can see that some people would consider that my only reason to be here is that I work here?" Ross nodded at this and Avalon decided the time was right to tell Ross something that he had wanted to tell him for some time, just not in these

119

circumstances. "But the truth is, I love this country and I love its people. I can honestly say that I have never felt so at home as I do here and that just isn't down to the country 'per se', it's down to the people I work with." Ross was stuck for words, he thought of several humorous replies, none of them seemed right. He shrugged, looked down to his drink and then back up to Avalon. He eventually found something to say.

"Ross is probably an old Yorkshire name." The tone was flat and matter-of-fact.

"What?" asked Avalon.

"Ross, it's probably from Yorkshire, I did some reading up on it once," explained Ross, still without any emotion, "it's possible that our part of the family could owe their presence here to my family buying land sometime in the twelfth century."

"That's immaterial my friend, your name *is* Scottish and it *is* etched into its fabric," insisted Avalon.

"Oh it is and I'm proud of that but I'm just saying that maybe the idea of 'buying' a national identity isn't new."

"Well if that *is* true," said Avalon, "you're in good company as your venerated 'Bruce' and 'Wallace' were probably Normans and the Normans just stole their lands by conquest," he paused for a moment, "at least your family paid for the land they occupied," and he took a drink. There was a little silence and then as the landlord walked past he said,

"Isn't it heritage that matters, not the fine detail?" and he turned to fill a shelf with bottles.

"That's right," agreed Ross and he pointed briefly towards the landlord, "heritage *is* what matters and Scotland's heritage has been made from countless generations that have worked the land and shaped its future."

"I agree," replied Avalon, "hundreds of thousands of Scots have died to keep Scotland," he paused to emphasise the point, "and the rest of Britain free from tyranny, but we're all just custodians," insisted Avalon shaking his head and leaning on the bar, "heritage is a collection of things, not just a single item, it's an 'historical soup'."

"Now you have lost me," frowned Ross taking several gulps of lager.

"Well," began Avalon in an attempt to explain his thinking, "Scotland wouldn't be Scotland as is it now if just one of the major factors of its history hadn't happened," explained Avalon.

"Well I realise that," said Ross with some hesitation, "history effects the people, o' course it does, without the Vikings and the Anglo Scottish wars we would now be living in some alternative history and none of us would be standing here now."

"Aye," agreed the landlord as he walked past, "we might all have ginger hair, freckles and bleached white skin." Avalon smiled at this and then shrugged towards Ross.

"See, there are some benefits from the inclusion of other cultures," smiled Avalon. Ross began to consider how the conversation would have turned out if DS Tom Murrey, a man with historical and sociological arguments, probably even PC Neil Dowd too, he would be able to put a different argument. As he thought through it he remembered a question that he had heard asked in a pub some years ago and no one really knew the answer.

"Scotland has an identity that has a little bit of Celtic, Pictish and even Scandinavian culture woven into it and that identity has developed the way we speak and the way we look, but what identity do the English have?" Avalon was troubled, he knew the only answer he could give would be disingenuous so he picked up his drink and took a sip and smiled at it.

"In England," he began, "you can usually tell a Scotsman living there, not because of his dress but because he has a stick-on saltire flag on the back of his car," he shrugged and then continued, "you rarely see English up here with a George Cross on their cars so you may have hit on a missing part of the English culture." Ross nodded as Avalon continued. "And I admit that when you see a Scottish truck on the motorway, the word 'Scotland' is always the largest text on the graphics," and he sighed a little. "And you have a national dress, as do the Irish and even the Welsh but the English?" He looked directly at Ross, "and I don't think the Beefeater costume would look good on me before you say anything." He decided that the subject needed to be changed and so he held up the golden fluid in the glass and took a sip, "but no matter what you say or what the argument, this English born detective with his own mixed heritage is at least 'spiritually' Scottish, and I'm proud to live and work here and partake of its fine wares."

"Why do I feel slightly patronised by that statement?" frowned Ross.

"I don't know," began Avalon with a passive expression, "probably because there isn't an argument for you to get your teeth into, and being truly Scot you are spoiling for a fight," he laughed a little.

"You should know me well enough by now to know I don't let anti-English sentiment taint my objectiveness," frowned Ross.

"Good," smiled Avalon, "after all, it was your

own Burns that said, *'We're bought and sold for English gold, such a parcel of rogues in a nation'* and he certainly was correct." Ross nodded and took another gulp of his drink,

"I thought poetry would rear its ugly head somewhere in the conversation," he said and then with a slight raising of his voice, "in any case, I like the idea of the English coming up here," and after a thought and in a quieter voice, "it makes me more proud to be Scottish."

"None taken," replied Avalon, "but I still don't understand why you drink that crap," he nodded to the glass in Ross's hand. He then held up his own glass once more with the remains of the amber fluid inside and toasted, "sludge," and then he pointed to Ross's drink. "So how do you toast in German? 'Prost' is it?" Ross scowled at Avalon for some moments then said,

"You need to develop a Scottish accent so I can deck you without being called a racist," then he lifted his glass too.

"Sludge," he announced and took a large gulp.

~~~~~~

Maybe they had stayed too long and had a few too many at the Castle Tavern, Avalon certainly felt non-too good the next morning. As he sat in his booth looking out into the Cave he noticed that Ross didn't look quite as bad as he would have expected. He then reflected how a couple of nights away could rejuvenate him and then he could reverse that good work in a few measures of single malt. He had planned to cut back on his drinking too and if this was the result, he would have to try a little harder from now on. He looked down at the computer screen and couldn't quite make out the words.

He didn't wear spectacles, his eyes were perfect so why couldn't he read the screen? Maybe that was a side effect of drinking too. He decided that a third cup of coffee might make a difference. DS Wilson and DC MacDonald were out of the office, Mackinnon and Pottinger were busy with paperwork and DC Boyd was helping B Section interviewing a distraught female victim of an attack in the city. Frazer was still working on her reports from the internal case she had been on and Ross was making phone calls that sounded like another missing persons case. Avalon shuffled back to his seat and slumped down heavily. He looked up to see Ross giving him a quick glance as he put his phone down. There was a whiff of a grin on Ross's face, it wasn't obvious but it was there. Ross's phone rang and about a half a second later his own phone rang.

"Avalon," he said with as much conviction as he could muster.

"*Et's Sergeant Gregory Jim, we've just had reports of a body up north, I've sent PC Kirk up with the notes but I thought I'd give y' the heads up.*"

"Thanks Bob, I'll get a response team ready," and he put the phone down.

"Body found up north," called Ross placing his phone down too and Avalon nodded as the door to the Cave opened and in walked Kirk with an incident sheet. Avalon took it from her and even before he read it he somehow knew it would be in Golspie. What surprised him was the fact that the body was male.

"Oh!" he exclaimed, "I wasn't expecting that."

"Golspie?" asked Ross.

"Yeah and looking at the address this could be very complicated," and he looked around the room then back to Ross. "Have you got a change of clothes you can

124

get to quickly?"

"Yeah," nodded Ross, "in my locker," Ross was one of the CID that kept a change of clothes just in case he got wet or dirty out on a case. Avalon nodded at the information and turned to Frazer.

"Megan, let DS Wilson know that I have to go back to Golspie and in the mean time you look after the shop." Frazer nodded. Avalon then looked back at Ross.

"We may be up there for a few days is there anything else you need?"

"Not really," replied Ross with surprise, "I can buy what I haven't got but what about you?"

"I still have my kit in the boot of the car," he replied returning to the booth for his phone and his keys. "Okay, get your things, we need to move."

The journey north was not quite as pleasant as the first time, it was lashing down with rain and they were in somewhat of a hurry.

"So what are you thinking?" asked Ross as they reached the Kessock Bridge. Avalon shook his head slowly.

"I thought it might be Mrs Stodart when I first heard, but the body is male and at the address is that of Peter Stodart so I'm assuming he's the victim."

"By the use of the word 'victim'," began Ross as he peered through the rain on the passenger window, "you suspect foul play."

"He was in perfect health on Saturday so yes, it's looking like it," frowned Avalon.

"It seems odd though, it sort of makes you think that the wife has disappeared so that she can come back and kill him if that's the case."

"I was thinking that," nodded Avalon staring

straight ahead.

"It has to be," added Ross shaking his head, "I'm struggling to think of any other reason there would be a body at the house."

"Like I said, complicated," shrugged Avalon and then added, "best not to jump to conclusions before we get there."

The single-track road up to the house was coned off and Ross braved the rain to move them and as they continued on past the house of Mr Sutherland, Avalon slowed and looked down the drive. He pointed the house out to Ross and then drove on to the Stodart's house. There were several police cars and half a dozen uniformed officers present and what looked like the SOCO team just getting ready. As Avalon stepped out of the car he pulled on his raincoat even though the rain had steadied off. He saw one of the officers was PC Gunn.

"Hello Detective Inspector, I didn't expect tae see you so soon," he said raising his eyebrows.

"No, it seems Golspie doesn't want me to leave, sorry I couldn't bring some better weather," he gave a slight smile, "do we know who it is?"

"Aye, we are pretty sure et's Peter Stodart, the postman saw bloody footprints and phoned us straight away."

"Did he go in?" asked Avalon.

"He says not, only myself and the sergeant from Brora have been in, we had a quick look in the other rooms and then secured the site," explained the PC. Avalon nodded then said,

"This is DS Ross from Inverness, he'll be assisting with the investigation."

"Aye I think we've met," smiled Gunn.

"Really?" asked Ross tilting his head, "I don't..."

126

"Et was two years ago, we were part o' the team on that terrorism exercise," he smiled and gradually the memory came into view along with a wide smile.

"Of course," Ross grinned, "Guzzler Gunn we started to call you down at the pub, you were-"

"Could we possibly leave 'all our yesterdays' for some other time seeing as we have an investigation to complete," interrupted Avalon.

"Sorry sir," apologised Gunn, Ross was still playing with the memory in his head as Avalon approached the SOCO team. He didn't recognise any of them but he spoke to the one that seemed in charge showing his warrant card.

"I want to have a peep inside before you start," he said.

"Aye, okay sir," nodded the man, "we're about ready though when you are." Avalon gave a single nod and he and Ross made a very careful way towards the house. The door was open and bloody footprints could clearly be seen coming from the house, they weren't clear but seemed too large to be from the diminutive Mrs Stodart. Avalon slowly made his way into the hall, following the footprints towards the kitchen being careful only to tread on the edges of the floor where it came to the walls. He was also careful not to touch anything but he could already sense that particularly sweet, twang that was a mix of blood and the early stages of decomposition. At the kitchen door he peered in and saw the body. They were not wearing forensic suits so Avalon stayed out of the room and tried to look around. He saw a pool of congealed blood around the body along with what looked like a smashed mug and something else he couldn't make out. To the right of the body was what looked like the weapon that had inflicted the damage, a bent bar or a pipe. There were other footprints around the area as if the person who had left them spent some time looking around after the act. One thing he couldn't see was the laptop that Mr Stodart had obviously been pre-occupied with. Avalon turned to Ross.

"Yeah, it's him, we better let the forensics team get on with it," and they exited the house as carefully as they had entered. Outside PC Gunn walked over to them.

"I thought that I better tell you, we had a report from the public of a car speeding away from this direction onto the moors," and he pulled out a notebook and read from it, "it seems he was driving in a dangerous manner and forced another vehicle off the road."

"Oh, do we have any details?" asked Avalon as the forensics team made their way past and into the building.

"Yes, a silver or grey hatchback, probably a Vauxhall, it sped off up the hill at about eighteen hundred hours on Saturday evening," explained Gunn still reading from his notebook. "The reason I mention it is that the vehicle was stolen from Inverness the day before. It was rung in before we knew about the body, but because we were given a registration number we were able to check it out."

"It could be unrelated but seeing as it's a stolen vehicle we'd better check it over, give the details to Ross," and he turned to look at the house. This was going to be an odd case now Peter Stodart had been killed. Ross had jotted down the witness's details and then said,

"You may want to look at this," and he handed the pad to Avalon. In Ross's unmistakable handwriting and double underlined was the name 'Mr David

Sutherland'. Avalon looked directly at Ross.

"PC Gunn, we're going to have a word with Mr Sutherland, has the coroner been sent for?" asked Avalon.

"I believe he has but he could be some time," replied Gunn.

"We won't be long," nodded Avalon as he returned to the car, "give me a call if anything crops up."

~~~~~~

"Er, Detective Avalon isn't it?" asked David Sutherland with a puzzled expression.

"Yes, may we come in and ask you a few questions?" asked Avalon.

"Yes, of course," nodded Sutherland showing them to the sitting room, "but I don't think there is anything I can add," he paused with a concerned look, "or, have you found something?"

"This is a slightly different line of inquiry, this is DS Ross by the way," he added pointing to his colleague.

"Oh I see," he frowned taking a seat opposite Ross and Avalon. "So this isn't to do with Muir's disappearance?"

"We don't know yet but I believe you reported a speeding car on Saturday night."

"Yes, the damn fool nearly knocked me off the road, I was coming back from a friends house near Tannachy, and this idiot came hurtling around the corner. I had to swerve, it was lucky there was a passing place," explained Sutherland.

"And you described the vehicle as a silver or grey Vauxhall hatchback and you gave a registration number I believe?" questioned Ross.

"Yes," nodded Sutherland, "I gave the details when I phoned."

"But how can you be so precise if you had to swerve out of the way?" asked Avalon.

"Because he left the road on the corner and had to back up," insisted the man. Ross and Avalon looked to each other.

"Can you be absolutely sure of the details?" asked Ross.

"I'm positive, I remember thinking, if I do nothing else I'll get the maniac's number," explained Sutherland, "anyway, I got a look at him to as he tried to reverse out."

"You got a look at the driver?" asked Ross.

"Yes, nothing clear, but I did see him, he had to lean slightly out of the window before he sped off again."

"Can you describe him?" asked Avalon.

"Small build, thin face with a pale complexion and scruffy looking, several days of growth on his chin I would think," explained Sutherland without a pause.

"Hair colour?" asked Ross as he jotted down the details.

"That, I can't say, he was wearing a hat, baseball cap I think."

"And he continued off away from Golspie?" asked Ross raising his pencil from the paper.

"Yes, but," Sutherland paused, "why the sudden interest in this area, there have been police cars coming and going all morning and now I get a visit by not one, but two detectives?"

"There has been an incident up at the Sutherland's house but I can't say more than that," insisted Avalon.

130

"It's not...?" the man spluttered with a look of shock on his face.

"It's not 'Mrs Stodart' Mr Sutherland but for now I can say no more," frowned Avalon and then continued with, "we may need to ask you more questions later if that's alright," and he stood with Ross following suit. "I would also ask you not to talk about the car or anything else to do with Mrs Stodart or this case." He nodded and stood too as the two detectives made their way to the door.

"He's an odd one," shrugged Ross as they drove back up the hill.

"Probably but I bet his description is accurate," replied Avalon.

"I don't doubt it, his eyes look everywhere, a bit creepy don't you think?"

"No," frowned Avalon, "just nervous, when I first interviewed him he was calm and co-operative. He's now second guessing the situation and is uncomfortable with the idea that something has happened at the house and Mrs Stodart is involved."

"Or he's involved," offered Ross.

"It could be, he's certainly changed from the first time I interviewed him, as I said before, he has a thing for Mrs Stodart but he was genuinely shocked to know something had happened up there," replied Avalon as he drove into the Stodart's drive.

"The coroner has arrived sir," explained PC Gunn, "he's gone straight in." Avalon nodded and arranged for two forensics suits. The scenes of crime officers were examining the other rooms of the house and the forensics teams were collecting anything they could find. In the kitchen was the coroner.

"Professor Lennox," announced Avalon and the white suited man turned from his crouching position by the body and replied.

"Ah, Detectives Avalon and Ross," his blue eyes giving away the smile that was hidden behind the facemask.

"Anything to tell us yet?" asked Avalon. Lennox looked back at the body for a moment and then up to the detectives.

"I haven't had much time to delve into the minutiae but at first glance it looks like blunt force trauma to the skull is the culprit," he said.

"Is that the weapon?" asked Ross pointing to the bent bar to the right of the body. There was a small yellow marker with a number on it by the weapon, a reminder that the forensics team had been through the room. It was clear that the bar was a large, heavy-duty wheel brace from a car or truck.

"Likely, detective, I won't know for sure until we get the body back, but it does look consistent with the wound." Avalon was looking around the room, he was looking for the laptop but it was nowhere to be found.

"Have you any ideas about the time of death?" he asked.

"Not as such but my experienced eye says at least a day or so ago." Avalon thought he could see the professor smiling again, he remembered Lennox found it amusing that the time of death was always one of the first questions.

"So he could have died on Saturday afternoon?" nodded Avalon.

"It's possible," agreed Lennox, "any particular interest in that day detective?" asked the professor light heartedly.

132

"I interviewed Mr Stodart on Saturday, that's all," shrugged Avalon.

"Then it is entirely possible that you have the dubious distinction of being the last person to see him alive," and Avalon saw his eyebrows lift before he returned to his work.

"Except for the bastard that clobbered him with the ironware," added Ross.

"Quite so," agreed Lennox without looking up. Avalon was looking at the broken items around the floor, there were obvious signs of a broken mug but there was a loose pile of black shards in the pooled blood too.

"What's that do you think?" asked Avalon pointing to the pieces. Ross carefully moved closer and bent down.

"Looks like it was a plastic box, hard to say what was in it though," and he stood, "we'll get forensics to test it," he added.

"We need to talk to the scenes of crimes," and he made a sideways nod towards the door. "There was a laptop on the table when I was here, we could do with finding it," explained Avalon when they were back in the hall.

"Shall I have a word with SOCO then?" asked Ross.

"Yeah, I need to talk to the sergeant and find out who the postman who found him was."

As Ross went to find the SOCO team, Avalon walked outside and was suddenly aware of a heavy feeling coming over him, it was difficult to explain and he had no idea what it was but it felt as if a dark cloud was hovering above him. He felt slightly nauseous too and he developed a serious headache. Was he ill? Was the job suddenly wearing him down? As he walked towards the car he felt slightly light headed and decided to lean on the car to catch his breath. He looked around the grounds and back to the house, no one was watching him and so he afforded some time to compose himself. Gradually the feelings subsided but the headache remained. By the time Ross had returned Avalon had still not recovered enough to continue and he was beginning to worry that it would affect his work. He opened the car door and sat in the seat.

"What's wrong?" asked Ross leaning in the car.

"Oh, nothing, I just feel a bit woozy," he knew it was the wrong thing to say even before the last word left his lips.

"Oh," was all Ross said as Avalon looked up at him. He could see Ross was wondering why his boss had found the sight in the kitchen a bit much, they had seen worse, the body they had attended at Beauly Priory the previous year had been much more gruesome a spectacle than this one. Avalon knew it wasn't the crime scene that had sent him into a sickening spiral, there was something else going on. He started to feel a little better as he concentrated and he got out of the car.

"I probably need something to drink," he announced, "I'll call in the village for a cuppa after we have done here." Ross just nodded, even he was a little parched and being in Avalon's car didn't have access to the emergency bottle of water he kept in his own vehicle. "See if you can get a name of the postman who discovered the footprints," continued Avalon, "we need to get a statement from him." Ross nodded again and set off to find the sergeant as Avalon made his way back to the house. Professor Lennox was coming from the doorway.

"Ah, detective," he smiled as he pulled off the

134

mask and the hood of the white forensics suit, "I think we can arrange to move the body if you are ready." Avalon nodded and replied,

"Any idea of time of death yet Professor?"

"As usual I can't be precise just yet but I would say he died sometime on Saturday afternoon."

"Oh, that's odd," frowned Avalon.

"Yes, it would mean you certainly were here close to the time of death," replied Lennox with a dry smile. Avalon thought back to the afternoon, he had seen no other cars coming up from the village so it was probably likely that the attack came from the other direction.

"But I suppose there is a larger window of error for the time?" he eventually asked.

"Oh yes," nodded Lennox, "it could equally have been later, the only thing we know is that it couldn't be before you left," he paused, "or are you investigating yourself?" he allowed a slight smile. Avalon's mind was elsewhere.

"Er what? Oh sorry professor, I was miles away."

"Yes," replied Lennox raising his eyebrows, "well I must get on, bodies don't get themselves to the mortuary," and he went off to speak to the forensics team. Ross approached.

"Feeling better?" he asked.

"Hey, what? Oh, yes," shrugged Avalon, Ross was beginning to think his DI was more under the weather than he first thought. Avalon seemed to be somewhere else than on the job and Ross said quietly,

"Look, do you want me to clear up here?" Avalon looked into the middle distance for a moment and then announced,

"No, no I was just thinking something."

"Care to let me in?" asked Ross. Avalon seemed to come out of his thoughts.

"Oh, it may be nothing, but I think we need to get Frazer working on some background to the Stodarts and to see if there is a link with David Sutherland." Ross nodded.

"It looks pretty clear cut to me, wife puts a contract on the husband and then disappears before the hit is made." Avalon nodded solemnly and said,

"I agree, Mrs Stodart is obviously the main suspect, I thought she was just covering her tracks so her husband wouldn't trace her but it looks like she was more concerned about *us* tracing her."

"So shall I get Megan to do some background?" asked Ross pulling out his phone.

"Yeah, we need to find this woman, whether she is involved or not we need to speak with her urgently." Ross dialled and then said,

"Oh, I've got the name of the postman who found the footprints," Avalon nodded and was about to ask his name but Ross spoke into the phone, "Megan, it's Ross, the boss wants you to do some digging." Avalon walked back to the house as Ross continued with the call, he couldn't help wondering why Sutherland and Mrs Stodart knew each other, they seemed so incompatible, and what significance did her little plan have to do with the man?

"And why do I feel so dreadful?" he said to himself looking round to make sure no one had overheard him. The body was being brought out of the house and Avalon decided to go and have a look around the kitchen now the room was fully processed. The scenes of crimes team had been busy, many of the tiny blood spatter marks on the wall had been picked out with small arrows and circles made with marker pen. On the floor the mark was still clear where the body had been and it looked like the mug and the black plastic box had not been broken before the man fell dead, due to the fact that nothing had been found under him. If the mug had been dropped by Peter Stodart, it meant that he could have been about to make the assailant a drink, which in turn meant he probably knew his attacker. That may or may not be confirmed once the broken pieces of the mug had been analysed by the forensics lab. The black box was another issue, though Avalon had an idea what it may have been, he had seen similar containers in his years down in Wolverhampton. A closer inspection of the wheel brace showed it was certainly an effective weapon, the end that would fit over the wheel nuts was quite a solid piece of metal. He needed confirmation that it was indeed the weapon but for now, results from the forensics would have to wait. He had a description of Mrs Stodarts car and they would have to find it if they wanted any clues to where she was. He looked around the room and then left to see if the SOCO team had found any sign of the laptop. Outside it was raining once more, he was beginning to think that the sun would never come out again. He gave the blanket of cloud a cursory glance and headed of to his car. Ross was on the phone, it seemed Frazer was already at work on the case and relaying information. To Avalon's right there was a slight knock on the window, it was the sergeant, his high visibility, yellow glowing jacket seeming even brighter in the fading light of a rainy afternoon.

"We cannae find a laptop Inspector," he frowned as Avalon sent the electric window down to its full extent. Rain was running from the edge of the officers hat and into the car, he pulled his head away as he continued, "both SOCO and our lads have searched for et but there's no sign of anythen like et."

"Okay sergeant, it was a long shot anyway," nodded Avalon.

"Do y' want somebody on tonight?" the sergeant then asked.

"I don't think there's any need, once everyone has finished just make sure it's secured," instructed Avalon, he knew finding personnel to keep an all night watch would stretch the local resources.

"Aye okay," nodded the officer, dislodging more rain from his hat and then he returned to the house. Avalon closed the window and turned to Ross who had finished the call.

"Anything?" he asked.

"Not much yet but Frazer says she has tracked down the company she thinks is Peter Stodarts internet gambling website."

"It's a start," nodded Avalon.

"The company is called 'Ebet' and is a dot co, dot UK website. It's mainly a poker-playing site," explained Ross.

"That sounds like it," nodded Avalon.

"Well if it is you would have thought it would make a fortune," frowned Ross, "there can't be many overheads once it's set up can there?"

"I don't know," shrugged Avalon, "but it doesn't matter how much money you make, if you spend it faster than you earn it you can quickly get into trouble."

"Maybe," replied Ross pursing his lips, "he must have been a total dick though if that's the case, I think most of those kind of sites make a shitload of cash."

"Probably but I'm betting that Mr Stodart had a 'shitload' of expensive hobbies," frowned Avalon, "and

I'm guessing one of them had something to do with white poison."

"Drugs?" asked Ross. Avalon nodded, "I bet he had his hand in the cookie jar too." Avalon looked over to Ross, "well," continued the DS, "he must have had some interest in gambling to run a gambling site." Avalon thought about this for a moment and looked out through the windscreen. Ross was correct of course, he could have easily lost as much, if not more than the company was making. If that was true, they needed to talk to anyone who may have had money interests in the business.

"Ask Megan to see if there are any partners or financial backers in the business." Ross nodded and took out his phone. Avalon placed his keys in the ignition and added, "and we better find somewhere to stay before it gets too late."

The rain had almost stopped by the time they reached Golspie and before he went to the Bed and Breakfast to see if they had spare rooms, he decided to call into town to buy some food for when they had finished work. Sandwiches and flavoured water were on the menu and he and Ross carried the items to the car and then went to the cafe for a drink. As they sat and looked out of the window the sky threatened more rain and Ross asked Avalon a question.

"You know, I just can't work this out. If Mrs Stodart did set all this up, why the elaborate plan to disappear?"

"I'm not sure yet," announced Avalon shaking his head slightly, "maybe it's a smoke screen, maybe she just has an overactive mind, I really don't know."

"It's too complicated for something so simple,"

continued Ross, "she could have just walked away."

"What, you think it's the work of the spirit from up on the moors?" smiled Avalon before draining the last of his coffee.

"The Brollachan? No I don't but there is just no reason for this deception, in truth, it's more likely to *make* us suspect her. She could have been abducted."

"Mmm, not likely." frowned Avalon, "I see your point but that would certainly put Sutherland in the frame and he's a bit too intelligent to think we wouldn't point the finger at him."

"Well it would be risky for him but money does strange things to some people," frowned Ross picking up his cup. He noticed Avalon craning his head towards the car park. "What have you seen?" he asked.

"What?" Avalon looked back slightly embarrassed, "oh nothing, I just thought I recognised a car." Ross raised his eyebrows and finished his coffee.

"Well," he announced placing the palms of his hands on the table, "we better make a move I suppose."

"Just a moment, wait here a second," said Avalon still looking into the car park and he stood and exited the cafe. Ross watched through the window as Avalon burst into a wide smile as a woman walked up to him. She was smiling too from under the hood of her raincoat. She wasn't exactly what Ross would call a 'belter', the raincoat was an old wax cotton type and she had tight grey leggings that seemed to be growing from a pair of tatty walking boots. She was quite attractive though and had a pleasing smile. She and Avalon seemed to know each other and they seemed to be discussing something. Avalon pointed to the cafe but the woman looked at her watch and shook her head. Then there were serious looks from both until Avalon nodded with a smile and they parted company. Ross stood and met Avalon outside.

"You're a sly fox," he smiled pulling the collar of his jacket up.

"Just someone I know," shrugged Avalon, "don't jump to any conclusions, anyway, she's offered us a room."

"*A* room?" asked Ross putting emphasis on the 'A'.

"Yeah," smiled Avalon looking at Ross in an upbeat manner, "it's a little bothy at the side of her house."

"I assume she knows what we do?" asked Ross with a slight grin, he knew from the body language that the two of them were only slightly acquainted.

"Yes... well, not exactly," stuttered Avalon.

"This is going to be interesting then," he smiled with a shrug and walked towards the car. Avalon hadn't moved. "Shall we go and explain then or do you want to abandon the idea and go and find a B and B?" Avalon grimaced a little and then answered.

"It'll be fine I'm sure, I won't say unless the subject crops up."

"You're a quick worker I'll give you that," nodded Ross.

"What's that supposed to mean?" frowned Avalon as he unlocked the car and slid into the drivers seat. Ross joined him in the front and replied.

"You were up here for two days and already you are impressing yourself on the local female population. I assume she isn't married?"

"I don't know," shrugged Avalon as he started the engine, "I have no reason to know so I didn't ask," and he drove out of the car park. Ross just shook his head with a slight smile and gave the usual comment.

"You're so full of shit."

~~~~~~

"What time is it?" asked Ross with a yawn as he put the phone back in his pocket.

"Twenty past ten," replied Avalon. It was dark and the rain had started for the twentieth time it seemed and even the air they breathed felt wet.

"Well shall we call it a day, we're not getting anywhere here?"

"I know, we'll have to wait until we get an incident room set up I think."

"What about the police station?" asked Ross.

"I don't think it's quite right, the truck will be here in the morning and we can set it up in the car park in the village."

"Okay, who do you want up here?" asked Ross.

"I don't want to pull the section off their duties," frowned Avalon, "we should manage for now with a few uniformed officers, we could do with Dowd too if we can get him."

"Dowd would love that," smiled Ross, "anything to get out of the station, as long as the Caley Jags aren't playing."

"We'll get it sorted in the morning," nodded Avalon.

"What about bringing Frazer up?" inquired Ross.

"I thought about it but she still has a lot to do, I'll leave her to tidy up her loose ends I think," insisted Avalon, "but I may get Rory up later," he added. He closed his notepad and put his phone in his pocket and said, "Come on, lets go and see what our room is like."

Julia Beattie looked genuinely pleased to see Avalon and she showed them into the little bothy that wasn't much smaller than the main house. There was a small kitchen and a single bedroom with a shower room and a cosy lounge. A log burner sat on one wall and the decor was what Ross considered 'homemade' and not being to his taste he almost 'tutted' as he walked in. Ross was a creature of modernity and functional fittings, what he saw in the bothy was typically female, and slightly hippy. It wasn't particularly to Avalon's taste either but it seemed cosy and comfortable.

"It's perfect," he said and he smiled at her. Ross saw them make eye contact and he could see that Avalon was more than a little taken in with her. She was a little too 'Arts and Crafts' for him but she did have a certain charm he confessed to himself.

"The sofa makes up into a bed and there is bedding in that trunk," she pointed. Avalon thanked her and said,

I'm not sure how long we'll be here, is that a problem?"

"No, not at all, the place just sits empty unless some of my family visit," She looked around to make sure everything was there and then she swung her arms nervously and asked,

"So, what do you do, are you reps or something?"

"Sort of," nodded Ross, "we represent the government."

"Oh," she said slightly alarmed.

"We're coppers," added Avalon before Ross tried to wind her up.

"You mean polis?" she asked wide eyed.

"Yes, Inverness's finest in the flesh," nodded Ross.

"So you must be here for that incident up on the hill," she asked, her demeanour had totally changed.

"News travels fast," smiled Ross patting the sofa to test how soft it was.

"Sorry, I didn't mean to pry, it's just that everyone is talking about something, I'm not even sure what it is," she frowned apologetically.

"It's alright, we can't discuss it anyway," said Avalon with a fake smile. She shrugged and said,

"Well, I'll leave you to it," and she turned to leave, "oh I nearly forgot, will you need breakfast?"

"No, that's fine, we'll be off quite early," smiled Avalon.

"It's no bother, I can-" she was cut off by Avalon.

"We'll be fine but thanks for the offer," he insisted and she nodded with a curt smile and left.

"Well done," frowned Ross as he walked into the bedroom to test the bed.

"What do you mean?" asked Avalon following him.

"Well, we get offered a breakfast and you turn it down."

"I didn't want to put her to any trouble," explained Avalon.

"You may have missed the point that 'B and B' stands for bed *and* breakfast," he insisted.

"Well this isn't strictly a bed and breakfast, she's just trying to make a bit of spending money," explained Avalon watching Ross return to the lounge and pull the bedding from the chest.

"So we get bed and no breakfast," sighed Ross throwing the bedding on the sofa, "or in your case, no bed and no breakfast." Avalon looked down at the sofa and then watched Ross carry his kit bag into the bedroom.

"I might pull rank on you," he said with raised brows.

"You can pull what ever you want in the privacy of your own lounge but when I sleep it's in my time and in my time, rank can go and..." Ross paused for a second and then continued, "in the words of DC Megan Frazer, 'spin on it'," and he returned to the bedroom. Avalon tested the sofa, it felt reasonable and he considered he may be able to sleep fairly well in front of the fire. Ross reappeared with two glasses and a small bottle of whisky.

"Nightcap?" he asked holding up the bottle.

Avalon nodded and Ross sat in the easy chair and poured out the liquid. Avalon held it to his nose and recognised the aroma of a good Highland whisky. He reached for the bottle and saw it was Glenmorangie. A fitting choice having passed the distillery on the way up.

"Sludge," announced Ross holding out the glass.

"Sludge," repeated Avalon. The whisky was consumed along with another and the sandwiches purchased earlier and then the two detectives made themselves comfortable for as much good sleep as was possible in the time given. As Avalon laid on the sofa in the dark with a small flame from the fire illuminating the room with a dim, warm glow, he thought about how his life had twisted and turned, of how he had been brought to the position he was in now. Was he happy? He wasn't sure, certainly he was content with Scotland and he was upbeat about his job, but happy? What was happiness? He wasn't completely sure he knew. When he thought back to memories he considered happy times, the images that entered his head seemed to involve his ex-wife Carol. Was that it? Could happiness only be achieved

145

with someone else? His thoughts began to wander and aspects of the case mutated into his thoughts, or were they dreams...?

Chapter Five

The mobile incident room arrived early in Golspie and was stationed in the car park with a few boards placed around it asking the public if they had any information about strangers, or suspicious cars in the area. It was the usual sort of thing, giving nothing away but expecting people to come forward or ring in to a special number. There were three officers stationed there and they manned the phones and recorded all calls they received, feeding the details into the computer. Avalon and Ross stayed with the vehicle until the operation was up and running and then they drove up to the Stodart's house where the forensics team were completing their search for evidence. The two detectives were quiet during the morning activity and even when they were alone neither of them spoke. Avalon was still feeling a little 'worse for wear' and Ross, although reasonably comfortable in the bed, hadn't slept too well. As they entered the house Avalon could feel another headache seeping into his brain and he wondered if it was the building itself. He dismissed the thought as he massaged his brow a little.

"Feeling rough?" asked Ross seeing Avalon reacting to the pain.

"It's nothing," he said as he sighed, "we better make a start," and he went to speak to the forensics team leader.

"No sign of the laptop at all," replied the man to Avalon's questions. Avalon frowned and looked over to Ross.

"It looks like it was taken then," shrugged Ross. Avalon nodded and looked back to the forensics technician.

"You found anything else?"

"Nothing out of the ordinary," replied the man shaking his head, "and there doesn't seem to be anything to point to the perpetrator visiting any of the other rooms." Avalon nodded and returned to the outside where he walked over to the garage. Ross followed and looked down at his shoes as he walked through the grass. It had been raining through the night and the early morning and although it had stopped, the grass was soaking and his shoes were beginning to look a little shabby. He stepped into the gloomy garage where the Stodart's Land Rover was still parked.

"If the 'perp' didn't go to any of the other rooms we have to conclude he was after the laptop and he found it," offered Ross. Avalon stared at the vehicle and after a moment he nodded.

"Yeah, I guessed that as soon as it was clear it wasn't at the house," he turned to Ross, "I wonder if they have processed this yet," he was pointing to the vehicle.

"It looks like it, it's covered in print dust."

"It was already like that from the previous investigation," explained Avalon.

"So this is the remarkable vehicle then?" asked Ross, Avalon simply nodded still looking at the scruffy truck. "I'll go and find out if it's processed," added Ross and he turned to leave.

"If they have done with it I want arrangements made to get it to the compound," added Avalon. Ross nodded and continued, leaving Avalon alone with the vehicle and his headache.

When Avalon returned to the car, Ross was half seated in the passenger seat trying his best to clean up his shoes.

"Don't get sludge and grass on my new carpets," insisted Avalon. Ross saw the irony of the statement as he noticed the foot well of the vehicle was splashed with mud and stones from previous usage of the car. With the weather so poor it was impossible to keep anything clean.

"It looks like you've been transporting farm animals in here," replied Ross without looking up.

"I know, what's wrong with the weather, is it ever going to stop raining?" asked Avalon leaning on the car.

"Get used to it," replied Ross, "this is a consequence of global warming."

"Whatever it is I'm sure it's causing my headache," frowned Avalon rubbing his brow again. Ross stood and looked at his shoes, there was a little improvement.

"Pressure," said Ross not taking his gaze from the footwear, "you're not used to it." Avalon was quiet. Pressure wasn't the issue Avalon thought, but lack of sleep could have been. Once again he hadn't slept well, the sofa bed wasn't the problem either, he had been comfortable enough, he simply kept waking up. "Oh," added Ross looking over to Avalon, "forensics have processed the Land Rover so I have arranged for a truck to pick it up." Avalon nodded and glanced back at the house. He then looked up at the sky, the clouds seemed close enough to touch and he could almost see the rain held in them, ready to drop at any time. Avalon sighed and was about to climb into the car when he heard a vehicle coming up the road, it was a police van and it entered the drive and parked next to the police car already there. It was PC Gunn and after having a quick word with the other officer he walked over to Avalon.

"Mornin' sir," Avalon nodded and Gunn continued, "I'm just off tae check on an abandoned car up on the moors, you might be interested en this one."

"Go on," insisted Avalon.

"Et was phoned en this morning by a guy who drives to work on that road every mornin', we checked the number of the vehicle, et's the stolen Vauxhall seen by Mr Sutherland," he raised his eyebrows. Avalon looked over to Ross and then back to Gunn.

"We need to secure the site," he insisted.

"I've got all the gear en the van but we're short on manpower,"

"I've got a couple of officers on their way up later but we need to make this car a priority," insisted Avalon turning to Ross, "get SOCO onto this," and he turned back to the PC, "where is the vehicle?"

"About five miles up this road, at a place called Loch Farlary," replied Gunn.

"Let's go," insisted Avalon as he walked towards Gunn, then he turned and threw Ross his car keys. "Don't scratch it," he said and left with PC Gunn to find the abandoned car.

The vehicle was parked in a pull-in by the side of a small loch in a remote area inland from Golspie. The first job was to cone off the whole lay-by and tape around the area. When it was done Avalon carefully moved over to the vehicle and noticed damage to the near side, probably corroborating Mr Sutherlands story of the

150

vehicle leaving the road. He peered inside, the vehicle wasn't locked but he decided to leave it closed to preserve evidence. He could see nothing out of the ordinary so he returned to the edge of the cordoned off area where Gunn was placing police incident signs. He was looking up at the sky now and then.

"I know, I'm expecting rain again too," said Avalon.

"I think the clouds are dropping," frowned the PC.

"What's that mean?" frowned Avalon.

"Well, we're not that high here but on a day like this ef the cloud base drops tae less than two hundred and fifty metres, then that cloud will push through this glen." Gunn was pointing to the cloud coming in over the moor. Avalon tried to quickly convert the metric measurement to something he could visualise. Just over eight hundred feet he considered, and as he looked out over the moor he wondered if he could actually see the ominous cloudbank dropping. As he stared to the hills in the distance he was aware that they were gradually blending into the cloud.

"So what does that mean, we'll get wet?" smiled Avalon as if rain was a rare thing.

"Not just wet, the cloud can be pretty thick, visibility will be an issue," explained Gunn. Avalon nodded, he didn't think it would stop the scenes of crime team from working and a little bit of fog seemed like the least of their problems. Avalon noticed the temperature was dropping too and he constantly looked under the cloud at the hills until he could see them no more. It looked like PC Gunn had an eye for the weather and his prediction was coming true. Looking back the way they had come was more depressing, the two large hills behind had lost their shape and their tops were now hidden. The cloud was lower than the peaks and he could see how the space between them was becoming a funnel for the cloud that was being pushed around them. He hadn't seen anything quite like this before, it was interesting to watch, he just wished it wasn't today. As the cloud pressed down on them he decided it may be worth scouting around the area before the visibility became too restricted. PC Gunn had decided to place the police signs further away from the lay-by as the single lane road could become dangerous for them in the fog. Avalon made his way towards the loch, searching on the ground for any signs of footprints or other evidence, all he found was wet grass and heather. He made his way around the outside of the lay-by and back onto the road as Gunn walked past him returning from placing the signs.

"Here it comes," he pointed to the heavens. Avalon looked to the hills but they had vanished and all that could be seen was the road the way they had come and *it*, was quickly being eaten up by the mist. There was something visible though, headlights. From the swirling cloud came Avalon's car with Ross in the driving seat and he carefully parked at the side of the police van on the edge of the lay-by.

"Bloody hell," he said to Gunn, "is it like this all the time up here?"

"Not very often but when the clouds come down..." he broke off as he shrugged. Ross walked over to Avalon.

"SOCO are sending a team up as soon as they can get, it could be some time though." Avalon nodded at the information as the fog descended to where they were. Gunn suggested they get in the van as the cloud could be

152

extremely wet. He wasn't wrong, it was odd, the air seemed drenched and the water ran down the windscreen as if it was raining.

"I think there are some waterproof jackets in the back," offered PC Gunn pointing to the rear of the van with his thumb.

"How long is this likely to last?" asked Avalon. Gunn shrugged and looked out of the side window.

"Anything from hours to days, I could radio for a weather report," he announced.

"It doesn't matter," replied Avalon gloomily, "we'll just have to deal with it."

"I could ring Frazer and see if she can get the weather changed," shrugged Ross.

"I don't think even Megan has that capability," smiled Avalon.

"Probably not, but she has dug up a few interesting items," added Ross raising his eyebrows, "remind me to tell you about them later," he added knowing the DI wouldn't want anything discussing in front of the PC. Avalon nodded with protruding lips and then said,

"I'll get my waterproof out of the boot of the car," and he climbed out of the van. To his surprise there was a strong breeze in the fog, it seemed odd that it could be so, shouldn't the wind break up the cloud? He reached into the boot and put on the bright yellow jacket already feeling the effects of the wet air on his suit. He zipped the front and closed the boot and tried to peer into the gloom and just for a moment he saw movement. He squinted but could see no definite shape. He moved into the narrow road to look closer as Gunn wound down his side window and asked,

"Problems sir?" Avalon didn't react at first, he

just kept his gaze on the area he had seen the movement.

"I thought I saw something," he eventually said, "yes there," he suddenly pointed and moved forward.

"Et's probably a deer, there're loads of 'em up here," added Gunn. Avalon looked around the area of the movement from the road but there was nothing to see, he decided to move closer and once again he saw a shape move, not thirty feet ahead of him. He made his way onto the grass verge and into the heather, continuing towards the shape. Behind him he heard the doors of the van close, which meant that Gunn and Ross were probably following but then there was silence, even the breeze slowed to the slightest whisper. The cloud thickened and he realised he couldn't see either the shape or the road. He looked down to try and find a rock or some other feature, to guide his way but inside he was feeling apprehensive. It could indeed be a deer moving about, but the shape had seemed taller than it was long and as deer tended not to walk around erect on their rear legs he began to have doubts about what it was he had observed. As he continued he recalled an old movie he had seen when he was a young boy, it had scared him utterly and completely, 'The Hound of the Baskervilles' it was called, a Sherlock Holmes film with Basil Rathbone in the title role. It had inspired him to buy and read the book, which scared him all over again and that image of the beast on the moor was inside his head. The local area in this empty landscape had similarities to 'Grimpen Mire' and he trod carefully just in case there were similar sort of bogs here. He was soon wishing that the dependable Dr Watson was with him carrying his service revolver for protection. Behind him he heard a noise and from the gloom he heard Ross cursing as he approached, he was probably ruining his shoes again.

154

"Where the hell are you?" he heard him ask. Avalon didn't answer, he looked forward to see if he could see the shape but there was nothing.

"Here, over here," he eventually called. Ross was already looking bedraggled as the borrowed day-glow waterproof broke through the steamy swirls of the mist.

"This is unreal," said Ross stepping carefully to reach Avalon.

"Where's the PC?" asked Avalon.

"He's staying on the road so he can redirect us back," explained Ross.

"Oh really?" said Avalon raising his eyebrows.

"So what did you see?" asked Ross also peering into the murk.

"I really don't know, the fog seems even thicker here."

"Well, it could have just been a deer," insisted Ross.

"You don't think I saw anything do you?" asked Avalon looking forward.

"You did say you had a headache," smiled Ross but Avalon didn't see his grin, he was still peering through the gloom.

"I saw something and I swear it looked like..." he broke off and turned to Ross, "let's go back my feet are soaked." Ross nodded and then suddenly pointed behind Avalon hissing the word,

"There!"

"What?" Avalon turned to where Ross pointed and saw the movement too. He dashed forward towards the area and felt his feet sink into soft ground, after two paces he stopped and held up his hand to stop Ross moving on.

"What was it?" asked Ross in a whisper. Avalon

shook his head slowly still looking into the curtain of fog. "If it's a deer, it's a bloody big one," added Ross.

"Quiet," hissed Avalon, "would you say it was here, at this point?" he whispered.

"Yeah, just about where you're standing," nodded Ross though Avalon hadn't turned to look, he was looking forward and then he said,

"Then look down here," pointing to the earth but still looking ahead. Ross looked and saw Avalon standing in mud, the brown mush oozing slowly over his shoes. Ross was about to ask why he didn't get out of the mud and then he realised why Avalon had mentioned it. He felt himself swallow. In that soft earth, there were no footprints, no marks at all. The whole area as far as he could see showed no sign that anything had walked, crawled or slithered across that place. He stayed quiet. Avalon felt the silence and looked slowly round to Ross who stared blankly back and shrugged.

"Come on, let's get out of here," insisted Avalon walking steadily away from the boggy ground.

Back at the roadside the fog wasn't as thick and they saw PC Gunn standing by the police van.

"Did you find et?" he asked.

"No, nothing, as you said, it could have been a deer," agreed Avalon and he returned to the boot of his car to find a roll of paper towels to try to clean his footwear. Ross's phone rang.

"Yeah," he said and there was a silence followed by, "Okay, we're at the site so we'll probably leave when they arrive," and he put the phone away.

"SOCO?" asked Avalon, Ross nodded.

"Yeah, they're in Golspie so they should be up here soon." Avalon nodded and then looked to where PC Gunn was standing then over to Ross and in a quiet voice asked,

"You said there was something to tell me from Megan."

"Oh yeah," nodded Ross returning from his thoughts and he too looked over to Gunn. He decided to speak quietly even though he was a way off in the fog. "She has found out that the Stodarts were in deep debt, even council tax and utility bills were unpaid and a large amount of credit was also in the red."

"I guessed they were in a bit of a pickle but it looks pretty serious," nodded Avalon.

"Very, it also makes you wonder if they had taken loans from more nefarious people," added Ross.

"I think we're going to find that there was a great deal more debt that seems credible here, but it leaves us with a more pressing question," sighed Avalon.

"The wife?" asked Ross.

"Exactly," nodded the DI.

"It still doesn't mean she had anything to do with it thought does it?" insisted Ross checking where PC Gunn was.

"No, not at all," agreed Avalon, "but as it stands, there seems little doubt she at least knew something was going to happen, even if she had no direct connection to his death." Ross nodded, it did seem damning, the timing was everything in these matters and the fact that she had gone missing a few weeks before someone killed her husband, looked bad in every way. "We certainly need to find her," continued Avalon, "and that damn laptop." Ross nodded and then looked a little puzzled. "What?" asked Avalon closing the boot of his car.

"So..." there was a slight pause, "what did we see out there?" and he nodded to the fog bank at the side of the road. Avalon shrugged.

"Something that as yet is unidentified," he announced walking back to the police van.

"Is that how you explain everything away?" frowned Ross. Avalon stopped and turned.

"If I have learned anything in my time in this job," began Avalon tilting his head to one side, "it's don't complicate matters by speculation." He then turned to continue on but as an afterthought turned back to Ross, "if there were no footprints, there was nothing there, end of story." Ross shrugged as Avalon walked away.

"And people wonder how you got the name Auld Clootie," he whispered to himself.

~~~~~~

Back at the incident room Avalon and Ross sat with a hot drink and listened to the utter silence in there. The phones hadn't exactly been busy and the officers looked thoroughly bored. At least it wasn't raining, as they had retreated from the moors and dropped under the cloud, the rain had ceased and by the time they were back at Golspie, it was a reasonably pleasant day, if a little cloudy. Avalon finished the tea and went outside to sit on a bench in the grassy area at the side of the car park. He looked out to sea and breathed in a large lungful of clean, fresh air and realised his headache had finally passed. After a few minutes, Ross joined him and sat, checking that it was reasonably dry first.

"The press want some information," he said.

"Point them to the press officer, that's what the facility is there for," answered Avalon grumpily.

"This comes *from* the press office, they have arranged for the television to come up," explained Ross. Avalon spun on him.

"You're trying to wind me up right?"

"Nope, a TV crew will be here this afternoon around four thirty," frowned Ross.

"Then you sort it, I've had my face on the television and I didn't like the repercussions."

"I will but I think you should do it, being the senior officer," sighed Ross.

"DCI Croker will be none-too pleased, he hates the idea of press and I wouldn't want to go against his wishes," explained Avalon.

"Well suit yourself but I still think it needs to be you, it was you they asked for."

"Specifically?" asked Avalon with a doubtful look on his face.

"You are the senior investigating officer and that's who they asked for," insisted Ross. Avalon looked back out to sea, he didn't like the limelight since his time in the Wolverhampton police where he had been labelled as the Ghostbusting Detective. It was certainly inevitable that he couldn't shirk the responsibility forever, the public needed facts and it could even stimulate people to ring in some information. He nodded.

"Okay, you'll have to be there too," he insisted. Ross shrugged and replied with,

"If you say so," and he stood and returned to the incident vehicle. Avalon breathed in some more fresh air and then he too stood, thrusting his hands into his trouser pockets and taking in the view over the bay, all the way out to Portmahomack on the peninsula and as far out as the Tarbat Ness lighthouse. Somewhere behind him a seagull began its raucous call, it sounded like a laugh, it sounded like it was laughing at *him*.

The television news team were on time and the anchor

woman was everything Avalon had grown to expect. She was well presented in every way, attractive, well dressed with perfect makeup and on camera very smooth and unflustered with a perfect speaking voice. Off camera she was utterly officious and as foul-mouthed as a Clydeside docker. He stayed clear of her as long as he could. There was no point in finding out what she would ask him as his previous experience had told him that she wouldn't stick to pre-arranged questions anyway. He went into his introspective side and decided to say nothing but the bare facts, he would ask the public for their help and assure them everything that could be done *was* being done. He was actually hoping it would start raining again so that the interview would be cut short but ironically the sky began to clear even more. She was introduced to him and she wrote something in her notes but gave him very little eye contact, he took that as a sign that she would be unpleasant to deal with. He gritted his teeth as the camera lights went on and stood slightly off camera waiting for a cue. It soon came with the words,

"...and we have Detective Inspector Avalon from the Inverness CID here with us who is leading the investigation. Detective Inspector Avalon, can you confirm that this is a murder investigation?" Avalon had anticipated that question of course and he had the standard, non-committal answer that he had been trained to give. Avalon rarely used any advice that his training had given him. He considered that in all walks of life and all professions, training was usually given by people who were not quite good enough to be doing the job they were training other people to do. So, he generally ignored it, but in this instance, it was right on the money. The idea was to say nothing that can't be confirmed by higher authority, that way you can't get into any trouble for making the wrong decision. The presenter was obviously ready for his unenthusiastic reply and asked,

"Then can you confirm that the deceased is Peter Stodart and he died by violent means?"

"As I said previously Sally, I can't confirm the identity of the deceased or the manner of his death until I receive the report from the coroner and a formal identification can be made." The use of her first name was designed to make him seem more 'connected' to her for the viewers, in reality he just wanted to beat her with a stick and go and have something to eat.

"Then can you tell us if this has anything to do with the disappearance of Muiranne Stodart, the wife of Peter Stodart some weeks ago?"

"The disappearance of Mrs Stodart is a separate investigation and bears little or no connection to this inquiry, we are however interested in finding Mrs Stodart at the earliest opportunity."

"And I believe you are asking for public help in finding her?"

"Yes, we would like to know if anyone has seen her or knows where she might be found, if anyone..." Avalon went through a rehearsed collection of numbers and contact information before another question was thrown at him. This one struck him straight between the eyes.

"In light of several other people vanishing without trace in this area over the years, most in unexplained circumstances, has Police Scotland brought you in as a specialist in this kind of case?" His heart raced, he knew what was coming, how the hell could he ever shake the spectre of his past? And what other disappearances? Rory had done his homework and said there was another recent one but that was it, or had he got it wrong? Either way he had to answer before the pause looked like he had been caught off guard.

"I must stress that this is a straight-forward investigation, I am just one of many detectives working from Inverness," he replied but he was looking for a disarming comment, he couldn't think of one.

"But you do seem to be given some unusual cases," she interrupted so he did the same and interrupted her.

"I don't know who does your research Sally but I can assure you that there is never anything *usual* about criminal activity, what I want to stress," he continued trying to change the subject, "is that we are keen to speak to anyone who may know the whereabouts of Mrs Stodart." The presenter tried to interrupt again so Avalon raised his voice and brought out his reserve option. "My colleague Detective Sergeant Ross has a full description of Mrs Stodart and her vehicle." The plan worked, it took Ross by surprise but the camera turned and faced Ross who blinked and then read from a sheet he was holding. Avalon knew the interview had a finite time to run and this was a way of getting the presenter off the subject of his 'unusual' cases. Back in Wolverhampton he had been tarred with the nick-name 'Spook' due to his previous successes and now it seemed a world away. He didn't want to go back to that at any cost and he didn't want it mentioning on the television either. He noticed a man behind the camera make a signal to the presenter and as soon as Ross had finished reading out the details, she turned back to Avalon as did the camera.

"Thank you Detectives Avalon and Ross," and then she turned to the camera, which enveloped her and brought her entirety back to the watching public. As

Avalon heard her say, "that was Detective Inspector Avalon of the Inverness CID," he sighed with relief and nodded to Ross to make a quick exit as she continued with her wind up of the interview.

"Unusual cases?" smiled Ross.

"Well," admitted Avalon, "we do seem to drop onto odd circumstances now and then."

"I suppose so but that is a tiny part of what we do," shrugged Ross.

"But the ones that hit the papers and the TV more often than not have the occult, phantom drummers or moor spirits tied in somewhere," added Avalon as they reached the incident truck.

"Let's hope we don't get the Giant Marshmallow Man on a murder rampage then," grinned Ross. Avalon cringed slightly at the reference to a character from the Ghostbusters movie.

~~~~~~

The rest of the afternoon dragged somewhat as they waited for any reaction to the TV interview. There were a few calls but no leads and certainly no new information. They would just have to wait for forensics or some lucky break. Frazer called Avalon later in the afternoon and gave him an update on her findings but there was nothing significant and he and Ross prepared themselves for a long investigation. Ross was returning from a local shop when he saw Avalon standing at the rear of the car park once more looking out to sea.

"I've had an idea," he said handing Avalon a sandwich.

"Is it, 'let's change profession and go and do something more gratifying?' if not I'll be very disappointed," replied Avalon removing the packaging and taking out the food.

"Well not quite, but I was wondering about the reason that Mrs Stodart may want to vanish rather than just leave."

"I'm listening," replied Avalon sniffing the sandwich to try and work out what it was. He had to wait for the reply as Ross had begun eating.

"It's probably a long shot but if you think about it, she set up something that would be fairly public and that is the key to this I think," he said and then took another bite.

"Are you going to stop eating for a moment and explain or should I try to contact you by ESP?"

"Sorry," announced Ross in a muffled voice and he tried to clear his mouth. The chewing didn't take long and he seemed to simply swallow the food, Avalon decided Ross had some seagull DNA in his blood and decided he would pass on the sandwich, placing it on a bench behind him. "She knew that disappearing like that would mean that it would make the news, or at least the local papers," continued Ross taking a break from his food, "and that means she *intended* it to become public."

"Well I got that part of the plan," sighed Avalon.

"But that means she was creating a sort of alibi," continued Ross and then he shrugged and looked across the bay, "I grant you it's sort of misfired but did she expect him to be killed?"

"Sorry but you're making as much sense as Morrissey lyrics," frowned Avalon.

"Right," began Ross once more, " we assume she knew her husband was up to no good, no good that could bring him, and her for that matter some serious trouble," he paused and Avalon nodded slightly, "so she is sick of

164

the whole situation, the money, the drugs, probably the gambling and anything else he is connected to," he paused again and Avalon made a slight shrug. Ross saw he was following and continued, "so she wants out, but she wants out to the degree that she needs to sever herself from him totally, so she comes up with a plan to vanish in an unexplainable way so that the media report it." Ross took another bite of the sandwich.

"She could have just walked away," replied Avalon, "and announce publicly that she was filing for a divorce."

"She could," nodded Ross, "but if the crazy hubby could work out where she was he could still bother her," and he finished off the food.

"But that still doesn't explain why the plan has to be so complex," frowned Avalon, "it's more akin to a magic act than..." Avalon trailed off and Ross realised what had triggered it. Avalon clicked his fingers, "that's it," and he looked at his watch, "see if Megan is still in the Cave, ask her to find out who Mrs Stodart knew in the entertainment business." Ross took out his phone and spoke to Frazer as Avalon paced up and down trying to think how the disappearance had been done. Nothing came to him, he thought back to the area where the woman had gone missing but still nothing came to him at all.

"She's getting straight to it," said Ross as he put his phone back in his pocket. He watched Avalon pace with his hand on his chin and then said,

"We know a magician."

"Do we?" frowned Avalon, "who's that?"

"Clive Smith, aka Damian Tennant, the brains behind the Drumnadrochit case."

"He's in the nick," insisted Avalon.

165

"Yeah," nodded Ross, "so we know where to find him. He may help us if you ask him nicely." Avalon thought about it for a moment.

"It's an idea if Megan can't find anything," he eventually said. There was silence for a minute or two and then Ross asked,

"Are you gonna eat that?" pointing to the sandwich.

"What? Er no, help yourself," replied Avalon and he looked back out to sea. "I always thought the water butt in the back of the Land Rover was the key to the disappearance but for the life of me I still can't see how it was done." He turned to look at Ross finishing the sandwich, "there's no wonder you are putting weight on," and he waited for the defensive argument.

"I'm not putting weight on, I have to eat to keep up my strength, I do more than you anyway." Avalon turned back out towards the ocean and let himself indulge in a slight smile.

~~~~~~

The little bothy at the side of Julia Beattie's house was a more inviting base for Avalon and Ross and so they made their way back there, with instructions to the incident team to ring if anything at all came in. The bothy was quite inviting after the damp of the day and Ross made sure the kettle was boiling soon after arriving. Avalon opened up his laptop and checked his emails. Ross came in from the tiny kitchen with the drinks and sat besides him.

"Anything we didn't know about?" he asked sipping the coffee.

"Not really, Megan has sent me Peter Stodart's

previous, nothing all that serious and well in the past it seems," frowned Avalon.

"So what about the gambling business then?" asked Ross.

"He's just a bad businessman it seems, oh and you were right, he had a gambling problem, he was ripping off his own business to gamble on other sites."

"No wonder she wanted out then," shrugged Ross, "he sounds a complete dick."

"Oh he was," agreed Avalon, "and it's probably what got him killed but by who?"

"Gangsters, loan sharks, unhappy business partners, take your pick," shrugged Ross taking another sip of the coffee. Avalon finished reading his emails and was about to close the laptop to take a drink but then a light came on in his head.

"Is there any way to find out what was on that laptop without actually having it?" Ross looked into space for a moment and then curled his bottom lip.

"I can't see how," he admitted eventually, "unless he backed everything up on a server, but you'd have to get permission to allow his ISP to give it you."

"Can you explain that in English please?" asked Avalon.

"Well," explained Ross, "if the contents of the laptop are so important to him it was probably backed up to his internet provider," and Ross placed his cup on the table and looked over to Avalon. "You know, he could have just been waiting for an email, and unless he purged the server after every contact, that email would still be on the server." Avalon's eyes lit up.

"Then we need to apply to get that information, get Rory to look into it," he looked round to Ross to tell him to get it sorted but he was already ringing out to

HQ. As Ross explained the situation to Mackinnon on his phone, Avalon put thought into what would trigger Mrs Stodart to plan her escape in such a theatrical way. There had to be more to it, by all accounts she was not a confrontational type and that probably meant she wasn't all that imaginative. Was she being manipulated then? Had a competitor or even a colleague of her husband managed to get to her? Ross came off the phone just as there was a knock at the door. Avalon looked over to Ross. Who knew they were there? The latch lifted and slowly, the door opened.

"I thought you were back, I'm not interrupting am I?" It was Julia looking a little apologetic behind the half open door.

"No, no not at all," said Avalon as he stood, "come in, would you like a coffee, the kettle should still be hot," offered Avalon pointing to the kitchen area.

"Oh, no, no thanks," she said as she entered slightly, "I don't want to disturb you, I expect you're busy." Ross had said nothing, he was just watching what he considered to be a pathetic and fawning conversation that was going on between the two. "I was just wondering," she continued, "if you would like to join me for supper tonight, it won't be anything fancy but you're welcome..." and she trailed off. Avalon wasn't one for formal entertaining or being entertained but Ross was always up for a free meal.

"Aye, I'll make one," he nodded. Avalon looked round to him and Ross wondered if the glare in his eyes meant 'change your mind quickly' but before he had time to say anything Avalon turned back to Julia and accepted.

"That's very kind of you, we'd love to join you, we'll bring the wine."

"Oh lovely," she smiled, "I think I was a little off with you last time we spoke..."

"No, not at all," said Avalon looking to Ross for support.

"I don't remember it that way," replied Ross shaking his head.

"Well..." she cupped her hands together and smiled again, "I don't often get the chance to entertain so..." and she raised her brows and then turned to leave.

"Er, what time?" asked Avalon.

"Oh sorry," she laughed, "and began to blush, "about seven thirty?" The time was agreed and Avalon warned her that they may have to leave if something came up, she understood and as soon as she left Ross said,

"It really makes me squirm when two forty-somethings act as if they are twelve years old."

"What are you on about?" said Avalon with remnants of the sickly smile still hanging on to the corners of his mouth.

"She's obviously interested in you and you in her, though I can't imagine why," frowned Ross, "so why don't you just get on with it?"

"And here speaks the voice of experience," replied Avalon in a derogatory tone as he sat on the sofa.

"Well I wouldn't arse about like you that's for sure," insisted Ross.

"So what about that barmaid that invited you round to her house, you walked away from that one as I recall," grinned Avalon.

"Don't bring that one up, she was too clatty even for me," he frowned.

"Clatty?" asked Avalon not understanding the word but Ross thought he wanted an explanation.

169

"Yeah," explained Ross, "she told me to take a seat but I had to tidy the room before I could find one never mind sit on it."

"So you just left?" asked Avalon.

"Yeah, well I instigated the Robertson Protocol."

"What's that?" frowned Avalon.

"Me and an old rugby club mate have a thing where we arrange a phone call just after the allotted time, it's a 'get out of jail free' card if you know what I mean."

"So your mate rings you up just after you meet and you have to decide whether to stay or not?" asked Avalon incredulously.

"Aye," nodded Ross seeing his DI's disapprobation, "it works and no one gets hurt," he then explained trying to lighten the situation.

"It sounds pretty shallow to me," sighed Avalon before adding, "so, what did Rory say?" It took Ross a couple of seconds to think back to his phone call with Mackinnon.

"He and Frazer are getting straight onto it, it could take a few days to get it through the courts though."

"Let's hope there is something to find."

"It's likely there will be, I can't imagine anyone deleting all their emails off the server," nodded Ross. Avalon's phone rang.

"Avalon," he said as he answered. Ross watched his reactions as he listened but there was nothing until he said, "and do we have a number for the car?" There was silence for a few seconds and he eventually ended the call. Ross watched Avalon put his phone away and then look at his watch before saying,

"Someone phoned in with a tip-off that Muiranne

Stodart may have had a lover, her car was seen parked up near Dornoch with another car and both drivers seemed to be in the other vehicle."

"That doesn't mean anything," insisted Ross.

"No but it may be an accomplice rather than a lover," suggested Avalon. Ross nodded and then asked,

"So I'm guessing we have an ID of the car but no number?"

"Yeah," nodded Avalon, "a white Volkswagen, probably a Polo or a Golf, but sadly no number."

"Is the tip off anonymous?"

"No, someone from the local force is going round to interview them," replied Avalon.

"Shouldn't we go?" asked Ross.

"Not yet, it could be someone just trying to stir up trouble or some other type of timewaster. I'm more interested in interviewing one particular owner of a similar car."

"Who?" asked Ross.

"David Sutherland, he had a small white VW parked in his garage as I recall."

"I didn't notice," admitted Ross.

"Maybe I ought to send you back for some retraining," frowned Avalon.

"Maybe, but if you did you would have no one to solve this one for you," he grinned as he stood. Avalon took the cue and they walked to the door as Avalon asked,

"So have you solved it already?" with a wry grin.

"I'm close," nodded Ross, "but I'm not ready to spill the beans yet, in Miss Marple tradition I'm waiting until I get everyone into the library."

"Miss Marple could be your new nick-name,"

"Don't even think about it," hissed Ross as he sat

in the passenger seat of Avalon's car.

They pulled into Sutherland's drive and as Avalon had suggested, a white Volkswagen Polo stood in front of them, just forward of open garage doors, Mr Sutherland washing the vehicle with a hosepipe. As Ross opened the door Avalon grabbed his arm and said,

"This could be someone trying to get him into bother."

"I know, I don't need that much retraining," insisted Ross as he climbed out.

"Oh, Detectives Avalon and Ross, I didn't expect to see you so soon," he said as he turned off the hose, "is there any news?"

"Not as such," began Ross, "we are just investigating an incident that happened a few weeks ago near Dornoch."

"Oh," said Sutherland raising his brows, "an incident?"

"Yes Mr Sutherland," began Avalon, "Mrs Stodart's car was seen parked in the car park at the Evelix fuel station late one Friday evening, it was parked close to another car and both occupants were seated in the other vehicle,"

"And?" asked Sutherland wondering why they were asking him about it.

"Do you know who the other person might have been?" asked Ross.

"I'm sure there are other people who can dig up dirt about her detective, I know nothing about her private life and I'm not sure I would tell you if I did."

"What if we told you the other car was identified as a white VW Polo?" asked Ross. Sutherland looked down at his car and then back to Avalon.

"That's impossible, I simply wasn't there, I have never met Mrs Stodart anywhere other than here or at the bowls club."

"Does your wife ever drive the car?" asked Ross.

"Well, yes on occasions but she has her own car," insisted the man.

"Is it white?" asked Avalon.

"No it's red, now look here," the man was becoming agitated, "my wife can't have anything to do with this, she hardly knew Mrs Stodart."

"Is your wife a member of the bowls club?" asked Ross.

"Yes of course, but she hardly ever goes," admitted Sutherland obviously under some stress as he began to see the implications of what was being asked.

"When did you last see Mrs Stodart at the bowls club Mr Sutherland?" asked Ross taking out his notepad.

"Er," he hesitated trying to think when it was, placing his hand behind his head, "the Wednesday before she went missing, yes that would be it."

"Did you see her there often?" asked Ross.

"Well yes, most weeks I suppose, but most people at the club would see her too."

"How often did your wife attend?" asked Avalon.

"About once a month, maybe less," he replied shaking his head and then he added, "is she a suspect now?"

"We will certainly have to ask her a few questions," replied Avalon, "just as a matter of course."

"She really has nothing to do with this, neither of us do," insisted Sutherland.

"As I said, Mr Sutherland," added Avalon, "it's just a matter of course and I'm sure we can clear this up once we speak to her, is she at home?"

"No, she's at work," replied the man and Avalon explained that he would send someone to speak to her later and then they left.

As they drove back to Golspie Ross asked,

"So what does your 'instinct' glean from that then?" Avalon stared at the road ahead and gave a slight shrug.

"I still think that he's telling the truth."

"But you have to admit, there seems to be an obvious scenario available," replied Ross.

"You mean the wife?"

"Of course, can't you see that?" asked Ross with a little surprise that Avalon hadn't considered it.

"I can't see any motive," said Avalon shaking his head slightly.

"So you don't think that a jealous wife might arrange to meet the queen of the bowls club to warn her off?" Avalon was quiet as he considered it.

"It's not impossible, it would explain a similar car to her husbands being seen in the car park but we would then have to assume that there was something going on between Sutherland and Muiranne Stodart."

"Not really, it just means Mrs Sutherland *thought* there was," insisted Ross. Avalon stuck out his bottom lip out and nodded, then said,

"I'm guessing that the Volkswagen Polo is probably one of the most popular cars on the road at the moment," and he gave a quick glance over to Ross. The younger detective looked back and then straight forward through the windscreen and shrugged.

"And white is probably the most popular colour but it doesn't mean the theory is flawed," he said.

They were a little late arriving at the main house of Julia

Beattie, it was the nature of the job but they had managed to clear up as much as they could before retiring for the evening.

"You'll have to forgive the place at the moment," explained Julia as she lead them to the dining room, "it's a bit of a brooach." Avalon didn't understand what she was getting at but he just smiled and apologised for being late. "Oh don't mind that, I was running a little late myself, it's so long since I cooked for anyone," she smiled seeming a little nervous.

"It smells nice whatever it is," admitted Ross looking at the formally set dining table and he then held up two bottles of wine and asked, "do you have the necessary?"

"Oh, yes," she smiled, "I'll get the corkscrew," and she returned to the kitchen. Ross raised his eyebrows a little to Avalon who shook his head slightly and looked at the bottles that he had asked Ross to buy. They were not the most expensive he had laid eyes upon but at least they weren't screw top. She soon returned and told them to take a seat and the food was duly brought out. The meal was simple but tasty and pleasant and the conversation revolved mainly around Julia's life previous to Golspie. She was divorced with one daughter who now lived in the USA, she was an ex-teacher who had decided that there must be more to life than teaching, only to find out there is more to life than looking for 'more to life'. She had spent the last two years just trying to make ends meet and was disillusioned with her lot. It was a story Avalon heard a great deal particularly from people of around his own age. Ross suddenly lifted his wine glass and proposed a toast to the hostess and then he said,

"Well, I must make a hasty retreat, it's been a

lovely evening but I have a few things to do before I turn in."

"Really?" asked Avalon, not sure why Ross was returning to the bothy.

"Yeah, a few emails to send to sort out a meeting with a magician?" said Ross as a question. Avalon saw the look on Ross's face, it was obvious he was leaving to allow Avalon and Julia to be alone. Avalon shrugged and then nodded. Ross thanked the host again and left.

"A magician?" asked Julia with a slight laugh, "I'm sure it must be some sort of code only you understand."

"Not at all," replied Avalon with a serious face, "he has fifteen children at home and he has to arrange entertainment for them, it's the birthday of number eleven, or is it twelve, I forget." Julia laughed again, she could see through Avalon's jest and took a sip of wine.

"So you've heard about *me* most of the night, what about you?" she asked.

"There's nothing much to tell, the life of a detective is fairly drab most of the time."

"Oh I don't know, it must be quite exciting sometimes," she said looking into his eyes. Avalon felt his stomach tighten, he hadn't had enough wine for him to be totally comfortable with her but he found it exciting, it was something that had been missing from his life.

"Don't believe what you see on the television," he smiled, "most of the job is paperwork, and when it isn't it's trudging through mud and slush."

"I'm sure you are underselling yourself," she returned the smile, "but I meant about you, about James Avalon." He noticed her finger playing with the rim of her glass, he found it slightly seductive and his stomach tightened even more.

"Same story really," he announced, "to be a detective you have to be a little methodical, which in turn breeds a boring sort of person." She decided to change tack.

"Okay, Mr Boring," she smiled again as she rest her elbow on the table and tucked her hand under her chin, "what do you get up to on your days off?"

"Well, for starters," he began, "there aren't many days off, but now and then I sometimes go for a ride on my motorbike." She raised her eyebrows a little but said nothing. "I sometimes play my guitar," this brought much the same reaction, "and when I get really bored, I free-climb tall buildings."

"Really?" she grinned, allowing her arm to fall flat on the table. She caught his arm as it fell, Avalon looked down at her hand which was still touching him.

"No," he gave a slight smile, "the last bit was a lie." She gave a grin at this but the grin faded and she leaned forward, it was a slow approach, so slow that he was sure time had halted for a second, and he thought that he could feel all the hairs on his hand move. Her face came closer and as he looked into her eyes, contemplating the blueness he had only just noticed. The room wasn't cold but he sensed the warmth of her as she neared him and the delicate aroma of her body struck him like an olfactory tsunami. She was so close now that he could no longer focus on her features and he let his vision drift off into the middle distance as she kissed him, his mouth automatically reacting to the connection.

Chapter Six

"No headache today then?" asked Ross as he sat in the passenger seat of Avalon's car.

"Er, no," answered Avalon thinking about the question. He hadn't noticed it until Ross had asked but there was no sign of the pain that had plagued him of late, "it's early yet though," he added.

"Interesting," grinned Ross.

"What's that supposed to mean?" asked Avalon as he looked over to Ross and started the car.

"Nothing," shrugged Ross and in an attempt to change the subject he continued with, "oh by the way, we are getting PC Dowd this morning." Avalon nodded as the car pulled away and they made their way to the incident vehicle.

"Good," he said, "he's just the man to co-ordinate the information coming in."

"There isn't any information coming in," demanded Ross, "the only details are coming from our own office through snippets that Frazer and Mackinnon are finding."

"Any further news on that score?"

"No," replied Ross shaking his head, "I checked

emails this morning but except for forensics saying they expect the results from the Stodarts house to take another day, there was nothing." Avalon parked the car by the side of the incident vehicle in the centre of Golspie and they stepped inside to check on the officers working there. Avalon informed them that a PC would arrive later who would liase between them and the incident room and then they returned to the car where Ross pulled out a thermos of coffee he had made earlier. The weather was cloudy but at least there wasn't any rain and so Avalon opened the window to breath in the sea air and to allow the pungent aroma of the coffee to escape. He sipped at the plastic cup as he thought through the case, he still couldn't work out why Muiranne Stodart had exited her relationship with her wayward husband in such a dramatic way. The other thing that was making him think that Muiranne wasn't exactly as innocent as people considered her was, 'why now?', why after all this time had she taken it upon herself to devise an elaborate plan to vanish just two weeks before her husband was bludgeoned to death? There were two options, the first was that it was pure coincidence, the other was that she had planned his death. If she had just left, he would be more inclined to think that it was coincidence but with this drawn-out plan to disappear, Avalon was erring on the side of her being involved. Ross was also thinking about the case as his next statement testified to.

"She can't have anything to do with it,"

"Who with what?" asked Avalon turning to him. Ross was staring out of the windscreen that had misted up in front of him from the heat of the coffee he was holding in his right hand. In his left was a copy of the photograph of Muiranne Stodart.

"Sorry," he then said turning to Avalon and

blinking several times, "Mrs Stodart, she can't be involved with the death of her husband."

"And why not?"

"It stands to reason that if you were planning something this big, would you go missing in a way that would bring the police crawling all over your previous life?" explained Ross as he turned his gaze back to the windscreen. For a moment, Avalon thought Ross was going to wipe the screen with his hand and he couldn't abide finger marks on windscreens, he instinctively reached down into the door pocket for a cloth. Ross didn't move however and so Avalon thought about his statement and replaced the cloth.

"You wouldn't think so," he simply said, "but that doesn't make me believe she's innocent."

"It's more likely to be a cry for help," mused Ross looking down to the photograph.

"A cry for help, how so?" asked Avalon raising his brows.

"Well, if she thought, or somehow knew her husband was in some deep trouble," Ross turned to Avalon to explain, "and was panicking about it, could she have come up with something to bring her plight to the eye of the police and the public?"

"Are you serious?" asked Avalon watching Ross return his sight to the image, "that sounds like a plot from a cheap budget Australian soap opera." Ross kept his eyes on the image of the woman and Avalon looked down to it too.

"She's a looker if this is anything to go by," offered Ross.

"She is, and her magic is strong," nodded Avalon. Ross looked round to him.

"What magic?"

180

"*Her* magic, she's captivated many men with it and it seems it's coming out of her image too," replied Avalon raising his brows sharply at Ross who was about to reply but Avalon cut him short, "and talking of magic, did Megan find any connection to entertainers and Mrs Stodart?"

"No," sighed Ross, "so we're trying to arrange a meeting with Damian Tennant."

"Okay, it may help if we can work out how she actually disappeared," nodded Avalon just as a car pulled in at the side of them, it was PC Dowd with another officer. Avalon got out of the car and began to explain the details of the case and set out Dowd's and PC Makin's duties. When he had done, Ross offered them a coffee from the flask.

"Sorry it's not better weather for your trip out," smiled Avalon.

"Ah, et's better here than anywhere else, it rained all the way up," explained Dowd, "as soon as we crossed over the river it brightened up." Dowd and Makin were shown inside the incident vehicle and made themselves at home. Avalon left and walked to the edge of the beach and looked out to sea. Most cases that were not solved in the first forty-eight hours could be very frustrating, there were long gaps where nothing happened, waiting for reports from forensics and pathologists, house to house interviews, sifting through reports from cranks and inquisitive locals but this case was different. There were the gaps for sure, forensics could certainly bring up some information and they would have to wait for that but the telephones were silent. Either no one knew anything or no one wanted to tell. The single piece of information about Muiranne Stodart's car seen with a white Volkswagen seemed to check out but that was it.

Ross came over to him and asked,

"Where do you want to start?"

"I dunno," shrugged Avalon, "there isn't much to pursue, we need to get a statement from Mrs Sutherland though."

"We could arrange that for when she gets home I suppose," admitted Ross.

"It may be better to approach her at work," replied Avalon. Ross raised his eyebrows.

"Put some pressure on her you mean?"

"Maybe," nodded Avalon, "though to be honest it feels like clutching straws," and he turned to Ross, "no on second thoughts, get Dowd to arrange to see her later." Ross nodded and was about to walk back to the incident unit when his phone rang.

"DS Ross," he said. There was some silence as he listened to the phone and then he asked, "really, that seems odd," and after a few seconds he added, "okay, thanks for that, I owe you one," and he replaced the phone in his pocket. "Sarah Underwood," he announced. Avalon gave a curt nod and asked,

"Some news?"

"Aye but not about the case," replied Ross, "a forensic locksmith has made some headway on that latch key I sent them."

"Oh," replied Avalon waiting for the rest of it, noticing a puzzled look on Ross's face.

"It's not a latch key, he thinks it's a safety deposit box key," explained Ross still puzzled. Avalon was also taken aback by the information, why would a homeless person have a key to a safety deposit box?

"Is he sure?" asked Avalon.

"He's a forensics locksmith, how much more qualified can he get?" frowned Ross.

"I suppose so," nodded Avalon, "it must be a key he picked up somewhere."

"I think it has to be, where would he get the money to rent the box anyway?" admitted Ross. Avalon hadn't considered that, a safety deposit box would cost money to rent and Arty Struthers didn't have the where-with-all to afford even that weekly sum.

"I suppose he just picked it up in the street and kept it in case someone reported it missing," offered Avalon.

"Probably," nodded Ross, "the locksmith is trying to track down where it's from by the serial number," shrugged Ross, "but even if they do, I don't see how we can track down who owns it."

"Not your problem," replied Avalon, "just send it to the company who runs the boxes if the locksmith can track it down." Ross nodded and then thrust his hands into his pockets. Avalon could see Ross was still running through the possibilities in his mind. This time it was Avalon's phone that rang.

"Avalon."

"*Et's Frazer boss*," said the voice on the end of the phone.

"Go on Megan, any news would be good news."

"*Nothin' spectacular but this magician, Clive Smith, or Damian Tennant as he was known, says he's willing tae talk to you.*"

"Oh," replied Avalon trying to hide his disappointment that the information wasn't something crucial, "okay, set it up for us then."

"*When do you want tae do et?*"

"Where is he incarcerated?"

"*Peterhead, well et's called Grampian now.*"

"Er, where's that, it's over on the east coast isn't

183

it?" asked Avalon remembering something about it.

"*Yeah, et's just above Aberdeen.*"

"Well it's going to make it a full day so try to arrange it as soon as, we are at a bit of a standstill at the mo." Frazer said she would do what she could and she rang off. Avalon put his phone away and looked to Ross.

"Fancy a trip to Aberdeen?"

"Aberdeen, why Aberdeen?"

"Damian Tennant, aka Clive Smith has agreed to see us about Mrs Stodart's vanishing trick," explained Avalon.

"Is it worth it, I mean, it's a long way to go, particularly as it won't forward the case?" asked Ross with a frown.

"Maybe it will, maybe it won't," shrugged Avalon, "what have we got to lose? and to be honest, there isn't much happening here, until we get the forensics and coroner's reports, we're treading water." They returned to the incident unit and waited for any information to come in.

"What do you know about the Brollachan?" asked Avalon casually to PC Dowd. Dowd frowned a little and seemed to sift through his mental cupboards but eventually said,

"Nothin, much, an old Gaelic folklaw demon as far as I can remember." Avalon shrugged, he thought Dowd would be the one to have something to say about it but as an attempt to begin a conversation in the quiet of the incident unit, the subject seemed a non-starter. Eventually, curiosity got the better of Dowd and he asked,

"Why the interest in folklaw?" Avalon looked lazily out of the open door of the unit, watching a seagull peering back at him from outside.

"Just a passing interest in local legends really, I keep hearing about this thing," he explained as the seagull saw there was nothing of interest and waddled away. He looked over to Dowd and gave a quick smile, "I like some of the local legends, they give you a sense of the place and the Sutherland Brollachan seems to have slight differences to other legends." Dowd nodded and then said,

"Well it isn't exactly folklaw or to do with the 'faeries' but if you step outside I'll show you something that has become local legend," replied Dowd but Avalon wasn't quite sure what Dowd was getting at but the three of them walked into the car park. Dowd pointed up the wooded hill behind them and continued. "That, is quite a legend in these parts." He was pointing up to what Avalon thought was just some kind of monument.

"It's called Ben Bhraggie I believe," said Avalon.

"That's the name o' the hill, the statue is called the 'Mannie' locally, he was the Earl of Sutherland," added Ross.

"George Leveson-Gower to be precise," explained Dowd, "born in 1758, the son of the Marquess of Stafford. He married into the Earldom."

"So what's the legend?" asked Avalon.

"Not so much of a legend, more of a notoriety I would think," offered Ross, "he was one of the instigators of the 'clearances', because of that he is labelled as a monster."

"It depends which side of the fence you are on, some say he just wanted better conditions for the labourers," offered Dowd.

"The evidence doesn't support that though," insisted Ross, "people were forcibly evicted, from a lifestyle they had chosen and that makes it ethnic

185

cleansing."

"Well true, the intensive sheep farming was more profitable and given the land raids after the first world-war, it would seem some people did indeed want the crofting way of life," agreed Dowd.

"For Christ's sakes, they had their roofs burned above them, they were forcibly moved to the coast and left without shelter," insisted Ross who had evidently studied the subject, "either way," he continued, "there have been lots of attempts to pull the thing down," explained Ross.

"Pull it down, it must be enormous?" frowned Avalon.

"Aye, about a hundred feet tall but that hasn't stopped them trying," smiled Dowd.

"I know the arguments over the clearances can be volatile, but was he a monster?" asked Avalon.

"Even for the time he seems to have dealt harshly so I would say he was," nodded Ross looking up to the statue.

"I have heard people say he was possessed by a demon," added Dowd raising his eyebrows, "so you never know," and he turned to point to the top of the hill, "that could be one of the last known possessions of the Sutherland Brollachan." Avalon let his eyes drop from the statue and fall on Dowd, there was a slight smile in the corners of his mouth.

"Could be," nodded Avalon and he slowly made his way back to the incident truck.

Avalon kicked off his shoes and leaned back into the sofa as Ross opened the lid of the laptop and began to check his emails.

"So we're off to Aberdeen in the morning?" he

asked. Avalon turned to him and answered.

"Yes, it's arranged for ten in the morning so we need to get an early start."

"We look like going to the chip shop tonight then seeing as we don't have the pleasure of our hostess's company tonight."

"She runs a pottery class down near Dornoch tonight," explained Avalon looking at his watch. Ross looked over to him but there was nothing being given away in his demeanour.

"So what happened last night," asked Ross.

"What do you mean?"

"Well you were alone with Miss Beattie for almost two hours last night and as you came in humming some tune I'm guessing you didn't spend that time discussing Highland Policing techniques or explaining the 'Stop and Search' laws." Avalon shrugged, sat up and then shrugged again.

"We just talked, about this and that," he eventually said.

"How much this and how much that?" grinned Ross.

"You know, I don't think it's something I want to discuss with you," frowned Avalon settling back into the sofa.

"What was that tune you were humming?" asked Ross with a theatrical puzzled look.

"I have no idea, was I humming? I hope I didn't wake you."

"I think it was something from the movie 'Titanic'," said Ross thoughtfully.

"No it wasn't," announced Avalon.

"I thought you didn't remember?" laughed Ross.

"Maybe I did, what does it matter?" replied

Avalon with indignation, "I had a pleasant evening in her company and that's all I'm prepared to say."

"I'm just interested in your welfare that's all," insisted Ross. Avalon began to massage his feet and then he looked over to Ross.

"I get it," he smiled, "you are after pointers, you want to know how a sophisticated English-educated man romances a woman,"

"I do alright without your elaborate preamble," insisted Ross playfully.

"Yeah, I've seen you in action but the promise of a tin of 'Export' and a fish supper doesn't appeal to the sort of females I wish to spend my time with," smiled Avalon.

"Who said anything about a fish supper?" frowned Ross. Avalon looked at his watch again.

"Talking of which," he said quickly replacing his shoes, "we better get off to the chippy, we need to get an early night."

~~~~~~

Avalon hated prisons, he had put many a crook behind bars and he dehumanised the inmates in his mind, he had to, they were the enemy. He knew a lot of detectives saw them as 'deactivated, decommissioned', but Avalon saw it them as a time bomb and with the right fuse they could explode spectacularly. Here in Scotland, the penalties for misdemeanour never seemed to fit the crime and you could easily put some insane killer away, just to find out eight years later he gate crashes your family barbeque. As he waited in the interview room at HMP Grampian, he wondered what Smith would make of his questions, he wondered if he ought to tell him anything about the case. Smith looked as if he had lost weight, he had none of the commanding presence he had demonstrated the first time Avalon had met him. Prison had brought him down, much more than the career criminals that Avalon usually dealt with. It was clear that Damian Tennant had vacated the man, he was now left with the remnants of Clive Smith. He smiled slightly as he was brought in. He sat opposite and the guard left them alone.

"I didn't expect to see you again Detective Avalon," he said and then nodded to Ross.

"No, it's quite a turn up for the books," said Avalon softly.

"How's the 'blackbird'?" he asked, it was a reference to Avalon's motorcycle

"Fine, I still manage to get the odd ride between the monsoons, how are you?" he asked. Smith shrugged.

"I'm not going to pretend it's been easy, I get by. The magic still comes in handy, I entertain the cons now and then, it makes sure they leave me alone." His reply was delivered as upbeat as he could manage but it was clear to see he wasn't built for life behind bars. "I'll be moving next month," he said with a slight smile, "good behaviour and all that." Avalon nodded and then said,

"Well if you can help us out we'll also put a good word in for you." Smith nodded and then leaned back in the chair a little.

"I have to confess," he began, "I have been wondering what I could possibly help you with, I'm sure you don't wish to learn magic tricks."

"Ironically, that's not far from the truth," smiled Avalon.

"Really," Smith frowned, "come now, there must be more to it than that."

"Well yes," explained Avalon, "we have come

189

across an unusual circumstance, a missing person actually. If I asked you to make a person disappear from a car as it was driving along, could you do it?" Smith raised his brows at this, he thought for a moment and then folded his arms.

"What's the vehicle?" he asked.

"A Land Rover," replied Ross passing over an image of a similar vehicle, "and there can be no alterations to the vehicle, or at least nothing forensics could track."

"Sounds interesting," nodded Smith, "are you telling me this has been achieved?"

"Yes," nodded Avalon, "and frankly, we have no idea how it was done, we suspect the missing person has arranged this through some third party, possibly in the entertainment industry."

"There are ways, but I need to know all the facts," he insisted. Avalon looked over to Ross who glared back and eventually nodded, Ross relayed all they knew about the details of the missing person pertaining to the vehicle. Smith listened and looked up to the ceiling several times and when Ross passed over Avalon's sketch of the water butt inside the vehicle he began to shake his head. "If the container was a square tube I would say it was easy, but a round container?" he paused, "that makes this a whole different project." Smith came alive, Avalon saw some of Damian Tennant making its way back into him, his eyes sparkled and his brain went into action.

"But it is to do with the water butt?" asked Avalon.

"Undoubtedly, but if this is a standard size I don't see how it could be done, particularly if the rear door of the vehicle was opened," he insisted. Smith borrowed a notebook and made sketches, he sighed, he shook his head several times, he paced the room and then made more sketches but at last he sat and sighed, tossing the pad onto the table. "I'm sorry but this one has me beat, I have to take my hat off to whoever did this," he exclaimed.

"Why does the shape of the container matter?" asked Avalon.

"Well, hiding something in a box is an old trick, but the box has to be square or the illusion can be worked out by looking into it, with circular walls..." he trailed off shaking his head. Avalon looked over to Ross and made a slight grimace.

"Well it was worth a try," said Ross.

"Have you given me all the details?" asked Smith folding his arms, "there is something missing here and unless I know everything..." he trailed off once more with slight frown.

"There are certain aspects that I have omitted," explained Avalon, "but as far as I can see I have included everything that pertains to the disappearance."

"Do you know for sure that the person was in the vehicle after it had stopped?" Smith asked.

"Yes," nodded Avalon, "as I said, the brakes were seen to be applied, the lights were on and then they went off." Smith frowned deeply and then began to shake his head.

"Well this man is a genius," he sighed, "I can think of several ways of doing this but the round container has me beat, I'd love to know how it was done." Avalon stood, there was nothing else they could get from Smith, he looked over to Ross who was also standing and shrugged.

"Well thank you for trying," began Avalon, "I

will certainly send you the details once we know how she did it," and he paused, "as long as you don't use the information to make *yourself* disappear," there was a slight smile on his face as he held out his hand to Smith. Smith didn't take the hand, his face became rigid and he seemed to have wondered off in his mind. Avalon let his hand drop and asked,

"Are you alright?" Smith looked as if he was working something out and then he looked directly up at Avalon.

"You said *she*, was this done by a woman?" Avalon realised he had inadvertently let something slip, it was most unlike him but it was done and now Clive Smith seemed animated once more.

"Well, yes it was a woman as it happens," Avalon admitted.

"What sort of build is she?" Smith asked looking into the middle distance.

"She's small, does it matter?" asked Avalon.

"Of course it matters detective, now how small was she?" Smith was slightly agitated by this news, he asked for the pad again and began making more sketches once he had the description of the woman. He then asked for the exact size of the water butt and after a phone call from Ross to Frazer to get the details, they watched Smith work on some calculations and then he sat on the floor in a tight ball. "Measure my height," Smith then insisted.

"What with?" asked Ross thinking the man had gone mad.

"And I thought you had to be clever to be a detective," scowled Smith up at Ross. Avalon could now see the man he had first met a year ago, that same Damian Tennant. His features once again resembled the feisty magician now he had something alive in his brain. "What size are your shoes?" he then asked.

"Size ten," shrugged Ross, "but what-"

"Don't dally detective, your shoes will be as near as damn it, a foot in length, take them off and measure me." Ross looked across to Avalon who simply nodded and Ross did as he was asked. With the information, Smith sprung to his feet and went back to the pad and added some figures. He then said,

"That's it, I have it," and he threw down the pencil and smiled up at Avalon. "It's not truly accurate," Smith continued, "but scaling her size to up to mine and then scaling the water butt up by percentages, I know how it was done."

"Go on," insisted Avalon.

"Two water butts were used," explained Smith, "one of them probably altered to fit inside the other."

"Not possible," insisted Ross, "as we said, forensics would have found the second one."

"Then at least the base of another one," insisted Smith, "they must have missed it, I'm telling you, that is how it was done." Ross began telling Smith how forensics were not in the habit of missing anything, particularly something the size of a water butt. Avalon was scouring the back of his memory banks and trying to recall exactly what David Sutherland had said about Mrs Stodart returning for a second water butt.

"You could be right about the two butts," nodded Avalon, "but what the hell happened to the second one and how did she get out of the vehicle and..." he stopped as he realised he was thinking aloud.

"I think you are dealing with a remarkable woman," said Smith and he added, "and I doubt she had help, if I were you I would check her bookshelves," and

193

he raised his brows with a whiff of a smile. Avalon held out his hand to Smith once more. "Thank you, you have been a great help," he said and he and Ross made their exit from the prison.

~~~~~~

Avalon sat in his booth and looked out into the Cave. It seemed like he had been away much longer and there was a mountain of paperwork for him to deal with. There hadn't seemed any point in returning to Golspie, the journey back from Peterhead had taken the best part of three hours and there was much they could do from the office. Ross seemed more at home too, Avalon considered that his DS has a symbiotic relationship with Inverness, and he was never quite himself when he strayed from it. Avalon was seeing that in himself too. Inverness had become his home and he felt comfortable there, the only downside was the fact that since they had left Golspie that morning, it had rained. A phone call to PC Dowd to explain that they were staying in Inverness had furnished him with the information that the sun was shining in the little village. He put that thought aside as he got down to the work at hand, there was much to do and he and Ross had just about formulated how Mrs Stodart had disappeared, they just needed to find out why and where she was now.

When DS Wilson arrived with MacDonald he made his way into the booth.

"How was the holiday?" smiled Wilson.

"Very amusing," replied Avalon, "anyway, why are you so happy?"

"I'm just a naturally happy person," smiled the DS, "anyway, you missed all the fun while you've been away," he added as he sat.

"Fun at this nick is impossible, you may find fun elsewhere, but not here," scowled Avalon.

"Oh, there are a few surprises," Wilson insisted, "for instance, Pottinger is getting married..." Avalon didn't react to the news, he already knew it was a possibility, "... we're getting a new face in C section...", that was of more consequence, "and B Section has found out why Croker was passed over." Avalon had to admit, the last two pieces of information were of interest.

"So who's the new detective?" he asked.

"DC Martin Rutherford, but don't get excited, he's not just new to us, he's new to CID."

"Great," sighed Avalon, "another one we'll have to hold the hand of, why can't we have experienced officers for a change?"

"Better than nothing," insisted Wilson.

"So what's this about the DCI?" asked Avalon not sure he ought to be asking. Wilson folded his arms and a more serious look came to his face.

"I don't know exactly what it is but someone in B Section used his resources and skills to do some checking up on DCI Croker," he explained, "but DI Lasiter has put a lid on it."

"So he should," nodded Avalon, "I don't think it would be good for any of us if the DCI has his authority eroded."

"It's gonna get out anyway, most of the nick will know about it by now I would think," shrugged Wilson.

"Probably," nodded Avalon, "but just in case, brief C section about it and make sure they realise I will take a dim view on anyone spreading any rumours." Wilson nodded and then brought the section situation up to date and then left to continue with his own work.

Avalon was about to continue with his own pile of paperwork when the door opened a little and DI Lasiter pushed his head inside and raised his eyebrows. Avalon stood and followed the DI to his office.

"I heard you were back, tak' a seat, want a cuppa?" asked Lasiter. Avalon declined and said,

"Is this about the DCI?"

"Sort of," nodded Lasiter as he sat, "one of my team inadvertently came across Croker's name during some checks he was doing." Avalon nodded but considered it was Lasiter's way of protecting his team.

"So is he 'Bible John'?" asked Avalon seemingly uninterested.

"He's old but not that old," glared Lasiter and then he continued, "et's not anything serious, en truth, I feel quite sorry for him and I never thought I would hear myself say that." Avalon sat impassively waiting for the DI to continue. "Et seems that Croker found out his wife was having an affair with one of Croker's colleagues, and he found out through the press."

"Ouch," frowned Avalon, "that must have hurt, no wonder he hates the press."

"Exactly, but old Croker doesnae mess about," continued Lasiter, "he goes straight down t' the colleague's office, an' punches his lights out." Avalon gave a slight smile.

"Good for him," he said.

"Aye, it wasnae though," continued Lasiter, "he was suspended and three days later he was at it again, he tried to feed a camera to one of the newspaper photographers."

"I'm guessing they would pursue him for a story," nodded Avalon, still retaining some of the smile, "so how the hell did he keep his job?"

"I'm guessing," said Lasiter, "and et's only a guess mind," he added holding up his index finger, "that the other officer did some back scratching to keep both their jobs, as the other one is now a well known Detective Superintendent."

"And Croker has been left out in the wilderness," frowned Avalon. Lasiter nodded slowly. "There's no wonder he's got a chip on his shoulder," sighed Avalon, "but I have to admit, I'm warming to him."

"Aye, et seems en his youth he was a man of action too," nodded Lasiter, "he was a good copper and a damn fine detective."

"Have you managed to can this or not?" asked Avalon. Lasiter shrugged.

"I've tried and I've told my lot ef I hear they have been spreading the story I'll chew their nuts off."

"My section know about it already," admitted Avalon, "or at least one of them does,"

"Aye," said Lasiter shaking his head, "et's like trying to keep fog in a box, let's just hope he doesnae find out where the information came from."

When Avalon returned to his office he looked on the computer for the file of DC Andrew Rutherford. There wasn't much on there, probably because he was new, it just said he was thirty two, had been in the service almost five years and had passed his exams six months ago. Avalon was beginning to think that Police Scotland saw C Section as a CID nursery but, it was an extra pair of hands and as long as Andrew Rutherford wasn't a complete idiot, he would at least help with something or other. He looked down at the desk phone and as he did it rang, was he willing it to ring or was he just developing an instinct for it?

"Avalon."

"*Ah, Detective Avalon,*" it was Sarah Underwood, "*I have a few details for you about the crime scene at Golspie.*" Avalon imagined her face as he listened.

"Oh, right, ...yes we could do with a little help on that one," he admitted.

"*Well we have one or two items that are in the report but I thought I would ring in with what was found in the curious black plastic box,*" she explained. Miss Underwood knew the need to act as quickly as possible and she usually rang in anything that may be crucial to an investigation.

"So it was a box," replied Avalon.

"*Yes, we have just about pieced it all together and it contained the broken parts of a syringe and a small glass ampoule.*"

"Contents?" asked Avalon.

"*Alpha Methylphenethylamine,*" she replied, "*not a great deal of it but enough to easily trace it.*"

"Amphetamine? I sort of expected something of that nature," admitted Avalon.

"*I see,*" said Sarah slightly disappointed she hadn't been any help.

"I was going to ring you on a slightly different matter,"

"*Oh?*" she said. "*and what was that?*"

"Did you find any scrape marks or any indications that something had been tightly fitted into the water butt found in the back of the Landrover?" She was quiet for a moment.

"*There were marks as if the container had been used and we did swabs for any residue but found nothing,*" she explained.

"Right, but nothing out of the ordinary?" he

asked.

"*Nothing, but we can go over it again if you like,*" she offered.

"Is it still at the lab?"

"*Yes, you can have a look yourself if you wish.*"

"Yes, I'll come over, I have a theory I would like to try out," he said as he considered how the vanishing trick was done.

It was late in the afternoon by the time he reached the forensics lab and Sarah was in her office with some of the other technicians looking like they were preparing to leave. He knocked on the door and walked in the office.

"I'm sorry, I didn't realise it was so late," he looked through the window to the people who were putting on their coats.

"It's alright," she smiled, "I rarely get away early, oh and the team have finished with the car found abandoned by the loch, you should get the results in the next day or so." Avalon nodded, he wasn't expecting much from the vehicle but sometimes mistakes were made and evidence is left behind. He just had to hope something may be there. "The water butt is in the vehicle bay," she added and lead him to a door at the rear of the lab. There were several vehicles in there, some surrounded by plastic, some almost totally stripped down and there was the car found at the loch. It looked like her team had done a thorough job on it, there were parts on racks and bits and bobs in bins, it was hardly recognisable and on a large rack was the water butt. "Help me pull it down," she said as they closed in on it. They placed it on its side on a bench. "So what's this theory you have?" He was no longer sure the theory had any merit, the green barrel looked smaller that he thought it would be. He leaned insided and looked down the sides and he was soon handed a flashlight and a magnifying glass. He smiled and re-examined the side of the butt.

"We have photographed the scrape marks but they are slight," insisted Sarah. He looked back at her and smiled from out of the barrel and then extracted himself.

"I suppose I'm making a fool of myself," he said as he stood upright.

"I would never question anyone's methods," she grinned. He put down the flashlight and the lens and sighed. "Don't you want to discuss your theory?" she asked.

"Sorry, I didn't mean to keep you out of the picture," he said with some embarrassment, he leaned on the bench and folded his arms. "I thought that the missing woman had hidden herself in this," he pointed to the barrel, "but it seems too small now I'm standing by it."

"Really, I would have thought a person could have got in there easily," she shrugged.

"But the person has to get in there and leave most of the barrel empty," he explained, "and I just can't see how it could be done."

"How tall is this woman?" she asked.

"Not very, she's a few inches shorter than you and very slightly built," he explained.

"Just one moment," she said and she walked away. As soon as she was gone Avalon examined the base, there was a natural line where the base met the sides, a sort of strengthening ridge. Sarah soon returned and was wearing a forensics suit.

"Let's put the barrel on the floor," she said and

they laid it on its side. "Now steady the thing," she asked and she sat and pushed her legs inside. It didn't take her long before all of her body was inside it and her head disappeared from view. Avalon peered inside, she was trying to wedge herself onto the base of the thing with her legs pulled up so her knees were at the side of her head.

"For Gods sake don't get stuck," he frowned, "this will set the rumour mill on fire if I have to send for help." She tried to laugh but she was so squashed into the butt she refrained. She had done it, her head was to one side but she was in there.

"Point proven?" she asked in a strangled tone.

"Yes, now lets get you out," he grinned. As she eventually stepped out he realised he was holding her hand and revelled in the soft warmth of it.

"Phew, it's hot in there," she said letting his hand go and removing the suit.

"Thank you for that, it does prove it can be done,"

"And if she is smaller than me it wouldn't be such a tight squeeze," she said as she straightened her hair. "So what does this prove?" she then asked.

"I hate to say it after all your exertions but relatively nothing, it's just bringing together a theory of how she went missing."

"Rather than being abducted by the Brollachan?" she smiled.

"You read the article in the papers then?" he frowned.

"I did but I think I'll go with the barrel theory," she smiled once more. Avalon hadn't seen her smile quite so much, it was like taking the lid of a box of sunshine, the whole room lit up. "So," she continued, "has this at

201

least achieved something?" Avalon realised he was staring and probably making her feel uncomfortable.

"Oh yes, certainly," he smiled, "it has also given me another idea, but that's just another theory." As he saw out of the corner of his eye another of the technicians wave over to Sarah as he was leaving, Avalon made his apologies for keeping her and thanked her for her help, and then although it went against his wishes, he left.

As he climbed the stairs heading back to the Cave he wondered why he still had a magnetic attraction to Sarah Underwood. It was clear she wasn't interested in him or any other copper for that matter so why did he still feel drawn towards her? She was attractive, she was intelligent and she was single, or at least that was the legend. But to some people she was distant and aloof, and in the main not that popular, so why did Avalon raise her on a pedestal? She did remind him of his ex-wife Carol, not the way she looked particularly but in her mannerisms and the way she dealt with her professional life. Maybe that was his problem, he was still emotionally attached to Carol and Sarah was his only connection, be it vague and a little odd. He was actually shaking his head as he entered the Cave. There was just Ross and Frazer in there and as he looked down at his watch he realised that most of them had probably left for home. Ross and Frazer seemed to have been discussing something but stopped as he entered.

"Don't let me interrupt," he said, but they didn't seem like they were about to continue, it struck him that they may have been discussing Croker. He sat on the edge of one of the desks.

"Are we off back in the morning?" asked Ross.

"Golspie?" said Avalon raising his eyebrows, "is

there any news from Dowd?" Ross slowly shook his head and then folded his arms. Avalon sighed and then said,

"Well, at least I now think I know how she dissapeared," he stood and paced a little, "David Sutherland said that she came back for a second water butt because the first one was damaged. I now think that she needed two barrels to hide herself."

"But there was only one found in the vehicle," insisted Ross.

"True, but I think she cut the base from one so that it would be a sliding fit inside the other," explained Avalon.

"A false bottom?" asked Ross, "so you're saying that she hid beneath the false bottom, that seems hard to beleive?"

"I have seen how it can be done," insisted Avalon, "I saw someone slightly larger than Megan occupy less than a third of the barrel." Frazer looked up at the mention of her name but said nothing. "Someone as small as Mrs Stodart would easily be able to climb in there," continued Avalon, "and then pull the false bottom into there too, as long as no one looked too closely at the barrel, and who would, seeing that it seemed empty? It would look as if she had vanished."

"So what happened to the false bottom?" asked Frazer.

"And more importantly," added Ross, "what happened to the woman, assuming she managed this weird trick, how the hell did she get out of the vehicle, hide the false bottom and get away before anyone saw her?"

"That part I can't work out but I still think she had an accomplice," insisted Avalon, "and it stands to reason someone could have simply driven past and picked her up."

"Or it was Sutherland," insisted Frazer and Ross nodded in agreement.

"I don't think it was him," said Avalon shaking his head.

"There were only his footprints found at the site," insisted Ross. Avalon could see his point but he just didn't think Sutherland was the type. He shrugged and said,

"Let's sleep on it, anyone fancy a beer?"

It was reasonably quiet in the Castle Tavern and so Ross and Avalon sat in their usual place, Frazer had declined to join them so they sat and complained about the weather. It had rained most of the day again and even for Scotland there seemed to be more than the average amount of rainfall for the time of year.

"They're predicting a hot summer though," announced Avalon taking a sip of the beer, he had decided against the single malt.

"Who're they?" asked Ross with a deep frown, "everyone says *they* but never explain who *they* are."

"Well, the weathermen I suppose," shrugged Avalon.

"It's all pish, they can't predict what'll happen tomorrow so why should we take any notice of what they say it will be months ahead?"

"True," replied Avalon taking a look around the pub, a few people came in and it looked like they were dry. Maybe it had stopped. He didn't care all that much, the case was dry and that was a problem. Even having some idea how Muiranne Stodart had achieved her disappearance didn't further the investigation, they needed something from the forensics or some other clue from their legwork. "So what do you think?" he asked looking back to Ross.

"The case?" he asked, Avalon nodded. Ross looked into the middle distance for a few seconds and then said, "I can't see any other option than she planned his murder and got Sutherland to help her do it, I'm not saying it was either of them who opened his skull with the bar but I do think they are both involved."

"I admit," nodded Avalon, "that there are bits of circumstantial evidence to that theory and it looks like Stodart knew his killer but the missing laptop holds more than a clue to this."

"If the courts allow us to investigate his emails I agree, but if they don't we have to pursue this in some other direction," frowned Ross and then he added, "and why the big interest in how she disappeared, it really isn't that important is it?"

"Maybe not," replied Avalon picking up his glass, "but there are two reasons, the first is getting into how her mind works, I really think she is much more than the sum of her parts," and he took a sip of his beer, "and the second thing is, was she working alone or not?" He replaced his glass on the table.

"And do you think she was?" asked Ross.

"I don't know yet," replied Avalon shaking his head, "even Clive Smith thought this was a worthy trick and so where is the magic connection?"

"Well let's take his advice and look on her bookshelves," said Ross.

"I'll get Dowd to arrange it with the local team and we'll check it when we get back in Golspie but we need more help, I wondered about taking Frazer up with us."

"She can't stay in the bothy, there isn't enough room," insisted Ross reaching for his glass.

"She can stay at the bed and breakfast."

"Hang on," interrupted Ross removing the glass from his mouth, "I'll go to the B and B, let Frazer stay at the bothy."

"That wouldn't be appropriate," smiled Avalon.

"More like you don't want Frazer coming between you and Miss Crunchy," added Ross before taking a drink.

"*Crunchy*? I wouldn't have said crunchy," frowned Avalon, "anyway, there's nothing between Julia and myself."

"Yeah, right!" was all Ross said as he placed his glass on the table.

"Oh and I forgot to mention," began Avalon, "Peter Stodart was using amphetamines, forensics found evidence of the stuff on the bits of plastic found at the crime scene."

"We did expect that, has the coroner's report come in yet?" asked Ross.

"Not yet, I'm expecting that and the full forensics report in the next day or two though," replied Avalon. Ross finished his drink and asked,

"Another?" Avalon looked at his watch, and then down to his glass.

"Why not," he said and he picked up his half pint glass and drained it.

"Well done by the way."

"It was easy, I just tipped the glass and swallowed," shrugged Avalon handing Ross the empty glass.

"I meant about changing the subject from Julia Beattie," frowned Ross turning to the bar.

"I've told you before," replied Avalon, "don't try to fill in gaps between the facts with conjecture." Ross stopped briefly as he moved to the bar and turned to Avalon.

"You missed your true calling, you should have been a solicitor," Avalon didn't say anything, he just threw Ross a questioning look before Ross continued. "You're annoying, you manipulate the truth and you never buy a drink." Avalon considered that part of that statement wasn't accurate, he distinctively remembered buying a drink when they were at the pub some days previous. As to manipulation of the truth? There wasn't much to tell, if he spoke the truth as it appeared in black and white no one would think it *was* the truth. For instance, if Avalon had told Ross that his time alone with Julia Beattie consisted of some heavy petting at the dining table until he tried to move his arm sending a half glass of wine across the table, and a fork into her right foot, Ross would have said he was exaggerating. But it was the truth. Two minutes kissing, ten minutes cleaning up spilled wine and another ten minutes trying to stop her foot bleeding. The rest of the embarrassing time had been spent with apologies, the possible antiseptic qualities of vinegar and the best way of removing wine stains from tablecloths. The whole episode had been a total failure and a joke but then again, it was the nearest thing Avalon had experienced to a romantic encounter since he and his wife had split up. Julia had taken it well however and saw the funny side of the situation. She even cracked a bit of a joke by saying 'the experience had provided her with a good forking'. Their laughter may have sounded like post-nuptial hilarity to Ross trying to sleep in the bothy if he had heard it but the cause was very different. Even if Ross had noticed

Avalon go straight into the shower when he returned, it was not as he may deduce to cleanse himself from the transfer of bodily fluids, but rather to try and remove the transfer of cheap French red. No, the whole truth wasn't always a good idea and sometimes owning a shovel didn't mean you had to dig yourself a hole. As Ross returned with the drinks and sat, Avalon was still considering what Ross was probably thinking about the incident.

"I bought a drink last Sunday," he said as he picked up the fresh drink and took a sip. Ross shook his head.

"Is that what you have been thinking about?" asked Ross with a very questioning tone, "I was just standing at the bar and I turned to look at you and saw you were deep in thought. I thought you were all wrapped up in the case and instead, you were trying to remember the last time you bought a drink?" Ross was flabbergasted.

"That wasn't all I was thinking about," answered Avalon tilting his head to one side.

"So what else was ambling along the dusty shelves of your mind? The last time you gave to charity, the last time you farted and blamed someone else?" Ross was using what Avalon considered his most sarcastic voice, "or how about, the last time you opened up and shared something personal with a mate?" and Ross concluded by taking a drink.

"I'm a private person, you know that," said Avalon defensively.

"Private person bordering on miserable bastard," added Ross. Avalon raised his eyebrows and then let them fall into a frown. He wasn't sure if he should wind Ross up more or offer an olive branch. He considered both would be good.

"Okay, if that's what you want, I could tell you something very personal, something I have never told anyone before," he said staring straight at Ross. Ross looked back, was this the moment Avalon broke down his steely defences?

"Okay, I'm listening," he said with some doubt.

"Some years ago, a long time ago now, I was coming back from Cadwell Park on the bike, I had been to watch the British Superbikes and on the way back it threw it down." Avalon paused to be sure Ross was listening. "I was soaked and freezing cold as I didn't have any waterproofs with me and I was really fed up. Then I realised I wanted a pee, but I didn't want to get off the bike as it was still hammering it down."

"I hope this isn't going where I think it is," frowned Ross.

"You're ahead of me," smiled Avalon.

"You mean to say you pissed yourself on the bike?" asked Ross with a frown, not knowing if he wanted the answer. Avalon opened his eyes wide and gave a slight nod.

"It was lovely and warm for two minutes," Avalon announced taking another sip from his drink. Ross screwed up his features and curled his lip as he considered what he had been told. "Obviously," continued Avalon placing his drink back on the table, "if the story gets out, I will deny it and put you on office duties for the rest of your career." He said it without emotion as if it was obvious, but Ross was still wrapped up in the imagery of it and felt slightly unclean. Eventually he broke free from it and said,

"Remind me *never*, to ask about your private life again." Avalon afforded himself a slight smile, if it meant keeping Ross from asking any more questions, the story had been well worth it.

Chapter Seven

The gravel of the drive crunched as the car rolled slowly along and stopped near to the portico door of the large house. The passenger door opened first and an Italian leather shoe carefully pressed down on the chippings. A second shoe joined it and the quality cloth of the trouser legs above them fell and folded over the tops to their former position. The driver's door then opened and two very different legs descended to the floor and made their way around to the boot of the vehicle. They were clad in old walking boots and tatty blue jeans. A black bin liner was then extracted and the boot of the car was closed, the four feet then moved towards the door crunching their way through the gravel until they reached the black marble doorstep and the bell pull was operated. A gentle bell sounded somewhere in the distance. The door was opened by a large man and the two people were lead inside, across exquisite oak flooring, over delicate Persian rugs until they entered a room with a thick wool carpet. They made their way to a desk made from exotic South American hardwoods, most of them now illegal to export. Behind the desk sat a man in his late fifties with a balding head, he was well dressed and was wearing a fist-full of gold rings and expensive spectacles. He looked up to the two visitors.

"Is et done?" he asked in a deep Scottish accent. The scruffier dressed of the two men who was holding the bin liner nodded and tossed the bag onto the desk. The sharper dressed man shook his head slowly and rolled his eyes. The man behind the desk looked grimly up to the shabby man and glared at him for a moment before opening the top of the bag and looking in. Without looking back at the shabby one, he leaned over and picked up a small briefcase and placed it on the desk. He clicked open the case to reveal several piles of twenty pound notes.

"Do you want me tae put et en the bin liner?" he asked sarcastically. The shabby man missed the point of the question and shrugged.

"Yeah, can do," he replied in a Liverpool accent before shrugging again. With a surprised look, the seated man was about to remove the money from the case but the sharper dressed man made a slight cough and gave a pained expression. The seated man sighed and left the money where it was and closed the case, then he pushed it towards the shabby man.

"Ta muchly," he said and he turned to leave. The other man gave an apologetic wince and then followed escorted by the large man. When they had left the room the man behind the desk rang a small hand bell. The slight tinkling sound it made attracted a younger man from an adjoining room. The man behind the desk pointed to the bin liner and growled,

"Get rid o' this." The other man nodded and took the bag back the way he had come. When the man behind the desk was fully alone he opened a small drawer to his right and lifted out a yellow powdery sweet and popped it into his mouth and began to chew. After a moment he shook his head.

"I dunna know what this country's coming to," he said to himself and swivelled the sumptuous seat clockwise to gaze out of the large window behind him.

~~~~~~

Avalon had only just paid for the coffee when his phone rang, he shrugged to the woman handing him his change and left leaving the two plastic cups on the counter.

"Avalon," he said as he reached the outside.

"*Boss, et's Frazer, I have some info for y',*"

"We could do with something Megan, what is it?" he asked. As Avalon listened he could hear another phone ringing in the background.

"*At first I thought et was nothin' but after diggin' around I have found what could be a lead,*" she announced.

"Go on," said Avalon looking back to the door of the cafe.

"*I was talking tae one o' the traffic boys tae see ef any of them were recording anywhere on the day that Peter Stodart was killed. I thought maybe someone may have a wee bit of video around that area. They looked on the logs but there was nothin'. There was however two logs on the day Muiranne Stodart's car was seen en the garage forecourt so I asked ef we could have a look through, just en case I could see the cars parked up, I knew et was a long shot but...*" she paused for a moment, "*et seems that day that one of the unmarked cars was following someone they suspected of using a mobile phone whilst driving so they recorded et for their records. I looked through et and bingo,*" she sounded almost excited, "*as they passed the garage at Evelix,*"

213

both Mrs Stodart's car and the white Volkswagen Polo could be seen parked up." Avalon was obviously interested in this information.

"Could you ID the drivers?" he asked.

"Not as such but we could clearly see the number plates which I thought was of more importance."

"So we can identify the car?" asked Avalon with a hopeful tone.

"Aye, et was a hire car," Frazer replied.

"We need to find the records for that day then," insisted Avalon.

"Done et," announced Frazer and then continued with, *"the car was rented by an Elizabeth Lithgoe, she lives en a rented house not far from Dornoch."*

"Text me the address," said Avalon.

"Aye, et's on ets way," she replied.

"Excellent work Megan," added Avalon.

"Aye, but that's not all," she explained, Avalon was sure he could almost hear her smiling, *"Rory looked through the council records to find out who owned the house and we eventually found et."* Avalon was silent, he knew what he was about to hear was the key to unlock the case. *"The house belongs to none other than Muiranne Stodart."* Avalon allowed himself a smile, this was the information to move the case further. It was a surprise to him but this was probably where she was hiding out.

"Fantastic, this is what we need, I'll get over there straight away, thanks Megan," and he ended the call. He was about to walk away but then remembered the coffee and went back for it. He walked back to the incident vehicle as quick as he could and as he crossed the road he saw Ross talking with Dowd.

"Oh inspector," said Dowd as he noticed Avalon

214

approach, "I was just saying tae Sergeant Ross, we went up to the Stodart house yesterday afternoon as you asked but there was nothing particularly interesting on the bookshelves, the usual pap, romantic fiction, needle craft and baking." Avalon nodded as he handed the coffee to Dowd who looked a little surprised.

"I thought that was mine?" asked a frowning Ross.

"You can't drink coffee and drive," explained Avalon handing him the keys.

"So why can't you drive?" asked Ross taking the keys.

"Same thing," he smiled holding up the other plastic cup, "I can't drink and drive," and he held up his phone with the other hand, "this address and pronto."

"Slave driver," announced Ross as he walked over to the car, Avalon followed. He explained the sterling work that Frazer and Mackinnon had done back at the office and Ross eventually commented.

"It doesn't mean she's there though."

"No it doesn't but it's the best we've got and it's a start," replied Avalon finishing his coffee. It didn't take long to find the address courtesy of Avalon's satnav and the house was a converted croft, quite some distance from the main road. As they pulled up into the rough drive and climbed out of the car, Avalon nodded to a gate between a barn and the house. Ross understood, there was a slight chance the woman may try to escape. Ross opened the door carefully and then nodded to Avalon who knocked on the small wooden door to the main house. Ross moved around the rear of the property but eventually the door opened and a plain looking woman in her forties carefully peered around it.

"Yes?" she asked half hidden behind the door.

"Elizabeth Lithgoe?"

"Yes," she replied looking past Avalon to the car.

"I wish to ask you a few questions," he continued showing her his ID, "I'm Detective Inspector Avalon from Inverness." The woman blinked, she was obviously not shocked but she still seemed unable to find the correct reaction. "I can get someone to come and take you to a police station if you would prefer?" he added after a moment.

"Well, what do you want to ask?" she said still guarded by the door.

"Can we go inside, my colleague is also here?" Ross appeared from around the corner. He looked at Avalon and made the slightest shake of his head.

"Er, well," she stuttered, "it depends what it's about." Avalon almost sighed but he was used to this kind of pointless reaction.

"You know Mrs Muiranne Stodart and you have been seen with her just before her disappearance," insisted Avalon.

"I..." she began and then ceased. Avalon considered she was about to deny it.

"You hired a car and met her at the Evelix garage," he added.

"You better come in," she eventually said moving away from the door. The house was small but well equipped and expensively furnished, Avalon took it to be the work of Mrs Stodart rather than the woman he saw in front of him as he sat.

"Nice place," he smiled, she nodded and looked over to Ross as he took out his notebook.

"How long have you been renting the house?" asked Avalon. She quickly looked back at him and was about to say something, he considered she was going to

216

say something but thought better of it. Ross noted something in the pad, he probably thought the same.

"I've been here about a year," she replied. Her accent was slight, Avalon couldn't place it but didn't think she was from this far north.

"When did you last see Mrs Stodart?"

"I'm not sure, about a fortnight."

"Do you have a car?" asked Ross.

"No," she paused, "no I don't," she added but Avalon noticed a slight flash of her eyes to the left wall. The barn was the other side of that wall.

"Is that why you hired a car?" asked Avalon.

"Look," she began, "I don't know where she is, I really don't." Avalon nodded.

"So why did you hire a car to meet her just a few miles away?" he asked.

"I think she thought her husband was following her, I don't think she wanted him to know about the house," she eventually said. Avalon didn't believe her and neither did Ross.

"So how did you get to the car hire company?" he asked. She was obviously fazed by this, she seemed to have no explanation. Avalon then added,

"You need to tell us the truth Elizabeth, Mr Stodart has been murdered so this is much more serious than a missing woman." This did seem to take her attention, her eyes opened wide for a moment and then she said,

"I heard on the news that something had happened but..." she paused and Avalon continued.

"So you see Elizabeth, this is very serious and we need to find Mrs Stodart, she could be in danger."

"I really don't know where she is, I really don't," insisted the woman. Avalon nodded sympathetically.

217

"Would you mind if we take a look around?" he asked softly. She looked to Ross and then back to Avalon.

"I, I don't know, you see-" she stuttered but Avalon interrupted her.

"We could do it officially and return with a search warrant if you wish but those things are never very pleasant."

"I suppose so, I really have nothing to hide," she eventually said and Avalon nodded to Ross who quietly went for a look around. Avalon kept her talking as much as he could.

"So how did you fetch the hire car?" he asked.

"I can't remember, I think I got someone to give me a lift, yes that's it," she said. He knew she was lying and so he didn't pursue it, it was pointless at this stage.

"How did you know her?" he asked.

"I met her a few years ago, I think it was at a charity bowls event, and then..." she trailed off and by her uncomfortable body language he saw she wasn't going to tell him the truth about that either. He needed a way to pressurise her but nothing came to mind. Ross returned and passed Avalon a book. It was called, 'Hiding The Elephant' by Jim Steinmeyer.

"Are you into magic Elizabeth?" asked Avalon showing her the book.

"No not at all, the book belongs to Muir, I don't..." she broke off for a moment seeing that she had been lead into a trap, "I, I don't read much," she ended slowly.

"How long have you and Mrs Stodart been lovers?" asked Ross directly, Avalon was taken aback and glared up at Ross.

"How dare you?" she spat.

218

"There is just one bedroom and if you don't read," growled Ross, "why are there so many books in that bedroom Mrs Lithgoe?"

"It's miss!" she insisted and then in a quieter tone she added, "I'm not married," and then in an almost apologetic tone concluded with, "I never got married," and she looked down at the floor once more. Avalon could see Ross had been absolutely correct though Avalon was concerned about his direct method. If he had been wrong it could have seriously slowed down the interview and even ended it. Eventually she looked back up.

"We did have a thing going for a while," she sighed looking down at the floor, "I don't think it was ever serious for her."

"In what way?" asked Avalon trying to be less abrupt than Ross.

"It was a one-way love affair you see, she didn't feel about me as I felt for her, it was just something I think she wanted to try." Her eyes looked up for a second and went to the floor once more.

"Did she still come to see you?" asked Avalon.

"Not often, once or twice each month," she shrugged, "but I knew she was becoming tired of me."

"Why was that?" asked Avalon.

"Why did she tire of me or how did I know?" she replied a little aggressively but then sighed and continued in a more reasonable tone. "She tired of me because I'm too ordinary and because I think too much of her." Avalon noticed Ross exit the rear door.

"So when did you really see her last?" he asked trying to keep her talking.

"A few days after I met her in the car park I think, she came over to make a few phone calls and we had a bit of a chat," she shrugged but Ross interrupted as he quickly entered the room.

"Boss, you need to see this," he said and he left the room to go back outside. Avalon looked at the woman, her face was flushed and she looked nervously to where Ross had been. Avalon stood and followed Ross and saw him standing by the open barn door. Inside was Muiranne Stodart's car.

"Fetch some gloves," he said to Ross who left passing the woman coming towards the barn with her arms folded, she looked deathly white.

"Why is her car here Elizabeth?" he asked.

"She left it here and told me not to use it," replied the woman in a quiet voice.

"Was this the last time you saw her, the time you were just telling me about?" The woman nodded twice. Ross soon returned with several pairs of latex gloves and a flashlight and Avalon pulled on a pair of the gloves and entered the barn. He could see the door locks were in the unlocked position and so he carefully opened the door and peered inside. The car seemed empty and so he slowly closed the door and made his way to the rear. He carefully pulled the catch of the boot and he felt it give and the boot opened just a little way. He looked up to Ross and instinctively Ross brought in the flashlight and turned it on. Avalon slowly opened the boot but the space was all but empty, there was a crowbar and a garden spade. Avalon looked over to the woman still standing by the open door and asked,

"Have you been in the boot of this car Miss Lithgoe?" She instinctively registered that the detective had ceased to call her by her first name and she had now become 'Miss Lithgoe'. She realised she may be in some trouble.

"No, I did as she asked and I haven't been near it." Ross was leaning in and examining the spade more closely.

"It's been used recently, I can see dirt still on it and the crowbar," he announced as he stood upright. Avalon carefully closed the boot and walked over to the woman who was looking very worried.

"Miss Lithgoe, I'm going to have to ask you to come with us for further questioning."

In the tiny room in the Golspie Police Station, Ross sat asking questions of Elizabeth Lithgoe who was becoming more and more agitated by the minute. Ross had spared no time in breaking her down and Avalon who was taking a break over in the incident vehicle had been ready to whisk her off to Inverness. Ross had said he wanted to have a try at getting more from her. He had maintained that he didn't think she had the "nerve or the capability to murder someone and bury them under the patio," and so Avalon had allowed him to try. The forensics team had been sent for to examine the car in the barn and to scour the grounds and house. It was now a waiting game and wait, they would have to do. Avalon spent the time looking through the book they had found in the house, there were some interesting passages in there and enough information to give someone like Muiranne Stodart the idea that she had come up with to disappear. Avalon eventually went back to see how Ross had gone on and found him sitting with Miss Lithgoe, both of them drinking coffee. Ross stood as Avalon entered and made it obvious he wanted to speak alone.

"What is it, has she said anything?"

"A little," nodded Ross, "she has confirmed in more detail what she has previously told us but..." Ross paused.

"What?" asked Avalon seeing something in Ross's expression.

"I was using the idea that she had been 'set up' by Mrs Stodart."

"Yeah," shrugged Avalon, "not a bad tactic."

"But I've convinced myself too, I think she *has* been set up and you were right from the start," explained Ross with a serious face.

"You think Mrs Stodart has done for her husband and is now trying to make it look like this woman did it?" asked Avalon pointing to the door of the room with an amount of disbelief in his voice.

"Sort of," nodded Ross, "this woman isn't tough enough to do anything like this, she genuinely doesn't know anything about the tools in the back of the car." Avalon considered this, he hadn't really thought she was capable of this kind of crime either but neither was this getting them closer to finding Mrs Stodart.

"Okay, I'll have a word with her," nodded Avalon and he and Ross returned to the tiny room.

"Miss Lithgoe," said Avalon as he sat opposite her, "the time has come to tell us everything you know, it's the only option you have other than being taken to Inverness and being charged with perverting the course of justice," he paused and then added, "do you understand?" She nodded.

"But I have told you everything I know," she said shaking her head, tears starting to form in the corners of her eyes, "I feel totally betrayed, this is so wrong."

"I can see this must be upsetting but the time has come to distance yourself from Mrs Stodart, I want to ask you a few more questions," insisted Avalon. She didn't react and after a quick glance to Ross he asked,

"Tell me, how did you really get to the car hire office to fetch the car?"

"Muir took me," she said dropping her gaze to the floor once more. Ross had done good work, this woman was now seeing that she *had* been used, even if she didn't know why.

"Did she give you any instructions?" he then asked.

"Not really," replied Elizabeth looking up to him, "she'd booked the car under my name and then told me to give her a few minutes start and then to meet her at the garage."

"Did she say why?" asked Avalon.

"She said she was going to sort out a future for us but she needed time," the woman's eyes were full and tears began to slip down her cheeks.

"And then what happened?" asked Avalon.

"We just talked, for about an hour or so, I asked if we should go into the cafe but she said it wasn't a good idea as her husband was looking for her."

"Did she say why?" he asked. The woman shook her head, tears cascading as she did. Avalon reached for his handkerchief and passed it to her. She wiped some of the tears away and then seemed to regain her composure.

"She just said that he had something up his sleeve that wasn't good for her health and that she was going to have to vanish for a few weeks."

"Did she explain about the hire car to you?" asked Avalon.

"I asked about it but she said she wanted to leave her car in the barn at the house so she needed it to get away," explained the woman but sniffling back the tears. She was getting control of herself and Avalon wondered if she would stop talking but she became more helpful.

223

"It occurred to me after we got back to the house that she wasn't telling me the whole truth but I didn't think it was my business, and I didn't want to interfere with her plans," she continued.

"How did she leave once she had left her car at the barn?" asked Ross, "did someone pick her up or did she leave in the hire car?"

"The hire car," explained the woman.

"So what happened after that?" was Avalon's next question.

"She gave me a mobile phone and said she would ring me on it but she didn't, I never saw her after that. When I heard she had gone missing I did think of going to the police but she told me that under no circumstances should I tell anyone about any of this." Avalon nodded and looked up at Ross for a few seconds, Ross gave nothing away, he lifted his brows slightly and then just stared back.

"Do you still have the mobile she gave you?" asked Avalon. The woman nodded.

"Yes, it's here, she said handing him the phone from her jacket pocket." Avalon had a quick look through the phone to search for numbers but soon realised the card was probably brand new.

"Do you have somewhere you can stay, I'm not sure you should go back to the house for a few days?" he eventually asked.

"I could go to my sister's I suppose but I would have to go and get some things," she explained.

"We'll get someone to take you," Avalon said and then he stood and nodded to the door. Outside he sighed deeply and said,

"This changes the whole picture." Ross nodded.

"Yep, Muiranne Stodart is quite something, it

224

looks like she's been using both Elizabeth and David Sutherland in this little caper," he admitted. Avalon thought for a moment and then said,

"Okay, let's move on this, get someone to take Miss Lithgoe to fetch what she needs and see that she gets off to her sister's house, then we need to talk to David Sutherland."

It was later in the afternoon when Avalon phoned Sutherland but there was no answer so he decided to put off the interview until the morning. He then got a phone call from Sarah Underwood who explained she would arrive at the croft where Mrs Stodart's car was found late in the evening. The site had been secured but due to previous appointments the forensics team would be working late on the house and the car. She did however explain that she had the previous reports and would bring them with her. Avalon was upbeat about what may be in those reports, he had to be, the case had become much more complicated and he needed more details. The lack of useful information coming in from the locality meant that the incident room would be winding down in a few days and the case would become much harder once it was out of the public's attention. He considered another press conference, and though he hated them he knew it might jog someone's memory.

The weather had been reasonably good through the day but light drizzle began as he and Ross set off to meet Sarah Underwood and her team at the croft. They were already at work when he arrived and after she had passed on the forensics reports to Avalon, he in turn passed them to Ross who began to read through the main points. Sarah asked Avalon about the background to the croft and then Avalon joined Ross back in the car.

"Found anything?" he asked. Ross just shrugged as he sat with a large folder full of notes, the topmost file had a thick wad of leaves folded back. He looked across to Avalon.

"The car abandoned up at the loch had Peter Stodart's blood on the carpet, and there was an imprint similar to the ones found in the kitchen and on the doorstep."

"To be expected," nodded Avalon, "it proves that the car was probably used by the murderer."

"But there was nothing else found in the car," frowned Ross. Avalon sighed and looked out of the window.

"Anything significant at the house?" he then asked.

"I'm still reading the report on the house but all I've seen as of yet is a partial footprint in the blood not consistent with the first prints."

"So someone else was there?"

"It looks like it," nodded Ross looking back at the report. He read a little more and then closed the folded sheets and let it drop to his lap. "The conclusion is that the mug smashed onto the floor at the same time or slightly before the body." Ross then turned to Avalon and continued, "so it's likely that Stodart knew his attacker, as his own cup was still on the worktop, he was probably making a drink for him."

"Or her," added Avalon.

"Well, yes," agreed Ross, "particularly if there were two people present."

"Did we get anywhere with the courts allowing access to the internet provider?" asked Avalon.

"It will take time," explained Ross, "Frazer is on it but even she can't hurry the legal process."

226

"So where the hell is Muiranne Stodart?" asked Avalon to no one in particular, his gaze moving off into the middle distance. Ross gave no reply. He looked out of the side window as bright lights of the forensics team were switched on just outside the barn. The natural light of the day was fading and Ross felt hungry.

"It's gonna be another late one," he eventually said. Avalon's thoughts and his gaze came back into the car and he looked to where Ross was still staring.

"Yeah, looks like it, though I doubt anything will be found here." Avalon was waiting for the forensics team to process the bedroom, he had asked to be informed when they had done and as soon as it was possible he climbed the short stairs to the small room. There was a double bed, an elegantly carved wooden example, probably French with fine fabrics and quality bed linen around the room. It was tidy and yet snug with several soft toys on a wicker chair under the dormer style window. There were two photographs, one of Elizabeth Lithgoe standing by some kind of monument and one of a younger woman who Avalon didn't recognise. He had a quick look through two drawers and then he moved back to the landing and into the bathroom. He found nothing of interest anywhere in those two rooms but before he climbed back down the stairs he looked back into the bedroom. Something struck him, mainly about the person of Mrs Stodart. She was from a reasonably wealthy background and had lived her married life in a large house with incredible views over the North Sea. How would such a woman adapt to spending time in this cramped house with a very ordinary woman such as Miss Lithgoe? As he stared at the large bed, it just didn't seem to fit with what everyone considered her character to be. She was

227

certainly chameleon like, so different in different situations. Far from being the demure little wife who opened gardening fetes and showed up at the local bowls club now and then, if the evidence was being read correctly, this woman could turn out to be a manipulative firebrand with no conscience whatsoever. If that was correct, she probably had some sort of history, a history that was so well hidden that no one had found it yet. When Avalon returned to the ground floor he met Sarah coming the other way, complete with white forensics suit and rubber gloves. He glanced around to see if they were alone and then asked,

"Climbed into any good water butts lately?" She smiled and then replied,

"I admit it was one of the most unusual things I have done in the name of science." She pulled off the gloves and then asked, "how is it going?"

"Okay I suppose," shrugged Avalon, "but we could do with finding more to point to who was in the Stodart's house."

"It seems they were careful, we found nothing significant there or the car, no fibres and no hair," explained Sarah with a more serious face.

"Which points to professionals rather than a crime of passion," nodded Avalon.

"Unless it was planned well in advance," she added. Avalon had already considered that, the problem was, there was no evidence to support that theory. "Oh well, no rest for the wicked, I must get on," she said and left the room to continue. Avalon walked to the outside and returned to the car to find Ross fast asleep in the passenger side, he pretended not to notice and opened the door and quickly got in.

"So what do you think?" he asked. Ross looked

puzzled, he struggled to stop his eyes closing again.

"Er," he tried not to stutter, "er, well, er what about?"

"About what I just said," explained Avalon trying not to smile.

"Well," said Ross and then paused, "it's not easy to answer." Avalon glared at him.

"Why?" he frowned.

"Well, several reasons," Ross paused again, blinking and looking slightly confused. Avalon began to regret the joke, Ross like most of C section, had to contend themselves with very little sleep and here they were on another late evening and without any chance of food or drink. Avalon looked at his watch as he said,

"I was just winding you up," it was a quarter to ten already, "I saw you were asleep," he smiled looking over to Ross.

"Yeah, I probably was," said Ross wiping his eyes, "sorry."

"Don't apologise, it's my fault, we should have just left this to Sarah and her team."

"At least we got to see the reports," yawned Ross.

"Yes but we didn't need to be here, I'm getting some flak from the DCI."

"You didn't mention it," replied Ross sitting up in the car seat.

"No point, there's nothing you can do. I've had two calls today," explained Avalon, "the recent lull is over it seems, we look like running this one from base."

"You mean drive up and down the A9 every day?"

"If we need to," nodded Avalon, "I think Croker thinks we are on holiday up here." Avalon's phone vibrated in his pocket. He looked at the message, it was from Frazer. "It seems we have the coroner's report," explained Avalon and then he looked at his watch once more and then phoned Frazer.

"Are you still at the office?" asked Avalon.

"*Er, yes boss, just a few wee bits tae clear up,*" came Frazer's voice.

"Has the DCI been pushing?" he asked, there was a pause.

"*I think he's been giving DS Wilson a bit of a hard time but Gordon can cope,*" she answered.

"Get off home now, that's an order and if anyone else is there, make sure they get off too," he insisted, "I'll be back there in the morning." Ross looked round at this comment, did Avalon plan on driving back tonight? The DI put his phone away and sighed. "I'll go and have a word with Sarah," he said and then got out of the car. Ross considered if *he* was up to driving, he got out and took several deep breaths of the cold air and walked to the croft. He found the kitchen and washed his face with cold water and then returned to the cold air. He was tired, hungry and had a severe headache. He felt like death but he probably felt better than Avalon. When Avalon returned to the car Ross was in the driving seat.

"So what now?" he asked as Avalon slumped into the passenger seat.

"Sarah says they can cope here so we can get off but everywhere will be closed now so we can't get anything to eat," admitted Avalon.

"Well is it Golspie or Inverness?" asked Ross. Avalon looked out of the window into the darkness, he seemed to be considering their options.

"I don't know, we still need to interview David Sutherland," he paused giving the issue some thought.

"We could go back to the bothy then or we could

go back to Inverness, I still have a tin of spaghetti hoops I think." Avalon turned to him to see a slight smile.

"That's convinced me that Golspie is the best bet," insisted Avalon and Ross started the car and headed off to the bothy.

Fortunately, Julia saw them arrive and she offered to make them some simple food, which was thankfully received. Avalon explained that they were returning back to Inverness in the morning.

"Will you be coming back up," she hesitated for a moment, "I'm guessing the investigation isn't finished?" she asked.

"It's likely," nodded Avalon as he finished the homemade soup, "there's still a great deal to do." She didn't add anything, she just nodded.

"Our boss has heard about your cooking," smiled Ross, "and he's so jealous he's called us back." She returned the smile but still remained quiet.

"It seems that it's become busy back at base and a few other cases are stretching our resources so we have to get back to help out," added Avalon.

"I can see it must be difficult," she eventually said collecting the dishes and carrying them to the sink, "I always thought detectives work on one case at a time but..."

"They do on the television," smiled Ross, "but the truth is quite different." He then pushed his chair from the table and stood. "Well, that was wonderful Julia but I, at least need my sleep so..."

"Yes, me too," added Avalon but Ross shot him a stern glance. Avalon saw it but ignored the response and thanked Julia for looking after them.

"Will I see you in the morning before you leave?"

she asked.

"Maybe, we'll be away early though," he smiled and then they left. Back in the bothy, Avalon counted out some money and left it on the small table under a large decorative shell. His eyes caught the steady frown of Ross.

"What?" he asked.

"So what was that about?"

"What was what about?" asked Avalon slightly agitated.

"You know damn well what I'm getting at, I was leaving to let you two be together."

"I know, but I didn't want to stay," said Avalon emphatically. Ross shook his head and turned to enter the bedroom.

"I give up with you," he said and he pushed the door closed. Avalon made the sofa as comfortable as he could and prepared for sleep. He laid there but sleep didn't come. He certainly wasn't the only police officer to suffer with insomnia, most seemed to suffer with it at some level. For Avalon it had become a curse, a situation he loathed. It was the loneliest place he knew, laid in the dark with his thoughts for company. He had tried many ways to combat insomnia and some things had worked, inane thoughts were best, something to occupy the brain until it got bored and entered sleep. That's why poetry had been important. He had found in the past that thinking his way through poems he had learned had helped him doze off but recently even that wasn't working. He could be absolutely exhausted but as soon as his head hit the pillow his eyes would spring open and the dark thoughts would appear. Most people had those dark thoughts, many people kept them in a small box hidden away in the back of their minds. Avalon had so many dark thoughts, they occupied a suite of rooms in *his* mind, and although they were behind a closed door, the door had no lock. He would walk past that mental door now and then and find it slightly ajar and those spectres were abroad in his memories. Some of the memories were regrets, he would find himself sifting through details of the issues that caused his divorce, other times, things he had regretted doing or saying, not just to his wife but to his friends. The worst moments were when images of the things he had witnessed, the things that once seen, couldn't be unseen, came forward. Some of those images had caused him to scream or shout out in his sleep, and in the past they had resurfaced to haunt both him and his ex-wife Carol, yet he had never shared those nightmares with her, not wanting her so see those same images. He had brushed them off as 'bad dreams' or due to something he might have eaten at work. He had just never admitted to her or anyone for that matter, that the things he had witnessed in his career sometimes haunted him. In truth, the job haunted him. As he lay, looking up at the dark ceiling, he realised the job was *still* haunting him. He liked Julia, he liked her enough to want to see her again, but he had decided that he didn't want to bring his nightmares to someone else. He didn't want to have to explain the unexplainable, or make excuses for one thing or another. He didn't want a relationship, and yet, he was at the same time desperate for a relationship. As he festered in his black depression, in this cocoon of darkness, all he wanted was for someone to hold him, to tell him it was okay to fear, it was normal to doubt, it was wrong to be alone. He sat up and switched on the lamp. Oddly, having a light on allowed focus on his thoughts, he could sleep easier with it on. It wasn't something he admitted to, as it seemed he was afraid of the dark and that wasn't the case. The dark could be comforting in some circumstances, it was only when he tried to sleep that the darkness became an enemy. It seemed to nurture the black thoughts. It fertilized them and allowed them to grow and even though he knew when the cold light of morning eventually eased its way into the room, those thoughts would seem trivial, in the dark, they were oppressive and all pervasive. He laid his head back down and tried to work through the lines of a poem by Alfred Lord Tennyson. The words didn't come easy and he struggled to remember them.

"*Below the thunders of the upper deep, far, far beneath in the abysmal sea, his ancient, dreamless, uninvaded sleep, The Kraken sleepeth, faintest sunlights flee.*" He swallowed as his mouth dried from the words, even the poem he was trying to remember had sleep in it yet it still evaded him. He began to look around the room and thought about the possibility of buying his own place and wondered about this kind of 'homely' house. He preferred the, easy-to-clean, smooth-sided kind of house. Maybe that was his problem, was he looking for an easy to clean smooth sided woman to go with his easy-to-clean smooth-sided life? Not that his life was either of those things, it may be what he craved but it wasn't at all what he had. He adjusted his pillow for the twentieth time and closed his eyes. He saw the image of Muiranne Stodart's photograph and before he knew it the case was buzzing around his head again. To purge the image he thought about what he knew of other police officers and their problems with insomnia. Some had tried all manner of remedies, many were taking prescription drugs too but that wasn't Avalon's way, drugs were always a slippery slope. Like Lasiter back at

234

Inverness, he too had lost a close friend in the police force. His old mentor DI Colin Woods had taken Avalon under his wing when he first joined the CID. Colin had carefully guided him, told him everything he knew about the job but at just forty-five years old, he had suffered a massive heart attack and died. 'Stress of the job' they had said but Avalon knew he hadn't lived a very healthy life either. He had been just a couple of years older than Avalon's current age. It was one of the reasons Avalon had decided on a healthier outlook and lifestyle, he didn't want to go down the route that poor old Colin had succumbed to, drinking heavily and over doing headache remedies on top of sleeping pills. He was then saddled with the memory of his old mate, he could see Colin in his minds eye and remembered his ways and little habits. He tried to purge those thoughts by working his way through the chord sequence of David Bowie's 'Heroes' but he was still fully awake. He turned the light off once more and thought about something else. The black thoughts still came back now and then. He was cursed, cursed with insomnia and the demon of a career that entrapped him to such a degree that the functioning of his brain was corrupted by habit and necessity.

As usual, he ended up lying on his back, his eyes wide open staring up at the ceiling he couldn't see in the dark, the dark so thick in this bothy that it pressed down on his eyes. Shutting them was no different to having them open, at least at his home in Inverness there was enough light pollution to see the ceiling. As the time slowly ticked by, he began wishing for the morning, this was usual too, even if he had no sleep, at least the morning would give relief from the depression that was overtaking him. Then, he saw her face, the face coming through the dark, the face he had seen so many times, getting closer, becoming clearer. Was he asleep? He was close but if the face was there, he would have to wake. He sat up, pulled the cover around his shoulders and walked outside into the cold air. For a few seconds, the face was still visible but looking up at the sky he saw stars, he saw there was no cloud and he could see stars. He could see the Milky Way so clear, like a faint cross of light set at an angle. Here was at least one benefit of lack of light pollution. He shivered, wrapping the cover around himself. He shivered again. Nothing seemed to work and as the shivering increased he returned to the bothy and slumped onto the sofa, ready to take on more demons.

Chapter Eight

Avalon walked back to the Cave from DCI Croker's office with a return of his headache. It was probably brought on by the DCI suggesting that Avalon's team were dragging their feet with the Stodart murder. Avalon had explained it was a complex case but remained vague about his progress, which had probably angered Croker even further. This in itself didn't concern Avalon, it was the job of a DCI to try to motivate, it was just that Croker didn't motivate, he simply wasn't supportive in any way. The slight amount of sympathy that Avalon had carried for Croker's situation had evaporated with the words, *"having yourself a bit of a holiday up north,"* and now Avalon considered Croker could go to hell. He would tell him nothing and continue as if the man simply didn't exist. There was still a great deal to do, he still had to re-interview David Sutherland and it was all going to be much more difficult now he was back in Inverness. As he opened the door to the Cave and strode purposefully to the booth, he wondered if the time had come for Detective James Avalon to become a 'proper' DI, a man tied to a desk, a man that delegated all the jobs to the real detectives? He knew some DIs were able to balance the job by doing both but he was struggling with the idea of spending more time behind a desk. It was difficult being a detective these days, but it was much more difficult being a DI. He sat and decided to damn it to hell and carry on as he was doing, if Croker didn't like that he could find someone else to take on the role. He looked through the glass partition to see who was in the Cave. Ross was there busily writing up his reports for the last few days and both Frazer and Boyd seemed busy too. Wilson and Mack he knew were out at Dingwall investigating two new thefts from business premises and Mackinnon and Pottinger were in court on a trial of two teenagers caught selling drugs on the street. He looked down at the pile of paperwork but he was focused on the Golspie case and couldn't shake it. He pulled out the coroner's report from the pile and began to read through it. Now and then his thoughts drifted to his time up in Golspie and the brief evening he had spent with Julia Beattie, it brought a smile to his otherwise sullen mood.

When he had finished the coroner's report he stood and carried it to Ross who looked up as if he had just been awoken from a deep coma. Reports had that effect on a person.

"This is fun," he said sarcastically.

"Well have a read through this when you get time, nothing we didn't suspect and no revelations but interesting nonetheless."

"Interesting?" asked Ross with a glazed stare, "the last moments of a person's time alive and you say, 'interesting'?"

"From a purely professional standpoint of course, but if you expect me to wax lyrical on a scumbag like Peter Stodart then you've got this cynical detective sadly wrong," replied Avalon and he returned to the booth. He then continued to try and whittle down the pile of work he had in front of him.

When Mackinnon and Pottinger returned just after lunch, Mackinnon walked to the office as Pottinger returned to his desk.

"Hello Boss," smiled Rory, "how's the case going?" Avalon looked up to Mackinnon's eager face.

"Okay I suppose, how has your day been?" Rory explained briefly that the court had adjourned for lunch and their case was running late, they would return to the courts in the afternoon. It was a problem for the police, they had to be at the court but the system wasn't always easy to predict how things would go. It was an enormous waste of police time and resources. Avalon had noticed that Pottinger was his usual grim self.

"What's wrong with Mr Happy now?" he asked nodding towards Pottinger.

"Oh," said Rory looking through the glass, "he's just had some potentially bad news," he continued not sure if he should relate the whole to his DI.

"Go on," insisted Avalon making Mackinnon's reticence pointless.

"Well, his fiancé works in the control room and the rumours of it closing and operations being moved to Dundee are becoming fact," frowned Rory.

"Really? that doesn't make sense, they're closing the Aberdeen one but to close ours is pretty short-sighted," insisted Avalon.

"It is," nodded Mackinnon, "but if it does close she'll lose her job."

"I suspect that most of them will have the option of moving though," insisted Avalon but Rory didn't reply, he just looked blankly at Avalon. The realisation came to him that Mackinnon had obviously already gathered.

"Right," Avalon nodded, "if she moves to Dundee control then Pottinger will transfer."

"It makes sense," nodded Rory, "she would struggle to find other work but with the shortage of detectives DC Pottinger will probably get a transfer quite easily, particularly to Dundee, they are really short of staff."

"So are we," frowned Avalon, "but I see what you're getting at, Dundee probably has precedence."

"We have a new chap though from what I've heard?" smiled Rory. Avalon nodded grimly.

"We do but he's another DC wet behind the ears," he sighed looking down to the paperwork but looking back up as he realised what he had said, "none intended," he added with a smile.

"That's alright boss," smiled Mackinnon, "it must be difficult having to hold the hand of a new detective?"

"Well you'll find out," replied Avalon with a playful smile on his lips, "I was thinking of putting him with you."

"Me?" asked Mackinnon with disbelief."

"Of course, as long as you don't tell him you're new, I won't."

"But..." gasped Rory but Avalon continued.

"Now, now DC Mackinnon, you're senior to him so you'll have to stand up to your responsibilities," insisted Avalon with a more serious face. Rory gulped and then blinked several times.

"Sir," he nodded and then returned to his desk. Avalon smiled, he trusted Mackinnon and thought the experience would be beneficial. The phone rang.

"Avalon," he said as he lifted it to his ear.

"*Detective Avalon, it's Sarah Underwood,*" came the reply.

"If you are ringing with the results from the croft then I'm impressed," he said.

"*Not exactly,*" she replied, "*but I do have something for you.*" He didn't speak, he just waited for the information hoping it had some importance. "*The first tests we did this morning have been on the crowbar and the spade, there were no clear prints on the tools but we did a quick examination of the deposits found on them,*" she paused.

"And I'm guessing you found something?" he asked.

"*Yes but I'm not sure what this means, it may make some sense to you however. We looked at the deposits under a microscope and realised they looked like salt.*"

"Salt?" he questioned.

"*Yes, or more accurately Halite,*" the word wasn't something he recognised, "*the crystals are made up of potassium, gypsum and sodium chloride,*" she explained.

"So what is Halite?" he asked.

"*Rock salt, plain rock salt,*" was her response. There was a silence until she added, "*I thought it might mean something to you, but it seems it doesn't.*" He hesitated and then said,

"No, no it doesn't," and he tried to conceive why rock salt would be important but nothing came. Sarah's voice continued.

"*We'll continue with the examination of the vehicle today, we have found a few fibres and hair but preliminary findings are that there is no blood in the vehicle.*" When she had finished, Avalon thanked her and then went to speak to the rest of the team.

241

"Does anyone know of a rock salt mine in Scotland?" There were blank faces and silence, all except Rory's keyboard clicking out some activity.

"It doesn't look like there is one boss," he eventually said looking up from his screen. Avalon nodded and then moved over to Ross who was waiting for some explanation.

"It's what was found on the tools in the boot of Mrs Stodart's car," he said as he leaned on the window ledge.

"Odd time of year to be throwing rock salt about," suggested Ross.

"We didn't even have snow through the winter did we?" frowned Avalon. Ross didn't answer, he couldn't see how the salt would have remained on the tools for such a long time. He like Avalon scoured his brain for anything that might include rock salt and then he thought of something. Avalon watched Ross as he got busily to work on his computer, he had a look on his face as if he had thought of something.

"Got it," he said with a grin. Avalon looked at the screen, there was a view from Google maps of a single-track lane on a hill. Avalon recognised it as the hill near David Sutherland's house and more importantly, the hill where Mrs Stodart disappeared. Ross moved the image around to the left and there on the screen was a yellow bin, the sort that is usually full of grit, or rock salt.

"Brilliant," nodded Avalon, "that's how she did it." He paced around for a moment thinking his way through the events but Ross wasn't so upbeat.

"It still doesn't give us any leads to her husband's murder though," and he began to read through the coroner's report.

"No it doesn't," admitted Avalon, "but it does tell

us more about this woman and that could go much further to explain her thinking." He paced again and then stopped and turned to Ross. "This means she is much more organised that we first gave her credit for, I mean to think ahead to clear the grit bin so she could fit into it shows a lot of planning." Ross nodded but Avalon hadn't finished. "She seems pretty ruthless, I mean," he paused for a moment, "on the face of it she was 'using' her girlfriend and one of her few friends."

"We could assume she is but we don't know that for sure," argued Ross, "she may have just been scared, we have no idea what happened between her and her husband before this incident and it's always you that says we shouldn't jump to conclusions." Avalon seemed to ignore the statement, he began to pace a little more and then leaned on the window frame looking out over the fields. The sky was grey with plenty of scattered clouds but at least it wasn't raining. He looked down at a small puddle and saw it was still, there wasn't a single raindrop striking its surface. He then looked back into the room, he needed to get another interview from Mr Sutherland but who could he send? If it wasn't Ross or himself, would David Sutherland be responsive? Ross's comment finally reached his brain and he decided to reply.

"Personally, I don't think Mrs Stodart is the sort of person that gets scared, I think she is a very different species than most people imagine." Ross glanced up to him.

"You're going against your own mantra with that statement," frowned Ross.

"What mantra?" he asked. Ross put the report down for a second and in a frank voice said,

"The one I've just mentioned, the 'don't make assumptions, use only fact' mantra," he insisted.

"Sometimes," replied Avalon, "instinct bears down on me to such an extent that I have to listen to it, this is one of those moments."

"Well my mantra is, 'instinct is total bullshit', and I'm going with it this time," insisted Ross picking up the report once more.

"That's because you don't *have* instinct," said Avalon looking down to Ross, "you work with facts alone, that's what makes you good at your job." Ross once again put down the report and pulled out his notepad.

"Was that a compliment?" he asked picking up a biro.

"Sort of, why?" asked Avalon.

"I just need to record it," he said and he looked over to the office clock, checked the time with his watch and then scribbled something down in his notebook. "That's one for my memoirs," he added with a straight face as he replaced the notebook and continued reading the report. Avalon gave a slight smile as he turned back to look out of the window.

"I suppose I better give Dowd a call, the incident room will be closing today," and he returned to the booth.

"*Hello, PC Dowd,*"

"Neil, it's Avalon, anything come in yet?"

"*Oh, er, no, well nothing of any use inspector,*" replied Dowd.

"Okay, this is the last day for you, back here Monday," said Avalon trying to keep the disappointment from his voice.

"*Yeah, et's not been quite as worthwhile as we would like,*" replied Dowd. It was quite an understatement, as far as Avalon was aware there were

244

only twenty-seven calls logged and very little of interest had been found.

"It was worth a try, did any of the reported sightings come to anything?" asked Avalon.

"*Of the five that came in,*" began Dowd, "*two were discounted as impossible and one was tracked down as a similar build of person that turned out to be male. The other two are unconfirmed.*"

"Not great then," sighed Avalon.

"*We're still trying to track down the other two sightings but PC Gunn says he's doubtful of anyone coming forward, one was in the middle of Golspie and the other one was near her house,*" explained Dowd.

"Why doubtful?" asked Avalon.

"*Er, well,*" Dowd seemed to hesitate, "*as the PC says,*" he continued, "*would Mrs Stodart go to the trouble of disappearing just to go walking casually through Golspie or up near her house so soon after?*"

"Probably not but unless PC Gunn has applied to join the CID he shouldn't be making his own decisions on the issue," insisted Avalon.

"*Et was just a passing comment he made sir,*" explained Dowd, "*we did still check them, the one up at her house was walking a small dog anyway and the Stodarts didn't have a dog, the one in the village seems a bit too vague.*"

"Okay," sighed Avalon again, "well, we'll see you back here on Monday," and he ended the call. Avalon was becoming frustrated by the case, to make things worse, the office was becoming busy with several new incidents and the team were under pressure once more. He began to wonder when the new face would be starting, they certainly could do with the help even if it was to man the phones or sort out the paperwork. He looked up at the clock on the wall and then checked his watch, the day was going much faster than he wanted, there was still a great deal to do and he knew he would soon have to 'ease' the case aside. Managing the time spent on cases was a particular area of the job he loathed. The only way to solve a crime was to put in the hours and yet time was always a rare commodity in detective work. There always seemed to be other cases or other obstacles in the way of retrieving information, and nine times out of ten those delays were detrimental to the case. He tried to alleviate his frustration by burying himself in the paperwork but it didn't help, the paperwork was part of the problem.

In the early afternoon Ross walked into the booth and sat opposite Avalon. The DI looked up and saw Ross staring at him.

"What?" he demanded.

"I've read through the coroner's report," said Ross.

"Well done, I'll put you in for a commendation," replied Avalon and he continued typing.

"Peter Stodart had amphetamine in his blood," frowned Ross, "and the black plastic box had traces of the substance."

"It was actually 'mephedrone' if you read the report correctly," insisted Avalon.

"Call it what you like, 'bubbles', 'bath salts', it's still a form of amphetamine," growled Ross.

"So what's your point?" asked Avalon looking up to him again.

"If the man was high when his attacker arrived it's likely he wouldn't be in a fit condition to resist the attack."

"So what? the report says he was killed by a single blow to the head which smashed his skull and he bled to death over several hours," insisted Avalon.

"But a single blow?" asked Ross with a puzzled look, "it's not exactly a frenzied attack is it?"

"No," shrugged Avalon, "but if they knew he was high they probably knew they wouldn't have to strike him more than once."

"But the report says he took several hours to bleed to death, that means the attacker wasn't trying to kill him," insisted Ross. Avalon raised his eyebrows and said,

"Probably, but anyone who hits someone with a wheel brace doesn't exactly have the victims health as a top priority do they? And what are you getting at?" Ross looked at the floor and sighed.

"I'm not sure, I just think that the pieces don't fit."

"Just think about it, they were after the laptop, hit him over the head and do a runner, that's all there is to it," insisted Avalon and he looked back to the screen.

"But you said it yourself," continued Ross pointing at Avalon, "lack of any trace evidence points to a professional hit, that doesn't fit with bashing someone over the head with an iron club does it, and neither does it point the finger at his wife?"

"Maybe not," shrugged Avalon, "then maybe it wasn't a professional job, maybe they just did their best not to leave evidence, and no, it doesn't fit with his wife doing it either but she could have taken the laptop just to make us think there was another motive." Ross went quiet, he linked the fingers of his hands together and leaned forward looking down at the floor. Avalon stopped typing again and stared at Ross, he knew there was a disparity in the crime but until something cropped up they had to sit tight. "We need the court's permission to retrieve those emails from the internet provider."

"We're on it but even if we get permission we have to track the IP address to find out which provider he was using," replied Ross without looking up.

"You lost me just after you said 'we're on it'," said Avalon.

"Rory explained some of it to me," said Ross looking up, "it seems it's not as easy as we thought," he paused, "but it can be done." Ross stood and began to return to the Cave.

"Look," began Avalon, "if you've got itchy feet over this, go and take another shot at David Sutherland."

"I thought you said he was telling the truth?" frowned Ross.

"I'm beginning to reassess that, I still don't think that he could miss the altered water butt."

"How do you mean?" asked Ross but Avalon's face lit up from a light that had switched on in his head.

"I've got an idea, do we know where the Land Rover is?" he suddenly asked.

"We had it brought back in seeing as the murder weapon was probably out of the vehicle," nodded Ross.

"Right then," said Avalon, "let's take a trip over to the compound and in the mean time, get someone to go and buy two water butts."

Avalon and Ross had arranged to have two water butts delivered to the vehicle compound and for an engineer to be on site to assist. They then set off to get the vehicle ready for Avalon's experiment. As they entered the foyer they saw DS Tom Murrey chatting with an enormous man with a shaved head. As they closed, Ross made what he thought was a quiet comment to Avalon.

"Jesus, he's a big ugly bastard." The man obviously had excellent hearing as he spun around towards Ross as he said in a thick Scottish accent,

"Aye, big enough tae rip your face off and wear et to the next fancy dress party." He obviously began to regret it as he realised the two men were probably detectives.

"Well isn't she touchy," said Ross to Avalon in his best sarcastic voice. This did little to suppress the anger the man was obviously feeling but Tom Murrey stepped in to completely defuse the situation. He looked over to Ross and Avalon and then said,

"This is C Section's new detective, DC Martin Rutherford," and he paused to watch the reaction and then continued staring directly at the big man, "Martin, this is your new boss, DI Avalon." The big man's frame physically deflated and his head seemed to sink into his shoulders. His eyes closed and he brought up a hand to cover his face for a few seconds and then he seemed to recover, standing up straight and saying,

"Oh, I'm sorry guv'nor, I dunna know anyone yet, I'm really sorry for that outburst." Ross was a big chap but he seemed to have to reach up to put his hand gently on the shoulder of the big man.

"Don't worry about it detective constable," began Ross, "I strongly believe that everyone is allowed to make one mistake," he paused removing his hand, "unfortunately you have made two because I'm DS Ross, *this* is DI Avalon, and he isn't as charming as me," Ross gave a thin smile as he pointed to Avalon.

"Shite," announced Rutherford sagging his shoulders once more, "how tae cock up before a' start," and he turned to Avalon who stood impassively with his hands thrust in his trouser pockets, the bottom of his jacket folded over them. "How do I get out o' this mess?" he asked though no one thought the question was directed at anyone present.

"I suppose you have to book yourself into an anger management course and then think about a career change," said Avalon and he walked on through the foyer towards the car park.

"You have a way with the new faces don't you?" smiled Ross as he followed Avalon through the door.

"If they sent us properly trained staff there wouldn't be a problem," insisted Avalon as he exited the building and walked into the car park.

"It was probably my fault though for goading him," added Ross as he followed but Avalon stopped and spun around.

"Then stop doing it," he snapped but calmed down immediately, "I mean, look at him, he's a gorilla, how can I send someone who looks like that to interview a sensitive victim of crime?" he was pointing back to the building, "or send him out to inform relatives that their child has been found dead." He dropped his arm and sighed. "His only use would be at the end of a strong chain, walking round Inverness scaring the petty crooks." Ross tried not to smile, he tried so much he ended up laughing. "And what's so bloody funny?" growled Avalon.

"Sorry," said Ross, "but it's just the image of Rory walking through Hilton with 'the Ape' on a long piece of anchor chain."

"I'm glad you see it as humorous," began Avalon, "I don't, we need detectives not misfits, or giants that are moved on from the beat because they can't get uniforms to fit them." Avalon continued across the car park.

"Have you ever considered he might be good at

his job?" asked Ross rooted to the spot. Avalon stopped and turned.

"If he can't control his anger in the station, what's he gonna be like out there?" frowned Avalon pointing to the gates.

"You didn't rate Rory when he arrived, or Alison, but would you swap either of them now?" asked Ross. Avalon thought about it, it was true Mackinnon and Boyd had become part of the furniture and he trusted both of them. He looked over to Ross and made his way back.

"I have an idea actually," he said in a softer voice and he walked back into the station. He found Rutherford talking to the officer on the desk.

"DC Rutherford," called Avalon. The man straightened and looked over.

"Sir," he answered.

"Cheer up man, you've got a face as long as a burglar's shopping list," began Avalon, "what do you know about the Peter Stodart case?" The big man searched his memory and then shrugged.

"Absolutely nothing sir, I don't think I ever heard the name before." He eventually replied.

"Good," nodded Avalon, "come with us," and then he hesitated and asked.

"Have you officially started yet?"

"No sir, not 'till Monday," and he saw Avalon give a pained expression, "but whatever et es, I'm en." Avalon gave a nod and then turned to join Ross at the door with Rutherford stepping confidently forward in his size twelves.

~~~~~~

Avalon was insistent that Rutherford should know nothing about the case, Ross had understood and had taken the big man for a tour around the compound whilst Avalon explained with a sketch what he wanted the police engineer to do with the water butts as soon as they arrived. When Ross and Rutherford returned they helped Avalon get the Land Rover into position and prepare it for his experiment. A police van soon arrived and out jumped PC Kirk. She quickly opened the rear doors and Ross helped her remove the water butts. Rutherford had once again been kept out of the way and he was becoming highly suspicious of what he was actually required to do.

"DC Frazer says you owe her forty quid sir," smiled Kirk.

"Forty quid for two plastic barrels, David Sutherland was knocking them out for a fiver a piece," complained Avalon.

"Are you sure there's no Scottish blood in your family?" asked Ross quietly. Avalon watched him move the barrels to one side and replied,

"Certainly not, I can't stand cheesy chips," which brought a smile to Kirk's face as she jumped back into the van and returned to the station.

"There's more to being Scottish than the lure of cheesy chips," shrugged Ross, as the engineer began work on the water butts. Avalon looked deep in thought as he walked into the small office in the compound.

"How would you describe David Sutherland at a glance?" he asked. Ross shrugged and said,

"It depends how you mean, he seems reasonably intelligent and for a retired sort seems to like to keep himself busy, why?"

"I just wondered if you would consider him

observant?" asked Avalon.

"Yeah, probably, he seemed to take notice of the man in the stolen Vauxhall and he remembered that the Land Rover brake lights were on."

"That's the impression I had, so you would think he would notice when something wasn't quite right?" said Avalon in a questioning tone.

"Yeah, I think he would make a good witness if that's what you're asking."

"So," continued Avalon, "if we put Rutherford in a similar situation, would he notice anything out of the ordinary do you think?" Ross smiled and gave a slight sigh.

"I don't know," he admitted, "I know nothing about him so it's difficult to guess but if he passed his exams to get this far he ought to, yes." Avalon nodded and then sat in a rickety chair by the door.

"Then this might not work as I expected but it's worth a try," he said.

"You can't set up the exact situation here, whatever happens, it isn't going to be the same as it was over at Golspie," insisted Ross leaning on the doorframe.

"I'm quite aware of that," admitted Avalon, "that's why I'm going to put him through the grinder, I'll put some pressure on him to try and recreate a similar situation."

"Oh," said Ross pursing his lips and then giving a momentary shrug, "this should be interesting." The engineer came to the office and informed them that the work was done and Avalon went to inspect the results. The bottom of one of the water butts had been removed and carefully shaped to fit snugly inside the other. The barrel was then loaded into the back of the Land Rover and held in place by the ratchet strap. When secure,

Avalon placed some items including two one-gallon containers full of water into the barrel to simulate a small person inside and then the false bottom was gently slid inside to hide the items.

"That's it, fetch our oversize DC and we'll give it a try." Ross soon returned with Rutherford who looked around the compound and then over to Avalon. The DI then began to explain.

"We seem to have got off to a poor start DC Rutherford but you now have a chance to redeem yourself." The big man nodded slightly but gave nothing away in his body language. "This is a simple test, it has a dual purpose but have no illusions about my seriousness over this." The man seemed to understand what he was getting at. "You see that Land Rover over at the other end of the compound," Rutherford nodded, "I want you to make your way over there smartly, check the vehicle over as quick as you can and return back here. There is an empty barrel in the rear of the vehicle, this is because we are trying to set up a similar situation to what is supposed to have happened in a case we are currently working on," The man looked down doubtfully at Avalon. "Yes, you're right, there is more to it than that. I will be timing you. All you have to do is make sure there is no one in the vehicle, assume it will burst into flames within the time allotted," Avalon felt Ross turn to him and knew he would be once again questioning his methods. He also noticed that Rutherford had seen Ross turn, but that was good, it meant he noticed things. "Is that clear?" asked Avalon. The man nodded suspiciously. Avalon looked at his watch for effect and then back to the big man then said,"

"You wont have much time, just thirty seconds to get there, check it and return to this spot, do you understand?"

"Aye, I think so, and what does this mean for me?" he asked. Avalon allowed what almost passed as a smile and he said,

"If you get there and back within the time then you're in C Section," he paused, "if it takes you longer, you failed and my first assessment of you sticks." The big man had an unsettling expression at this, he looked at Ross for a moment and then back to Avalon. They could see that Rutherford knew this was completely out of order and against all police protocol but he would do it, if only so he could complete it and tell Avalon exactly what he could do with C section and the job. He had put up with some crap from senior officers in his life but he had decided long ago that those days had gone. He nodded slowly and gave a deep frown. He took a deep breath, turned, and said,

"When you're ready then," and he looked over to the target vehicle and focused, assessing it to be about thirty good paces away. It was almost impossible to do it in the time allotted but he'd give it a go. Avalon made a show of looking at his watch once more and he seemed to be getting the thing ready to record the time.

"Go!" he called and Ross noted that the watch was forgotten as soon as Rutherford darted off towards the Land Rover. For a big chap, the DC wasn't a slow mover, he was up to the vehicle in seconds and instinctively went to the driver's door, he opened it, looked in and into the rear and slammed it shut, he then looked under the vehicle before opening the rear door and quickly slamming it shut and darting back to the spot he had started from. Avalon had no idea how long it had taken him but he asked,

"Was the vehicle empty?"

"There was no one in the vehicle, just a plastic barrel in the back," he panted.

"Did you notice anything about the vehicle that you may find suspicious?" asked Avalon. The big man soon regained his breath and began to explain what he found.

"Aye a few things, for starters, the print boys have been all over et several times as it was covered in dust, the tools have been removed by the look of et as all the clips are empty, et has an aftermarket CD-radio fitted on the passenger side of the dashboard, the front offside tyre is barely legal and the recorded mileage is 42,676." Avalon looked over to Ross and raised his eyebrows with a slight grin. "En the back, the green water butt es secured with one o' those one inch ratchet straps an' there es no spare wheel."

"Pretty good and well within the time I gave you," nodded Avalon.

"With respect *sir*," Avalon heard a slight amount of anger hidden in the word 'sir', "what es this load of bollocks really about?"

"Okay Rutherford," nodded Avalon, "you deserve an explanation," Avalon noticed Ross make his way slowly to the Land Rover but ignored it, "I wanted to see what you might notice about the vehicle if you were under some pressure, you noticed much more than I expected but the experiment has backfired somewhat," admitted Avalon with a slight shrug.

"Why's that, did y' not expect me tae notice anything about the vehicle then?"

"It's a long story, I had a hunch about a witness, I wondered if he was telling us the whole truth, the barrel in the rear is the key to the whole thing, not the actual vehicle," explained Avalon. Ross called over.

"The mileage is over seventy-eight thousand not forty two and the offside tyre is like new." Rutherford looked over to Ross.

"Aye, that was shite I made up, I guessed y' wouldnae know what et was," and he turned back to Avalon, "so you were wondering ef I would notice the water butt had a false bottom or no?" Avalon smiled at this.

"So why didn't you say so?" he asked.

"You asked specifically about the vehicle, I wouldn't have thought anyone could be en the space behind et and you wanted tae know ef there was a person en the vehicle." Avalon shook his head still smiling.

"I did," he admitted.

"So what's this really about then?" asked Rutherford.

"Well DC Rutherford, firstly, welcome to C section, secondly, why do you crop your hair so close?"

"Because there isnae much of et so I keep et well mown," replied the man thinking it was an odd question.

"Well a less harsh look would go some way to helping you blend in with fellow humans," smiled Avalon.

"Blending en, isnae somethin' I have noticed comes easy tae somebody my size," replied Rutherford allowing himself to drop the frown.

"Then think of it as a PR exercise, anyway," paused Avalon for a second, "thirdly, I think you have just proven that one of our witnesses is lying through his teeth."

~~~~~~

"You're quiet," said Ross.

257

"Is there any wonder, I am angry with myself for getting David Sutherland wrong," frowned Avalon.

"You might not be wrong, he may have told the truth," shrugged Ross finishing the cup of coffee he had just poured. Avalon hadn't touched his, he was stewing in the thought that he was losing his touch, he was convinced Sutherland had been a genuine sort and was telling him the truth, for the first time his instinct had let him down.

"I realise that DC Rutherford may be more observant than one of the public but you said it yourself, you thought that Sutherland seemed almost creepy the way his eyes took everything in."

"Yeah, he seems to notice things but..." Ross paused for a moment, "the surprise of seeing Mrs Stodart had vanished from her vehicle may have caused him to miss things."

"So when you can't find your car keys," said Avalon looking directly at him, "and you try the usual place in the cupboard, the drawer in the kitchen, the little fruit bowl where you keep other keys, down the back of the sofa and all your pockets, and still can't find them, what do you do?"

"I start from the beginning and look through all those places again," smiled Ross.

"Exactly," nodded Avalon, "and the same would happen in these circumstances, a friend vanishes from their vehicle in front of your eyes, do you look several times or do you put it down to the Brollachan?"

"But this is different," insisted Ross, it's not like you can misplace a friend down the back of the sofa is it?"

"You know what I mean," insisted Avalon.

"I do but it's different," replied Ross and then he

paused for a moment, "and do you have a fruit bowl to keep your keys in?" he grinned.

"No," replied Avalon and then in a more relaxed voice said, "but I noticed you do."

"So is that why you insisted in bringing him in, just anger?" asked Ross.

"No not just anger," insisted Avalon, "I want to put pressure on him, bringing him fifty miles for an interview late in the day will make him sweat, particularly as his wife will know all about it."

"Yeah but it means yet another late night for us," said Ross standing to rinse out his cup.

"I told you, you didn't need to be here."

"Yeah, I know that but I also know you don't like doing interviews on your own," shrugged Ross.

"I wouldn't be on my own, Rory will be back soon with the Land Rover," insisted Avalon.

"True, but that's why I wanted to stay, I want to see Sutherland's face when he sees our little surprise," smiled Ross. Rory entered the Cave.

"Ah, Rory, is it ready?" asked Avalon as the office phone rang, Ross answered it.

"Yes boss," nodded Mackinnon, "just as you asked." Avalon nodded and Ross turned to him replacing the phone.

"He's here, interview room two," he said.

The three of them made their way to the ground floor and into the interview room. Mackinnon went into the area behind the two-way mirror and Ross and Avalon entered the room with the attending PC leaving soon after.

"This is highly irregular detective, as I said on the phone I have nothing further to add," insisted Sutherland as soon as he saw Avalon. They sat at the table opposite the man and Avalon explained.

"This case has taken an unexpected turn Mr Sutherland and as such has become more serious."

"But couldn't we have done this over the phone, it's over an hour's journey for me to come into Inverness," insisted the man.

"I'm aware of that Mr Sutherland but we need you here for something specific," added Avalon.

"Well can we get on with it please?" he asked. Avalon nodded and led him outside to the station car park where it was almost dark. The compound lights were on however so there was no lack of light. Sutherland immediately saw the Land Rover.

"Is that the same vehicle?" asked Sutherland.

"It is," nodded Avalon, "and that is why we needed you here, we want to go through the exact movements of that day when Mrs Stodart went missing using the actual vehicle."

"I see," nodded Sutherland raising his eyebrows. Neither Ross or Avalon detected any stress or panic in the man, he was taking it in his stride and Avalon was beginning to doubt his theory once more.

"My colleague DC Mackinnon will drive the vehicle down the car park and try to re-enact as close as we can what happened, he will however extricate himself from the vehicle in the normal manner." Sutherland shrugged and Avalon told Rory to continue. He drove the vehicle around the almost empty car park and brought it to rest by the waiting men. Avalon explained that the moments prior to the loading of the barrel were of no interest and they would start by placing the water butt into the rear of the vehicle. At a signal, Rory reversed the Land Rover up to the point where they were standing and Avalon opened the rear door.

"The barrel is in here as you can see," explained Ross, "so we'll fetch it out so that it can be loaded as you did it on that day." The barrel was placed on the floor and the ratchet strap in the rear of the vehicle, it was clear to see that there was nothing else in the back.

"I will play your part for the moment Mr Sutherland," explained Ross, "all you need to do is direct me through the motions that you went through that day," and with this Ross climbed into the vehicle, Rory remained in the cab of the vehicle looking back.

"Well, I just lifted it in like this," and he placed the barrel in the rear, Ross moved to hook the ratchet into position it was found on the day and he then tightened the strap.

"Is this correct?" asked Ross and Sutherland nodded. Ross jumped out and closed the rear door.

"We don't have the hill or the room in here to recreate the distances but that isn't important," explained Avalon, "we just need to establish how the events happened." Avalon called to Rory to continue and he drove off towards the gate, he revved the engine and stopped the vehicle at an angle similar to how the Land Rover was found. The brake lights shone bright as Sutherland had explained and then went off.

"Now then Mr Sutherland, we have to use our imagination a little here but is this good enough to simulate the incident?"

"I suppose so," agreed the man.

"And you will be able to show us how you proceeded?" he asked. The man nodded. "Then we'll continue," added Avalon and he called to Rory in the vehicle to get out. After a few seconds the young detective got out of the driver's seat and made his way towards them.

261

"If you would walk us through it Mr Sutherland?" said Avalon holding out his arm towards the Land Rover with its engine still running. Sutherland nodded and walked casually to the vehicle, he opened the driver's door, looked in and then closed it.

"I think I looked around, up and down the lane and then back to the cab," he explained and he looked into the cab through the window. "I then went to the rear of the truck and opened the door," he continued and walked to the rear and opened the rear door of the vehicle fully, "I then looked in and..." he trailed off. He stood motionless until he realised he had gone silent, "I then er, I looked to make sure she wasn't in and... and then..." he was now visibly shaken.

"What is it Mr Sutherland, did we get something wrong?" asked Avalon.

"No, no... not at all, I... I just can't remember what I did next," he stuttered the words.

"Or is it that you have seen something you didn't expect to see?" asked Avalon abruptly. The man looked from the rear of the vehicle and turned to Avalon, his face glowed white in the lamps of the car park.

"I think I need to speak with my lawyer now," he said.

"Very well but you are free to go if you wish, we haven't arrested you," nodded Avalon, "not yet," he added. He was disappointed that the man hadn't come clean but it was obvious they had him, they were correct, David Sutherland knew about the water butt with the false bottom and that meant he was an accomplice.

They returned to the interview room where Avalon arranged for the man to be given a drink of tea and then he was offered the phone. He didn't pick up the phone and he seemed deep in thought so Avalon shot a question his way.

"I wonder Mr Sutherland, did you realise she was playing you for a fool before we brought you in?" Sutherland hesitated for a moment.

"I really don't know what you are talking about, and as you said I'm free to go so I don't need to answer any more questions," and he began to stand.

"Yes, as I said," shrugged Avalon, "free to go but I still have to ask you if you knew she was using you."

"I suppose detective it's the sort of thing you would ask me, but I'm not going to be drawn into the seedy world you live in, I'm sorry but I can't help you any further."

"Did you know that she had a friend who she had hire a car exactly like yours to implicate you in the crime?" added Avalon casually.

"That's just a coincidence and you know it," spat the man.

"Not at all," added Ross, "we have a sworn testimony from Mrs Stodart's lover that the car was sought out specifically, a car identical to yours."

"Lover? that's ridiculous, she wasn't the sort of person to go with another man."

"You're probably correct, but I didn't say the lover was male," added Ross casually. This took the man by utter surprise, he looked as if he was about to choke and he slumped back into the chair. He dropped his head into his hands and then looked up.

"I can't believe that would ever be the case," he eventually said.

"I'm afraid Mrs Stodart manipulated a great many more people than you, but it's true, she had even bought a house for the lover to live in." explained Avalon. Sutherland began shaking his head, it was obvious that the news was a total shock, it had clearly taken him by surprise. His head went back into his hands and Avalon turned to the two-way mirror and made a drinking gesture towards his reflection. Less than a minute later there was a knock at the door and in came DC Mackinnon with a tray of drinks. Sutherland didn't react to the offer of a drink but Avalon could clearly see he was wrestling with some inner conflict and hoped the pressure had worked. Without any warning Sutherland looked up to Avalon and asked,

"Do you believe that Muir is involved in her husband's demise?" Avalon took a second or two to consider his response.

"It's possible of course," he nodded, "that is the problem, until we have the opportunity to interview her we just don't know how she was involved." Sutherland looked down to the floor, wrung his hands feverishly and then sat up straight and placed them flat on the table.

"I'll tell you what I know," he then said as if he had just been asked the correct time. Avalon nodded and looked at Ross who instinctively knew it was his turn to question the man.

"So, Mr Sutherland," began Ross, "what really happened that day when Mrs Stodart went missing?" Sutherland swallowed hard, he looked down at the cup and took a drink of the tea and then began to explain.

"Muir came to me and explained that her husband had lost his wits and was planning something that might cause her harm, and before you ask she didn't elaborate," insisted Sutherland placing the cup back on the table. "She asked me to help her to leave him, she said she didn't want him to be able to track her down but I refused at first," he paused and looked up to Ross. "I told her I would never be involved with anything illegal but she assured me that there was nothing illegal about it and she just wanted to disappear." His eyes flitted around the table, not seeing anything there but viewing the images in his mind. "She then said she had a plan, all I would have to do was tell the police a story which she said would work. She told me the story and I said it was a terrible plan, she assured me it would work but again I refused on the basis that it was a lie. She then asked me how I would feel about it if it were true. I said I may consider it but I would have nothing to do with it if I had to break the law."

"So you didn't consider perjury against the law?" asked Ross.

"As I didn't take an oath it was never perjury," explained Sutherland seeming slightly more at ease, "in any case, it really happened and so it wasn't even a lie."

"So you are saying you actually went through with the whole scenario?" asked Avalon. Sutherland nodded.

"Yes, exactly as I told you, she drove down the hill, crashed into the field and I watched the brake lights go off. I waited a few seconds and then ran down. I looked in the vehicle, moved to the rear and opened the door, I even wished her good luck, then I turned and came back to the house to phone the police."

"And did you return as you said?" asked Ross.

"Yes," replied the man, "I even went through the process of checking the vehicle again and when I got to the rear I saw she had gone..." he tailed off as he recalled seeing the false bottom of the facsimile that the detectives had arranged.

"And what happened then?" asked Ross.

"As I told you, I looked over the fields to see if I could see her but I couldn't. I was quite surprised how she had got away so quickly." Sutherland looked somewhat calmer now he was telling them the truth.

"So she didn't tell you how she planned to exit the locality?" asked Ross.

"Not at all, I think she said she would make her way across the fields but as I say I just couldn't see her," he explained. Ross nodded and made a few notes on his pad.

"Were there any plans beyond that?" asked Avalon.

"No," replied the man, "she said she would contact me when she was safe but I never heard a thing from her from that day forward."

"So you don't know what Peter Stodart had threatened her with and you have no idea where she is?" asked Ross.

"No, and that *is* the truth detective," announced Sutherland.

"I have to ask this question again Mr Sutherland," began Avalon, "were you having any kind of relationship with Mrs Stodart?" Sutherland began shaking his head before Avalon had finished the question.

"No, I admired her but I never thought I had anything she would want from me. We were good friends..." he paused, "or at least I thought we were but now I see I didn't know her at all." His demeanour changed a little and he recoiled back into himself considering the past events and then continued with, "I mean she is charming, sophisticated and utterly captivating and I would have given anything to think she saw something in me detective, but..." he paused again and shrugged, "I'm too much of a realist to think she ever saw anything in me in that respect." Avalon decided on a short break and he stepped outside with Ross and explained that they needed to get everything he had told them into a statement for him to put his name to.

"So you think this is the truth then?" asked Ross.

"Don't you?"

"Yeah, probably," nodded Ross, "I'll get someone to sort the statement out and get him back home." Ross looked at his watch. "We might just get the last ones if we hurry," he added.

"Not for me," replied Avalon shaking his head.

"So what else you gonna do?" asked Ross.

"Home, shower, bed," replied Avalon emphatically.

Thirty minutes later, Ross and Avalon spilled into the Castle Tavern just in time to get the last drink before closing time. It was quite busy and so they braved the cooling air outside in the beer garden. Avalon leaned over the railing cradling his Glenmorangie, looking out over Castle Road and the River Ness beyond. The twinkling shine of the streetlights and the buildings of Ardross Terrace over the river danced across the water, smashed and buffeted by the tiny waves, returning whole as the water calmed, ready to be split into many specks over the next waves.

"It's not a bad evening," he said as Ross joined him.

"Well, it's not raining if that's what you mean?" replied Ross. Avalon smiled and gave a curt nod, he took a sip of the single malt and sniffed the clean air of the river through the slightly peaty fumes of the whisky. He sighed, not the usual sort of exasperated sigh but the sort of sigh that leans on the side of relaxation. Ross had been correct to convince him to go to the pub, it did indeed help wind down the pressures and stresses of the day, particularly a long day like they had just experienced.

"What day is it?" he asked. Ross thought for a moment and then replied with,

"Saturday, not for long though," he looked at his watch, holding it up slightly to catch the glimmer under the beer garden roof lights. "Why?" he eventually asked, "you got plans?"

"Sort of," nodded Avalon, "I have to go to a police station and try to work out a bit of a problem with too few clues and very few staff."

"Oh, that," nodded Ross taking a drink, "well, what else would you do on a Sunday?"

"Oh, maybe the sort of thing other people do," replied Avalon languidly, "get up late, sit on the patio with a cup of strong coffee, eat two slices of toast with home made marmalade spread over them, read the paper in the sun wondering if I had the energy to do the crossword. Then I'd watch the wife bring me out a cold Pimms and argue that it was a little early for drinks but laugh it off as it was such a lovely day. Then I'd notice the cat stroll over the immaculate lawn and collapse by the pool watching the fountain spray water up through a tiny rainbow falling back down on the brightly coloured carp milling around in the crystal clear water," he paused for a quick breath, "and there in the distance, a cuckoo. But then again, I hardly heard it because over to the left in the park the village team are playing cricket and the sound of leather on willow can be quite noisy sometimes. But I'll have to get up soon because my two daughters and two sons are coming round for Sunday dinner and then we're going down the river on a leasurely cruise." He stopped, not because the images ceased but because it felt pointless.

"Didn't you do that the week before?" asked Ross

casually. Avalon turned to him.

"Did I?" asked Avalon, "that's the problem living the perfect life, it all becomes one long day." He looked up at the sky but couldn't see a single star. "So, you know what I'm doing," he asked looking back to Ross, "what about you?"

"Me," smiled Ross, "oh nothing like you, I'm taking Angelina Jolie out on my speedboat, I mean, I feel responsible for her marriage break up so I have to spend some time with her." Avalon nodded.

"Yeah it's only right," he said and looked back out over the river. "A meal somewhere after?"

"Nope," announced Ross, "we're off to that little place I bought last year in the south of France and I'm gonna shag the spine out of her," and he took a drink.

"Well, if you change your mind," said Avalon sounding a little uninterested, "you could always give me a hand down at the station." Ross thought about it for a moment.

"Well, I suppose I could manage a couple of hours if you're struggling," and he downed the rest of his drink in one.

~~~~~~~

Avalon sat in his chair looking out from the booth into the office. The Cave wasn't very busy but it was nothing to do with it being Sunday. Wilson and Mack were having a rare day off but Pottinger and Mackinnon were out tidying loose ends on two cases they were working and DC Boyd was helping Frazer with a minor issue at Dingwall. Ross was busy catching up on paperwork and he looked up as PC Dowd entered. Avalon had arranged for Dowd to come and update him on the last logs taken from the incident vehicle. The vehicle was now closed and a press release had been sent to most of the local newspapers and websites, but it was clear from Dowd, nothing more of interest had been logged. Dowd was still upbeat about the progress but he admitted that there was now not much likelihood of more information coming in.

"I think that it could simply be that nobody has seen anythin', ef the woman has done a runner abroad then et's likely that you'll have to wait for her tae make a mistake," he explained. Avalon gave a semblance of a shrug.

"Possibly," agreed Avalon, "thanks for helping out anyway," he smiled.

"Och, y' know me, anythen tae get out of the office."

As Dowd left Avalon stood and walked into the Cave and sat on the desk opposite Ross.

"When I got into bed last night I began to wonder why the spare wheel was missing from the rear of the Land Rover."

"I've already given that some thought," answered Ross looking up from his work.

"And what did you come up with?" asked Avalon.

"When we were in the compound with Rutherford, I had a look seeing as he had mentioned it, there is only one anchor point in that vehicle for the spare wheel and it's on the rear bulkhead. She would have needed to remove it to lay the water butt in there, I suppose that's why it's been left in the Stodart's garage."

"You checked it on the forensics report?" questioned Avalon. Ross nodded.

"Yes, there was a list of items in the garage and a

'large wheel and tyre for a Land Rover' was on the list," explained Ross. Avalon looked out of the window. It was a reasonable sort of day, there were clouds but no sign of the miserable rain that had visited of late.

"We'll just have to wait for the forensics report from Mrs Stodart's croft and car," sighed Avalon.

"Yeah, I suppose we'll have to wait until tomorrow, I can't see it coming in today," agreed Ross, "come to think of it, I haven't checked my email this morning," and he made a few key presses on his key board.

"Expecting one from Angolina Jolie?" asked Avalon as he stood to returned to his booth.

"Yeah, I bet she doesn't want to go to Monte Carlo this year," smiled Ross watching the emails flood in.

"Take her to Eyemouth instead," called back Avalon as he entered the booth. He sat and began to type up the report of the previous night and the interview with David Stodart. It wasn't long before Ross slumped down in the seat opposite with a far-away look in his eye.

"What's wrong, has she called it off altogether?" asked Avalon but he noticed Ross hesitate before he said,

"I've got an email from that forensic locksmith, he's identified where the key came from that was found in Arty Struther's pocket."

"And?" inquired Avalon. Ross seemed a little shocked but he snapped out of his thoughts and said,

"It's for a safety deposit box in Glasgow." Avalon frowned and then asked,

"Does that fit with him?"

"Do you mean does a homeless wino have the means and a reason to keep a safety deposit box?" asked Ross sarcastically.

"I meant does he have connections in Glasgow?" growled Avalon. Ross dropped his stern look and said,

"Yes he does."

"So what are you gonna do?" asked Avalon.

"I don't know, I suppose I could get the key sent over there, they probably won't let me open it anyway," explained Ross.

"It may have escaped your notice but you work for the CID," replied Avalon raising an eyebrow.

"Yeah, I suppose," shrugged Ross, "but I could just get the company who run the boxes to open it up and check the contents."

"Or get the local force to check on it," added Avalon and then he asked, "who paid for the box anyway?"

"It seems Arty paid for it," explained Ross, "well if it was his, he did, they informed the locksmith that the particular box that goes with that key paid the rent in advance every six months."

"Well either way," insisted Avalon, "you need to check this one out." Ross nodded and stood.

"I'll get on the blower to them in the morning, for sure I haven't got time to go over there myself," and he returned to his desk. Avalon watched Ross every now and then, it was clear he was troubled with what he may find in that box. Avalon still considered it may be nothing to do with the homeless Struther, it could indeed be a lost key that he had found. But then again, the company running the boxes would have known the key had been lost. Whatever the reason, and whatever was in the box, Ross seemed apprehensive about what it may contain. Avalon busied himself with his work and hoped that it wouldn't be such a late finish that evening.

Chapter Nine

The sky was full of broken cloud yet still, the sun did its best to force through but as Avalon drove into work he assumed it would be raining soon. He turned off the roundabout and found his way into the car park where he stopped the car and pushed back from the steering wheel. He took several deep breaths, this was going to be an awkward day if something didn't turn up in the Stodart case. DCI Croker was already making trouble and he could feel that there was more just around the corner. He made his way into the foyer and up the stairs to the Cave and as he opened the door the welcoming aroma of coffee massaged his nasal passages. DS Wilson and DC MacDonald were already pouring themselves a cup and further examination showed DC Mackinnon was already at work. He was consistently an early starter so it was usually he who made the first pot of coffee for the day. He knew Pottinger would be late as he was needed at court over a case that he had worked on before he joined the section. Avalon nodded to the room as several voices said good morning to him and he went to the booth to remove his jacket and find his cup. Back at the coffee machine he heard Boyd enter the Cave talking to Frazer about something she had seen on the TV the night before. He wondered how anyone found anything worth watching on the infernal machine, every time he sat down to watch something it was an unfeasibly impossible plot in a soap opera or even worse, a police drama. In the nineteen nineties he remembered a program called 'Cop Rock' which still made him wince as he thought about it. It was a musical delivered as an American cop drama and it was truly diabolical. Since then he had considered that TV executives must make their bad dreams into programs. The door opened again and brought him out of his thoughts, it was Ross. He immediately looked round at Avalon and before he got to his desk he asked,

"You got a minute?" Avalon nodded and carried his cup into the booth with Ross following.

"Problems?" he asked as he sat.

"I was thinking about the disappearance of the Stodart woman on my way in," explained Ross sitting opposite, "if she jumped out of the truck when Sutherland went back to his house to phone, why were no footprints found?" Avalon thought about it, the ground was soft and everyone else left at least one print.

"It's a point but would it make any difference either way?" asked Avalon.

"I think it would, yes," frowned Ross, unless there are prints to show she left the vehicle, it could be the case that Sutherland is still not telling us the truth."

"It could, but equally, it could mean she didn't leave any prints, maybe she was careful," suggested Avalon.

"Why would she do that if she and Sutherland are going through the motions just to keep him in the clear?" explained Ross and continued with, "it just doesn't make sense." Avalon sipped at his coffee and thought about it,

274

something was rattling about in the back of his mind. Ross stood and walked to the coffee machine and poured a cup. Mackinnon looked up at the large jug and sighed, the damn thing needed filling again. Ross returned and sat opposite once more.

"I think I can possibly explain it away," Avalon said, "when I interviewed Sutherland and got him to take me through what he did on that day, he told me a pair of his wellies had gone missing and he only ever found one of them."

"So what?" shrugged Ross.

"Is it possible *she* took them so that she didn't leave her own tracks, she could probably have worn them over her own shoes?"

"Could be," said Ross, "but did he know she had arranged that, he certainly didn't mention it?"

"I don't know," replied Avalon as a couple of phones rang in the Cave, "but I don't think it's all that important, if she was trying to implicate Sutherland in her disappearance, she may have done it to cement his guilt." Ross nodded and considered if that was true, she was a very nasty piece of work. It meant that she had attempted to make it look as if David Sutherland was responsible for her going missing. Frazer entered the Booth.

"Sorry tae interrupt boss but we have an email from the courts,"

"Go on," he said.

"We have permission to ask for the emails from Peter Stodart's ISP," she explained raising her eyebrows.

"How long will it take?" asked Avalon.

"Not sure," replied Frazer, "but Rory has done as much background as he could, we think we know who the ISP es because en the pile of the Stodart's paperwork

275

there es a printed email invoice. Et seems et was the only bill he was paying."

"Okay," nodded Avalon, "you and Rory stick with it, let me know if you find anything." As Frazer left the booth, he looked to Ross and raised an eyebrow.

"It doesn't mean there will be anything there, he may have deleted everything," said Ross.

"It's all we've got at the moment," shrugged Avalon taking another drink of his coffee. Avalon felt his phone vibrate in his pocket so he pulled it out and checked the text. It was from Julia Beattie but he decided not to read it while Ross was there and so he placed the phone back in his pocket. "I wonder what has happened to DC Rutherford, he said he was starting today?" asked Avalon not really expecting any sort of explanation.

"He's probably getting all the trimmings from PC Kirk," replied Ross with a half smile, "mind, that won't take long." Avalon gave a slight laugh, he remembered when he first started at Inverness, she was on 'super quick' mode as she showed him around, but then again she did try to play a prank on him. Maybe she was trying the same on Rutherford. He picked up the desk phone and called downstairs.

"*PC Dowd*," came the voice.

"Neil, it's Avalon, have you seen anything of DC Rutherford? He's our new chap."

"*Oh morning sir, er no*," he hesitated a little, which was uncharacteristic for Dowd, "*but on the other hand a cross between King Kong and an angry bulldog brought two minutes of shadow to the front desk ef that helps*."

"I detect PC Dowd," smiled Avalon, "that you may have met our newest recruit to C Section."

"*Well ef he es, I reckon you may have to vacate*

276

the Cave and find a hangar down at the airport," added Dowd, "*he's just gone off with PC Kirk, et looked like a bison being led by one of et's fleas*," Avalon smiled and thanked Dowd.

"What's so funny?" asked Ross as Avalon replaced the phone.

"Dowd just met Rutherford," and he continued with the smile.

"So I assume Neil imparted some wisdom upon you?" Avalon nodded and said,

"Kirk is with him, I suppose they'll be up here soon."

When the knock came, Ross was back at his desk and he looked round to the door as Kirk entered, with the oversize detective following. To Avalon, Rutherford seemed to fill the whole door and the spectacle wasn't lost on the rest of the room and there was more than one gaping mouth as Kirk ushered the big man to the booth.

"Detective Constable Martin Rutherford reporting to C section sir," said Kirk with an amused glare.

"Thank you constable," he said to Kirk who smartly left and to Rutherford he said, "take a seat Martin." The big man sat lightly on the chair opposite and looked across to his new boss.

"I realise that you are new to both the CID and the section but I don't have much time to ease you in to our methods," he began, "we're as busy as ever so you'll have to move around where you're needed." The man nodded. "We work as a team in here, if that goes against how you expected to work then you won't last long in C section. There are some basic ground rules which one of the team will let you into I'm sure, any questions?"

277

Rutherford took in breath and said,

"No questions guv'nor, but I just want to apologise-"

"Don't apologise Detective Constable, you weren't officially working for C section when you made your outburst and in any case, DS Ross was in the wrong. As I see it, if you have to apologise you have made a mistake, I don't like mistakes so I don't expect apologies, is that clear?" Rutherford nodded and so Avalon held out his hand across the table and Rutherford shook it. Avalon felt the size of the man's hand, it looked like a father shaking the hand of the child and Avalon was the child. He stood and took Rutherford into the Cave. There was silence.

"People, this is DC Martin Rutherford, yes he's big, get over it," announced Avalon, "show him the ropes and let him know how we work. Mack, he'll have to share your desk until we can find room as you are out most of this week." Mack nodded, still mesmerised by Rutherford. "Megan, can you sort him out with all the relevant computer access,"

"Aye boss," she nodded and she pointed to a chair near the coffee machine, "Y' better bring that over here," she added for the benefit of the big DC. Avalon returned to the booth and tried not to look back into the Cave to see how they were reacting. If he couldn't see it, it couldn't be a problem.

Over an hour later, his work pile seemed just as large as it had when he started and he stretched his legs under the table as he noticed Rory on his way to the booth.

"We're in," smiled Rory.

"To Stodart's email account?" asked Avalon excitedly. Rory nodded and they both went to Mackinnon's desk where Frazer was already looking

278

through them. She looked up as Avalon approached.

"He's got 211 new emails so I'm checking through them first boss," she explained.

"Do them later," insisted Avalon, "I'm more interested in the week or so leading up to Mrs Stodart's disappearance, I need to know if there is anything still there." It took Frazer several minutes and she confirmed their fears, Stodart had erased all his emails from the server. The ones showing had come in since his death.

"Et looks like we need tae find the laptop boss," she sighed.

"I can maybe get around that problem," added Rory.

"Then do it," insisted Avalon and Frazer moved to allow Mackinnon to have access the keyboard.

"If I set up an account on this machine based on his own login, I can probably get his address book."

"Will it do that though?" asked Ross who had joined the group around the desk.

"Not sure," shrugged Rory as he furiously tapped away at the keyboard, "it depends on the ISP's system but it's worth a try." Rory set up the new account and asked the machine to import the contact list.

"It's bringing something in," he said. Avalon watched as the copy account refreshed and then stabilised. Rory then clicked to open the address book.

"Bingo," smiled Rory, "he didn't delete his contacts."

"Right," said Avalon, "you and Megan go through all the contacts, I need to know who each one of them is and as soon as you have something, let me know." He turned away and caught Ross's eye. "Let's hope this goes somewhere," he said raising his eyebrows. Ross nodded. The process didn't take long and both Frazer and Ross entered the booth.

"We might have a possible," frowned Frazer.

"Go on," insisted Avalon.

"We found one email address from a company called B.I.F.S. which is a dodgy set-up with connections to Charlie Sands," Frazer explained.

"Never heard of him or the company," replied Avalon with a shrug.

"He's a well known scammer," explained Ross, "who tries to legitimise his crooked methods by fronting it by registered companies, in this case Black Isle Financial Services. The contact is backed up by the fact that another email contact is 'Garbh', another name that Sands goes by."

"What's his angle?" asked Avalon.

"Money laundering, loan sharking, dodgy land contracts an' on occasions he's been known tae work as a fence," explained Frazer.

"He tries to live the high life," added Ross, "doing his best to stay out of trouble and making out he's legitimate."

"Big house, flashy cars, gold jewellery, y' know the sort," explained Frazer. Avalon was nodding.

"Is he the sort to whack a customer on the head with a wheel brace if they don't pay their debts though?" he asked.

"He's been known to rough people up, he has a few 'heavies' for that job," explained Frazer, "but he's not a killer, a complete bastard but not a killer."

"Well, he's all we've got at the moment, where's he live?" Avalon asked.

"Just outside Muir of Ord, he had a place built, I think it's called 'Ormond'," replied Frazer.

"Strange name, Irish isn't it? I recall the Earl of

Ormond fought in the Wars of the Roses," frowned Avalon.

"I don't know about that but Sands styles himself after William the Lion and *he* was Scottish," explained Ross, "I think the name Garbh means 'the rough' which was the nickname of William the Lion."

"Aye, he takes it all serious, he's somehow related through his mothers side to the Munro family, historically they had land on the Black Isle," added Frazer.

"So if you know this much about him, you must have had plenty of contact with him?" asked Avalon with a serious frown.

"Yeah," nodded Ross, "he was sent down for fraud when he was young and came onto the radar some years ago in another fraud case but he more or less got away with it. Since then he's known to engage in very dubious commercial deals with high-return loans but so far he has kept his nose relatively clean."

"I once had him on surveillance during an investigation into money laundering," nodded Frazer, "but he is pretty careful these days," then she lowered her voice which was a pointless gesture as everyone was close enough to hear. "He has been know to point certain coppers in the right direction on occasions." Avalon went quiet. He leaned back in his seat and looked up at the ceiling for some moments and then sat up and asked,

"What's happened in the past can stay in the past, I want to know about the here and now. You know enough about him, what do *you* think?" Frazer looked over to Ross who looked back in turn and then he turned to Avalon.

"I can see he would be involved with Stodart, he's exactly the sort of person Peter Stodart would seek out to raise cash but..." he trailed off shaking his head.

"I agree," cut in Frazer, "he'd certainly be someone en the frame for the loans but I just can't see Sands getting into murder," she paused, "not intentionally anyways."

"Okay," nodded Avalon, "we need to speak to Mr Sands." He stood and looked directly at Frazer. "Find out anything you can on Sands, not just criminal activity I want to know more about him, someone that styles himself on an historical character must have a complex lifestyle." Frazer nodded and Avalon turned to Ross. "You and I," he continued, "are off to Muir of Ord."

As they walked down the stairs to the car park, Ross's phone rang.

"DS Ross," he said and he stopped walking, Avalon turned but Ross gave nothing away in his face. "Oh, right," he said and then he added, "just one moment," and he held the phone to his chest and looked to Avalon. "I'll just be a minute." Avalon nodded and walked into the passageway and left Ross to his phone call. It must have been personal because as Ross caught up with Avalon he was quiet and said nothing about the call.

Ross drove and as they went north, Frazer rang Avalon to update him on everything she could find on Charlie Sands. It wasn't much and it wasn't important but Avalon liked to know the enemy before he went into battle. During the journey, Ross had been unusually quiet and Avalon couldn't help thinking it was to do with the phone call he had taken earlier. Twice Avalon had tried to start conversations, mainly about the information that Frazer had equipped him with, but Ross was unresponsive.

"Something wrong?" Avalon had asked but Ross

glanced over, shaking his head and said,

"No, why?" Avalon didn't pursue it, if Ross wanted to talk Avalon was there. The problem was, Ross was like Avalon in that respect, he kept his personal thoughts and troubles to himself, it wasn't healthy but neither of them could change. As they arrived at the large house called Ormond, Avalon had decided to forget about Ross's problem for the time being, whatever it was. In the drive was a new Jaguar and a Porsche Carrera.

"He makes more than a detective inspector then?" said Avalon nodding to the cars. Ross just shrugged and walked to the large door. The house was quite a property, built on a single floor it was much more than a bungalow. The layout was typical of a bespoke build and the grounds were extensive with some woodland to the rear. The views were excellent, it was obvious the spot was chosen well. The drive wasn't the usual cheap gravel sort either, the whole area was a sea of red brick sets in swirling designs. The drive probably cost more than Avalon could afford for a house. Ross had pulled the doorbell which made no sound outside and the large, impressive door swung open to reveal a smartly dress man who looked almost as well built as DC Rutherford.

"Yeah?" he asked and Avalon had already guessed that this wasn't Charlie Sands.

"Is Mr Sands available?" he asked.

"Name?" the man asked. Avalon noticed the man look them both up and down as if someone had dropped a couple of dog turds on the doorstep.

"Avalon, Detective Inspector Avalon," came the reply.

"Appointment?" he asked. Ross didn't seem in a very patient mood and turned to Avalon.

"A single word warrior," and then he turned to the man, "he probably struggles with two together." The man glared at Ross.

"No appointment but we just want to talk to him for a few minutes," insisted Avalon.

"No appointment no interview," he replied and then leaned forward to Ross, "an' that's four words gobshyte." Ross smiled but Avalon knew Ross was fuming. The man was about to close the door but Avalon stepped closer.

"You better tell Mr Sands that we are here to talk to him about his involvement with Peter Stodart, we'll wait here for..." he looked at his watch, "sixty seconds and then we leave to get a search warrant and then I'll be back to take Mr Sands in." The man closed the door and Ross walked towards the Porsche, he bent and looked inside.

"We're in the wrong business," he said as he returned to the doorstep. Avalon made no comment, he looked at his watch and as soon as the minute was up he turned and stepped purposefully back to Ross's BMW. The door to the house suddenly opened and the man said,

"He'll see y', he's on the phone." The man had a thick accent, probably from the other coast but Avalon felt a little easier as he lead them into an anti room. The house was sumptuously decorated, Avalon knew little about art but he realised most of the ornaments and the antique furniture for that matter were not fakes. The man didn't ask them to sit, he just waited staring at them until Sands was ready, Avalon was used to this, it made these sort of people feel they were in control. Ross however seemed agitated and Avalon could sense he was boiling up inside. The anti room was fairly large with two polished wine cabinets near the double doors that Avalon assumed was the room where Sands was, and to the left was a French polished table with an old style nineteen seventies desk phone on it. The room looked more like the hall of a colonial consul than the entrance to a Scottish crook's home. Avalon looked back to the man, he was glaring directly at him and Avalon could feel himself becoming agitated too.

"What do you know about Peter Stodart?" he asked. The man curled his nose as he spoke.

"I don't answer questions and I particularly don't answer questions from your sort," he turned to Ross, "what the hell are you doin' working with the English?" he added. It was a mistake, Ross had probably been waiting for a chance to wind the man up.

"It's funny," he smiled, "I don't particularly dislike anyone, no matter what country they are from, I tend to assess everyone as an individual. I don't even mind some Glaswegians," and then he instantly dropped the smile and hissed, "but I've wiped better things than you off my arse." Avalon tried not to laugh as he turned away but then there was movement and a crash. He spun quickly to see the man sprawled on the floor and Ross leaning over him with the nineteen seventies phone in his hand above his head and it looked like it was about to come down on the prostrate figure.

"DS Ross!" called Avalon. Ross stopped. "I hope you are going to use that telephone to call for an ambulance and not comb this gentleman's hair." He walked closer as Ross dropped the phone onto the French table with a crash and crouched by the man who was holding his private region and seemed in terrible pain. "Oh, I should have mentioned that Ross here has special police training in just about everything except dinner party small talk and inventive needlecraft." The man was still rolling in agony. "Now then, tell me where Sands is or I'll let Ross continue with his phone call." The man seemed loath to remove his hands from his privates but he gradually did with one of them and pointed to the double doors. Avalon made straight to the door shooting Ross a withering stare and walked through to find a smartly dressed man behind an extremely large desk, a large cathedral-style window lit the room. The man was on the phone and as he saw Avalon and Ross he said,

"Er, I've got to go, something has cropped up." He put down the phone as he looked to the door behind them.

"Your man is..." Avalon paused, "er, indisposed, now then Mr Sands we can do this the easy way or the very hard way, it's up to you." The man gave another quick look to the doors and then gave a weak smile.

"Please gentleman, take a seat, I was on the phone to my solicitor." His accent was probably of the Inverness locality thought Avalon.

"Have you need of his services Mr Sands?" asked Avalon.

"I don't know yet Mr..." the man waited for Avalon to explain.

"Detective Inspector Avalon, Inverness, this is Detective Sergeant Ross, we are investigating the murder of Peter Stodart." To Avalon's surprise, Sands who was probably in his sixties nodded and steepled his hands on the desk.

"Yes, I wondered if that would eventually bring you here."

"So you know something about the case Mr Sands?"

"Yes unfortunately I do," he nodded again. "Peter Stodart was a customer of mine."

"You loaned him money?" asked Avalon knowing the answer. The man nodded yet again.

"That's right, he was in some financial trouble and came to me, but sadly at the time I didn't realise how much trouble, or any of the other kinds of trouble he was in."

"So I'm guessing you asked for your money back?" asked Avalon.

"Of course, it was all done through Black Isle Financial Services, I have all the paperwork," insisted Sands.

"So I'm also guessing he couldn't pay it back?"

"No he couldn't, he even had the temerity to ask me for more and when I refused, he threatened me," explained Sands removing his hands from the table.

"He threatened you?" asked Avalon.

"Yes, he said he would tell the police what I was doing but as I explained to him the loans were totally legal."

"Except for the money laundering workaround," interrupted Ross.

"There is no money laundering involved Detective Ross," smiled the man.

"So knowing he had no money to pay you back what did you do?"

"The only thing I could, I threatened to take his house from him, I had a contract, it would take time but I could do it," explained Sands. Avalon knew the man would employ other methods but there was nothing he could accuse him of.

"Did you kill Mr Stodart or have him killed Mr Sands?" he asked. Sands leaned back shaking his head, a slight smile entered the corners of his mouth.

"It's not my style, it's not profitable, I like my customers alive and well. Dead men can't pay their debts," he said.

"So do you know *who* killed him?" Avalon asked but he wasn't prepared for the answer.

"I believe I do." Avalon looked at Ross then turned back to Sands.

"Care to explain?"

"I made the mistake in employing two people for my courier work, unfortunately they turned out to be utter misfits." Avalon stared at Sands and raised an eyebrow, it was clear he wanted names. The man nodded a little and then said, "They are known as the Thompson brothers." Ross made a stilted laugh.

"You employed *them*, they are also known as the Twisted Thompson Twins?" he remarked and looked around at Avalon with surprise. Avalon looked vague and Ross realised Avalon wouldn't have heard about them.

"Two bad sorts, not real brothers, but they have the same name," he began, "from Liverpool, Tony likes to dress like a gangster, he's sort of in charge though even he can't control Eric," he paused turning to Sands, "you know these two are subhuman."

"I have to employ certain unsavoury sorts but I admit I made a mistake with these two,"

"So you sent these two to threaten Peter Stodart?" asked Avalon.

"Far from it detective," sighed Sands, "Peter Stodart hatched a plan and he actually rang me to tell me about it, I told him never to ring me but he was like that. He was always more important than anyone else."

"I take it you didn't like him then?" asked Avalon.

"Of course I didn't like him, but I'm not Tesco's, I

don't have to smile as I do business," insisted Sands with a little venom, "he was a cheap, conniving little bastard who got nothing more than he deserved." He paused and composed himself. "Even so, I have never resorted to killing a person just because I don't like them, half of the county would be floating in the Moray Firth if that were the case."

"So tell me about the call," insisted Avalon.

"He said he had come up with a great way to raise cash, but his 'get rich quick' plan needed my help. He suggested that I could kidnap his wife and then between us we could demand money from her family. As soon as he suggested it I refused and I knew I had to sever all contact with him. And I did. I more or less wrote off the money he owned me, I knew he had lost all sense of reality. When she went missing I thought he had decided to do it by himself and being a 'crack head' I knew it would turn out bad, the problem I had was that all my business was done by email." Sands paused and sighed again. "It was then I knew I had to get hold of his laptop, his communications could implicate me, and killing people is very much against my ethic no matter what the police think about me."

"So you sent these two men to get it?" asked Avalon.

"Yes, but only after I got a tip off that he was out."

"From who?" asked Avalon.

"Unfortunately, I can't tell you, I wish I knew who it was. I thought it was someone who had financial interests in him at the time but I rather think it may have been someone who doesn't like me a great deal. It was a text message that seemed to come from another business associate but it wasn't. It seems you can use an Internet site to send anonymous texts and emails. The text said if I wanted the laptop I should go straight away as he was out," he paused, "but I gave the Thompsons strict instructions that the laptop was all I wanted. They had been the couriers for the money so they knew Stodart, and they did find the laptop and brought it back. They failed to mention that he was dead, so when I heard about it on the news I asked them what happened. They assured me that he was dead when they got there. Of course, I didn't believe them and severed contact with them straight away." He paused again and looked out of the large windows, "I've been talking to my solicitor ever since."

"I'm guessing he doesn't know what to tell you?" said Avalon, the man shrugged.

"Where's the laptop?" asked Ross.

"I disposed of it," answered Sands.

"This doesn't get you off the hook Mr Sands," insisted Avalon.

"I realise that, but I don't want blood on my hands," he said looking back to Avalon.

"I think it's too late for that," said Avalon but Sands said nothing.

"Do you know where we can find the Thompsons?" asked Ross.

"I have a couple of addresses but I made it very clear I was furious about this and I warned them to stay out of the area."

"From what I know of the Thompson Twins they won't give a shit about threats," frowned Ross. Sands shrugged.

"Maybe, maybe not," he said.

"You're taking this very calmly Mr Sands," frowned Avalon.

"I rarely get excited about anything these days detective," replied Sands with a distant look.

"You could be looking at a long spell at her majesty's pleasure," added Avalon, "and I'm sure the conversation with your solicitor was about that possibility but even if you dodge under the radar over your *business* association with Peter Stodart, you are certainly guilty of not reporting a crime and could be charged with perverting the course of justice and that carries a maximum of ten years."

"And that's if you can prove you had nothing to do with the murder," added Ross. Sands looked over to Ross and then back to Avalon.

"Bodies are not something I want on my conscience," he frowned, "as I have said, neither are they my style, yes I made a mistake employing the Thompsons but-"

"That makes you complicit," insisted Ross, "employing these two arseholes makes you guilty."

"My solicitor sees it differently, particularly if I help you sort this out," shrugged Sands. Avalon sighed, he knew what Sands was getting at but Avalon wasn't in the mood for making deals, people like Sands were just as bad as the Thompsons, even if he was telling the truth. He stood.

"I'm not sure this needs sorting out Mr Sands," he announced, Ross got the message and also stood, "it seems to me that we know exactly who is responsible and the course of justice will be implemented."

"I see," frowned Sands leaning back in his chair. Avalon expected Sands to make further comment as he and Ross left but he didn't, as the two men left, he opened a small drawer and took out a powdery, yellow ball and placed it in his mouth. Out in the anti room the large man was still in agony and another man had joined him. The injured man looked up at Ross and gave him a deathly stare saying,

"You an' me are gonna meet again."

"I dearly hope so," hissed Ross, "and next time the Englishman won't be there to hold me back." As they walked back to Ross's car Avalon made no comment but by the time they were back on the main road he slammed Ross for his behaviour. Ross didn't think he had seen Avalon quite so angry, it was such a shock to him he made no 'smart' comments, no jokes, he made no comment whatsoever. Avalon said nothing else all the way back to Inverness. The only other noise he made was to phone Frazer to put out a 'Be On the Look Out' for the Thompson Twins. Back at the station Avalon walked off quickly from Ross and by the time the DS was back in the Cave Avalon had still not arrived there. He had taken a route through the station and out of the front door, he then went around the building and re-entered the car park through the gate. He jumped in his car and drove quickly out.

~~~~~~

Avalon didn't quite know how he had managed it, he was in Drumnadrochit, for him at least, it seemed all roads lead to the little village beside Loch Ness. He pulled into the car park and got out of the car into some of the first sunshine he had seen in weeks. He crossed the road and went to purchase a coffee and returned outside to glory in the brief rays of sunlight. As he sat he realised that he was being a fool, had things really got on top of him? That seemed doubtful, he had lived through worse times than this in Wolverhampton so what the hell was going wrong with him? He had just severely berated Ross for losing his temper at Charlie Sand's house, not just because of Ross's outburst but because something was obviously going on in Ross's life and yet he hadn't spoken of it to Avalon. Yet here he was, running away from his responsibilities for much the same reason, simply because he had no one to talk to. His short time with Julia Beattie had given him a feel of what real life was like, the stomach churning, the childish laughter, the company, all things that Avalon had thought were no longer possible and yet for that evening that Ross had left them alone, he had once more enjoyed those things. Then the cold reality struck him. Julia had sent him a text but he had forgotten about it, the case had taken precedence and he had damn well forgotten about it. He pulled the phone out of his pocket, after all it was just this morning, wasn't it? He couldn't remember, he really couldn't remember when it was. He read the text.

"Hello you, just wondered if you were heading north anytime soon?" He swallowed hard, here he was wishing he had a normal life and yet he was reading a message that was probably a way to experience just that and all he could feel was fear. He rarely felt fear, not in the usual sense of the word but this was unadulterated fear. Fear that he had to make a decision to either see her again or save her the heartache of a detective's cruel life and tell her the truth that he wouldn't be going back to Golspie. Not to socialise at any rate. He sighed and put his phone back in his pocket, he could answer later, at the moment he was struggling with other issues, how to explain why he had run away? He didn't have to explain it to the office, that was a perk of being a DI, but explaining it to himself was a whole different matter. Had he actually run away? Probably, it was easy to

explain it as 'needing some air' or 'needing time to think' but it still felt like he had run away. He began to feel a little childish and so he tried to think of a more rational reason he was sitting outside a cafe in Drumnadrochit. He looked at the coffee and took a sip, it tasted fine so he tried to consider his next move. He then took out his notepad to make a few notes and noticed some scrawled verses, they were attempts to write lyrics for the song he had written, but they had turned out more like a poem by Wordsworth than lyrics to a song. He looked around the village, people were going about their business and even this early in the season he could see several holidaymakers. He wasn't sure what made them so obvious, maybe it was the way they looked around as if they were wearing special spectacles that made everything look rainbow coloured. Avalon glanced down at the notepad again, pulled the pencil from the spine of the pad and looked at the paper and crossed the verse out, he wondered what the song should be about. Maybe a love song? He had fallen in love with Scotland but maybe that wouldn't quite do. Should it be about Julia? Probably not, particularly if he wasn't going to see her again. What was he doing? He was swimming through the deep end of a major case and here he was trying to write words for a love song. Was he truly mad? Probably, and yet the pencil was writing away, word after blessed word and the thing was, they were the best lyrics he had penned yet. Why was that? He examined his thoughts deeper and what he saw annoyed him somewhat, he could see an image of Sarah Underwood. Was he so besotted by her that he had even driven to where he last saw her, Drumnadrochit? That must be it, he must be infatuated with her.

"Well, fancy seeing you here?" he heard her

voice, the way she spoke, that slight but sweet Scottish lilt that the tones of her speech made. He could see her face, smiling down, her hair silhouetted against the thin rays of a cool sun. "Has this become a regular stop?" Avalon blinked, this wasn't in his mind, what a fool, she was there, standing in front of him and he was sitting like a lunatic with his mouth open, his head drizzled with stupid thought. He jolted upright and almost knocked the lightweight table over, coffee spilled onto it.

"Oh, er," he shot to his feet stuttering, "oh I was miles away, would you like a drink?" He took out his handkerchief and mopped the table.

"Oh, not thanks, I've just had one at my sister's, are you alright?" she asked as he threw the hankie into a nearby bin.

"Yes, fine," he lied, "I was just trying to piece together some aspects of the case," he lied further.

"Do you mind if I sit?"

"No, not at all," he said, "you sure you wouldn't like a coffee or something?" She shook her head.

"No thanks, I'm sure."

"So what are you doing down here," he asked sitting once more, "I would have thought you would be sweating over a hot microscope."

"I am actually working, it sounds odd but we want a test example of Thunbergia alata for the lab, and I just happen to know my sister had one on her patio. It's better known as Black-eyed Susan," explained Sarah.

"Oh," replied Avalon, not knowing the slightest thing about gardening, "quite a coincidence seeing you here then."

"Well, actually, I was going to bring in the reports from the Stodart's house and vehicle so I rang your office, they told me you weren't there."

"Oh," smiled Avalon finishing his coffee.

"And DS Ross told me he didn't have a clue where you had gone," she further explained but Avalon just gave a thin smile, "he seemed to think..." she paused, Avalon dropped the smile.

"Think what?"

"Oh, he said you may be out of the office for the rest of the day," she eventually said but Avalon began to wonder if she and Ross had been talking about him. It was doubtful however, he hadn't known the two of them have any other type of conversation than a professional one.

"I needed a bit of a break from the office," he shrugged. He noticed her look down at the notepad, which was still open, he gathered it up wiping a splash of coffee from it saying,

"Just making a few notes about the case," and he gave a weak grin and placed the pad back in his jacket pocket. He wondered why he was being so defensive, was he still trying to impress her? He knew this childish behaviour wouldn't, so he sighed deeply and decided to tell her the truth. "No that's not correct, I was writing down some words, a verse."

"Of course, you're into poetry," she smiled.

"It's actually for a song, it's not a great song and the words stink but..." he trailed off with both a shrug and a smile.

"A song? Do you play then?" she asked.

"I torture a guitar now and then, I can't play very well so I wrote a bit of a tune from the chords I can just about manage," he explained.

"I'd like to hear it one day, what's it called?"

"I don't know because as soon as I write some words I scribble them out."

"It must be difficult writing a song," she smiled.

"More than I can describe," he nodded.

"Well, as soon as it's finished I'd love to be the first to hear it."

"Really?" he asked with surprise.

"Yes, of course," she returned the smile with a slight amount of embarrassment. Avalon always felt childish and giddy when he was with her but the embarrassed look made him wonder if she really did like him, after all this time, could he still have a chance with her? He passed it off has his weird imagination.

"Okay, it's a date," he grinned, "but don't say I didn't warn you," and she gave a slight laugh at this.

"I'm sure it will be fine." She began to stand and Avalon followed suit. "Well I must get on, my plant specimen needs to be fairly fresh," she said patting her small shopping bag.

"Yes, me too, I better ring in and let them know where I am." He had no intention of ringing in but he did need to move on. He accompanied her towards the car park and after she handed him the reports they parted company but Avalon's phone rang, he was surprised that it wasn't anyone from the office but rather a number he didn't know.

"Avalon," he said as he watched Sarah's car head off towards the far end of the village. It was Charlie Sand's solicitor trying his best to convince Avalon that his client had nothing to do with the death of Peter Stodart and assuring him that Mr Sands would co-operate fully to the mutual benefit of both parties. Which in legal parlance meant that Sands would squeal as long as Avalon wouldn't prosecute. The man also furnished him with two address in Inverness which he implied were known contact address of the so-called Thompson

Twins, the real murderers in the case. Avalon feeling much more positive told the man that he couldn't promise anything but agreed that if Mr Sands did indeed co-operate he could assure them that he would only pursue lines of inquiry connected directly to the death of Peter Stodart. This in turn was Avalon's rhetoric for 'if your client doesn't squeal I will take great care to find all the 'dirt' there is on Charlie Sands'. There was no positive reaction however, he just told Avalon that he and his client would review their options and contact the police with their decision. Avalon ended the call staring at the phone for a moment, promising himself he would contact Julia Beattie before the day was done.

Once again Avalon climbed the stairs to the upper floor and headed to the office they all knew as the Cave and entered with purpose as if he had just returned from an important mission. He didn't look into the room at fist but Frazer called over to him.

"Boss, the DCI wants tae see you." Avalon raised his eyebrows and turned to leave the way he had just entered. He may as well get it over with, Croker was probably going to tear a strip off him for going off the radar. He knocked at the door and entered.

"Ah, Avalon, take a seat." He didn't seem angry, he didn't even seem his usual agitated self but Avalon was cautious as he sat. DCI Croker looked at Avalon over the top of his tiny spectacles and said,

"I have been speaking with the Superintendent this morning and we have decided to review the procedures of your section." To Avalon that mean he had been told that he wasn't happy with Croker's system and so Avalon listened with interest to what that would mean for him and his team. "I accept," he continued, "that the numbers and let us say 'quality' of the recent recruits to B and C section have been lacking somewhat."

"Honestly sir, I'm reasonably happy with the new staff, of course I have no experience of Rutherford but-"

"Ah, yes, Rutherford," interrupted Croker removing his spectacles and massaging his eyes, "Rutherford is quite an anomaly. His record in the force is reasonable enough but he doesn't seem to be CID material."

"Well, he's observant," smiled Avalon remembering his 'test' in the vehicle compound.

"Quite, but as we know," continued Croker, "being observant isn't the only quality we require." Avalon didn't answer, he waited for Croker to tell him the alterations. "As it is, the Superintendent and myself think that given lack of staff we should revert back to the situation as it was previously, I have updated the other DIs to the decision."

"So we'll be working in Inverness again?" asked Avalon.

"Indeed, B Section have come under a great deal of strain of late and from what I can gather your section to a degree has had some respite," frowned the DCI.

"We still have twenty three ongoing cases with over thirty long-term investigations," said Avalon but Croker simply nodded and added,

"I realise the workload DI Avalon but the nature of those cases is quite different to the inner city work of B Section," insisted Croker and then he shrugged returning his spectacles to his head, "if things change in the nature of the staffing I have assured the Superintendent that I will be more than happy to continue with the system." Avalon nodded, he didn't want to say goodbye to the rural cases but he knew some of his team saw their work as less important than that of B section.

He left Croker's office and made a further attempt to return to the Cave and he made his way straight to the booth. He was still angry with Ross who seemed to be gazing out of the window. It was a sure sign he had something on his mind. He looked around his staff, Wilson and MacDonald were back in but they were still busy with their cases. He considered sending Mackinnon to check the address he had for the Thompson Twins but he didn't think he was quite ready for the likes of those people. He just didn't want to send Ross. It would have to be Frazer, she could take Rutherford with her as protection, not that Frazer necessarily needed any protection. He stood and put his head around the corner of the booth.

"Megan, got a minute?" he called. She stood and entered the booth.

"Boss?"

"I have a couple of addresses for the two Thompsons, I want you to check them out and see if you can see signs of them at either address."

"Are these the same two that they call the Thompson Twins?" she asked folding her arms.

"The very same so be careful as they may be the killers of Peter Stodart, and take Rutherford with you."

"Rutherford?" she questioned, "et's going to be a very inventive surveillance with the big man, can't I have a normal size officer?" Avalon saw what she was getting at, he would draw attention to himself even sat in a car. Avalon looked over to the large DC and tried to imagine him in the passenger seat of Frazer's small car, it would look like an inflatable rescue dingy had accidentally gone off in a telephone box.

300

"Okay, I'll see what Rory is up to," and he stood and walked into the Cave. "Rory, are you up for a drive out with Megan on a surveillance job?"

"Aye, no trouble, I'm just writing reports at the mo boss," Mackinnon was always eager for something different. "What is it?" he added.

"Two nutcases so no heroics and follow Megan's orders to the letter," replied Avalon and he returned to the booth as the two officers prepared to leave. Ross was soon in the booth.

"So why am I not on this?"

"I think you know why," answered Avalon, "your earlier outburst makes me believe you have something on your mind and as such you are making some errors in judgement."

"That bastard over at Sand's place went for me," hissed Ross.

"I know, but kneeing him in the nuts was enough, you didn't have to smash his skull in with an unfashionable telephone, that could have cost you dearly." Ross backed off slightly.

"Yeah, he did get to me, but I wouldn't have actually done it," he shrugged.

"I don't know that, so what is on your mind?" asked Avalon. Ross stared at him and sat.

"I may as well tell you, maybe you can come up with an answer." He sighed and then rubbed his brow. "I got a call from the people who run the safe deposit boxes, the one that Arty Struther rented," Avalon raised his eyebrows, "they opened it up and looking inside, it had a photograph of a baby, some other paperwork, almost six hundred in old cash and a letter. "

"Six hundred quid, and so what happened?" asked Avalon.

"Well I asked him to read the letter, he didn't want to at first but I reminded him who I was and he agreed," Ross paused, he seemed under some pressure, Avalon was beginning to wonder what was in the letter. Ross sighed and then continued. "The upshot of it is, Arty had a daughter, from his marriage, he didn't know until after he left and it seems it bothered him for the rest of his life so he tried to save money to send her later in life. He never managed anymore than just over six hundred or so," Ross paused again as he heard Frazer enter.

"We're off then Boss, we'll just check around and then start a proper surveillance en the mornin'," she said. Avalon nodded but Ross added,

"Watch yourselves, those two have a reputation."

"Okay dad, I'll try tae get back before et goes dark?" she replied and Ross just shook his head as she and Rory left.

"So, you were saying," said Avalon. Ross looked at him and then sighed once again.

"Well, the silly old sod had this six hundred quid to give to his daughter, I mean six hundred?" Ross held out his arms in a questioning manner, "it may have seemed like a lot twenty years ago but these days it wouldn't buy her a new phone."

"I don't think that is the point, he somehow managed to gather all that money over the years and keep it safe, can you imagine how difficult that was for him?"

"Yeah, difficult," nodded Ross, "but it would have been much better if he had cleaned himself up and gone to see her," answered Ross in a bitter tone, "instead he expected me to go to her with a few hundred quid and say 'this is from your old man, go and get your hair done', it just seems awkward to me." Avalon nodded, he could see Ross's point but he had options.

"Do you know where she is, or even who she is?" he asked. Ross shrugged and said,

"There are some clues in the letter and I suppose it wouldn't be too difficult to track her down but then what?"

"Parcel up everything you have and post it on as his effects, I don't think she'll lose many tears over him anyway," suggested Avalon.

"Yeah probably," he replied but Avalon could see he was still troubled by it. There wasn't much else he could suggest, it was something Ross had to sort out, all Avalon could do was be there for him.

"Do you want to go for a wet tonight?" he asked thinking it may be a way to get him to talk about it. Ross looked up, it wasn't usual for Avalon to suggest a trip to the pub.

"Why, do I look like I need it?" he asked.

"It was just a thought, I understand if you want to be by yourself, you know, to think it over," said Avalon.

"Have you ever known me refuse to go for a drink?" frowned Ross.

"The Castle Tavern, eight thirty then?" smiled Avalon.

Chapter Ten

As he sat in the booth on yet another busy morning Avalon noticed his phone vibrate and light up. It was another text from Julia Beattie. Luckily he had remembered to send her a message the night before but three factors made that an irresponsible thing to do. Firstly he was tired, secondly he wasn't a 'texty' sort of person and thirdly, but more importantly, even though he didn't wear spectacles, in dark places he struggled to see fine detail. So, while they were at the pub the previous evening and trying not to let Ross see he was texting, he waited for his drinking partner to visit the lavatory before sending the reply. This meant that it was a hurried message in the low light of the Castle Tavern. Needless to say, Julia had sent another message asking him what 'geespmetime' meant. He felt embarrassed, he made a mental note that he should not text people, ever, just as soon as he had sent a reply - by text message explaining that his phone seemed to be making up some strange words and he would get it sorted out. He also added he would ring her later. That part he wasn't sure of, he didn't know what to tell her. Frazer entered the booth.

"How did you go on yesterday Megan?"

"No' bad, we didn't see any movement at the

Hilton address, we did see a shifty looking type at the second address though. But then again et's one o' those estates," she replied.

"What sort of estates?" asked Avalon not sure what she meant.

"Och, y' know, where every house looks exactly the same so they have tae paint their doors different colours tae know where they live," she frowned with distain.

"We can't all live in a farmhouse in six acres of woodland," explained Avalon with a frown.

"No comment," she shrugged, "so what do y' want us tae do?" Avalon thought for a moment, he couldn't see any reason why the Thompsons couldn't be brought in if they were there.

"Okay, let's set up an arrest, contact uniform and see if we can gather some bodies as assistance," nodded Avalon, "let Ross know and keep Rory on the job too."

"Tactical?" she asked.

"I don't think they're particularly dangerous, if they killed Peter Stodart they did it with a wheel brace not a shooter so I don't think so, but don't go with too few people." Frazer nodded. "In the meantime I'll get the warrants sorted." Frazer left the booth to prepare and Avalon got straight on the phone, when he had set the operation in motion he went to tell Croker. It was his modus operandi to keep the DCI informed, he had been caught out in the past. Avalon decided to be present at the operation but he would let Ross do the actual arrest.

Some hours later, they sat in several cars and an unmarked van, parked on the road close to the address that the two men might be using. As soon as movement could be seen in the house the operation began. Ross and

Frazer moved to the property with the uniform team, several secured the area and the others were present to support Ross. Another pair of officers arrived with the 'big key', which was a small battering ram to break down the door if the occupants were unhelpful. Ross knocked at the door and stood back. An untidy man opened it and Ross read him his rights and cuffed him as the rest of the officers poured into the house. Just over an hour later, Eric Thompson was in custody at Inverness police station but Tony's whereabouts was unknown. Avalon had seen Frazer under many situations and he did consider her to be a hard working and thorough police officer, but due to her past and just a tiny bit of doubt, he decided to allow Ross and Boyd to conduct the interview of Eric Thompson. Then, to Avalon's surprise, before the interview of Eric was complete, the other suspect, Tony Thomson gave himself up and was also in custody. Avalon decided to take Mackinnon and interview the man himself.

Avalon made sure that Ross knew that both men were in custody, it may help with the interview by giving Ross a bit more leverage. Avalon set about questioning Tony Thomson. He was a pure opposite of his dishevelled partner in many ways. He was dressed smartly with a reasonably expensive suit and high-quality accessories but he didn't speak much and as Avalon sat opposite him in interview room two he quickly decided that if the man had given himself up he must be prepared to at least tell him something, even if it was lies. Tony hadn't asked for a solicitor so none was provided but Avalon asked him questions before he decided to change his mind. As he looked at the charge sheet, he noticed that Tony's name was spelled without the letter 'P'.

"So why have you handed yourself in Tony?" he

asked. The man made no response for a moment and then he looked over to Mackinnon before his eyes once more fell on Avalon.

"Why have you arrested Eric?" he asked in a calm and clear voice. There was a Liverpool accent there for sure but it wasn't as broad as Eric's.

"I think you know that," replied Avalon, "we think you and he are involved with the murder of Peter Stodart up at Golspie."

"That's not true, did Sands tell you we did it?"

"Were you involved?" asked Avalon.

"You need to talk to Sands, that bastard is trying to set us up," replied Thomson.

"We know you were there," added Avalon, "we have evidence that you were at the house at the time Peter Stodart was killed." It was an exaggeration, they had bloody footprints and Avalon knew that they would probably find a match with footwear from the address, but as of yet Avalon was just guessing. Thomson was quiet. He sat and stared into space. "We have your partner as you know," said Avalon, he knew the two men had previous convictions and he knew they were not likely to succumb to obvious tactics but Avalon just thought he would remind the man anyway. Tony stayed tight lipped. Avalon decided to wait and let him stew a little, Tony wasn't going to tell him anything at this point. Ross was waiting outside and he spoke to Avalon as they returned to the Cave.

"Well, as to be expected he's saying Stodart was dead when they arrived."

"So he's admitted being there?" asked Avalon turning to Ross as they walked.

"Yeah," nodded Ross, "he seems pretty angry that Sands has grassed them up."

"To be expected," shrugged Avalon, "but it does make me think."

"You think he's telling the truth?" asked Ross as they entered the Cave. Avalon went to the coffee machine to pour them both a drink.

"I don't know but think about it," frowned Avalon, "if Sands did want Stodart dead, what better way to stitch up the Scousers, get someone to knock the troublesome Stodart on the head and get 'yin and yang' downstairs to walk straight into a murder scene." Ross raised an eyebrow.

"It fits the situation," agreed Ross, "Eric is vehemently denying it and Tony just strolls into the station once he hears his mate is arrested." Avalon gave a slight nod. "It just seems out of character for Sands, he's never been against slapping people around but murder?" added Ross.

"Well I'm not interested in the psychological profile of Sands," replied Avalon, "but we still have to keep an open mind on this one, in the mean time we continue with the Thompson Twins."

The forensics reports were piled at the side of Avalon's desk, he had stacked them neatly after reading everything in there and no matter how hard he looked, they, and the evidence pointed to one thing, that the only people that could be proved to be at Peter Stodart's house around the time of the murder were Eric and Tony. It had been considered that the bloody footprints found at the house matched a pair of shabby trainers that Eric wore and he was quite convinced that forensics would confirm that soon enough. There was also a slight chance that the partial footprint was that of Tony Thomson but that would be harder to prove as the print was not a complete foot. He had arranged for David Sutherland to be present at an 'identification parade' to try and see if Eric was the person driving the speeding Vauxhall that forced him off the road and if the ID was positive, it would help with a conviction. Avalon stared into space and thought through the events of that day, but he was still considering that the suspects could have been double-crossed and if it was true, Sands had made it look easy. What was nagging at Avalon was why would Sands go to that much trouble to hide the fact that he had ordered Stodart killed. Sending the two men into a trap with the premise of looking for the laptop was always going to implicate himself, and that simply didn't add up. There was still a piece of the jigsaw missing and he couldn't see what. Ross walked into the Cave, he had been with Mackinnon and Boyd formally interviewing the two men with a solicitors present.

"Anything?" asked Avalon seeing from Ross's blank expression there wasn't.

"Not really," replied Ross, "officially they are now admitting to being there but deny killing him." He sighed and sat opposite Avalon. "Their version of events is that they went to get the laptop as instructed by Sands, it seems Sands had told them that Stodart wouldn't be there so it would be straight forward."

"Well they're bound to deny it."

"I realise that but I'm starting to believe them," frowned Ross.

"Really, any particular reason?" asked Avalon. Ross sighed again, this time making a show of blowing the air out.

"Eric says that he went into the house as the front door was slightly open and Tony stayed outside by the entrance to watch for anyone arriving," explained Ross, "but when Eric reached the kitchen he saw Stodart in a pool of blood so he picked up the laptop and left." He paused and turned to the wall trying to think through the interview. "He says he then went out and told Tony, who went back in to have a look, but Tony saw the prints that Eric had made but decided it was best to leave." Ross then turned back to Avalon and continued. "They got in the car and left but for the life of me I can't help thinking that the whole thing is a lie."

"You just said you believed them," frowned Avalon, "make your mind up."

"I believe them when they say they didn't kill Peter Stodart, I just don't believe their version," explained Ross, "for instance, David Sutherland saw a single occupant in the car that went speeding past him and there were blood stains in the drivers floor well of that vehicle and not in the passenger side." Avalon nodded slowly, he saw the argument but why would they lie? Ross provided what he thought was the answer. "Tony Thomson has a distinctive car, it's a bit of a classic and so they decided to steal one from Inverness for the job. Then they drove to Golspie and arranged to meet up at the loch a few miles out of the village," he paused to catch breath, "Eric went to the house, found Stodart on the floor and because he's not all that bright, he lifted the laptop and left a load of prints. He drove off quickly in a panic and met his partner in crime at the loch, telling him what he had found." Ross stopped for effect and to be sure Avalon was keeping up. "Tony may have decided to go and have a look and whether he thought Eric had done it or not, decided to say he had been there to protect his slow-thinking mate." Avalon made a pinched face, it was clear he wasn't thoroughly convinced but he eventually conceded.

"It's possible, have you tried using that tack on them?"

"No," said Ross, "it's a long shot and we decided to have a break as we're not getting any further with the questions," he stood, "and he can't tell me why they didn't inform Sands what they had found. Sands heard about it from the news."

"I suppose they thought they wouldn't get paid if they admitted to it," offered Avalon.

"Well, I better get back to it," said Ross thrusting his hands into his pockets.

"It may be time to bring Charlie Sands in," suggested Avalon.

"Maybe," nodded Ross, "give me another half an hour," and he left.

~~~~~~~

Charlie Sands was looking out through the enormous windows of his cavernous office wondering if the little bird table at the end of the lawn was too far away from the woodland. He hadn't seen many birds on it of late and the food on there was just rotting. Maybe it wasn't the proximity of the table to the trees, maybe it was the fact that his new girlfriend had a stupid little yapping dog. She just let it out on his lawn and the damn thing crapped everywhere, yes that was probably the reason. He wondered how upset she would be if the dog went mysteriously missing. Was it worth the hassle? She would only go and buy another anyway, it wasn't like she really cared for the thing, it was just another ornament. He sighed, turned to his desk and opened the drawer and took out another lemon bon-bon. He was probably eating far too many of them lately, he just couldn't resist them. He tried to cut down by keeping the tin in the drawer so that he had to open it every time he wanted one but it was just wearing down the runners of the drawer. He turned back to the lawn, he could see small dog turds here and there and he scowled across his once pristine garden. Yes, the dog would have to go, or maybe the girlfriend. That was a laugh, she wasn't a girl, she wasn't even a friend. She was younger than him true but she was no spring chicken by any stretch of the imagination. She had no class either, he couldn't really remember why he still put up with her. He heard the doorbell ring. He instinctively looked at the clock on the wall, he wasn't expecting anyone, it was probably her, back early from the salon. He thought she spent so much time on the sun bed she was beginning to look like a cross between David Hastlhoff and a blood orange. The bell rang again. Charlie picked up his little bell and rang but no one came. He looked back out of the window and saw his gardener trying to shovel up a pile of faeces so he opened the window and called.

"Brian, come and open this frigging door, I pay five people to run this house and I'm damn well sure I ain't opening the thing myself." The gardener nodded and dropped the turd back onto the grass. Charlie shook his head and hissed to himself.

"I bet the bleedin' queen doesn't have this much trouble with her servants." He slumped back into the sumptuous chair as the side door to the room opened.

"Sorry Mr Sands," apologised the grim looking man who entered, "I didnae hear the bell, the gardener just told me."

"Just get the door f ' Christ sake, there could be six dead Jehovah's witnesses on the step by now," spat Sands and the man obeyed. Sands had hardly had time to reach for another lemon bon-bon before the man returned. "Well?" he asked angrily.

"Et's the coppers again," he replied with a sheepish look.

"That's all I need, don't they have some parking tickets to issue?" he was visibly agitated. He considered ringing his solicitor but his previous experience had taught him that they wouldn't wait so he pointed to the door.

"Okay, let them in," he called. As Sands watched the door, he heard voices in the antechamber and the main door close then the double doors swung open and in walked the grim looking CID man that had been previously, and this time his partner was an extremely large man with an equally grim face.

"Oh, you again detective, have you decided that you didn't hospitalise enough of my staff on your first visit?"

"I would have thought that under the circumstances you would be a little more contrite," said Avalon.

"Well, you don't hear that word every day of the week, but if I recall, it means to feel remorse for something I have done wrong," Sands paused, "and yet it strikes me that it's you that keep coming here and harassing me."

"We need to talk to you about the Peter Stodart murder," insisted Avalon refusing to be drawn into an argument.

"Talk away, but make it quick, I'm busy," frowned Sands.

"At the station," added Avalon.

"Inverness?" smiled Sands with an amount of incredulity in his voice, "I don't think so," he continued

313

changing the smile to a deep frown. Avalon looked to his colleague.

"Arrest him," he said calmly and the big man moved forward.

"Whow, hold your horses," exclaimed Sands holding up his hands, "on what grounds?" The big man stopped and Avalon looked directly at Sands.

"Perverting the course of justice, failing to report a crime, receiving stolen goods and possibly murder," he explained raising his eyebrows at the last item. Sands let his hands fall to the desk, he looked over to the phone but abandoned the idea of phoning his legal advisor again. He sighed.

"Okay, but *you* know, and *I* know you've got the wrong man."

"We'll see Mr Sands, we have the Thompsons in custody and they seem to think you've stitched them up, so as I say, we'll see." Avalon wanted to raise the stakes, he let Sands know the Thompsons were probably revealing all they knew.

"No surprise there then, those two thick bastards will do anything to try to shrug off the blame," replied Sands as he stood. He looked back at the drawer in the desk and sighed again then turned to Avalon. "Crooks are so dishonest these days," he said.

~~~~~~

"Still not resolved the Struthers issue then?" asked Avalon. Ross had been gazing out of the window of the Cave, his eyes unseeing, unfocused. He turned back to Avalon and drew in a long breath and then combed his hand through his hair before letting it out.

"Yes, I sent it on, the daughter was easy to find,

314

she isn't married and there aren't that many Struthers over there."

"So why the glum face?" asked Avalon pulling up a chair. Ross shrugged and turned back to the window.

"I don't know, I sometimes think that life is just a joke, like it's all designed to make our time here miserable and there is no way to enjoy it."

"It's about choices, we make them and we have to live with what we chose," offered Avalon.

"That's not always the case though is it," replied Ross turning back to his DI, "Maria Struthers didn't choose to be born to a down-and-out father who ran off because he couldn't cope with responsibility did she?"

"No, she didn't," began Avalon realising Ross had made some guesses why Struthers was the way he was, "and it's true, some of us are dealt a better hand than others," he added, "and I suppose in that respect life is a joke." Ross usually had a mechanism for dealing with the job, he larked about, he made inane comments, he pretended it was all 'water off a duck's back' but it was a very fragile mechanism and now and then the slightest thing could trigger depression. All the team suffered it, Avalon too but Ross's mechanism was ill-conceived and rarely worked.

"Did you send a message with the money?" asked Avalon trying to keep him talking.

"Just the basics, I sent her the photograph and the money, I changed it first though," explained Ross looking back through the window.

"Changed it?" asked Avalon. Ross nodded still looking through the glass.

"Yeah, some of that money was ancient, it made sense to change it into something she could spend,"

"Just the six hundred?" asked Avalon knowing

315

the answer. Ross was silent for a moment, his eyes flicked around the view over the fields before he turned back to Avalon.

"I added a bit, it was such an empty gesture, I couldn't just send her and old photograph and six hundred quid," admitted Ross.

"And she'll probably throw the photo away and go and blow the money on a spray tan and Vodka," suggested Avalon.

"Yeah, probably," nodded Ross with a fake smile, "anyway, we better get back to it."

The interviews continued and one thing soon became clear, no one was going to admit to killing Peter Stodart. It was going to be down to evidence and they didn't have a great deal of that, there was an amount of circumstantial evidence but nothing concrete. Avalon knew they didn't have enough to convict Charlie Sands of the murder and even minor charges would be difficult. How convenient it had been that the informant saying Stodart was out had phoned in anonymously, it all seemed to let him off the hook. He had been clever in other ways too, he had tried to help the police by pointing to the killers in the shape of the Thompson Twins. That meant it would be difficult to convict him of perverting the course of justice, maybe they could prosecute him for failing to report a crime and receiving stolen goods, but that was small beer. On the other hand, there was a case to present against the Thompsons. It was clear to see that it was Eric's footprints in the blood and they had now admitted to being there and even taking the laptop, but they still denied murder. But then again, Avalon couldn't remember the last time a crook stood in the dock and announced, 'it's a fair cop, society is to blame,' so he shrugged that off. There was still a nagging doubt however, it still *could* be Sands who had hatched a very clever plan to be rid of the troublesome Stodart.

Avalon went to see DCI Croker to explain the situation and to warn him he was going to charge the two brothers but as usual, Croker was ambivalent to the information. He was more concerned that he would need to inform the press about the arrest, it caused Avalon to think about Croker's past and wonder how embarrassing the whole event had been for him.

It was late in the day by the time all the paperwork was processed and as Avalon got ready to leave Ross came up to him.

"What's the situation with Sands?"

"We may as well drop anything against him for now. I let him go about an hour ago, I wish we had more but we don't," replied Avalon with a blank expression. Ross nodded.

"Ah well, no point in dwelling on it, we'll just have to put a good case together against the brothers," shrugged Ross and then added, "do you fancy a drink?" Avalon shook his head.

"Not tonight, I'm whacked, I'm spending too much time at the pub anyway." Ross nodded and picked up his jacket.

"Yeah, you're probably right," he said but Avalon suddenly felt guilty, what if Ross wanted to talk about the Arty Struthers issue?

"Mind you," he said, "I could always get something to eat there I suppose."

Avalon had been correct, Ross did want to talk about it

and as they had waited for their food to arrive Ross had gone through the whole thing again and finally admitted to putting an extra thousand pounds in the pot that Arty Struthers had collected. Avalon had accused him of being too much of a softy but Ross didn't reply, he just made a slight shrug. Avalon could see there was a great deal going on in his mind over the incident. As Ross returned to the bar to order a second drink Avalon thought of Ross's predicament and it gave him an idea, he pulled out his little notepad and jotted a few lines down.

"Working on your resignation?" asked Ross as he returned. Avalon hadn't noticed him and quickly put the pad away.

"No, I've been writing a song and the words are harder to write than the music," explained Avalon.

"Wasn't there a TV program some years ago called the 'Singing Detective'?" mused Ross.

"Probably," nodded Avalon but you can't call what I do singing, it's more of a groan."

"The 'Groaning Detective' works for me," smiled Ross sitting down with the drinks, "anyway, you're taking this guitar thing seriously aren't you?"

"I don't get much time but I do a little bit when I can," he shrugged.

"So what's the song called?"

"Everyone asks that, it hasn't got a title until the words are finished."

"So let's hear what you've got then," demanded Ross, "I might be able to help."

"Not likely," frowned Avalon, "with your rugby background it will probably turn out as an alternative version of *'Four and twenty virgins came down from Inverness'*," and he took a drink.

318

"The Inverness song is called 'The Ball at Kirriemuir," smiled Ross.

"Oh, right," replied Avalon with a lack of interest, "either way, it's a personal thing and it's just about finished so I don't need help."

"So it's a love song," smiled Ross.

"I didn't say it was a love song," insisted Avalon.

"It is though, I'm guessing inspired by the meeting with Julia in Golspie," chuckled Ross.

"Wrong,"

"How wrong?"

"It's a love song."

"So am I correct in thinking there is someone else in your affections?" asked Ross with a little surprise.

"No," replied Avalon raising his brows, "it's just a love song to no one in particular."

"Yeah, right, so when do we get to hear it?" Ross asked with a doubtful look and took a drink just as their food arrived. Avalon remained silent as the attractive woman laid the food on the table but he noticed Ross eying her up and down. When she had left Avalon looked directly at Ross and said,

"She's got a partner."

"Who?" asked Ross starting on his food.

"The barmaid," replied Avalon with a wry smile.

"How the hell do you know that?" asked Ross stabbing another chip.

"I'm a detective remember," replied Avalon unfolding his napkin. Ross leant on the table and pointed at Avalon with his fork.

"That's your stock answer and it's getting on my nerves." Avalon laughed, "and do you know what else gets on my nerves?" continued Ross, "the way you change the subject and think I don't notice."

"I don't change the subject," frowned Avalon, "so how's the scampi?"

"You see, there you go again."

"Sorry, I promise not to do it again," smiled Avalon, "oh and I need to think about looking for my own house." Ross made a soft tutting sound and looked up.

"It's like talking to three people at once," he frowned. They both ate a little and then Avalon asked,

"Where might be a good place for a house do you think?"

"Are we staying on this subject for a few seconds or should I ignore the question?"

"It's a serious question, I need to put my money into some property," insisted Avalon cutting a piece of his food.

"Maybe Kinmylies," suggested Ross, "but it depends what sort of place you're looking for."

"I'm not sure," replied Avalon, "just somewhere reasonably quiet but not far from the centre of the city."

"Difficult then, maybe somewhere up Island Bank Road on one of the back streets," suggested Ross reaching for more tartare sauce, "to be honest as long as there are no retired sorts near, anywhere up there would do."

"So what have you got against retired people?" asked Avalon. Ross discarded the sauce wrapper and looked at Avalon.

"Generally nothing, but I wouldn't want to live next door to one, they have no sense of what goes on around them. They wake early and start mowing the lawn or cutting the hedge when everyone else is still sleeping," Avalon grinned at this, "and then they go inside and fall asleep in front of daytime television and then swear that they are rushed off their feet." Ross paused to bring a scampi to his mouth but he stopped mid way to continue, "and they change the subject almost as much as you," and the scampi went into his mouth whole.

"Maybe I should retire then?" smiled Avalon. Ross shook his head and decided to continue with his food.

~~~~~~

"For Christ's sake will y' stop doin' that?" Ross turned to look at Frazer, she had her face set in a scowl that would turn away a storm. He blinked and then asked,

"Doing what?"

"That stupid tapping with your pen," she growled.

"I didn't realise I was doing anything," he replied, "anyway I'm thinking."

"Yeah, an' we're gettin' a pay rise," she said looking back to her computer screen.

"Are we?"

"No, et's fantasy, like you thinken'," and she shot him another scowl.

"It's nervous energy then," he suggested with a thoughtful expression.

"But you're tapping a pen," she insisted, "you don't use a pen, you have got a computer to do your writing with." Ross could see it had annoyed her, he considered doing it again but abandoned that idea as she had been known to throw the contents of her cup over people who annoyed her. Ross noticed Mackinnon grinning but trying not to look at either of them. He thought maybe he could wind up Rory a little but his heart wasn't in playing the fool, he was sick of writing the reports up for the interviews. The truth was he was becoming sick of the whole paperwork side of the job, more so than usual and having to work on a less than straightforward case wasn't helping. They had the two Thompsons in the sheriff's cells and they had evidence to suggest they had at least been at the crime scene but was there enough to convince a jury of that? He wasn't even sure the two of them had actually killed Peter Stodart, and neither was Avalon. They were going to saddle the Thompsons with some lesser charge so they could keep them in custody until more work had been done on the case, but they were running out of options. They had released Charlie Sands even though they both thought he could have had something to do with the murder. Avalon was out, he was having a meeting at the procurator fiscal's office to see if they had enough evidence to pursue the case against the brothers. In the meantime it was back to the piles of paperwork. Wilson and Mack walked into the Cave.

"Where's the boss?" asked Wilson seeing Avalon was out.

"Down at the PF, got problems?" asked Ross.

"Not a problem, we just need a search warrant for this job we're on," explained Wilson, "I'll have a word with the Toad," and he left the office. Ross considered that one day Croker would hear about his nick-name and someone would be in serious trouble, he just hoped it wasn't him. His phone rang.

"DS Ross," he said picking up the phone.

"*It's Avalon, I've just come out of the meeting with the procurator fiscal,*" said the voice, Ross listened intently, he knew what was coming as he had expected

322

as much, "*they're issuing a release for the Thompson Twins.*"

"It looks like we were a bit previous releasing the news of their arrest to the press then?" frowned Ross.

"*Well, I suppose we knew it was dodgy,*" said Avalon, "*but at least with a release we can go after them later once we get more evidence.*"

"So what now?" asked Ross, "we're at a bit of a loose end."

"*I know, but we have to keep at it, there must be something we have missed,*" insisted Avalon, "*get back onto the forensics evidence and I'll be back as soon as I can.*" Ross put down the phone and did as Avalon had suggested, he took out all the files and began to systematically work his way through the reports, hoping there was something that would jump up from the pages and give him that little nudge in the direction he needed to look. By the time Avalon was back in the office he had found nothing, or at least nothing he thought would lead anywhere and he told him so.

"Then we need to look again," insisted Avalon pulling a chair up to Ross's desk, "is there nothing you have found?" he added.

"No, well nothing I can put any reason to," insisted Ross.

"What do you mean by that?" asked Avalon.

"I read the report from the murder scene, particularly the part about the black plastic box."

"And?" asked Avalon with a questioning frown.

"Well, I don't quite understand why it's giving me an itchy feeling but," Ross paused to try and find the best way of explaining himself, "the report says the box looks as though it was crushed, either by a sharp blow or being stood on and after recalling how it looked, I would go

323

further and say it was stamped on."

"All that means is that whoever killed him probably had an aversion to his habit," insisted Avalon.

"But that's it," explained Ross, "why would the Thompson Twins do that? During the interviews, neither of them said anything about him being a user, and Eric even has convictions for possession on his record."

"So you think this points more to Sands," nodded Avalon, "because he did take a dim view of Stodart being a user?"

"Or his wife," added Ross, "and until we find her, we can't rule her out of this."

"No, I agree with that," nodded Avalon again, "but equally Stodart's drug kit could have been trodden on accidentally too."

"That I doubt, the damage to the metal parts of the syringe is severe," insisted Ross. Avalon looked at the floor thinking through the possibilities, certainly Ross had seen something that could be significant, but as it was, it meant nothing. Avalon stood and walked over to the board on the wall where the collected information had been pinned. He looked at the photograph of Mrs Stodart, she was obviously the main suspect but without being able to interview her they couldn't go very far forward with that side of the case. Then there was the name, Charlie Sands, he had probable cause, Stodart owed him money and was suggesting that they ransomed Stodart's wife to raise cash to pay it back. Sands could indeed have taken a dim view of that and sent out someone to get the laptop and destroy any information to connect him to Stodart. But that left its own set of unanswered questions. Then there were the Thompson Twins, they were incompetent but they didn't seem to have an issue with Stodart's drug abuse. Avalon looked up at Ross.

"Which ever way you look at this it all comes back to Mrs Stodart," he insisted, tapping his finger on her photograph.

"I know," nodded Ross, "that's what I thought but if it is her, why only one blow to the head?"

"Well it certainly did the job," shrugged Avalon.

"But she couldn't have known that one blow would kill him," insisted Ross, "and from the pathologists report it didn't. Stodart was alive for some time after and bled to death. You would think an angry wife coming back to kill an abusive husband would make a more frenzied attack." Avalon nodded slightly and he noticed Frazer look over to the board. She had sat quietly working at her own computer until now but she had stopped and was turned facing the board on the wall.

"Unless the revulsion of the act shocked her and put her off," offered Avalon.

"But it was a severe blow for a small woman."

"Maybe," shrugged Avalon, "but anger can do that." Now it was Ross's turn to think through the attack. The pathologist report said the wheel brace was the weapon used and it struck the victim from the rear and could be from a right handed person who may be smaller than the victim. The problem was, Eric Thompson wasn't very tall so it could point to him being the killer. Sands was at least as tall as the victim which ruled him out being the person wielding the weapon but not ordering the contract. In truth, the actual attack gave nothing away except that the attacker would probably be strained with blood spatter, yet nothing had been found on any of the Thompson's clothing. Just traces of blood on Eric's trainers, which fit the footprints found at the scene.

"Anger can make the smallest person strong,"

said Frazer eventually as she turned back to her computer. Avalon had thought she had seen something they had missed and he was surprised by the statement, it seemed Frazer was probably thinking aloud. He looked to Ross who also seemed surprised by the comment. He raised his eyebrows to Avalon.

"Does the broken cup offer anything?" he eventually asked.

"I have been through that before," shrugged Avalon, "and to be truthful, no it doesn't. All it means is that he probably knew the person and that includes all the suspects," he looked back to the board.

"But just one person being there?" asked Ross.

"Not necessarily," replied Avalon turning back to the room, "but I see the point. The cup itself was very similar to the others on the rack and we know it hit the ground about the same time as the body," he added. They both fell silent, Ross looked out of the window and Avalon returned to the seat and looked down at the floor once more.

"What does the murder weapon tell us then?" he eventually asked without looking up. Ross sighed and said,

"It's from the toolbox in the Land Rover, no prints were found on it, the garage or the vehicle."

"That's not what I meant," insisted Avalon in a serious tone looking directly into Ross's eyes, "if the vehicle was in the garage the perpetrator would have to go specifically for it, why did they end up going into the garage, then into the vehicle to find something to strike him with?" Ross shrugged and shook his head slightly.

"I can't explain that."

"And neither can I, and it's making me think we've missed something obvious," frowned Avalon.

"Et's small but heavy," suggested Frazer still typing. Avalon looked across to her, she was a strange one. There were complicated thought processes going on in her head but she rarely showed it, she just allowed small drops of information to trickle out.

"Meaning?" asked Avalon. Frazer stopped, she turned to Avalon and explained her thinking.

"Stodart saw the person who was going tae kill him and yet he reached for a cup tae make a drink for that person," she said, "so I'm thinking that the person didn't come in with the weapon raised above their head."

"It was concealed you mean?" asked Ross.

"Exactly," she replied glancing over to Ross, "the 'perp' sought out the right weapon, they probably wanted it t' be reasonably heavy that could be hidden up a sleeve or somethen'." Avalon nodded.

"So they could have searched around for something before going to the house?" he offered. Frazer nodded and then turned back to her computer.

"Okay," said Ross, "but it still seems weird to me. This person arrives to kill Peter Stodart, unarmed and hopes they will find a weapon on the site? It seems a bit far fetched."

"What if the person had already been to the house?" cut in Avalon, "we're assuming they turned up and killed him but it's just as possible that the person had argued with Stodart and got angry enough to go and look for a weapon before returning to whack him on the head."

"Which brings us back to his wife," insisted Frazer pointing to the board. Avalon nodded, he saw that Muiranne Stodart was the obvious choice, she had been the principal suspect from the start but without knowing where she was and a complete lack of any solid evidence that she was there at any time since she had gone missing, it was impossible to conclude without reasonable doubt that she was the murderer. They all went quiet and eventually Avalon stood and said,

"Where the hell is she and have we exhausted all avenues to find her?"

"As far as I can see we have tried everything," said Ross folding his arms, "her friends, family, even people who knew her professionally, no one has any ideas."

"Then we are pretty much at a dead end," sighed Avalon but as if showing an inner determination to his team he added, "for now," and he walked back to the booth.

Wilson soon returned from arranging his search warrant and spent some minutes with Avalon bringing him up to date on his case then Avalon sat alone in the booth. He stared into space and thought back to the first time he entered the Stodart's house. He remembered the door being open, the kitchen with the body on the floor and the broken cup in the pool of blood. He then tried to visualise the moments before Peter Stodart was killed and whatever he tried, he couldn't see anyone else but Muiranne Stodart with him in the kitchen, and yet it just didn't fit. He just couldn't see her returning to the house and the husband saying, "Hello love, would you like a cup of tea?" It almost made him laugh. No, there had to be another explanation, there had to be something else Was the smashed mug nothing to do with those moments? He sighed and looked out of the glass partition seeing the members of the team at work, all except Ross. He was once again staring out of the window. Anyone else would probably reprimand him for wasting time but Avalon knew it was a sign that his DS was thinking, not day dreaming.

Maybe Avalon needed a window to look out of, cooped up in the booth there was no direct view to the outside world though he could see the broken clouds moving from the south and heading off inland. He thought back to the case and the motive of Muiranne Stodart to kill her husband, if indeed she had done it. Then he considered that Charlie Sands had said that Peter Stodart rang him, what if Muiranne heard the phone call? What if she became aware that he planned to kidnap her for money? That would probably change the character of this once quiet and demure woman, but again, there was no evidence. Then he had an idea, he stood and walked into the Cave and straight to Ross.

"Can we get hold of the murder weapon or an exact copy?"

"I suppose so," nodded Ross, "why, you got an idea?"

"I'm not sure, I want to be absolutely positive that the murder weapon came from the Land Rover, and the only way we can know for sure is to put it back where it came from," insisted Avalon.

"But forensics have already done that," insisted Ross and he reached for a file on his desk, "it says somewhere on the report that it even has scratched where it clipped into place."

"I did read that," explained Avalon, "but I want to try it." Ross dropped the file and looked up to Avalon. To him, it was just a waste of time to go through something that forensics had checked.

"Okay," nodded Ross giving in to Avalon's obvious hunch, "I'll find out if they have done with it," and he rang the forensics department to ask.

They were soon in the car and off to pick up the wheel

brace to take over to the vehicle so that Avalon could try out whatever it was that was bothering him.

"So is this a secret?" asked Ross as he drove.

"No," shrugged Avalon looking over to Ross, "I just think there is something I'm missing and as I can't find it I want to cover everything myself," but he realised how the statement sounded and so he added, "I know they have done it properly but I just have to check." When they had the wheel brace and they approached the vehicle in the compound, Avalon was beginning to see the stupidity in his decision to check the placement of the tool in the vehicle. He could see the scratch marks on it even through the plastic evidence bag and he began to have doubts. They opened the passenger door of the Land Rover and Ross looked for the clips that held it. He found the clips under the seat, they had been a later addition on the vehicle to allow stowage of the extra strong brace that removed the special wheels the vehicle had. Avalon took the tool out of the bag and handing it to Ross who lifted his brows and then thrust the wheel brace into the clips. It snapped into position with a positive click. Ross looked at Avalon and shrugged.

"It definitely came from here," he said expecting Avalon to make a comment, but he didn't, he just stared into the distance. Ross wondered what Avalon was thinking and he eventually interrupted his DI's thoughts by adding, "So does that clear anything up?" Avalon blinked several times as he came back to reality. He shrugged.

"Sort of, we know it was taken from here but it's got me wondering exactly when."

"We can't know that, the vehicle was used by both Stodart and his wife," insisted Ross. Avalon wasn't so sure and he frowned deeply, he looked at the vehicle as a whole, it still had stickers and marks on it from the forensics team and it still showed a great deal of residue from the fingerprint dust.

"This vehicle has been processed several times," said Avalon pointing to it unnecessarily, "and for each time it's been processed we have a report."

"True," nodded Ross climbing out of the vehicle, "it's certainly worth a look through again."

"I agree," Avalon replied and he stood back from the Land Rover and thrust his hands into his pockets, "it's ironic, this vehicle has been central to this case, it would be more than coincidental if the clue to finding the murderer was here all along."

"I think there's more to it than that but I get your meaning," nodded Ross.

"Come on," said Avalon, "let's go and have another look through those forensics reports." They left the compound and jumped in the car and headed back to the station. Avalon looked up at the sky, it was bright and there were few clouds and he wondered if it was sign that they were making some headway. Maybe not, it was Scotland and the seasons come and go as they please, there is little pattern and he was getting used to that. In that respect, the weather was like a difficult case, just as you think all the evidence is coming together, the rains come back. He smiled to himself, inside he felt that he would find something in those reports, something slight that would change the barometer from 'changeable' to 'fine and sunny'. His phone rang.

"Avalon." Ross glanced round as he answered the phone, he hoped it was good news. Avalon listened for a few seconds and then said abruptly, "Right, on my way," and he put the phone back in his pocket and turned to

Ross. "Back to the station and step on it." Ross didn't know if it was one of those situations where he needed lights and siren so he waited for the explanation he knew would follow. "We have a celebrity guest in interview room one," he added and paused for a moment as he looked to Ross, "Muiranne Stodart."

Chapter Eleven

Avalon looked through the two-way mirror at Muiranne Stodart as PC Kirk took her a cup of coffee. As Kirk left Ross entered with his notepad in hand and sat opposite. He began to ask her questions to confirm her details as Avalon had asked him to do. She was a striking woman, she looked tired and pale but beyond that he could see pleasant features, exacting dress sense and an aura of command that comes from only the most organised personalities. He could see how David Sutherland and anyone else for that matter could be taken in by her. Yet she was small, very small, sitting opposite Ross she looked no larger than a schoolgirl but she also looked perfectly proportioned. Avalon unknowingly frowned as he tried to think what possible reason she could have seen for marrying Peter Stodart. Her husband had been brash, unfeeling and most of all, broke, and yet here was a woman who could have carved out a life for herself that would have been the envy of her peers. Maybe Stodart had been a different person when she met him, maybe she was different to what people saw, either way, it was time for him to go and meet her himself.

"This is Detective Inspector Avalon, he's in

charge of the case," said Ross as Avalon entered and sat at the side his DC. He gave a slight smile to her and then stared into her eyes. They were blue and deep, he could read nothing except what she wanted him to read, and at the moment she was the model of contrition, now a widow but not tearful nor mournful, just sad yet composed.

"Mrs Stodart," began Avalon with a serious look, "as you can expect, we need to ask you a great deal of questions, I believe you know your husband is deceased?"

"Yes," she said but sat motionless, "I understand there's a great deal you need to ask me." Avalon was surprised that she had a Scottish accent, he didn't know why but he expected her to have little to none. He thought about the way she spoke and he was reminded of the singer Lulu, she sounded similar and for that matter resembled her slightly.

"Where have you been since you disappeared?" he asked.

"I stayed in a friend's holiday cottage, I have access to it and I knew it to be empty. The place is further north, near Lybster."

"The address?" asked Avalon and she dutifully told them the address and Ross jotted it down.

"And so why have you decided to come and talk to us now?" asked Avalon. She looked down to the table and cradled the coffee cup for a moment then looked straight at him.

"I'm not going to pretend that my marriage was good," she began, "but I didn't hate my husband, I didn't love him either but when I heard he was dead I became afraid. I knew something like this might happen, he seemed to have plenty of enemies."

"So you expected it?"

"No, I didn't expect him to get murdered," she insisted opening her eyes wider, "but I did think someone would eventually take some sort of revenge."

"Is that why you left?" asked Ross. Her gaze turned to him as she answered.

"I had considered it previously," she paused and looked back down to her hands around the coffee cup, "but no it isn't the reason. I actually heard him speaking on the phone, he was planning to have me taken hostage," she paused again and looked at Avalon but he sat impassively, "he must have thought that my family would pay a ransom," and she shook her head and looked to the table once more, "so I decided it was time to leave and make sure he couldn't find me."

"You still haven't answered my question," insisted Avalon.

"Sorry," she looked up to Avalon with a puzzled expression, "what was the question?"

"Why now, why have you decided to come to us now?" She seemed to understand the question but was hesitant to answer.

"Well, I suppose when I heard that the people who had killed Peter were in custody I assumed it would be safe," she explained.

"I see," said Avalon, "so you assumed that the people who murdered your husband were probably after you too?"

"I suppose I did, I was afraid."

"Of being abducted or ending up like your husband?" he asked quickly.

"Either, both," she replied, "I just didn't know what would befall me to be honest."

"Well, honesty is all we are after Mrs Stodart,"

sighed Avalon leaning back from the table. The woman let go of the coffee cup and gently rubbed her brow. Avalon continued.

"Why the elaborate plan to vanish and was it your plan?"

"I saw a television program about a similar situation, it may have been a movie, I'm not sure but it seemed the best way to ensure I wasn't followed."

"By your husband?"

"By anyone," she insisted.

"And you thought that now that Eric and Tony Thomson had been arrested that the danger was over?" he asked.

"Yes," she nodded, "I suppose I did, it was quite a shock when I found he had been killed. I didn't love him but I wouldn't want that to happen to anyone," she began to shake her head slowly and her gaze fell to the table once more. "I read that two men had been arrested for the murder so I felt a little more confident of being safe," she continued.

"We have to get a prosecution first Mrs Stodart," frowned Avalon.

"Where did you hide your car?" asked Ross.

"I was under the impression you had found it?" she said looking at Ross with a questioning glare.

"We have but I didn't know if that was where *you* placed it," added Ross.

"Oh, I see," she nodded with a softer look on her features, "I left it with a friend near Dornoch."

"Who was also your lover," added Ross. Muiranne wasn't at all phased by the comment, she nodded and looked directly at him.

"I'm embarrassed to say I treated her badly, she was there to comfort me when I was upset and I completely abandoned her," she paused and looked to the table once more clasping her hands together in front of her. "I hope she'll forgive me one day."

"And what part did David Sutherland play in the plan?" asked Avalon. This brought a slight smile to her face.

"Dear David," she began, "I thought he would do anything for me but when I told him about my plan he would have nothing to do with it, he said he wouldn't break the law so we had to come up with something real. That's why we had to go through the whole thing."

"Ironic then that in doing so you have both broken the law," insisted Avalon but he continued before she had time to react. "So why was it that you orchestrated a charade to make it look like you were having a liaison with Mr Sutherland?" She looked surprised, for a moment she was lost for words and then asked,

"I'm not sure what you mean."

"You hired a car and arranged for Elizabeth Lithgoe to meet you near Evelix," explained Avalon.

"Oh, yes, so I did," she agreed looking away from him, "but I don't see why that had anything to do with David."

"So you don't think it rather peculiar that the car you hired was almost exactly the same as Mr Sutherland's vehicle?" insisted Avalon.

"Was it?" she said with some surprise, "oh, I didn't know." Avalon glared at her for some moments and it obviously made her feel uncomfortable because she began to make excuses. "You have to understand detective, I was under extreme pressure and I was doing things by the second, maybe I made some severe mistakes."

337

"I was under the assumption that you had planned it for some time," he said raising his eyebrows.

"Not really, I became very anxious when I overheard him talking about my abduction however, I think that was when I began to plan it."

"But you see Mrs Stodart, we spoke to your husband just hours before his death, he said that your car had been missing for some time," insisted Avalon.

"That's true, I admit that I had moved my car, I had thought about moving out some days before that," she conceded.

"Who helped you move it?" asked Ross. She turned to him.

"A friend but I'd rather not say a name, I think I have hurt too many people already," she said as she frowned and looked down at her hands once more.

"Can we get you another drink or something to eat?" asked Avalon as he stood. He noticed she hadn't touched the coffee, he didn't blame her, the stuff was vile but he wanted to let her stew for a while.

"Oh, no thanks," she gave a brief smile.

"Well, I'm sure you won't mind if we get a drink, I'll get PC Kirk to stay with you."

"Am I under arrest or in some sort of trouble?" she asked.

"Did you murder your husband or arrange for him to be murdered?" asked Avalon in a matter-of-fact way. This took her by surprise but she composed herself.

"No I didn't, and the last time I saw him he was still alive," she insisted.

"Then you're not under arrest and free to go but," he paused for effect, "any questions we don't get around to today will have to be answered at some other time." She thought for a moment.

338

"Could I have a cup of strong tea then please?" she asked.

Outside in the corridor Ross asked Avalon what he thought.

"She's done it," he said emphatically.

"I think so too but I'm not as sure as you," nodded Ross.

"I'm not sure, I'm positive."

"Really, what gives you that impression?"

"She's lying about things she doesn't need to lie about," began Avalon counting the fact theatrically on his fingers, "because when I first asked her a question she didn't answer it and gave me a pre-rehearsed statement, because she thinks we've got someone for the murder, because I can feel it in my water, because-"

"Okay, okay, I get the picture," interrupted Ross, "what gave it away for me was her body language, she's not the actress she thinks she is." Avalon stayed quiet, he leaned on the wall in the corridor and thought about his options.

"The problem is now," he said, "how the hell do we prove it?" Ross shrugged.

"Back to the beginning," he eventually said.

"Yeah, seems like it," agreed Avalon, "we better get someone to find who the owner of the address is she says she stayed at and send local to check it over and get the site sealed for forensics. Get someone to sort out the warrants." Ross nodded and went to the Cave to put someone on it. Avalon looked up at the strip light on the ceiling, it was buzzing as if it was designed to make noise rather than light and he left to find somewhere better to think. He ended up in the car park and breathed in the cool air and considered what was the next best move. There was so much about Muiranne Stodart that was captivating, she was easy to talk to even under present circumstances and it was easy to see how David Sutherland had been taken in by her, but he could also see something else, something unpleasant. If he was correct and she had murdered her own husband, then there was a mind at work here that must be given the respect it demanded. It was possible that every eventuality had been anticipated and planned for and if that was the case, then Avalon would have to think about every move before he made it. He shivered a little from the cool air and returned inside. Ross was waiting and strangely, he was casually playing with some clear sticky tape he had wrapped around his hand.

"Been wrapping Christmas presents already?" asked Avalon staring at the tape.

"This?" Ross held up the hand, "no, not quite," he smiled and with a sterner expression added, "just a hunch." Ross didn't explain any further he just asked, "Plans?"

"I'm not sure but we have to think this through," insisted Avalon.

"A full statement then?" suggested Ross, it wasn't going to crack the case but it was certainly the best place to start and so Avalon nodded and they returned to the interview room. Once Mrs Stodart had explained her story fully, the statement was signed and she was told she was free to go. Ross seemed eager to show her to the door and squeezed past Avalon to open it and let her through. Avalon wondered if Ross had begun to like the woman, but as soon as they were in the corridor he stood back and showed no further interest in her. Avalon frowned at him slightly and then showed Mrs Stodart to the foyer and opened the door to the outside for her. In any other situation, Avalon would have been impressed by the lady, but he had to keep an open mind, however, he still had one more trick up his sleeve.

"I suppose that we will see more of each other detective," she said looking up at him, "I mean, there are bound to be developments as this goes to trial."

"Not until we have someone for the murder," replied Avalon following her through the door.

"Oh, I thought..." she paused but Avalon made no comment, "I read in the newspaper that the two brothers had been arrested for the murder," she continued. Avalon jutted out his bottom lip and thrust his hands into his trouser pockets.

"They were a little previous, we had to let them go, not enough evidence to proceed," he replied. She obviously knew nothing of this, her gaze drifted and a worried look passed along her features for a moment.

"But after you left Peter at the house, if they were the only people to have seen him after you, surely they must have done the deed?"

"You would assume so," nodded Avalon, "but without evidence, we have to look elsewhere," explained Avalon.

"Well," sighed the woman, "I'm sure you'll find them detective inspector." He didn't reply, he just watched her walk off to find her car and he turned to head inside. Then he stopped and waited a moment before taking a look where she was going. It was obvious she had arrived on foot, or at least walked from her transport to the police station. He returned to the foyer where Ross was waiting, in his hand he held an evidence bag and when Avalon pointed to it and asked what it was Ross said,

"My hunch," and he held it up. Avalon could see

that it was the discarded tape from his hand.

"I'm not sure what you're after but it's no good as evidence, it's contaminated," insisted Avalon.

"I know, I just need to find out what it is."

"From where?" asked Avalon.

"I noticed some fibres on her jacket, it got me thinking," smiled Ross, "I could be wrong but we'll see."

"A trip to Miss Underwood's lab maybe, we can also assess the forensics reports from there?" asked Avalon. Ross nodded.

~~~~~~

"It looks like animal hair," said Sarah holding the small bag under a light source.

"It's not evidence, I just need to establish what animal," explained Ross. Avalon was leaning against the wall with his arms folded, he still wasn't sure what Ross was doing and why he had found the need to lift the fibres from Mrs Stodart's coat. He had explained that when he helped her through the door he had gently rest his hand on her back, hoping that the sticky tape would do its job, it had, three small hairs plus other fibres were present. Sarah placed the fibres under a microscope and looked at them for several minutes.

"I'm sure they are dog hairs but with the other fibres in there we need to separate them," she explained and removed the slide from the microscope, "I'll get one of the team to have a better look," and she walked off down the lab with Ross in tow. Avalon sighed and followed on but became aware that he had a nagging doubt as though there was some evidence very obvious and yet he was not seeing it. He hated nagging doubts, they could be annoying but equally they could also turn up something interesting. He watched the technician set up the machine and then turned to Sarah.

"Have you got copies of your reports on the Land Rover from the Stodart's case?" She nodded.

"Yes, I can get to them in the office," and she walked back the way they had come, once again Avalon following. Sarah entered the office and sat at her desk.

"It shouldn't take long to sort out the fibres, is it important?" she asked.

"I have no idea, it's Ross's baby and as usual he keeps it to himself until he's sure," smiled Avalon folding his arms again

"Like most detectives," said Sarah returning the smile, "here you are," she added and stood to allow Avalon to view the reports.

"I just need the inventory lists to be honest," he explained.

"They're right at the bottom of the files," she pointed at the screen. Avalon could smell her perfume, it took great concentration to stick to the job at hand. She sat in a chair at the side of the office.

"Have you finished that song yet?" she asked.

"Oh," it took Avalon by surprise, "er, yes I have, well sort of, the lyrics are done and..." he hesitated, "yes I suppose it is."

"So when do I get to hear it?" she smiled again. He turned to her.

"When you wish, but as I said, it's not very good and I'm a dreadful musician," he replied with a very embarrassed expression. He had completely forgotten he had promised to play it for her, maybe he shouldn't have admitted it was finished. It was quite a shock to his system.

"I'm not busy this Saturday," she said and then

added, "late afternoon would be ideal for me," but then she saw Avalon's face bathe itself in doubt. "Oh, yes, I'm sorry, you'll be busy," she said with a weak smile. Avalon quickly thought through the work schedule for the week, could he manage to sort some time off? He was desperate to make that date, an actual date of sorts with Sarah Underwood. His stomach did several nervous summersaults and his heart seemed to be pumping for several people at once.

"Er, no, no, I think I actually may be able to make it." Of course he would damn well make it, this was Sarah, this was a woman he would give his career up for. Nothing would keep him from that date. Nothing. Then he saw a problem. He looked back at the screen for a second and then back to Sarah.

"The only thing is..." he stuttered, "I er... I don't know if my housemate has anything planned..." he knew he should have put some time into finding his own house. He knew Angie would still be sleeping after her Friday night shift at work, he couldn't really invite anyone round.

"Oh," she said with a certain inevitability, "well," she paused, she seemed to be thinking her way through something, "I suppose you could come round to mine," she added but Avalon distinctly heard a lack of enthusiasm in her voice.

"We could do it some other time," suggested Avalon as optimistically as he could muster.

"No, it's fine," she eventually said and she jotted something down and passed him the card with her address. He looked at it as casually as he could and placed it in his pocket.

"Great, it's a date," he announced with a smile but inside he was laughing out loud. He knew it wasn't the sort of date he would have wanted but it was a start and he was very excited, so much so, he didn't hear the door open and Ross walk in.

"We've got a result," he announced and then left. At the work station where one of the technicians was studying the hairs and fibres, Ross pointed to the computer screen that showed what the high-powered microscope was seeing.

"These are wool fibres which are dyed, they are from the coat," explained Ross pointing to the screen with a pencil, "these other three fibres are the hairs, one is human but the other two are dog hairs." A smile broke out around the edges of his mouth.

"If you give me a few hours I can tell you the colour and the breed of the dog," added the technician looking up from the equipment.

"I already know the colour, and I'm guessing the breed is Skye Terrier," replied Ross, the smile turning into a smug expression.

~~~~~~~

Mornings were usually the time that C Section assessed their previous days work and this Thursday morning was no exception. When all the other items were cleared, Avalon recapped on the Stodart case with Ross and Frazer. He stood at the wall looking at all the photographs and other details and turned to the others saying,

"So, we now think that Mrs Stodart had both the motive and opportunity to return and kill her husband, we also know from the forensic reports that the wheel brace from the Land Rover had already been removed prior to it being returned to Peter Stodart," he looked back to the board and pointed to the photograph of the weapon, "which means that the weapon couldn't have been removed the day that the murder took place. So we have the fact that this is a pre-meditated murder, what we don't have is a busting amount of evidence." He picked up the evidence bag with the fibres. "I'm not sure that putting this little find forward is enough to warrant going out on a limb but I have to say, well done DS Ross." Avalon raised his eyebrows to the DS, "care to explain what made you think of it?" Ross just shrugged and then said,

"I was reading through PC Dowd's reports from the Golspie sightings," began Ross, "the woman who phoned in the information was sure she had seen Mrs Stodart, albeit with darker hair and a dog, a Skye Terrier. That made me think the witness was attentive, so, when I saw several long hairs on Mrs Stodart's coat, and her own hair isn't all that long and blonde, it made me wonder. I hoped she would take the coat off but she didn't so I took a gamble and used the tape. Forensics can now confirm that the hairs are consistent with coming from a dark grey Skye Terrier or similar."

"So," announced Avalon, "with this being dubious to say the least, where do we go now?" and without warning that nagging doubt suddenly turned into something positive. It was something that Mrs Stodart had said but he couldn't quite recall if he had prompted her or not.

"Did you record the interview with Mrs Stodart?" he asked staring straight at Ross.

"Well, yeah, I always do, I know it can't be used for-"

"But you did record it?" interrupted Avalon slightly agitated.

"Yes, logged under my name with the date," insisted Ross. Avalon fled the room and went to find the recording.

~~~~~~

Ross stood at the bar gazing into his glass, watching the bubbles raising from the base of the thick bottom in a constant stream wondering what chemical process was causing the bubbles to form.

"Bloody hell," said a voice from his left, "you lost a pound coin?" Ross glanced to the source of the voice, it was Avalon.

"Yeah, depressing isn't it?" Ross shrugged, Avalon ordered a half of beer.

"Let's take a seat," suggested Avalon paying for the drink.

"You got something?" asked Ross picking up his glass and heading to the only free table by the window. Avalon sat opposite and began to speak quietly.

"I want her brought in tomorrow, I'm not sure we have enough yet but we have warrants to search the house and I'm hoping things fall into place. The sterling work that Megan has done should also help."

"It still feels a bit dodgy though," frowned Ross, "we've got so little real evidence."

"I know but like I say, we have to hope that all the pieces fit together, we really need to push this or I'm gonna get my nuts chewed by DCI Croker." Ross nodded, the case hadn't been running all that long but the general feeling was that Croker was becoming impatient, the section was becoming busy and the DCI wanted results for the work he had put in to secure new staff for the sections.

"Okay, but he'll be more aggressive if we get it wrong," insisted Ross.

"Oh," began Avalon with a thought, "I could do with Saturday afternoon off too."

"Well you're the boss, you don't have to ask me," smiled Ross but he noticed Avalon's gaze. Ross sat back in the chair and gave out a grimace. "Oh, I get it, you want me to cover, I was suppose to be off Saturday."

"I know," nodded Avalon, "but Wilson and Mackinnon are over at Invergordon with the Port Authority most of the day." Ross sighed and picked up a beer mat and began to tap it on the table as he looked out of the window towards the river. He was planning some time with the rugby club, it was over a month since he had seen a full day off from work.

"Is it important?" he asked looking back to Avalon.

"No," replied Avalon, "not crucial, not life threatening or even beneficial to our cause but..." he trailed off with a deep shrug of his shoulders. Ross looked casually through the window once more then dropped the beer mat and said,

"You owe me." Avalon nodded and smiled, it was important to him but in a way that Avalon couldn't admit to. The chance to spend a little time with Sarah Underwood was to him, something that would make him feel alive once more. He knew it was childish and he realised it was naive in its way but that's who Avalon was, he was excited by things that most people took for granted, by things that other, 'normal' people experienced every day of their lives.

"I suppose you're off to see Julia?" asked Ross but Avalon just thinned his lips and shrugged. Ross shook his head and smiled, "you're so easy to read," he

348

said.

"Yep," nodded Avalon and he took a sip of his drink. Ross was close but not quite on the money, Avalon would probably tell him the truth eventually but at the moment, he was cautious, he knew no plans survive contact with the enemy. There was a short silence until Ross said,

"What do you think of Rutherford?"

"I haven't had much chance to get to know him yet but the team seem okay with him," admitted Avalon, "I spoke with him when we went to Charlie Sands place and he seems very bright but other than that I can't say."

"For a big guy he's surprisingly nimble, I thought of getting him involved with the rugby club, he's a one man front line," smiled Ross.

"The problem is, his size will limit how we can use him," insisted Avalon, Ross nodded, it was the case that Rutherford stood out even in a crowd. They went silent once more, they both knew Friday was going to be a big day and in the back of their collective minds, they were thinking about the case. It wasn't long before they decided to have an early night to be ready for an early morning. Avalon walked home through the city. Inverness hadn't been a city for very long, it still felt like a big town and even at night it was reasonably quiet. He walked steadily through the streets looking into estate agent windows, seeing if there were any houses he may take a liking to. He didn't really know what he was looking for, houses were just places to sleep for him, maybe a flat of some sort would be ideal. His walk home from the Castle Tavern took him about thirty minutes and if he was going to continue any sort of social life with Ross it would have to be no further away than that. He shook his head at the prices and continued to the rented bungalow he shared with Angie.

Friday morning dawned and Avalon sat at his table in the
small kitchen waiting for the woman who lived opposite
to leave for work. He had previously known her as Mrs
Pink but that name had become redundant as she had
generally ceased to wear the colour on a regular basis.
As soon as she came out and waved to him and drove off
in her car, Avalon readied to leave. If he found a new
place to live he would miss the regular habits of the
strange woman opposite.

It wasn't quite raining but the sky was threatening with
menaces and as Avalon entered the Cave he put the
problematic weather aside and looked to the busy day
ahead. It had already been agreed that Mrs Stodart would
be brought in under caution and one other person that
had been found by the persistent work of DC Frazer. As
soon as Muiranne Stodart arrived at the station, Avalon
and Ross made their way to the interview rooms. In one
was Mrs Stodart, in the other a man in his forties by the
name of Proctor Mackenzie. Frazer had certainly put
some work in to the case in the last few days. She had
sent local officers to the address that Muiranne Stodart
had given them. They had found that she was indeed
given permission to use the house and they were allowed
to look through it, fortunately, a letter had been found
from Mr Mackenzie. It was a matter of course that he
was now in the interview room. He was formally
identified and Ross began the questions with Frazer by
his side. The man had a solicitor with him so Avalon
watched from behind the two-way mirror.

"How long have you known Mrs Stodart Mr
Mackenzie?" asked Ross. It seemed Mr Mackenzie was
a more recent 'friend' of Muiranne and was at a loss to

know what was going on.

"Just over a month," he replied.

"And how long did you know that her husband had been killed?"

"Not until one of the police officers told me this morning," he replied.

"So you're saying that you know nothing of Muiranne Stodart's previous life?"

"Nothing at all," replied the man shaking his head.

"Do you keep a dog Mr Mackenzie?" Ross then asked.

"Aye," he replied, "a small Skye Terrier called Somer," he looked slightly embarrassed and then added, "it's short for Somerled."

"And would I be correct in thinking that this dog is a grey colour?" asked Ross. The man nodded.

"Aye, how did you know that?"

Avalon left the room, he now realised why Ross had pulled the fibres from Mrs Stodart's coat, it could prove that the woman seen at the house was actually Muiranne disguised. He entered the hidden room of Interview room two. There was PC Dowd and a woman officer in the interview room with Muiranne.

"Has she said anything Neil?" he asked.

"Not yet sir, just griping about being arrested," replied Dowd.

"Right, we better get her solicitor in and I'll bring Rory down.

Avalon and Mackinnon sat opposite Mrs Stodart and her solicitor and once the formalities were done the questions began. Avalon laid out the facts, there weren't that many but it was clear to see that the woman was backed into a corner.

351

"No matter how much you deny ever being back at the house, you were seen, you were seen with Proctor Mackenzie's little dog," insisted Avalon.

"But there must be more than one grey Skye terrier in Scotland," she insisted.

"I also happen to know," continued Avalon, and here he was taking a liberty. He didn't know, he had just guessed, "that you were hidden in the summer house when I was there interviewing your husband."

"That is utter nonsense, I simply wasn't there," she insisted raising her voice slightly. Avalon placed a iPod device on the table, he looked up to her and said,

"This is a recording of a previous interview with you Mrs Stodart, it has you telling me that you felt safe knowing the two suspects had been arrested, which was why you came forward."

"Yes, that's right," she nodded.

"But when I told you later that we had let them go you said that those two suspects must have been the last to see your husband alive after I left there after an interview with him." The woman was quiet for a moment.

"Well it does make sense doesn't it?"

"Why is that?" Avalon asked but the woman had become cautious, she could sense a trap. He watched her face as her mind went through the facts, obviously, she wasn't aware of Avalon's final trick.

"Because of what I read in the newspaper, he was killed around the time you were there," she said.

"Nowhere have any times been mentioned."

"Then I must have assumed it, you said you were there on the Saturday and he was killed that day," she insisted.

"I didn't say that to anyone but that isn't what got

me thinking," frowned Avalon, "when I said *we* interviewed your husband, I was speaking from the collective point of view meaning 'we the police', but when you mentioned it you were more specific, you meant it to mean that only I was there," he insisted. She went silent, Avalon could see the solicitor was about to speak so he continued, "I told no one I was there alone, only I, your husband and you knew that." The woman went white. "You were there Mrs Stodart, you were hidden in the summer house and I'll guarantee that forensics will be able to prove you were there." Avalon knew that it meant nothing, it was highly likely she had been in her own summer house previously but he was banking on the pressure of the moment making her worry about her situation. Then Avalon unleashed his coup de grâce, it was nothing more than instinct that brought it out at that moment. He had assessed that the timing was right for him to mention something that he had no proof of but was just that tiny piece, that straw that the camel wasn't expecting. "When you saw me leave you sent a text to Charlie Sands to tell him that your husband was alone and the laptop that incriminated him was there." She glared at him and asked,

"So who is Charlie Sands?"

"He's the man you overheard your husband talking to when he was planning your abduction, and you know that because you checked his phone afterwards," insisted Avalon. Muiranne just sank her stare into Avalon, she made no further comment, the next utterance came from her solicitor.

"I need to speak to my client alone please." Avalon announced he was turning off the recording device, picked up the iPod and left the room with Rory close behind. Avalon knew it was a very tenuous argument, he also knew he needed time. At that very moment Mackenzie's house and the house that they had stayed at were being searched by forensics. He just hoped they found something. Avalon looked at Rory, he looked troubled.

"What is it Rory?" he asked as he leaned on the wall of the corridor.

"Nothing boss," stated the young DC.

"Out with it, I can see by the look on your face."

"It's just that..." he paused to bring up the courage to tell the truth, "I've... I've never seen you look worried before." Avalon laughed, it was a stilted sound, not that many people knew what Avalon's laugh sounded like.

"I'm always worried lad, but I admit, this one is close to the knuckle." He considered he used the word 'lad' as if he was an elder statesman in the force, almost like he was much older. It was probably the nerves that Rory had noticed that had brought out a phrase he didn't think he had ever used before. The door to the other interview opened and out came Ross, he walked up to Avalon at the end of the corridor.

"Mackenzie says he'll help as much as he can," he said with a half smile.

"Which isn't much if he didn't know anything," insisted Avalon.

"Well, that's not exactly correct," insisted Ross, "once he realised what Mrs Stodart might have been up to, he began to put certain things together, he also admitted that she had taken to going out with his dog," Ross paused, "and the dates match up to the sightings of her in Golspie." Avalon raised his eyebrows at this. Ross continued. "He also says that she had several wigs, and they are still at his house."

"It still isn't anything concrete though is it?"

354

sighed Avalon.

"It might be if forensics find a match to that other footprint in the blood, or a fibre from the wigs in the summerhouse," suggested Ross as the solicitor came out of the interview room.

"Have you got anything more than circumstantial evidence Detective Avalon because I really think you are pushing the limits here?" she asked.

"I don't move until I'm certain Mrs Donahue," replied Avalon. The woman looked deep into his eyes and saw he meant it.

"You have evidence?" she eventually asked.

"Enough to go to court," he insisted though he held doubts that a jury would actually convict her. The woman nodded and returned to her client. Just under an hour later they were talking to Mrs Stodart who was reconsidering her position and making noises that meant she was considering some sort of plea bargain. Ross was left with the woman and her solicitor as Avalon considered his own position. He decided it was better that he agreed. Mrs Stodart would admit to striking her husband if she could plead that is was done under duress and not a frenzied attack to kill him. Later in the afternoon, Ross found Avalon at the rear of the station leaning on his car looking into the middle distance.

"She gave in pretty quickly," said Ross.

"She realises we know she was there, with the evidence of the weapon being taken before the murder, forensics sniffing around the summer house and the fact that the partial footprint is probably hers, she knows we have enough to pursue her," explained Avalon, "and Megan is looking at phone records of Mrs Stodart, she says that a tower in the Golspie area picked up her mobile signal just prior to Charlie Sands getting his text.

She was in or near Golspie at the time Sands received that text." He shrugged a little and began to nod, "We know it's her, she knows she did it and she now knows it's just a matter of time before more evidence is found."

"One nil to us then," said Ross thrusting his hands in his pockets and looking into the same nothingness as Avalon. The DI looked round.

"More like a draw," he said.

"I don't know, we got her and that's what matters."

"It doesn't feel right that she'll probably get a light sentence and yet we know she'd planned it for some time."

"To be fair, she was backed into a corner though," insisted Ross.

"There is nothing that can justify killing someone, she could have come to us," insisted Avalon.

"Do you really think we would have listened to a little rich girl screaming that her husband was going to hold her for ransom?" shrugged Ross.

"I hope we would have," said Avalon looking back to his nothingness. Ross took a deep breath, sighed and then said,

"I would have never got her down for something like this, she doesn't seem the type."

"I think she bottled it at the last minute," replied Avalon still looking into space, "that's why there was only one blow and the weapon was left at the scene." Ross shrugged unseen by Avalon.

"It figures," he said and then he looked at Avalon, his boss looked tired, he looked like he was deep in thought too. "So have you got a poem for this situation then?" he asked with a slight smile. Avalon stood upright and turned to Ross.

"Not really, nothing I can bring to mind," he said and then he seemed to remember something, "but there is a quote from a German philosopher which would apply," and he stopped and tried to remember it. "I don't think I can recite it verbatim but it goes something like, *'He who fights with monsters should beware that he does not become a monster, and if you gaze long into an abyss, the abyss also gazes into you'*." Ross raised his eyebrows and said simply,

"Oh."

"It's a passage that every copper should have tattooed on his heart," added Avalon and he walked back into the building.

~~~~~~

It had taken Avalon hours to get ready to go to Sarah Underwood's house, he had fussed about his clothing, what would look good but casual, he had hesitated on whether to take a bottle of wine or not and he was very undecided on how to approach the whole scenario. All she was expecting was him to make a complete fool of himself so why all the preamble? He decided on a casual look, something comfortable and he would take the wine for his own benefit, as for everything else, he would just have to busk it. The house was easy to find and he pushed the doorbell and waited. She came to the door wearing jeans and a baggy tee shirt, he was glad he was dressed as he was, the first box was ticked.

"I've brought this," he said holding up the bottle, in his other hand was the guitar, "it is vegan wine," he added. She smiled.

"There's really no need," she said taking the

bottle from him.

"Not for you maybe but I need some Dutch, or should I say French courage," he grinned slightly embarrassed.

"Come in, where do you want to sit?" she asked. The room was modern but cosy, he pointed to the easy chair.

"Here?" he asked.

"Yes of course," she nodded, "shall I open the wine?" Now he wondered if this was her way of saying she didn't want to join him in drinking.

"Only if you want to, I will sound terrible whether I drink or not," he raised his eyebrows. Sarah smiled again.

"I'm sure you're not that bad, anyway, I'm not a musician so I can't say one way or the other," she replied and he noticed the bottle had been placed on the cupboard by the door and she was making herself comfortable on the sofa. Avalon began to realise he had read the situation wrong, she really did just want to hear his song, and his heart sank a little. He became slightly self-conscious and somewhat embarrassed but he soldiered on and asked if he should make a start. She shrugged.

"Yes, when you're ready," she smiled pulling her legs up onto the sofa. Avalon strummed a chord to see if the guitar was in tune and made himself comfortable. He strummed again to get a feel for the instrument and then began to play. He tried his best to control his voice and by the second chorus he was feeling more confident. He decided not to look up to her and kept his gaze on the guitar, forcing himself to remember all the words and get the chords in the correct order. As the song came to its conclusion he wondered about the end, he hadn't really thought about it but he just let it happen. In his mind he could hear the big ending like a well-known power ballad and to him that's how it sounded. As the final chord drifted away through the house he looked up. Sarah's face looked blank, he didn't know how to react.

"Wow, was it that bad?" he asked. She was staring at the guitar, her eyes didn't move and he thought he had caused her to suffer irreparable shock but then she looked up to him.

"That was wonderful," she said.

"You don't have to humour me, I know how bad I am," he smiled.

"No, honestly, I like it," she said standing, "I want to hear it again, let me open that bottle." She brought in the wine in two fine glasses and passed him one.

"So you must have written songs before," she said sitting on the sofa again.

"No never," admitted Avalon shaking his head.

"I can't believe that James, you certainly should write more." Avalon didn't miss the use of his first name, maybe he hadn't got it wrong, maybe Miss Underwood was just the sort of person who needed to break the ice. He felt his phone vibrate and then it rang. He sighed and took it from his pocket.

"Sorry, I forgot to turn it off," he said.

"Don't worry, I understand, just answer it," she smiled taking a sip of the wine.

"Are you sure, I won't be a second," and he answered the nuisance device.

"Avalon," he said as gentle as he dare.

"*Boss, et's Frazer,*" Avalon could feel the tension in her voice.

"Hello Megan, what is it?"

"There's been an accident, et's DS Wilson and DC MacDonald." Avalon went suddenly cold, he didn't say a thing, Frazer continued, *"Ross has already gone down to the hospital."*

"What's happened," he asked fearing the worse.

"We're not sure yet but it seems a truck hit them."

"I'm on my way," he said and put the phone quickly away. "I'm sorry but I have to go, it's my team, there's been some sort of accident."

"Of course," she replied standing to help him out. He said nothing to her, he just left and got into his car and raced to the hospital.

He met Ross just outside the accident and emergency entrance, he was seated with Wilson who was covered in blood and looked in shock. Ross had his arm around Wilson shoulder but when he saw Avalon he stood and walked towards him.

"Gordon's fine, he's got some cuts and bruises but he's okay," insisted Ross turning Avalon back into the corridor.

"But he's covered in blood," insisted Avalon sensing what was coming next. He could tell with Ross's demeanour that something was wrong.

"Most of it isn't his blood," said Ross solemnly. Avalon brought his hand up to his mouth but resisted biting his hand.

"Mack?" he asked. Ross sighed.

"Not good, but he's in the operating theatre at the moment."

"What happened for Christ's sake?" asked Avalon with desperation in his voice.

"A truck overran a junction and T-boned them, Mack was trapped in the passenger side." Avalon wanted to scream but he looked round to Wilson who was staring at the floor with tears running slowly down his face.

"Have you informed Gordon's wife yet?"

"We sent a car round, we thought it was best to tell her face to face," said Ross, "Gordon's pretty ragged at the moment as you can imagine." Avalon nodded, took a deep breath and went to sit at the side of Gordon, he gently took his hand and held it. Gordon didn't look up, he just began to cry like a child. Avalon held him and Ross turned and left.

Two hours later Wilson had gone with his wife to the station, Avalon thought it best that he wasn't left at the hospital, Ross had returned and had obviously been dealing with it in his own way but Avalon had just sat staring at the far wall of the corridor. It was bringing up Avalon's old demons, images he had held at bay for so long, spectres and imps that dwelt in his mind were threatening to run riot in his head. He shook himself and looked up at the ceiling, taking deep breaths and then a doctor came through the doors. Avalon shot to his feet.

"Any news Doc?"

"He's comfortable though he is still in a serious condition but we think he'll pull through," there was a hint of doubt in the doctor's voice, "the friend who was with him saved his life, a piece of the car door went into his thigh, the other officer managed to stop the bleeding out from the artery. If he hadn't..." the doctor left it to the imagination what the outcome may have been.

"But he'll survive?" asked Avalon.

"Yes, I'm fairly confident he will but," the doctor paused and looked a little sympathetic, "he may still lose his leg," the doctor replied, "time will tell however, he's young and fit, you never know," and the doctor left. Avalon looked over to Ross.

"Has he got any family?"

"Not to speak of, Gordon is more like family than anyone," replied Ross.

"We better let Gordon's wife know then, she'll know best how to tell him."

~~~~~~~

It was just another morning in the Highlands, the clouds were thick and heavy and the air was crisp and biting. Avalon stood and shivered as he looked out over the Cromarty Firth from Saltburn Pier. It was barely dawn and the lights from the pier twinkled out across the water as he sucked in the cold air. He heard the car door open and then close behind him and soon Ross was beside him pulling on his overcoat.

"It's bloody cold this morning," he said raising his collar against the cool air slipping along the water. Avalon nodded, his gaze still on the calm water stretching away into the darkness and more twinkling lights in the distance. He could feel the cold but he let it force its way into his flesh, it made him feel like he was alive, it made him think clearer. "They've forecast snow for later, they say that there could be a blizzard tomorrow," added Ross fastening up a few of the buttons as he too looked out across the firth. Avalon stood upright and shivered deeply. Over the water in the far distance the rim of the sea was becoming lighter and the sun was making its power felt as rays danced now and then across the firth, only to be constantly extinguished over and over by the heavy greyness that was held in clouds as thick as Orkney porridge.

"This could be a complete waste of time," said Avalon his teeth almost chattering.

"It could but Gordon said his contact was sure the boat would land here," replied Ross. They were working to a tip off that DS Wilson had been given that a boat with some sort of contraband was landing on that tide at the pier. It wasn't even known for sure what the cargo was but Wilson had been adamant that his contact had always been reliable so here they were with a tactical team to greet any vessel that tried to land. Avalon at last gave in to the cold, he turned and pulled his overcoat out of the car and fed his arms into the sleeves. It felt better but he was still shivering. In the air they began to see the tiniest grains of snow.

"For Christ's sakes it's nearly May and it's snowing," he growled. Ross looked up to the heavens watching the flakes grow in size until they were fully recognisable as traditional, honest to goodness snow. He turned to Avalon and tried to assess his mood.

"Did you go to the hospital last night?" Avalon glanced over and nodded before looking back out to sea.

"Yeah, he's awake and all that but he looks terrible," he admitted.

"Any news from the doctor?"

"Nothing solid," replied Avalon, "it's the usual percentage bullshit, they say there's a seventy-five percent chance he'll keep the leg, but a ninety percent chance he won't be able to walk properly," he sniffed as his nose began to drip with the cold.

"So it's the end of his career then?" asked Ross quietly. Avalon shrugged.

"Who knows? It's Mack, he's a fighter."

"True, best not write him off hey?" but Avalon didn't answer, he took out his handkerchief and blew his nose and then stamped his feet to keep the circulation flowing. Ross tried to think of something to change the subject, the last couple of days had been difficult enough and they still had a job to do, that job was going to be more difficult too without Wilson and Macdonald. DS Wilson had been given a little time off. Avalon had insisted and even gone to the DCI to make sure Wilson stayed at home. It would mean that DC Rutherford would be thrown in at the deep end but 'needs must'. The next few weeks were going to be difficult for Avalon and his section, he had decided that he would throw his weight behind making sure his team were kept busy so they had little time to brood over the recent events. He looked round to Ross, his friend seemed to be taking the whole thing in his stride but Avalon knew Ross was deep in thought.

"So what are you thinking?" he asked. Ross blinked into the twilight and then glanced to Avalon before clapping his hands together several times.

"Oh, I was thinking about the way life moves," he began, "it's like a snake, we never quite know what's coming."

"Probably a good thing too," offered Avalon.

"Undoubtedly, and what would it be without mystery," Ross continued, "and on that note," he paused for a moment, "what did we see in the fog that day up at Golspie?" Avalon raised his brows and looked out to sea.

"As I told you then, there was nothing there, it would have left some sort of print in the mud.

"Does nothing like that faze you?"

"Not really," answered Avalon turning back to his DS, "I've spent too many nights in graveyards waiting for someone to turn up, too many cases going through so called 'haunted houses' for clues and too many wasted leads that were more to do with superstition to believe anything odd is going on." He looked back over the water and leaned on the railings. "All I have ever seen that could be considered inhuman, has come from human hand," he concluded.

"So you never have any doubts?" asked Ross. Avalon raised his shoulders for a second and let them fall with a sigh.

"I wouldn't say that," he said standing upright, "when we were on the banks of Loch Ness that night when we pulled that security van from the water, there was quite a splash out in the loch and I couldn't explain what that was and equally, I can't explain what we saw up at Golspie, but," he paused again, "if you ask me if I thought it was the Brollachan, I would have to say that it wasn't." Ross gave a slight smile, it was exactly the sort of answer he would expect from his boss.

"Well here's a question you should find much easier to answer," said Ross in a more upbeat voice.

"I'll try," said Avalon wiping his nose again.

"How did you get to the hospital so quickly?" and he turned directly to Avalon before continuing, "you were there not long after me."

"What do you mean?" asked Avalon with a frown.

"I thought you were off up to Golspie?" added Ross.

"Golspie? No, I was only at..." Avalon cut the explanation short, "clever," he added with a half smile and then looked back out to sea. "You're getting good at this detective lark aren't you?" he added.

"Just curious that's all," Ross shrugged then continued with, "so where were you?" Avalon looked directly at Ross, his face clearer in the growing light, the snowflakes beginning to whirl and dance on the rising breeze.

"Let's just say I wasn't at Golspie," he eventually replied. No he certainly wasn't. He thought back to what might have been, at last he was with Sarah Underwood and the damn job got in the way again. He suddenly felt guilty for thinking that way, he would give anything to turn the clock back and have Mack safe and sound.

"I figured that," nodded Ross beginning to feel the cold himself, "so was it the girl who works at the pub?" added Ross.

"No," replied Avalon, "and even if you guess where I was I will never admit it," he frowned and then turned back to the inky water, then as an afterthought, "not that you would ever guess it." That piqued Ross's interest even more, he began to wonder why he wouldn't guess it, that meant it was something that would seem so unlikely that... An image came into Ross's head, he thought he knew in that moment where Avalon had been and who with. He was about to say too but Avalon reacted first.

"There!" he said pointing across the water. From out of the lightening horizon, lights could be seen, lights of a vessel, Ross went back to the car and fetched out binoculars.

"It could be our boat," he said still looking through the glasses. Avalon pulled out a flashlight from his coat pocket.

"I'll let tactical know." He aimed the torch at an unmarked van on the pier and flashed the light twice. The sidelights on the van flashed once and Avalon looked back out to sea. "Is it them?" he asked.

"Could be," replied Ross still looking through the binoculars, "we ought to alert the coastguard just in case,"

"Right," announced Avalon, "let's get into position, it's going to be another long day."

The Avalon Series, by Peter Gray.

The Drums of Drumnadrochit
By Peter Gray.

Introducing Detective James Avalon, a man in turmoil. Both his private and professional life is at an all time low and to make things worse he is seen as a liability to his senior officers. He has to make a change in both aspects of his life, but how? Though he is still on good terms with his ex wife she is beginning to despair with his lack of compromise in his life until a chance meeting with another officer shows promise of opening new doors to his future.

Auld Clootie
By Peter Gray.

James Avalon faces a new menace in the second book in the Avalon series. Change and upheaval within the police forces sees him struggle with the problems of a reorganisation of the team. Trouble visits once again in the shape of a major crime that seems to have no clues or motives and Avalon has to work with limited resources to solve a crime linked to religion, ritual and legend.

The Brollachan

By Peter Gray.

After just twelve months based in Inverness, Detective Inspector
James Avalon now feels more at home than any other time in his
career. With his personal life still a shambles, Avalon takes solace in
the landscape and his work, but when a woman disappears from her
car in plain sight, he wonders about the accuracy of the report.
When a body is found, the case becomes more serious. Is the
woman's disappearance linked to the body or does Avalon need to
reassess his methods?

The Black Clan

By Peter Gray.

When Avalon becomes embroiled in secret societies and Masonic
rituals he soon finds out how far up the food chain the rot has
climbed. Once again the Inverness detective is on the streets and
this time he's angry.

Out 2018

Caledonian Flame

By Peter Gray.

Out 2019

See website for details.
www.avalon-series.co.uk

Also by Peter Gray

A Certain Summer

Sam's Kingdom

With Feeling

Please visit:

www.petergrayauthor.co.uk
www.acertainsummer.co.uk
www.avalon-series.co.uk

www.trickyimppublishing.co.uk